The year is 2384. The small survi coping with the now hostile envi- .... The future looks bleak.

One possible lifeline is the Litchen Probe that promises to enable the transportation of a present-day soul into the body of an ancestor.

As the project nears completion, Dr Gemma Western decides to take the law into her own hands. She slips unnoticed into the laboratory early in the morning and activates the Probe using herself as the subject.

By setting the co-ordinates so that a minute of laboratory time equals a year in the past, she plans to rewrite her own history and cause herself to have been born rich and powerful, and then return before anyone can discover what she's done.

A slight miscalculation places her in the wrong body at the wrong time, triggering an unimaginable chain of events.

Essentially, a sci-fi thriller, *Dilemma* is an engrossing adventure story that will have wide appeal.

Janice Bosma is a descendent of Percy Bysshe Shelley, and perhaps more significantly, of his wife, Mary, the author of Frankenstein.

She was born in Epping but grew up in Barry, South Wales. She has worked as a stewardess for British Airways, as a model and has also taught to City & Guild standard.

She married a Dutch master mariner and moved to Holland, taking Dutch citizenship in 1978. She has two sons and three grandchildren. She is now based in Cornwall.

This, her first novel, was written during the 6–8 months she spends every year at sea with her husband.

*For my husband Lubbe (Louis)
With love and gratitude:
your enthusiasm at all stages
was more important than you
can ever know.*

DILEMMA

Janice Bosma

Temple House Books
Sussex, England

Temple House Books
is an imprint of
The Book Guild Ltd

This book is a work of fiction. The characters and situations in this story are imaginary. No resemblance is intended between these characters and any real persons, either living or dead.

This book is sold subject to the condition that it shall not, by way of trade or otherwise, be lent, re-sold, hired out, photocopied or held in any retrieval system or otherwise circulated without the publisher's prior consent in any form of binding or cover other than that in which this is published and without a similar condition including this condition being imposed on the subsequent purchaser.

The Book Guild Ltd
25 High Street,
Lewes, Sussex

First published 1995
© Janice Bosma 1995
Set in Baskerville
Typesetting by Acorn Bookwork, Salisbury, Wiltshire

Printed in Great Britain by
Athenaeum Press Ltd,
Gateshead.

A catalogue record for this book is
available from the British Library

ISBN 0 86332 999 3

INTRODUCTION

The Year: 2384. The Planet: EARTH.

The last four hundred years had been a dramatic time for earth; its face had changed beyond recognition.

In the year 2070, the war to end all wars had occurred, contaminating the air and making the land barren for almost two hundred years.

Privileged and fortunate people, forewarned of the coming holocaust, fled underground to specially constructed shelter cities, taking animals and suchlike, to a modern-day Noah's Ark.

Many nations were completely destroyed. Ten generations were born, reared and educated before the year 2250, when the slow migration to the surface began.

The entire weather pattern of the planet had altered. Winter now lasted seven long months of the year, from October through to May, with varying temperatures from minus 5c to minus 50c. June by stark contrast brought a rapid rise in the temperature to 51c and, as June gave way to July, the temperature would soar in most parts to 72c where it would remain until mid-September.

As the new generation made their way to the surface, a complex of Domes were erected from special materials which could withstand rapid rises and falls in temperatures of up to 200c, thereby affording the inhabitants a near normal life as was possible.

Each apartment within the structures came equipped with a guardian computer, controlled by a main computer, which regulated the individual flow of oxygen, lighting, water purification and temperature.

On March 11th, 2270, in the Boston Dome City, a meeting took place between the heads of the remaining nations. Their objective was to amalgamate and unite their resources and assemble a World Government.

By late June of the same year the newly-elected World Government Supreme, based in the world capital city of London, had set up and installed a subcommittee, made up of a senior member of each of the twelve remaining nations. This Counsel of Elders was based in the Boston Domed City.

Whilst London-based scientists continued with the search, as had their ancestors before them, for another habitable planet, Boston scientists, and in particular Dr Eric Swartz, a much-acclaimed scientist, experimented in time travel in the hope of returning to a suitable historical period long before the occurrence that was the "Great Holocaust".

In 2384 came a breakthrough. Dr Swartz and his hand-picked team of six, bound by a two hundred year old oath, *To Protect and Keep* had successfully concluded his experiment of detaching and transporting his own soul back through history, into a body of another age, of another century. A short while later, on 17th October, 2384, the middle-aged doctor and his deputy were called before the Counsel of Elders to detail their experimental results.

Each member of the Counsel listened intently, their eyes portraying great excitement as Dr Swartz told how the entity that was his soul had entered his ancestor's body close to his time of death. Functioning within that body causing a short remission in the chosen ancestor who was dying of leukaemia, he'd felt the pain and suffering of the old man's tired body and described in great detail the muddled thoughts of a dying mind as it neared the end and then the great rush of the powerful vacuum as the main computer withdrew his soul after the twelve hour inhabitation, the agreed time of occupation and his subsequent return to the present day.

When a transported soul first entered an ancestor's body, there was an initial awakening period lasting from one to five minutes, before it lapsed into a state of unconsciousness. This period was known as "Zone Time" and, although not a definitive period of time, previous experiments had proven it could last up to three years of the inhabited body's lifespan.

Time, however, could now be minimised in the chosen age, by the use of an Electromagnetic Radiation Space Clock an E.R.S.C. the theory and workings similar to the process of a Caesium Space Clock. By breaking down the present it allowed time as we know it to be not only independent of the observer, but permitted the transported soul to choose how long they initially wished to lose from their lifespan in the past.

This time loss, if the user chose to align on the safest span, that being a minute-to-a-year basis, would allow three years in the chosen history, with a loss of not more than three minutes from the present.

Zone time, although at that stage of the experiment it could not be shortened, was the time a transported soul needed to adjust to the new body it had inhabited and get the feel of its new environment. As the experiment progressed it developed a rebounding echo, a "flash" that sprang back from the future, mirroring in the first section of the soul, sending thoughts and deeds in the form of an inner hologram through the mind, allowing the transported soul an insight into the immediate future or past.

Dr Gemma Western's research on that particular subject had proven that if a transported soul were to concentrate hard enough, it would be able to induce the "echo" facility on any particular subject it chose.

While Dr Swartz worked on the time barrier, unbeknown to him Dr Heinrich Litchen had invented a probe. His objective was to abolish the Zone Time period.

The Litchen Probe, as it was later known, was made up of five parts, each one capable of working independently. Its potential was vast. . . .

After Dr Litchen's sudden and mysterious death Dr Swartz had been summoned to attend Counsel's Chambers where he'd been given the Litchen Probe's unfinished research papers. Sketchy as they were, with pages missing, he'd felt proud and privileged to have been chosen. He admired Dr Litchen's ideas and achievements greatly and worked diligently with his second in command Dr Harry Turner to fill in the blanks.

Both doctors' dedication to the advancement of the Litchen Probe, meant that they were close to obliterating the Zone Time Period.

Although the Probe was still in the experimental stages the secretive and, as yet, unlogged results they'd obtained through the last experiment were excellent. The genetics however, had proven to be more than an initial problem, and one that both he and his assistant had experienced great difficulty with, working long, painstaking hours together on the late Dr Litchen's vague scripts and unsubstantiated, incomplete explanations.

The long and the short of it was that a soul from the future could only be transported into an ancestor within a direct family line. It seemed the acceptance or rejection of the transported soul was based on the same principles as a blood type being given to save a life. The blood that pumped through our veins today is a mixture of that of our forefathers so if a transported soul went back into an ancestor, it would identify with the type of blood, and therefore be accepted. On the other hand, as was proven during past experiments, if it found itself inside a body with no link to its family line, it would be rejected.

1

BOSTON MAIN DOME CITY: 17TH OCTOBER, 2384.

Just after 6pm, Dr Eric Swartz, a tall, broad-shouldered man with salt and pepper hair, in his late forties and head of The Litchen Project, walked deep in thought, along the long, wide staff corridor to his own apartment in the annexe of the great dome, unaware that his student, Dr Gemma Western, a petite, pretty 26-year-old redhead was only a short distance behind.

The questions that the Head Elder had thrown at both him and his deputy during the meeting, had been nothing short of an interrogation. The Head Elder's voice still rang in his ears; his questions still nagged away in his subconscious. Way back, when the experiment was incomplete, he hadn't given their questions much thought. His own vanity had led him to believe that the Head Elder's keen interest had been the same as his own. But now that it was complete, what exactly did they plan to do? He walked on, still oblivious to his student behind, as he tried to reason the Head Elder's previous questioning.

'What would happen if a soul was transported into a body that was not dying and therefore still had an occupying strong soul. And is that possible?' was the first question he'd asked.

It was indeed possible for a soul to gain entrance in those circumstances, but it would be extremely foolish to do so, he'd conceded. His research had proven that a conflict of souls would occur; a fight for leadership within. And the winner would not necessarily become the victor.

He'd had many thoughts on that particular subject but scientist as he was, he did not add a further explanation at that time.

'How would a soul exit a body that was not dying, if the computer failed to do its job at the given time?' the Head Elder had persisted.

'By inducing death!' he'd answered quickly, then explained in more detail. 'On the death of the body the soul would automatically be returned to the present day, unharmed, and untouched by the circumstances. This of course would most definitely change the course of history, and as we are all aware, the Oath that we have taken forbids us to do that, so it would be only an emergency form of escape if all else fails.'

At this point he'd caught the Head Elder's eyes. What he saw there had greatly influenced his way of thinking.

'It is mandatory to thoroughly research your ancestor before transporting any soul, thereby eliminating any problems of this nature,' he'd concluded, still studying him.

But before he'd finished anticipating his next question and while his thoughts were still on the defensive the Head Elder had immediately pressed.

'Could a soul be transported into both male and female bodies, regardless of the soul's gender?'

'There are no hard-and-fast rules as to whether a male soul could be transported to a female body although the probability is such, in my opinion:'

He'd chuckled at this point, before resuming as he caught the eye of Zoniac the Resident Elder, a slim brunette in her late thirties.

'Either she or I would have great difficulty in coming to terms with it.'

Zoniac's large hazel eyes had held his meaningfully, returning his humour with a soft suppressed laugh. But in contrast the Head Elder's had narrowed and his disapproving glance toward her left no doubt in Dr Swartz's mind of his silent implications. Flushed but stern and angered by her indiscretion he'd arched a brow and asked his final question.

It was the last question that had really aroused his suspicions. Suspicions that he hoped were not founded, that he hoped would prove to be entirely in his imagination.

'When a soul is transported into history to inhabit another body, can it lengthen that life indefinitely, even if recorded history showed that particular person was shot dead at, say, forty years of age?'

'I believe you will find that our research speaks for itself Sir. But, yes, it can be done.'

As he approached the junction of the main laboratory, he bore right. Dr Western, just a few steps behind, turned left towards the side exit. As she neared the door a broad grin spread across her full lips and her light green eyes sparkled. She had the power to change history, to rewrite her future, to change her life and make an absolute fortune, then destroy her present . . . for ever!

She slid her small hand over the door lock beam, the exit slid open and she stepped outside. The sharp cold smell of the winter air embraced her as the exit closed quickly behind.

The snow promised earlier was in full flow, masking out the grey heaviness of the sky and becoming thick and wild in its turbulent descent, covering previous falls of well-trodden snow, leaving a crisp white sheet of unevenness on top of the frozen ground.

Soon she'd have to use the underground route as the temperature would fall to minus 30c and beyond. But she wouldn't have to concern herself with that for a while, because tomorrow, during the early hours of the morning, whilst most inhabitants of the city slept, she'd send her own soul back into history. She'd change the past for ever. She'd live out the life of her ancestor Lillian Becket, who'd died in a fire. But instead of dying poverty stricken at thirty-four, she'd give her forty more years of life! A life that would enable her to amass a fortune. A life that would produce a child that hadn't existed, enabling her to redistribute her new-made fortune, and the power that would come with it, to her side of the family tree, before her final return to the main laboratory, where she'd wipe her invasion from the computer's memory. No one would know and she could enjoy her unearned wealth.

She hurried on, excited at her own thoughts, not feeling the cold that the night exuded.

As she approached her apartment dome, the bright welcoming lights shone out into the white swirl highlighting the thick particles as the snowflakes descended and settled around her. Quickly she ran the last few steps, her hands and feet suddenly as cold as the snow and ice.

She placed a shivering palm over the door lock beam to the side of the entrance, the door slid aside and she stepped into the warmth of the foyer.

At the same time Dr Swartz neared his own apartment, his thoughts still centred on the Head Elder's questions.

A few hours later, as the darkness of the night gave way to the dawn, Gemma Western pulled on her blue regulation suit and hooded cape. Silently, she slipped out into the early morning. It was 5.58am. The storm had waned but the sky was still heavy with more of the promised snow. Hurriedly she crossed the compound to the main dome laboratories, the crisp snow crunching under her blue ankle boots.

As she approached the students' door, a blast of strong wind gusted the loose snow from the bankside. Like a giant slap of icy fingers in a grim warning, the chilling snow struck her full in the face. The hairs on the back of her neck stood up, the strange, bitter sweetness of the snow melting in her mouth as she fought against the sudden unexplained panic that surged through her. The loud beat of her heart vibrated throughout her entire being as she gasped, recovering from the unexpected assault. Then with her head bowed, she hurried on.

At the side entrance of the main dome she placed her hand over the door lock beam. Obediently the door slid open and she stepped inside. The long white corridor was deserted. As the door slid closed behind her she made her way up the dimly lit passage, towards the main laboratory doors. The same shivering handprint opened the double glass entrance and she stepped inside. The isolated research room was eerily silent and she felt strangely alone. The sudden "whoosh" of the doors as they closed behind her was unexpected. Her head whiplashed around, her heart beating double time, before the noise had registered and she felt safe again. Slipping off her cloak, she sat down in front of the screen.

For well over six months she'd been carefully studying and planning her journey. Soon she'd be in and out of history, a richer and more powerful woman, and no one would be any the wiser.

The programme would take about twenty minutes to set up. She'd allowed herself more than enough time. Entrance to the 1977 Time Corridor wasn't until 6.30am.

She grinned and licked her lips, fantasizing as she tasted her greed, then promised, 'I am your resurrector! Your life! You'll have remission for forty years! Be rich, and powerful beyond your wildest dreams. . .'

The next twenty minutes of checks went quickly. It was almost time. The laboratory clock showed 6.23am. She had just five minutes to feed in the programme, then on a ratio of one minute per year, forty minutes of local time would give her forty years of Lillian Becket's life.

Avidly she digested the computer's written confirmation. At 7.11am precisely her soul would be returned. Nineteen minutes exactly before her colleagues would arrive. No one would ever know. She had it all planned. . . . . .

Disconnecting the computer's failsafe, she slid her hand over the beam lock of the life support unit and the thick clear lid slowly opened. Eagerly she climbed inside and lay down. The lid slid back into position and sealed her inside.

In a few seconds the computer would take command, checking the programme with her as was the normal procedure before it began. . . .

First came the programmed check on co-ordinates.

She heard her excited voice answer, 'Affirmative!' Then came the date that she'd chosen, 4th August, 1977. Her answer was the same.

Then finally the computer's main question, 'Do you wish to proceed?'

'Affirmative!'

The excitement surged through her as the computer's voice confirmed its intentions to start. She watched as the laboratory's overhead lighting dimmed, the computer drawing maximum energy for her soul's transportation.

Suddenly she could sense the icy fingers of fear as they brushed against her. She could taste the sweet acid of panic on her tongue from the beads of sweat that somehow found their way into her mouth. Shouldn't she be unconscious by now? . . .

Determinedly she tried to raise her right hand. It wouldn't move. It was numb. She had no control! Her thoughts were misting, fading, just like the overhead lighting. A hazy red glow engulfed the entire room as the lead computer's firm voice echoed around her crosschecking its programme, filling her mind as she heard it instruct its sibling computers. Then fading . . . . fading . . . . as she fought an overwhelming feeling of terror that exploded inside her.

She lay there paralyzed, her eyes wide open, as an immense blackness edged its way closer. Above her, the transporting chamber was filling with long vibrating tentacles . . . . . reaching out, moving rhythmically closer and closer, towards her. Her whole being screamed inside as she lay gripped by the great fear of the unknown. She willed her eyes to close, but they wouldn't obey. She could only lie there, watching helplessly, as the enormous blackness began sucking her into its sphere. An irresistible force drawing her into its centre, blanking out her fearful thoughts as she succumbed to the warmth that the blackness held.

Slowly she drifted upwards, looking down at her still body. Her eyes were closed, but she could see. She was floating now, high above the support unit, melting into the warmth, becoming one with the darkness. Turning around and around cocooned in its safety. Slowly at first, then faster, faster. Spinning, the force pulling. Pulling until she caught up with it and went freely.

As the mistiness cleared, Gemma Western's panic returned.

People . . . . . People were close by . . . . . Voices . . . . . She could hear voices. What was that smell? Burning. Something was burning. She could smell smoke. She couldn't breathe! A man knelt to the side of her. She felt him touch her arm and opened her eyes.

'Maria . . . Maria.' He whispered.

His voice was deep but gentle. Warm, caring light brown eyes looked softly into hers. What did he say? Where was she?

He spoke again. 'Maria . . . Maria.' What did he call her?

At the same time as Dr Western had neared the end of her co-ordinate check the soft female voice of Dr Swartz's apartment computer awoke him.

'Good morning Eric. It's 6.15am.' Yawning he sat up and stretched.

'Good morning Zoe.'

Then, pulling back the bedcover, he made his way across to the shower cubicle.

'You may turn on the shower Zoe.' He instructed and felt the warmth of the water as it cascaded over his head and on to his freckled back.

By 6.30am he'd shaved and dressed and had sat down to his breakfast. As he looked out over the vast whiteness of the snow-covered scenery, he felt truly invigorated. His subconscious suspicious fears of the Elders' questions the previous day had gone, vanished, as had the tiredness he'd felt before his much-needed, long, deep sleep.

He'd been exhausted. The past two experiments had taken an intense, trying two years. But now they were over, completed, proven!

Exhilarated, he sipped his juice and took in the beauty of the landscape, contented and relaxed.

The thick branches of the tall maple trees were coated with snow. How virginal, how pure it all was. From the comfortable warmth of his second-floor apartment he could almost smell the sharpness of the winter as he watched the snowflakes fall. This was indeed the best part of the day. In a short while, the great outer dome that covered and protected the trees from the severe cold that was to come, would close tightly. But for now he could enjoy the sight before him.

As his unsuspecting eyes gazed over the land beyond the laboratories, they were suddenly diverted. Through the clear roof of the Laboratory a red haze of light glowed. An icy chill replaced his serenity.

'Inform Security!' he heard himself bellow to his guardian computer. 'There's someone in the lab!'

The urgency in his voice matched the expression on his face as he hurried out of the apartment and ran full speed along the deserted corridors towards the main laboratories.

Breathing hard, he placed his hand over the beam lock of the laboratory entrance and the double doors slid aside. At the same time two uniformed security police arrived.

With a fleeting glance of acknowledgement he stepped inside. And as his anxious dark eyes swept over the large room coming to rest on the life support unit containing Dr Western's comatose body, his anxiousness became sheer horror.

Quickly he slid into the fixed seat in front of the main computer screen, verbally requesting an explanation.

Obediently, the firm female voice of the main computer repeated its given instructions, the hologram that was the screen quickly filling with co-ordinates in a secondary confirmation of her complete programme. Studiously he checked the programme, his eyes wide in disbelief as they darted from one set of co-ordinates to the other.

'NO! . . . NO! . . . The programme. She's miscalculated. She's entered the wrong body!'

As the full realisation of her miscalculations hit him his shaking fingers sought out the speak keys in anxious appeal. Hastily he inserted an emergency interception code then stared at the screen, impatiently awaiting the computer's acceptance.

The laboratory was uncannily silent, save for the ghostly hum of energy that the computer drew.

The code he'd given would release section one of the Litchen Probe and "freeze" Gemma Western's soul within the body she'd infiltrated in the historic period she'd chosen, hopefully invoking a limbo period, a period of unknown time he wished to extend indefinitely to try to rescue her.

The loud throb of his pulse beat wildly in his ears as he wiped the nervous beads of sweat from his brow that his confused and undirected racing thoughts had encouraged.

'How could she do this?' He reasoned silently. He'd trusted her! Impressed with her previous work, he, Eric Swartz had personally selected her to join his team. He'd trained her, taught her. She was his protégée.

'Freeze mode functioning,' the computer's voice informed, breaking in on his private panic. Swallowing hard he tried to lubricate his dry throat with his spittle.

'Give me time elapse since beginning of programme?'

'Affirmative.' The computer replied, the screen quickly clearing before the luminous green flashing figures of the date and time appeared, 25th September, 1984. 2011 hours.

After verbally confirming the date and time the computer asked, 'Do you wish visual?'

'Affirmative,' he replied, voicing his thoughts aloud, 'Seven years in seven minutes!'

The hologram screen sprang to life, displaying a fast moving car. He watched, a lone witness from the future as the car zoomed forward striking a woman pedestrian. A microsecond later the computer had frozen the image. The date and time clock flashing intermittently as it confirmed the freeze.

'Give me visual of Dr Western's infiltration and intended infiltration?' he continued. His frantic thoughts raced ahead as he spoke.

A few moments later the computer had cleared the screen and started a re-run of Gemma's experiment, beginning with the three minutes local time it had taken to transport her soul back into 1977.

He watched in silence, unaware that the two security police were now standing either side of him facing the hologram, their obdurate expressions unchanged as the computer narrated the scene.

He witnessed her first awakening. Shared the initial horror she'd felt as she discovered her mistake, tasting her panic as she lapsed into unconsciousness during the normal Zone Time period, the period that had lasted three years before her awakening in Maria Becket's body, the daughter of her intended ancestor.

As the computer moved on, the degrees on her soul monitor

grew stronger. His eyes took in every detail before him as her soul fought the conflict with Maria Becket's soul for domination of her body. Determinedly she battled, gaining control any way she could, using the Echo facility to its fullest extent, to win the amount of ground she needed to remain safely within.

Dr Western's soul had bonded fast, but just how greatly he was unable to tell. The Probe had the facility, but he hadn't yet developed that part of the section. That was to have been the next step. . . .

'It was a mandatory procedure . . . . mandatory!' he thought, 'How could she be so stupid as to transport her soul. And without the failsafe? This should never have happened!'

Dr Western had emerged from Zone Time as a peripheral voice getting stronger each day for the last four years. He'd watched, the same silent witness from the future, as Maria Becket, seemingly guided and protected by Dr Western's renegade soul, had murdered her aunt, shot her ex-boss and driven the car that had almost killed the lone figure.

Was he responsible for the accident . . . the murders? Had he, whilst releasing the Probe's section, thereby freezing her programme, interrupted Maria Becket's concentration at the wheel for the precious seconds she would have needed to avoid the woman? Had his decision, with Dr Turner, to withhold his much-needed detoxification on completion of the last experiment somehow been responsible? Had he truly misled her into believing it was that straightforward? Had he inadvertently provoked her actions? His questions were endless. If he had only warned her . . . told her! He shook his head, wracked with guilt.

Just then the hologram dimmed, emphasising the moment of intervention and the Probe, in the form of a small luminous green arrow, edged its way closer to its target, moments away from freezing her soul.

She felt something watching her, luring her. Her senses now razor-sharpened, her chilling fear playing with her imagination. What was that? A voice, an unfamiliar voice, calling her. In a strange way part of her.

Suddenly, a rushing sound . . . . louder and louder . . . but closer, much closer now. A force, a terrific force, pulling her, its powerful current surging through her. Weakening her defence as the evilness of Maria's soul, that she'd fought against for so long loomed up on her.

She moved quickly, the strong wind propelling her forward; pushing her onward, the evilness close behind. The sound of its menacing laughter, a hurricane force rebounding from invisible walls in the dank darkness, until it crashed down on her, like giant breakers.

Suddenly, a long frenzied scream pierced her whole being, 'B I T C H.'

At the same time, unseen by Dr Swartz and the guards, the energy readings of the life support unit that housed Dr Western's comatose body shot up to maximum and her eyelids sprang open. . . .

Two scarlet, burning hollows began to simmer. Swirling, deeper and deeper, faster and faster, the sudden surge of energy feeding their foreboding crimson glow, illuminating the life support unit in murderous revenge as the lid of the unit depressed in readiness, preparing to open.

Just then, a blaring siren broke the silence. The icy chill of a ghostly presence ran up his spine. The sudden harsh, grating noise made him gasp for breath. His heart raced wildly, pumping a rapid surge of blood that pounded against his eardrums. He looked up at the temperature gauge. The charged energy had reached maximum.

His darting eyes sought out the control lever. He had to release it, burn it off! His quick actions, remote control-like as he lunged forward, his swift interception redirecting the pulsating mass. And the lid snapped back into position.

From inside the life support unit, the demonic presence howled in silent anguish. Its mounting strength sapped by Dr Swartz's sudden intervention. Gemma Western's once-still body writhed in contorted twists of pain as the entity struggled to keep its hold. The evilness, like the energy had earthed and the inhuman burning orbs dimmed, her eyelids closing as the redirected power waned. The unnoticed scarlet hue faded, blending into the red haze of the laboratory's emergency lighting.

Dr Swartz watched the screen. The darkness surrounding the glow of life that was Gemma's soul, lightening as a distant green glow beckoned. The pulsating light of the probe, burning brighter and brighter as she approached, drew her through the thick mist like a magnet. Then suddenly she could see it! A green translucent light, enticing her inside to bathe in its warmth.

As she floated towards it, arm-like tentacles circled her entire being, pulling her into its centre, protecting her from the dangers she knew were close. Slowly she went with it, becoming one with its strength.

At 6.37am, 18th October, 2384, the Litchen Probe had functioned well. Dr Gemma Western's soul was frozen within Maria Becket's body. He slumped back against the seat. But a second later, the flashing luminous green script broke his short-lived calm.

'Malfunction . . . Malfunction.'

The screen once again filled with co-ordinates. His anxious eyes read quickly. Section one of the Litchen Probe had disintegrated due to the mass energy surge. The thought level of the section was completely burnt out.

'Would Dr Western's soul be safe?'

He hadn't realised he'd spoken aloud until the main computer assured, 'Affirmative Dr Swartz but the thought level of this section is unable to transmit.'

'Explain!' he ordered.

'Dr Western's soul is frozen within section one of the probe,' the computer's voice confirmed, 'but her thoughts are inaccessible.'

'Is she safe?' he persisted.

'Affirmative, Dr Swartz.'

He sank back into his seat and into his own thoughts.

The Litchen Probe's tests were not fully completed. He'd taken a great risk in using the section, not to mention the fact he'd had no authorisation. He'd used it without the prior knowledge of the Counsel of Elders but to him there had been no alternative.

He stood up and rubbed his eyes then went over to the life support unit. The two security police stood aside, their eyes following his every move. He looked down at her comatose body. She was so pale, so still.

In the seven minutes Dr Western's soul had lived inside Maria Becket's body, a total of seven years from 1977 to 1984, had elapsed in Maria's life.

The Zone time had taken up the first three years of the seven, after which she'd emerged as a peripheral voice, inside Maria's thoughts. At this stage he had no idea how Gemma's ancestor was reacting to the infiltration. She may or may not have accepted it. But he knew that had he not frozen Dr Western's soul when he did, she would not have remained a peripheral voice for very much longer. She, a scientist like himself, would use all her knowledge to look for a stronger and lasting hold on her ancestor's soul, thereby forging an incontestable bond. A bond, he knew must never be allowed to develop.

The section of the Probe he'd used to freeze her, although functioning well, was nevertheless still in experimental stages. His main concern now however, was not so much how long it would hold, but how greatly Dr Western had bonded and if he could get her out! If after it all, he couldn't return her soul to her own body, then it wouldn't much matter. The paradox he feared would have happened and history would have already been changed, both in their future and the future, that was her ancestor's past.

He rubbed his brow, protesting to the ache in his head to leave him in peace, silently wishing that he'd had more than the last two years to further develop the probe's facilities. If only he'd been able to master the sections that could, as he suspected, separate the bonding, however much of a depth there was between the souls. This he was sure would come. He'd studied Dr Litchen's notes on the subject and felt sure that the doctor had more than just touched on the area of depth. If only Dr Litchen were alive, what a partnership they would have made.

His next task was one which he was not going to relish, but a job that had to be done nonetheless.

As he turned to walk back across to the main computer a lone tear ran unnoticed down Gemma's pale cheek.

Speaking into the Direct Communication Link, he informed the secretary to the Counsel of Elders of the dilemma he faced. He waited, impatiently drumming his fingers on the consul, watching the small hologram fade to a vision of musicians playing the choice of music for the day, before several seconds later it vanished abruptly and the Resident Elder appeared, sitting behind a consul in her rooms. He could tell nothing from her manner as she ordered his immediate attendance at Counsel's Chambers.

A short while later he stood before the large "U" shaped table in the Chambers of the Elders. The twelve stern faced members were seated behind it, their eyes trained directly on him as he explained his alarming discovery in great detail.

'Dr Western's soul is at present frozen in 1984,' he finished.

He was still not convinced that the Probe's section would hold. A worried crease deepened in his already furrowed brow.

'How long will it remain so?' the Head Elder asked.

He shook his head and felt an anguished ache gnaw in the pit of his stomach. For the Elder's question had been his own thought.

'The exact period of time, I can't predict,' he said, trying to mask the probe's malfunction, 'As you are aware sir, we are still in the process of testing this section's capabilities.'

He paused a few moments, trying to find the right words. But there were none, and he was all too aware of the deafening silence.

Reluctantly, his solemn words still undecided, he admitted, 'It could mean . . .'

His voice trailed off, the Head Elder finishing, 'Infinity?'

He nodded his head. 'Yes.'

The strained expression in his eyes told it all and if the Head Elder had not looked away at that very moment, he would have seen it. His single word had hung heavily in the air before the Head Elder broke in on his muddled thoughts.

'What do you propose to do?'

'The only thing I can do!' he replied curtly, then, realising to whom he was speaking said apologetically, 'I will try, with the Counsel's permission, to place another soul as close as possible to Dr Western, so that we can get a clear insight into the dilemma we face. Through a suitable candidate we'll have an open line, via the Probe's contact facility, and I can attempt to rescue her.'

The Head Elder nodded gravely, digesting his words, before

questioning in a statement-like manner.

'There's no other way? It's not possible just to take Dr Western's soul by inducing her ancestor's death? You could simply re-run the programme, could you not, after you've reprogrammed the normal events?'

'If only it could be that simple,' Dr Swartz replied, rubbing his chin, aware that he had been moments away from laughing at the stupidness of the Head Elder's statement.

'You see sir, with the greatest respect, Dr Western has infiltrated a body that already has a soul. And as I previously predicted a conflict between the souls has occurred. For the present I have stopped this progression, but I have no idea as to the depth of the bonding. The bonding being the normal result of the conflict, between the two souls. What I am trying to say sir is, if Dr Western has taken a part of Maria Becket's soul as would be stage one of the procedure, then there may be nothing we can do. If we should do as you suggest, then yes, we would retrieve her soul, but we would also retrieve the part of her ancestor's soul that Dr Western will have bonded with. . . .'

He fell silent again, not wanting to admit that the thought level of section one of the Probe had burnt out, and hoping that his answer wouldn't prompt the direct question, 'How did that happen?' for he had no answer. . . . At least the answer was not one he could or would discuss with them.

He swallowed hard. 'On the other hand, if we were to send another soul back, we could be sure of just how far this stage has gone. The freeze mode will stop Dr Western's further bonding, but sadly, it won't regress it. We are walking new paths Sir. We have not covered anything like this, in our previous experiments.'

'If the Counsel should permit you to send a further soul back, what would be the risk factors involved?' the silver-haired Head Elder asked.

'There would be risk factors Sir,' Dr Swartz confirmed, 'But it would be a controlled transportation, with a thoroughly re-searched programme, thereby we could and would eliminate most of the risks the second soul is likely to encounter.'

'The change in history.' the Resident Elder began, seizing an opening in the immediate pause. 'There obviously will be an initial change in history. You will, of course, reprogramme any changes immediately the rescue has been completed.'

'Yes ma'am, naturally.' His tone was more confident now as he realised the way the Counsel was thinking.

'You feel sure you are able to do that? The previous data you have supplied to this Counsel shows. . .'

'I understand that ma'am,' Dr Swartz interrupted, 'but since my last findings were filed with the Counsel, I have covered a lot more ground . . . within the scheduled curriculum, i.e. "freeze" and "thought projection". The results of which have been excellent. Ideally, I would have preferred to run a few more experiments as is my normal way before submitting my conclusions, but nevertheless, I'm one hundred per cent certain we have the experience now!'

His dark eyes briefly challenged hers before he finished, 'Besides ma'am, what alternative do we have?'

With heads bent close together the Counsel of Elders discussed in lowered voices the situation Dr Swartz had presented to them.

A few anxious moments passed before the Head Elder finally spoke, 'There is no doubt in our mind, Dr Swartz, that you have acted responsibly in your immediate use of the Probe. In the circumstances, you have our permission to continue. This Counsel will await your results. You will inform the Resident Elder of your findings?'

Dr Swartz dutifully nodded and confirmed that he would. But there was no doubt in *his* mind, as the dark-haired woman usher escorted him from the chamber, that the aged Head Elder's last question had been a direct order.

The two red uniforms, that were the trademark of the security police, stood out like a warning light as Dr Swartz hastened towards the laboratory.

Each man had taken up position in front of the main computer, arms folded across their chests, an arrogant expression on their faces. Their cold steel-blue eyes fixed firmly on the team.

'What's happening Dr Swartz?' Dr Maxwell asked as he entered. Her questioning hazel eyes gestured to the life support unit that held Dr Western's comatose body. But Dr Swartz's dark eyes flared . . . and Dr Maxwell's honest concern was greeted with such frustration and anger as he told of the stupidity of Dr Western's actions, it nigh reached intimidation.

When he had finished, a still silence fell over the team, before Dr Turner's calm voice defused his hostility. 'Have you seen the trace?'

Dr Swartz nodded, then with Dr Turner close behind, he strode across to the main computer. Hesitantly the rest of his team followed.

'You may resume your posts either side of the doors. Outside the laboratory!' he instructed the guard immediately in front of him.

His dark eyes met the cold blueness of the guard's, defying him to argue. And with an obvious reluctance, that had nothing to do with Dr Swartz's authority, the guard broke away from his glare and glanced at his colleague. Unspoken words passed between them before they repositioned themselves in the corridor, one each side of the exit. Dr Swartz followed them with his eyes until they had settled. He hated their attitude, their very existence. It felt more like a prison than a laboratory, with him and his team their inmates.

'Let it be, Eric!' Dr Turner whispered.

He put his hand on his colleague's shoulder, his eyes enforcing his words before Dr Swartz relaxed and turned his attention back to the miscalculated programme.

When Dr Gemma Western's soul had infiltrated the body of Maria Becket, she had been a sixteen-year-old teenager who had almost died due to smoke inhalation.

'I suppose,' he told his team, 'Dr Western could think herself lucky to a certain extent, because if she had miscalculated, and there had not been a void to which she could have gained access, then her soul would have been in limbo, floating around in the abyss of time forever, with no way of returning.'

'But how did she gain access to Maria Becket's body?' Dr Maxwell asked, the heavy, dark fringe of her hair, hiding the puzzled lines of her brow.

'There again, she was extremely lucky. Her miscalculations directed the computer to this ancestor's body because at the very same time as Dr Western started her journey, Maria Becket's heart had actually stopped beating, thereby giving the computer a green light. The medic that had been called to the fire, restarted her heart but during those few precious seconds Dr Western's soul had a void to infiltrate.'

'What happened to the failsafe?' Dr Grey questioned. 'It should have picked up any miscalculation, immediately, aborting the programme?'

'The failsafe had been discarded. At this stage I can only assume that Dr Western turned it off herself. Programming illegally as she did, she'd have had less chance of discovery. The security scanner would home in on the power surge, but would have had to search to find it. Therefore she would gain valuable minutes, enabling her to complete her journey. But that is not what should concern us right now.'

He paused briefly, pointing to the hologram of Julie van Slijk, the victim of the hit and run. The young lawyer was in a coma and her parallel history showed no such accident having occurred.

'I want you all to pay particular attention. This, as far as I can determine, is the first change in history, and one that we have to correct.'

'My intention is to run Dr Western's history change through to the end, to see if we can infiltrate the body of this comatose young woman, to aid our correction. If it is possible, and the computer has a suitable candidate, then we will send her soul back, cutting through the Zone Time with the Litchen Probe.'

'The Litchen Probe!' Dr Grey exclaimed, running his hand through his jet-black hair.

'Yes! Dr Grey.' Dr Swartz enforced.

'But.' he started.

'Dr Grey,' Dr Swartz said determinedly, cutting him off mid-sentence.

He turned to face the rest of his team and for the second time that morning explained. 'The probe, as we are all aware, has not been fully tested, but we have no choice in the matter if we are to have any chance of succeeding. I have successfully frozen Dr Western's soul for the present, but we have no way of knowing just how long it will remain so . . . and if, indeed, we'll be able to get her out! So to minimise the risks involved I have no alternative!

The results that both Dr Turner and I have obtained from previous tests, have been excellent, and if it continues to function properly, and at this stage there is no reason to think it shouldn't, then we will have the added advantage of a direct link. A two-way communication between ourselves and the rescuing soul. The Elders have been fully informed of my intentions, so for the present I would appreciate your fullest co-operation, in taking up your posts.'

His eyes passed from one member of his team to the other as they nodded their understanding before he motioned them to their various stations.

'Dr Turner,' he concluded as he sat down and took up his post, 'I'd like you to monitor the trace. We'll use the smaller screen to release the necessary sections of the probe.'

A few seconds later the computer had confirmed that Julie van Slijk's body, during her comatosed sleep state, could be safely infiltrated by a direct member of her family line. The chosen descendant that the computer suggested, was Commander Irinka van Slijk, at present serving with the World Aeronautic Space Administration Centre, based at the Long Island Dome.

At just twenty-eight years of age, Commander van Slijk, a slim, but fit six foot, with long blonde hair and bright blue eyes, could have been her ancestor's double. Graduating from Flying School with honours, she now commanded a fleet of a hundred deep spacecraft.

Dr Eric Swartz stood in front of the Counsel of Elders, updating them on his progress.

A short time later the Elders were unanimous. . . Air Commander Irinka van Slijk would be detailed to Boston.

It was 7.30am exactly, when the Head Elder, having imparted Counsel's decision, closed the hologram Direct Communication Link on Dr Swartz.

'Will Swartz have to be told?' his equally-ageing white-haired assistant Edwardo questioned.

'No, we can monitor his every movement,' the Head Elder confirmed.

'He has no idea of our intentions?'

'None,' he assured. 'In a way it's not such a terrible calamity. It will bring us much closer much sooner to our objectives. When Dr Western's soul has been safely returned and we have the results to hand, we will be closer to beginning our own history change. We can think of this as merely a trial run.'

He paused a moment, enjoying his thoughts, concluding, 'It was a shame about Dr Litchen. I admired his achievements greatly.'

'There was no alternative,' his assistant quickly defended. 'He knew too much. He had to be eliminated.'

'Let's make sure that it doesn't happen again,' the Head Elder stressed as he motioned his assistant to leave.

Meanwhile, in the still-guarded laboratory, Dr Swartz and his team studied the next phase of Dr Western's miscalculated programme, the hologram settling on 19th September, 1984.

Maria Becket was asleep in a motel in Portland, Oregon.

2

Maria awoke from a restless sleep bathed in a nervous sweat. She sat up and wiped the dampness from around her eyes, her heart pounding rapidly in her chest as the nightmare lingered in her thoughts. Then, with a distressed anger, she threw back the bedcover, swung her legs over the side of the bed and stretched across to the bedside table, flicking on the bedside lamp. The hour on her digital travel clock showed 2.44am.

She felt so tired, so drained. Her knuckle-white hands gripped the mattress each side of her legs as a wave of nauseating fear returned, its tight ghostly fingers washing over her again before tearing at her insides as she battled to keep the terrifying images of the awakening dream from her mind.

Suddenly, the buzz of the clock alarm went off like a police siren. Instinctively her shaking hand reached out to silence it. Still trembling, she slipped her blue towelling bathrobe over her nakedness and walked barefoot the few steps to the motel bedroom window.

Drawing back one of the faded drapes, she wiped a section of the pane and looked out onto the deserted street. A bright full moon shone, highlighting the two-storey grey brick buildings opposite. From out of the dark shadows a black scraggy dog wandered aimlessly across the road, his battle-scarred nose close to the ground, sniffing randomly.

She watched motionlessly as the dog turned over a trash can, pawing through the garbage in its quest for scraps before disappointedly moving on and out of her line of vision.

Sluggishly she turned away from the window abruptly halting in mid step as her bloodshot eyes locked on to the black leather attaché case she'd laid on top of the plywood coffee table.

Pulling her bathrobe tightly around herself, she crouched down beside it, unsteady hands reached outward, her long slim fingers resting momentarily on the two metal clips each side of the case before she sprang the lid free and once more she ran her fingertips across the neatly bundled rows of thousand dollar bills. Confused thoughts swirled around inside her head as she recalled the last few days.

From four hundred years in the future Dr Eric Swartz and his team observed as section one of the Litchen Probe raced, receiving the data.

'Open Thought Section and Relay,' Dr Swartz instructed the main computer.

Less than a moment later they listened as Maria Becket relived the night of September 17th, 1984.

* * *

She could still smell the bitter ozone aroma in the evening air of the promised lightning to come; still feel the force of the rain as it beat across her face and the wetness of the puddles underfoot soaking her jeans, that she'd splashed through as she'd hurried up the second alley to the dimly-lit parking lot and the shelter of her car.

From the dark depths of her subconscious, she drew Bernie's embittered voice. His cold angry words echoing in her ears.

'Get the fucking bitch out of my office! Out of my life!'

Her hands rose protectively, covering her ears in a vain attempt to block out the sounds. The muscles in her face tightened in an expression of repugnance. It was all so vivid now . . . . .

She could hear the heavy thunderous rain hammering down on the roof of her car. . .

The fast swish, swish of the wipers beat in rhythm with Maria's heartbeat as she reversed the two-year-old Pontiac into a parking space in the large, darkened parking lot opposite Bernie's office building. Switching off the lights and engine, her unsteady hands searched the dashboard for her packet of *Kool* cigarettes. She took one from the pack and lit the end then drew on it urgently, whilst her eyes acclimatized to the surrounding darkness. Watching as the rain lashed at the windscreen, sending a steady stream of water down on to the bonnet, that seemingly steamed back as if in revenge.

Tilting the rear-view mirror toward herself, she swept a stray tawny curl under her black bobbled hat, her thoughts remaining across the road on Bernie's office building. She switched on the ignition and the wipers jumped to life, sweeping a viewing path through the rain-soaked screen. Setting them on intermittent, she drew again on her cigarette and pictured the inside of the renovated two-storey building, running through the well rehearsed plan in her mind.

The rear door she'd use opened onto a cream-tiled foyer, at the side of which was a maplewood spiral stairway with a bordering waist-high wall. To the right of the stairs was a horseshoe of grey leather chairs; a clients' waiting area. At each end of the chairs was a mock marble pillar and a display of large potted shrubs; adequate cover from prying eyes outside. In the centre of the rear door was a small oval window that would give her a good view of the foyer before she made her move.

Ned, the night guard would be sitting in his usual place, behind the counter of the security section, by the elevator.

There were two security guards, Ned and Phil. Both were retired Police Officers nearing sixty, who worked the five-day, twenty-four hour shifts between themselves. At weekends the building was covered by Seecor. Maria herself had contacted the company a year ago, when they'd just moved in.

Bernie had bought the old building and had overseen extensive renovations throughout. On the ground floor were two office suites occupied by a finance company and an insurance company. She'd used both to buy her Pontiac, her one bit of luxury. Both closed their doors at five thirty.

On the next floor was Bernie's office suite and two others. The first was empty, the occupants having been evicted for rental arrears a few months previously. To her knowledge Bernie had not yet relet the offices.

The remaining suite was let to a young lawyer George Nault. He'd asked her out several times over the last six months or so but she'd never accepted. A tall dark-haired man of around twenty-five, with deep brown eyes, the sort that could hold you spellbound; or so the girl in the insurance office had assured her one morning as he'd passed them in the foyer. He always finished at five, so would be long gone. She drew again on her cigarette, savouring the taste as she stared up at Bernie's light.

The modern darkened-glass frontage had two wide double doors much different from the old, grey terraced building they'd occupied for two years previously further up the row. But strangely enough she'd felt at home in that building. This one left her cold, with its long white-painted corridors and two-tone lemon and cream offices.

She took another cigarette from the pack and lit it with the butt of the other then dropped what was left of the filter in the ashtray. With narrowing eyes she inhaled deeply, then blew out a continuous line of grey smoke, her thoughts now centred on that humiliating morning four weeks ago today, when Bernie Walters had so callously dismissed her.

She'd worked for him for over three years; been his personal assistant, his only assistant, sharing his workload, his problems and worries, his life, and, finally, his bed! She'd listened to his moans about his fat wife Marney, his ungrateful kids and his cheating accountant Myers, who grew steadily fat on his money. She'd stayed with him through the bad times, when the business had hit rock bottom. When he'd been scarcely able to pay her, refusing him nothing. Entertaining his clients at all hours, she'd been nothing more than a piece of his furniture, his equipment; a perk to his clients and, in return, she'd received his insincere praises and the fortune of watching his business grow. He'd used her. . .

Her refusal to entertain the Las Vegas client had brought about Bernie's anger and her subsequent dismissal. She remembered the client vividly. A short thin swarthy-skinned bald-headed man, who resembled a weasel, with close-set penetrating eyes. One Matt Figorelli.

Bernie had seemed unusually nervous when he'd mentioned his name. It was on Bernie's insistence she'd accompanied them both at dinner.

The evening had started off well enough, although for most of the dinner Bernie and his client had spoken in whispers. She ate alone, the third in the couple. She felt it wouldn't have mattered if she'd been there or not. Then came the downer. The waiter had just brought the dessert trolley. Bernie had offered this weasel of a client, this Matt Figorelli, her services so casually. Just like one would hand cigars around after dinner. The old man had leant back in his chair and stared, mentally undressing her with his eyes. A salacious grin spreading across his thin mean lips. Her skin crawled as he eyed her through the endless smoke of his foul-smelling cigar. She watched as he drew the smoke into his mouth, his lecherous eyes narrowing as they moved lustfully over her whilst the blue smoke of his cuban cigar curled around his yellow teeth. She'd glanced pleadingly at Bernie, her eyes holding his in a silent appeal. He'd laughed, ignoring her plea, and with the flip of his hand told her to go powder her nose. Just then, she felt the old man's bony fingers on her knee. His hand slid quickly up to the top of her thigh. The disgust of his action galvanized her into life. She remembered it well. . .

Grabbing her purse, she'd fled from the table and hailed a cab. From the comfort of her apartment she'd taken the phone off the hook, had a hot bath and slipped naked between the fresh white cotton sheets of her bed, her mind cleansing her body of his smuttiness.

When Bernie had hammered on her apartment door an hour or so later, she'd ignored him and, after several hours of tossing, had finally drifted off to sleep.

Now, now she'd been thrown out, just like an old rag doll; not given a second thought and for what! She drew again on her cigarette, nervously taping her toe as she always did when she could not make any sense of her feelings.

She'd seen her replacement, a tall thin blonde of around her age, trailing alongside of him. Watched whilst they'd laughed the way she used to laugh. Her getting in and out of his much prized "E" type Jaguar.

She'd seen them. . . . She nodded to herself in the mirror as she smeared a coat of scarlet lipstick over her upper and lower lips. She'd show him. She'd show Mr Bernie Walters.

He'd used her for the last time. . . .

Returning the lipstick to her blue jeans pocket, she stubbed out her cigarette in the dashboard ashtray, then stretched across to the glove compartment to unlatch the flap. Obediently it dropped down and her full round eyes rested upon the gun. A sardonic grin spread across her lips as she took hold of the barrel and stroked it sensually, her long slim fingers finally closing around the length of the silencer.

Headlights from an oncoming vehicle suddenly lip up the interior of the car. Instinctively she ducked down into the shadows until it had passed by, listening, whilst Bernie's excited words ran through her subconscious, as she recalled his victorious summing up of a difficult case he'd finally brought to a close.

'Assess the situation. Formulate a strategy. And be in at the kill!'

She grinned again at her reasoning. She'd most certainly done that! In her macabre thoughts, he'd be proud of her!

Taking a yellow duster from the driver's side-pocket, she wiped the .32 clean of prints.

'Just a safety precaution,' she whispered to herself.

Her eyes gleamed as she quoted, 'Assess the situation.'

Placing the gun on the front passenger seat, she returned the duster to the side-pocket and pulled on her black leather gloves (one of the rare gifts Bernie had given her) before placing the gun in her raincoat pocket.

A further probe into the glove compartment produced a neatly-folded piece of cardboard, which she tucked inside her left hand glove. Then, removing the keys from the ignition, she slipped out from behind the wheel and locked the door. With the car keys safely in her blue jeans back pocket, she drew her black raincoat tightly around herself and knotted the belt. A moment later she started down the first narrow alley to the junction of the main road, collar turned up against the approaching storm. It was 10.05pm. The dimly lit alley was deserted.

When she'd reached the junction of the road and alley, she

looked up and down. There were a few parked cars but no pedestrians. Hastily, she made her way across the four-laned street to the cover of the adjoining alley that would lead her to the rear of Bernie's office building.

For the last three weeks she'd gone over and over it in her mind. The voice would let her think of nothing else. Just like her stepfather all those years ago . . . . . .

She'd listened as her mother had told her, 'You can never trust a man, not any man!'

She'd listened, listened good that day; the day she'd helped her mother roll her stepfather's body into the shallow grave in the woods; visualizing her mother's scarlet, full lips whispering close to her ear as together they'd dug into the earth. Her mother with a spade and she, with her hands. All those years ago. . . .

Tears mixed with raindrops on her cheeks as, head bowed, she hurried on. Thunder rumbled in the distance forcing her to quicken her pace. The elderly night guard would be watching television from behind the security desk in the foyer.

At 10.15pm when the show finished, he'd switch off the set, check the doors both front and rear, then make his way down the corridor to the rest room where he'd habitually plug in his kettle for his nightly coffee.

As she neared the rear door, she felt a thrill of excitement course through her, stimulating her senses. Her scarlet lips grinned silently; her whole being that of a huntress, in search of its prey. . .

When Ned had checked the doors and made his way to the rest room, she'd make her move and slip up the rear stairs to Bernie's office on the first floor.

'Step two,' she thought, her eyes wide and alert, 'Formulate a strategy.'

She had it all planned: if the night porter was lucky he wouldn't see her. If he was not, she knew exactly what she had to do. Some tiny part inside her hoped she wouldn't have to. But then, he was a man. Still, he'd been kind to her and wanted nothing in return.

'Not like Bernie,' she whispered vengefully, patting the gun in her right hand pocket. Enjoying her thoughts before promising herself, 'He'll get his. He'll get his!'

At the rear door she stood on tiptoe, peering through the oval window. She could see Ned clearly now. He leant back in his chair, feet up on an open drawer, his hands intertwined behind his head, laughing at the contestants of a game show on the small portable television he had positioned on the counter in front of him.

She glanced at her wristwatch. It was 10.13pm, the show would finish at any time now. Flattening herself against the wall, she waited, her thoughts returning to the morning she was so callously dismissed. It was all so vivid.

She'd stood facing Bernie across his desk. She hadn't even had the time to take off her jacket. He'd turned on her the moment she'd walked in, his face blood red with rage. His pale blue eyes cold as they mirrored his anger. His words biting into her. She'd begged, pleaded with him . . . . .

At first she hadn't minded the socialising. It was part of her job. But over the last year things had changed.

'Be nice to them. It's good for business.' Bernie had begged. When she'd objected he'd assured, 'Just this one.'

But there was always an excuse, until the next whisky-loaded, clammy-handed client, pawed her. She shuddered at the thought, losing count of just how many.

She felt used and she'd told him! And he'd . . . he'd just laughed, laughed loudly at her as, betrayed and powerless, she'd stood almost glued to the spot. Callously, he'd depressed the intercom switch to the security section and spoken to Ned, who'd just come on duty. A tall broad-shouldered man in his early sixties, with strong powerful hands.

Bernie had continued with his verbal abuse until the guard had arrived. Then Ned, seeing her distress had put his arm around her shoulders, picked up her things and steered her gently out of the office. Bernie meanwhile, his face still as red as his hair, continued his foul-mouthed rangings. His voice would always haunt her.

In the guard's restroom Ned sat her down and made coffee. She was sobbing as she'd handed in her office keys. He'd comforted her. Rather like the peripheral voice. Still, he was a man, and men could not be trusted. She'd listened . . . . listened good that day, the day she'd made her stepfather stop.

He'd been shouting at her mother, shouting loudly. She'd been asleep. She heard her mother scream. A loud piercing scream that had awoken her. Frightened, she'd sat up.

When her mother screamed again, she'd jumped out of bed the sudden tears blurring her vision as she called out, 'Mamma. . . . Mamma!'

But her mother hadn't come. It was dark and she was scared. She'd opened the bedroom door wide and listened. Her mother always left the bedroom door ajar in case she called her. She didn't like it closed tight. Her stepfather always closed the door tightly, but that was when he'd climb into bed with her, when her mother went out. When he'd touch her. She didn't like it when her stepfather touched her. But she couldn't tell because he said her mother wouldn't like her. Her mother would get hurt. He'd hurt her Mamma she thought. So she never told. Never.

Fresh tears stung her eyes, as the memories came flooding back and once again her mother's screams filled her ears. She held her stomach. Her head span as the nauseousness returned.

'He can't hurt you now. He's dead,' the voice calmed, soothing softly whilst she continued to recall.

She'd crept out of her bedroom and on to the landing, peering through the wooden balustrade down into the lounge. She could see her stepfather straddling her mother. His big calloused hands formed in fists, punching her as he shouted, 'Lying Bitch! Fucking Whore!'

Her mother cradled her head with her arms, protecting herself against the fury of his blows.

'Mamma . . . . Mamma!' she'd cried out again rubbing her eyes as she'd hurried downstairs. Her tiny hands tugged at her stepfather's shirt. He span around and grabbed her small, thin arm with one hand, then swung his powerful fist and punched her away. She could smell his whisky breath; hear her mother's pleading voice. 'No . . . No! Fred, not my girl. Not my girl!'

And she felt the pain as the force of his blow sent her reeling, crashing against the wall.

As he turned his drunken anger back towards her mother, she'd found her feet. Then suddenly, something was in her hand. She couldn't remember. It was heavy. Summoning all her strength she'd hit out again and again, the dull, heavy sound of her blows thudding in her ears. It was silent then. Her mother had stopped screaming.

She'd stood there, cold and shaking, watching through salty tears as her mother struggled to push her stepfather's hefty, bloodied body away from her. She felt her mother's hands wrench the blunt object from her grip before her warm, safe, secure arms folded around her in a tight hug.

She was sticky. Her mother gently bathed her. The water felt warm and soothing. Her mother was crying. She'd reached out her hand and touched her hot tears.

'It's alright little one,' her mother assured, 'It's alright now.'

Through the deep rents of her subconscious the sound of a car's horn blasting brought her thoughts back to Bernie. Wiping the moisture from her eyes, she took a deep breath and exhaled, her body seemingly losing some of its tension as the flashback faded.

Standing on tiptoe, she peered through the oval window. Ned's chair was empty! Where was he? Her heart quickened its pace with panic, thundering in her chest. Her anxious eyes searched the lobby. Suddenly his head appeared just above the counter. He'd bent down behind the desk.

She watched, her heart settling to a more steady beat, as he switched off the set before walking across to check the front doors.

She had anticipated his move, waiting as he satisfied himself they were secure before checking the rear door. As he approached, she slid back from the small window, hugging the wall mentally counting his steps. A moment later she heard him check the handle. In six minutes it would all be over . . . . . .

Her heartbeat raced again and she pressed herself tightly against the wall, continuing her mental count. Seventeen . . . eighteen . . . nineteen . . . twenty . . . until she pictured him in her mind's eye, safely filling his kettle to make his nightly coffee. A further glance at her watch showed 10.16pm. She had planned well. He was almost on time. She looked again through the oval window. Her path was clear.

Taking the bunch of keys out of her raincoat pocket, she inserted the larger one into the lock.

'Yes Mamma,' she whispered, 'I kept my spare keys.'

Her mother had been cross with her, very cross. She'd been careless. It was raining. A day much like today. A boy had followed her, teasing her on the way home from school. A tall, ginger-haired, freckled-faced boy, a few years older than her. When she'd shouted back at him, he'd shoved her. Her books and keys had fallen into the road. As she bent down to collect them up, he'd kicked out, sending the keys clattering, skimming the surface of the road and down through the slats of the grating on top of the drain. She could see them, resting on the ledge just inside. Rolling up the sleeve of her jacket, she'd stretched her arm through the grating, her fingers just brushing the top of them. The freckled-face boy laughed loudly then pushed her again, just as she had almost reached them; then suddenly they were gone. A deep "plop" echoed back from the drain. She withdrew her hand and stared at the draincover. The freckled-face boy laughed again before he ran off. She'd waited a long time out in the cold.

It was dark before her mother came. She hadn't listened, or she would have known where the spare set was.

Thunder rumbled overhead, jarring her thoughts to the task at hand.

Slowly but firmly she turned the key in the lock. A light click followed and the rear door became free to her touch.

Quickly she stepped inside onto the small carpet square. From inside her glove she removed the neatly-folded piece of cardboard, wedging it between the door and the lintel, then gently pushed the door shut. She'd seen her mother do this many times to the old barn door, before she'd put a new lock on it. The door held firm.

Replacing the keys in her raincoat pocket she slipped off her loafer shoes. With her shoes in her hand she ascended the rear stairs to the first floor, listening as Ned whistled, busying himself making coffee.

The long dimly-lit corridor stretched out before her. Silently, she crept onwards towards Bernie's open office door. Suddenly, the sound of a telephone ringing caught her unawares. A gasp escaped her as she hugged the wall, riveted to the spot, until the familiar sounds of Bernie's voice found their way into her ears.

Like a hungry black panther stalking its prey, she moved closer to the open door, stopping as she drew near the gap between the door and the frame. Her heartbeat thundered in her ears as she peered through the narrow slit, her eyes making contact with Bernie.

He sat sideways on to the desk, feet up on the extension leaf, elbow resting on the desk top, the telephone to his ear. Unobserved, she watched, listening intently as he spoke with the caller. Her pulse raced with anticipation as she turned to glance back over her shoulder, confirming she was alone. The hallway was clear.

It was only Bernie who worked late on Fridays. She'd never quite known why, although she had her suspicions. He'd always been careful to send her off at 5.00pm sharp.

One time she'd been curious enough to watch from outside, but no one had come into the building. She'd done the same for the last two weeks and, apart from a uniformed messenger late last night, delivering what looked like an attaché case, no one had entered. And, as was usual at 11.00pm, Bernie's office light had gone out and he'd emerged a short while later. Last Friday she'd followed him. He'd gone to the Chinese Restaurant at the end of the street, where he'd met that blonde, her replacement.

The sardonic grin reappeared as she peered through the gap repeating her whispered vow, 'Oh yes, Mamma. He'll get his.'

Suddenly there was another voice. A woman's voice. A soft Californian accent calling him from the direction of the washroom.

'Bernie, I'm about done here. What do you want doing with these others?'

'Leave 'em there. I'll be through in a minute,' he replied then turned his attention back to his phone call.

'It's the Shady Pine Motel. Should be there around 11.15pm. I'll park outside the cabin. What time can I expect you?'

He listened a moment then nodded his head, finishing, 'Good.'

Replacing the receiver, he slipped on his jacket and walked across to the washroom.

Fearful of her discovery she stepped back, the sudden panic that tore through her sending the beat of her heart wildly erratic. They were about to leave. All her carefully laid plans.

'Mamma help me!' she pleaded silently.

Just then the voice spoke. 'Follow them!' It boomed back, urging, 'Go now!'

Meanwhile, Bernie had picked up the internal phone and buzzed Ned. Deftly she turned on her heel, retracing her steps back along the corridor and down the rear stairs.

As she neared the last few steps, Ned's approaching footsteps echoed loudly in the corridor and she froze in mid step, the heavy thud of her heartbeat thundering in her ears.

Just then, the sharp piercing sound of the front door buzzer broke the stillness. A low gasp of relief escaped her, as she listened to the sound of Ned's footsteps pause briefly before changing direction. Crouching down on the stairs, hidden by the waist-high wall, she listened as he walked across to the front doors and opened the grill.

'Special delivery and collection for Walters' Investigation Bureau,' the express rider called.

A moment later, satisfied Ned's attention was on the front door, she peered over the top of the wall then crept around the bend in the stairs to pull open the rear door.

The small piece of folded cardboard fell to the floor and she snatched it up, returning it to the inside of her glove. Then slipping on her loafers she stepped silently out into the alley, locking the door behind her.

At the same time as Ned was checking the express rider's papers, the elevator door slid open and Bernie and his assistant stepped out.

Maria meanwhile, had neared the top of the first alley. With a quick glance left and right, she sped across the road and into the safety of the adjoining alley's shadows.

A few seconds later Bernie and the blonde, preceded by the express rider, came out of the building. The stormy night air carrying his words in her direction, as he bid a "Goodnight" to Ned before they were drowned by the roar of the despatch rider's motorcycle as he sped off.

She watched them walk across the road in the direction of the darkened parking lot. Then she hastened up the second alley parallel to the lot.

Suddenly the sound of an empty can's clattering stopped her

flight. She looked up at the high bordering wall. A black cat, with luminous yellow eyes looked down, arched its back in a hissed warning before it jumped down hissing again, running off into the dark shadows as she returned its menacing stare.

At the end of the alley she turned left, running the short distance to the safety of her parked car and slipped in behind the wheel.

Bernie and the tall blonde were already in his car.

She waited until he'd started up the Jaguar, the exhaust spitting out an initial cloud of grey smoke. He turned on the lights and drove slowly across the wet surface onto the side road. She slipped the key into the ignition and the Pontiac sprang to life. She followed, keeping well back, so's not to be seen.

The rain had ceased but the damp night air spat at her windscreen as the tyres gripped the wet road. The westbound traffic was light as she followed his tail lights out of the city.

At 11.16pm Bernie turned into the entrance of the Shady Pine Motel, stopping outside the reservation office. A large neon sign with the motel's name hung over the door flashing red and blue intermittently.

She pulled into the side of the approach road and waited. A few minutes later Bernie came out of the office, slipped in behind the wheel of the car and moved slowly off towards a row of whitewashed wooden cabins, stopping midway along the building.

She watched as he stepped out of the car and walked around to the trunk, the porchlight on the corner of the building casting his long lone shadow before him as he opened the lid and took out a small overnight bag and attaché case. Placing them both on the ground, he reached inside again for what looked like an oblong package. As he closed the trunk the tall blonde joined him.

Handing her the overnight bag he picked up the attaché case then slung the strap of the oblong shape over his shoulder and unlocked the cabin door. As Bernie switched on the bedside lamp, the tall blonde closed the door.

Maria watched and waited until she was sure that they had settled then, slipping the shift stick into drive, she turned into the dimly-lit motel parking lot and drove slowly towards the rear. Reversing into a space between an old station wagon and a rusting pick-up she switched off the engine and got out of the car. Then she hurried through the damp mist and across the rain-soaked surface of the lot into the shadow of the corner building. The porch before her was as deserted as the cabins behind.

With the agility of a she cat, she mounted the wooden porch rail, loosening the bulb to put out the light. Then swiftly returned to the shadows at the side of the building, her light green eyes searching the darkness, before she crept silently towards Bernie's cabin window.

The drapes were slightly parted. She edged closer and looked inside. The blonde was en route to the bathroom, her painful voice harmonising with a song on the portable radio she had in her hand. Picking up a white towelling bathrobe she slung it over her shoulder and disappeared into the shower.

Bernie meanwhile had seated himself on the side of the double bed facing her, absorbed in the contents of his open attaché case. She couldn't see what it contained, but from the ecstatic expression on his face, he was more than satisfied. He turned around and placed the case on the bed, his back to her.

She crept past the window to the cabin door and took the gun from her raincoat pocket, running her gloved hand over the long slim silencer towards the safety catch. A moment later she was ready and her hand reached out towards the handle of the cabin door. With a firm steady grip she turned the knob. The door became free to her touch.

Slowly, with measured footsteps, she moved around the door silently closing it behind her. Bernie, oblivious to her presence, was still absorbed in the contents of the case. The noise of his assistant's shower and radio blocked out the sound of her entrance.

The wide, sardonic grin reappeared, as the pleasing southern accent of the voice incited, 'Kill him!'

Suddenly, as if he sensed someone standing there, he swung around. But Maria had moved quickly, anticipating his move and stood just a few feet away, her slim pale face vivid in the dimness of the bedside lamp. Her green almost glowing eyes fixed meaningfully on him. Her painted, full lips a deep scarlet. His startled, ice-blue eyes lowered, locking on to the gun she held in her hand, pointed straight at him.

Nervously he attempted to stand. The silence of the room was almost deafening, against the sound of the shower and radio beyond. The hand that had just closed the attaché case, instinctively held out in front of him in a half protective gesture, only to be cut down as Maria in cold deliberation, fired three times, point blank . . . . .

The muffled noise of the shots blended into the radio station's canned applause and, as the bullets found their target, he fell backwards halfway on the bed. His unbelieving eyes seeming to plead silently with her, before his legs buckled beneath him and he slid to the floor, the last seconds of his life ebbing away.

For a few moments she stood there, the smoking gun still in her gloved hand, her vengeful eyes, unmercifully trained on his sightless stare as Bernie's lifeless body lay slumped before her. Then, slowly, she aimed the .32 once more and pulled the trigger. The bullet found its target dead centre between his eyes.

Stepping over his still body, she pulled the attaché case towards her. Curiously she tried the two metal locks and the lid sprang free. As she lifted the lid a silent gasp escaped her, before her mouth fell open in disbelief as her eyes digested the contents.

Picking up a thick wad of thousand-dollar bills, she ran her fingers across the stacks.

'Thousands. There must be thousands!' she exclaimed, the excitement in her eyes equalled by her whispered words.

At the same time the voice within refuelled her excessive desire, urging excitedly, 'It's yours . . . take it!'

Her lips parted in a wide greedy grin. . . .

Just then Bernie's assistant called out from the bathroom, asking him to pass her the towel she'd left on the bedside chair. Her wide grin disappeared as her head whiplashed around at the sound of the intruding voice, her eyes darting frantically from side to side, before locking on to the woman's waiting hand emerging from the half open bathroom door. The blonde. She'd forgotten.

With her anxious eyes locked on the offending towel, two deft movements took her over the bed. Her pulse raced wildly as she snatched up the towel and dropped it over the woman's hand.

The interposing hand clasped at the towel, then disappeared back behind the door, a muttered thanks hanging like the bathroom vapour in the air. For a few, silent moments, she stood watching the fading steam before a sudden flash of lightning lit up the entire room.

Her accusing eyes darted to Bernie's lifeless body, as if he was somehow responsible for the sudden panic that surged through her. Then, replacing the bundle of money, she snapped down the metal locks of the case and gripped the handle tightly, her eyes sweeping around the silent room. Her mouth felt dry. A dull ache in her temples threatened. It was then that she saw it and the ache was forgotten. The rifle, Bernie's rifle, the rifle he'd lent her when she'd joined the shooting range last year. The year she'd won the Ladies Sharpshooters Trophy at the Portland Rifle and Handgun Club. It was standing in the corner of the room propped against the wall, the strings of the cover tied tightly around the long, sleek barrel.

The blonde's attempt at a high octave leap went unnoticed as Maria's obsessional need for the rifle surfaced. Preoccupied with the single thought she made her way across to it . . the expression on her face ecstatic as she slung the rifle strap over her shoulder before letting herself out of the cabin. Thunder rumbled in the distance as the storm circled.

She opened the door of the car and placed the rifle and attaché case on the rear seat then closed the door and slipped in behind the wheel.

At the same time a black Trans Am turned into the Shady Pine approach road.

The blue Pontiac moved smoothly off across the darkened parking lot. As she switched on the headlights the blonde's loud, curdling scream echoed in the dank mist behind her.

A soundless flash of lightning lit up the dark clouds as Maria turned out onto the deserted road. Her blood-red lips parted in a familiar sardonic grin, before her mouth opened in a piercing shriek of laughter.

He'd used her for the last time . . . .

3

A short while later, as Maria searched for another motel, a solitary candle lit up a large rubbish-strewn room further down the coast.

Fred Hall glanced impatiently at his wristwatch. The red illuminated numbers glowed 23.53. The date 17th September.

'Where the hell is Gino?' he asked himself, absent-mindedly kicking a piece of crumpled, yellowing newspaper cross the floor of the dusty, rat-infested warehouse, his hands buried deep inside his trenchcoat pockets. Suddenly, the noise of an approaching car engine, filtering through the old brick building's shattered windows, broke the silence. He pushed through the broken wooden crates and hastened towards the window. It was Gino at last.

He leant against the wall watching as Gino, flashlight in hand, made his way into the building and up the stairs.

'In here,' he called out, walking across to meet him, his eyes portraying his greed. 'You got the money?'

'You got the merchandise?' Gino retorted, shining the flashlight on his face.

Fred raised his hand to his eyes to block out the glare, his other hand reaching inside his pocket.

'No need for that Gino,' he said, and held out two bullets in the palm of his hand.

'And the gun?' Gino questioned, lowering the flashlight as he took the bullets.

Fred slid his hand into his inside pocket and withdrew an evidence bag, inside of which was the offending gun.

'Bin taken care of. Saw to it myself,' he confirmed.

'No problems?' Gino pressed, taking the bag.

'Nah,' Fred assured. 'Not a one.'

'Good,' Gino grinned, 'You done good Fred.'

He took the gun out from the evidence bag and slipped it into his suit pocket, along with the bullets, then looked up as Fred questioned.

'Buck Western. How long d'you want the list buried?'

'One, two days at the outside,' Gino replied casually, 'What you do with it after won't matter.'

Fred nodded he understood, then opened the wrapper of a Hershey Bar he'd just taken out of his pocket.

'And the money?' he questioned, looking at Gino as he bit into the bar.

'Later,' Gino replied.

'Deal was, I switch the evidence, and hold on to the list.' He bit again on the Hershey Bar and Gino grinned.

'C'mon Fred . . . You ain't done that yet.'

'Now hold on there,' Fred protested, 'You know I'm as good as my word. The paperwork's buried! The five thou'll just ensure it stays buried!'

A complacent smile edged its way around Fred's mouth. Gino threw his head back in a short exaggerated laugh then menaced, 'You'll keep the paperwork buried alright, Fred, otherwise we'll bury you! Get my drift?'

The weak smile faded from Fred's face. 'C'mon Gino. There's no call to be making those kinda threats. You asked me to do you a favour and I done it. Deal was $5,000.'

He paused a few moments, watching Gino, then resumed, 'What's five thou to you anyways?'

Gino's sarcastic grin returned. 'Tell you what, Fred, you keep the paperwork buried and not only will I not bury you, but I'll personally see to it that you get what's coming? Come see me in, say, two, three weeks,' he finished, still grinning as he winked his eye, cocking his forefinger, like a gun, before turning to walk down the stairs.

Fred followed him with his eyes until Gino had disappeared from his view. Then, silently, he moved across to the window to watch as he climbed into his car and drove off down the shadowy alley.

'Shit!' he cursed and threw the half-eaten Hershey Bar onto the floor. He hated having to deal with Gino! The old guy, Gino's father had been tough. But Gino . . . Gino was crazy! Switching on his flashlight he blew out the candle and made his way out of the building.

Fred was fast approaching forty, with thinning red hair he'd inherited from his Irish grandfather, but retaining the same slim figure he'd had in his early twenties. He'd met and married his wife, June, a year after joining the force. She was three years his junior, a curvaceous brunette and mother of his two children, Sammy-Jo, now thirteen, and Phillip-Paul, just eighteen months old.

He smiled to himself as he straightened his tie. He might have to wait a while, but he'd earned himself $5,000. That would sure keep June happy for another few weeks. . . . .

As Gino turned onto the freeway, the light on his car phone flashed. He picked up the handset. A few moments later the colour had drained from his face as his brother Marco gave him the news.

'When Sondra came out of the shower she found him lying there. . . .'

'And the money?'

'Gone.'

'Where is she now?'

'Here, with us.'

'Keep her there, I'm on my way.'

Meanwhile, Fred made his way up the alley towards his parked car, his guilt-ridden thoughts, on his partner Tony Garnet. They'd been together for almost three years. Tony was just about the most honest cop he'd ever met.

He pulled up his collar. The rain had become heavier. A dull rumble of thunder echoed in the distance around the early morning sky, as the northerly wind pushed the storm out over the sea.

He quickened his pace, his feeling of guilt forgotten as he neared the end of the alley and hurried across the deserted street.

Slipping in behind the wheel he started the car and moved slowly off, turning right into Main Street that would lead him on to the main highway, South East to Los Angeles.

He'd transferred to Los Angeles in 1978 as a newly-appointed Detective. It had proved quite an upheaval. After selling the house in Paybac, they'd rented an apartment for a few months before what turned out to be a relentless search for the "ideal" home.

They'd finally settled on a detached, three-bedroomed, older-type house, with enormous scope, he recalled the realty woman having said, west of the city in the suburbs.

It had cost him every penny he had, and would cost a whole lot more before June was finished. But even he had to admit the property had certainly been a bargain. The only problem was, it sure took some money. Money it turned out that the police force couldn't provide.

* * *

For the next few days Maria stayed in her motel room, ordering in, whenever the fancy took her, from the local diner and pizza place.

* * *

Dr Swartz and his team watched patiently as the Probe's facility provided them with an in depth hologram detailing her thoughts and moves.

From the re-run of Dr Western's miscalculated programme, it seemed she'd emerged as a peripheral voice. A voice that for the present would elude them, for the Probe's malfunctioned section couldn't relay it. But a voice, nonetheless, that Maria had undoubtedly begun to accept as the voice of her dead mother.

Just then the doors of the laboratory opened and took his attention. The Resident Elder, a tall brunette in her late thirties, accompanied by a taller fair-haired woman entered.

'Freeze the re-run,' Dr Swartz told the computer, and he turned to face the Resident Elder. The computer obeyed.

'Ma'am,' he nodded, as Zoniac approached.

'Dr Swartz,' she acknowledged. 'I'd like you to meet Commander Irinka van Slijk.'

'Commander,' he said, his dark eyes warmly meeting the deep blue of hers. He offered his hand in a shake.

'This is Dr Turner, my assistant, and the rest of my team.'

'Dr Turner.' Irinka said nodding, before acknowledging the rest of the team.

'Commander van Slijk has been briefed as to the problem.' The Elder informed, 'so I will leave her in your capable hands. You will let me know your progression.'

It was an order and he knew it. 'Indeed I will ma'am,' he managed before she took her leave.

For the next half hour Irinka van Slijk listened as Dr Swartz explained their predicament, answering her many questions and, he hoped, allaying any fears as he went.

'I won't say there aren't any risks,' he concluded, 'but I am sure that they won't be any greater than the risks you encounter every day in the job that you do at the present.'

He paused a brief moment, his warm brown eyes smiling reassuringly, before he resumed.

'We are at this moment in time, an approximate half way through the re-run of Dr Western's miscalculation. So, if you'd like to join me at the main computer, you'll have a more in depth view of the problem we face.'

She sat down alongside him and together they watched as the miscalculation unfolded.

The hologram was now showing Maria Becket as she booked out of the cheap motel. The Probe's thought section sending loud and clear signals of her intentions to drive to Las Vegas; the date and time flashing in the corner of the screen. Friday 24th September, 1984. 1200 hours.

*　　*　　*

The fast-moving Pontiac sped on, the late summer weather, returning to its former warmth as Maria drove. The hologram provided a breathtaking view of the immediate countryside, of nature in all its natural beauty, before the great holocaust had occurred, forcing future generations to flee underground.

Maria drove without stopping for a continuous eight hours.

Just before eight in the evening, she had reached Red Bluff. Exhausted, she searched for a motel. They watched as Maria pulled into the parking lot of the Travellers Rest Motel, where, after a light supper, she took a room for the night.

A red September sun hung low in the deep blue sky, as she pulled the drapes for the night.

Dr Swartz and his team listened as the thought section of the Probe sped on revealing Maria's dreams whilst she slept.

She was just four years old, a slim child with long, curled, tawny hair and large, full, green eyes. It was a Sunday. Maria sat in a straight-backed chair in her grandmother's kitchen, her mother at the stove basting a chicken. She could smell the aroma of the roast as it drifted into her nostrils. Her stomach rumbled with hunger.

Maria's memory, projected a doting mother, tall and beautiful, with long, dark brown hair and brilliant blue, happy eyes. She was wearing a long black dress. It was because grandmother had gone to join the angels.

'What did you say, Mamma?' Maria said aloud, talking in her sleep.

The dream. Maria's private, subconscious memories, transported through four hundred years of their history, into the future. A courtesy made possible, by the late Dr Heinrich Litchen's Probe.

'I'll get it. . . . I'll get it Mamma,' she assured aloud, turning over in her sleep as the dream became deeper.

The hologram showed her running . . . running quickly across a large farmhouse kitchen. They could hear the sound that her bare feet made padding on the wooded kitchen floor. Slap . . . slap . . . slap. She ran across to the swing door that led out onto the back porch. The dream was so vivid she could almost feel the breeze as it gently brushed her face, the kitchen door swinging back and forth in her wake, while she filled her clean, white apron with large, green apples that her mother had stacked inside a wooden barrel.

The hot summer sun glowed like a large red ball, high in the azure sky. She had on her Sunday Best dress. It was a deep green cotton with a cream lace collar.

'It brings out the colour of your eyes.' She heard her mother's voice say. She smiled contentedly and continued to dream.

Taking the apples from her apron, she placed them on the long wooden kitchen table, then climbed up on a chair, swinging her legs back and forth, watching as her mother took four of the apples to clean and peel, for the intended pie. 'You'd better wash up now, Maria,' her mother's gentle voice said, 'Your aunt'll be here soon.'

'I don't like her, Mamma! What d'you want t'invite her for?' she questioned, with a pout and a frown.

'Now, now, Maria,' her mother chided, 'It's for grandpa's sake, he likes to see her.'

Her mother had turned to face her, smiling, taking Maria's hand in hers.

Dr Swartz and his team watched in silence as the hologram continued to relay Maria's dream.

She saw her mother's smiling eyes, her scarlet lips kissing her forehead as she said softly, 'Go on now, dear, go get cleaned up.'

Still pouting, Maria jumped down from the chair, then skipped around the other side of the table.

Just then, one of the two remaining apples rolled off the table and across the kitchen floor.

She stopped skipping and watched it, looking back briefly at her mother, her dream state in slow motion now. The sound of her mother's musical laughter dying away interweaving with the grey smoky mist that crept into her subconscious; wafting through the hologram before her mother's apparition and the mist became one and faded from her dream as the hologram returned to Maria's face, her eyes following the apple's progress as it continued to roll, abruptly stopped by the shallow kitchen baseboard. Moments later the dream was gone; the sound of the apple's bump awakening her.

Still sleepy, Maria eased herself up in bed and switched on the bedside light. A fresh moistness formed in her eyes as she looked around the unfamiliar motel room. Reaching across to the night table, she picked up her wristwatch. It was 6.02am. She'd been dreaming.

Dr Swartz and his team watched as Maria rose early, ate a hearty breakfast, then checked out of the motel. An hour later she was back on the road.

The day was bright and fresh, the sky blue and cloudless. The golden sun behind her, seeming to propel her onward. She drove continually, the eight hours of landscape passing in a blur.

'We're almost to the point where I froze Dr Western, Commander,' Dr Swartz said, indicating a still hologram showing a frozen sequence of a speeding car.

Then, turning to a point at a larger hologram above it, he said, 'This next part will introduce you to the victim, your ancestor; the body your soul will infiltrate.'

The time was fast approaching: 7.25pm, Saturday, 25th September, 1984. Maria had almost reached the outer boundaries of Paybac City. In exactly forty-six minutes, they would witness the freezing of Dr Western's soul, and the first change in history.

Dr Swartz glanced at the laboratory clock. It was 7.28am exactly.

'Run a parallel hologram, of Julie van Slijk's movements, prior to her accident,' Dr Swartz instructed the computer 'Pick up at 1925 hours, merging both holograms on a five second countdown, thirty seconds before impact.'

'Affirmative,' the computer's firm voice replied.

They watched as the hologram's "eye" sped quickly across the Tehachapi Mountains. Like a giant eagle it soared, skimming the tree tops before slowing down then widening the viewscope as it rested at the base, homing in on Paybac City. To the South East lay Los Angeles, and the North West, San Jose. A few moments later they could see her.

Julie van Slijk, a prominent lawyer just 28 years old was a tall, slim carefree young woman, face free from make-up, dressed in faded blue jeans and T-shirt. Sneakers tied by the laces draped across her shoulders. Silky blonde hair that almost touched her waist was tied back off her face in a ponytail. She ran barefooted across the lonely shore of Jackson Beach on the hard-packed sand, throwing a stick for her dog Dobie, to retrieve.

The dog jumped high into the air as the stick twisted and turned in its flight, before its descent into the dog's open jaws. The young woman laughed as the dog released its hold on the stick and teasingly barked at her before the dog's thoughts centred on the various seabirds that had descended on the beach searching for food. The wet sand bore the markings of the sea and waves.

As the playful dog approached, the birds took off, rising high on the wind into the evening sky, circling then descending again further on down the beach.

Julie ran after her dog, leaving her smudged imprints in the hard-packed sand. The dog was a doberman, a bitch, and very protective towards her. She'd raised her from a puppy. It was Saturday evening and as was usual this time of the year, the beach was deserted.

All week was a chaos of courtrooms, but here she found complete peace, just her, her dog, the birds and the wide, wide ocean.

Heavy dark clouds moved steadily across the pink streaked sky. Like giant hands with long broad fingers, they blotted out the end of a beautiful day.

The young woman, oblivious to her forthcoming fate, and her dog made their way across the sandy cove, their energies almost spent, to the steep cliff path that would lead them up to the main highway, four miles from the centre of the city.

Some fifty yards off the highway, stood the great black wrought iron gates of the van Slijks estate. Just beyond, standing tall and proud, were four Dutch Elm Trees, branches outstretched like welcoming arms.

Irinka van Slijk watched as the seconds passed. She felt so strange. It was almost as if she was watching herself. Her heart beat wildly in her chest. If only she could call out, warn her; prevent what was to come. But it was history, a hologram. It had happened; there was no way she could.

Just then Dr Swartz accidentally brushed her arm. Her flinch went unnoticed, as he studied the remarkable likeness between the Commander and her ancestor.

The hollow sound of the seconds falling away from the parallel clocks as they started their countdown, tore into her. Each tick brought the impending tragedy closer. She closed her eyes trying to block out her mounting emotions and felt icelike fingertips brush against her arm, leaving the telltale signs of goosebumps in their wake. She opened her eyes. A silent scream welled inside, as she witnessed the speeding car's approach. Julie couldn't see it yet. She heard her unsuspecting voice as she called her dog to heel. The playful doberman obeyed.

As the red September sun slipped slowly behind a large dark cloud, they started across the main highway. Irinka's throat muscles tightened; her throbbing pulse racing, as the hologram showed the fast-moving car rounding the bend. She glanced at the flashing clock; the impending accident was only seconds away.

As the holograms merged, the Pontiac zoomed forward, Irinka's hands rose quickly to her mouth, covering the gasp that escaped; the sudden bump of the impact coursing through her in a quick violent shudder as she watched her ancestor's body twisting and turning in flight. High in the air, landing abruptly with a hard thud on the side of the private pathway.

The fast-moving car swerved and swayed, righting itself before speeding onwards, as if the driver was unaware of the tragedy left behind, before the hologram abruptly froze the image. The computer's verbal confirmation of Dr Western's freeze, sounded far away. Irinka's ribs and head ached. It was almost as if she could feel some of her ancestor's pain.

The penetrating voice of Dr Swartz broke in on her confused thoughts. She listened, the muscles still tight in her throat as he logged the necessary information before instructing the computer to continue. Then she watched as the distressed doberman bitch howled dolefully, whimpering as she licked her mistress' face, before turning to run full speed in the direction of the great house. The dog's loud harsh cries pierced the stillness of the evening air. She ran back and forth impatiently, her constant barking bringing the butler and the housekeeper out into the garden to investigate.

As the housekeeper stepped back into the kitchen to find a leash to put on the troubled dog, the butler moved towards her. The hairs on the back of the doberman rose and she growled fiercely, backing away from him.

When the housekeeper returned he warned, 'Leave her Mrs Beale. I'll fetch Mr van Slijk.'

The hologram clock in the corner of the screen flashed 2014

hours. The excited dog had taken just three minutes to raise the alarm.

At 8.16pm Rogers the butler, a grey-haired man nearing sixty, stood before Piet in his study, an agitated expression on his normally cheerful face, twisting his hands nervously in front of him as he spoke, his English accent voicing dismay.

'Sir,' he started, 'Mrs van Slijk's dog has returned alone, growling and barking excitedly. Neither Mrs Beale nor myself could catch her.'

Piet, normally a quiet and well-balanced man, looked up from his paperwork, his clear blue eyes wide with concern. 'Where's the dog now?' he asked, a tremulous note creeping into his normally firm voice.

'In the garden Sir,' Rogers replied and motioned to the french window in front of him.

Quickly, without another word being spoken, Piet pushed back his swivel chair from the desk and hurried across to the window. Sliding the door open he stepped outside. Rogers followed closely behind, running in half steps to keep up with his determined strides.

Commander van Slijk watched as Julie's husband stepped onto the lawn. The emotions she felt were the strangest yet. She knew it wasn't possible, but it was almost as if he were her husband, not her ancestor's.

She watched as the grey-haired housekeeper bent forward, the leash held out in front of her, trying to creep closer to the angry dog. The Doberman's teeth were bared in a meaningful snarl and she stood her ground. The housekeeper backed slowly away, her face flushed with fear. She'd never seen the dog behave like this.

As Piet came up on them she breathed a sigh of relief.

'It's okay Mrs Beale,' Piet called. Then commanded the dog, 'Stand still!'

Dobie turned her head in the direction of Piet's voice and whimpered. As Piet approached the whining dog, she lowered her head warningly but her anxious eyes remained firmly on him.

Taking the leash from Mrs Beale's outstretched hand, he slipped it on Dobie's collar then stroked his hand over her head in a calming manner.

'What's the matter girl, where's your mistress?' he said softly.

The dog licked his hand and whined again before suddenly like a frightened colt she pulled him forward. Piet held on to the leash tightly as the powerful dog lead him through the tall hedging and on to the pathway that Julie always took for her walks.

An eerie shiver ran up the Commander's spine. She knew that pathway; she'd walked it many times. She watched as he let the dog lead him, signalling Rogers to follow. Mrs Beale remained on the lawn, a troubled expression clouding her still-flushed face, watching in silence as the two men disappeared behind the hedging and out of her sight.

Leaves crunched underfoot as the trio hurried along the twists and turns of the narrow pathway. Just before the last bend Piet slipped the dog's leash and rubbed his aching arm. He was a fit man but the dog pulled full force. The panting Doberman sent leaves scattering in her wake as she bounded on at full speed ahead of him. A few moments later she came to an abrupt halt, whining and barking loudly.

As Piet rounded the bend his eyes fell on his wife's crumpled body lying at the start of the pathway, just off the highway, almost opposite the beach.

Kneeling down beside her, his eyes filled with tears. Gently he took hold of her wrist and felt for a pulse, his heart pounding out a beat at double its normal rate. Her pulse was very weak but she was still alive.

At the sound of Roger's labouring footsteps he turned his head and shouted, 'Get an ambulance!'

Rogers, needing no further prompting, puffed and panted his way back along the pathway in the direction of the house. Dobie sat shivering alongside her mistress licking her hand.

Dr Swartz and his team watched as the hologram eye moved away from the scene. High above Piet's head, it soared across the fields to the city, zooming in on a stationary police cruiser, parked outside a cafe, the two officers inside enjoying the first of their nightly coffees and jelly doughnuts. Just as the driver took his first bite, the call came over the radio.

'ACCIDENT .... VICINITY .... COAST HIGHWAY....'

For the next ten minutes, Irinka watched in silence, her eyes fixed firmly on the screen. Soon her soul would be transported back through the pages of this history; back into the body of her comatose ancestor to become a part of this era; back into a life she was strangely familiar with.

Her heart ached as the hologram returned to Julie's grieving husband Piet in the emergency section of Paybac's Memorial Hospital. She watched him pick up the telephone and dial before the hologram sped to the person he was trying to contact.

It was almost midnight. Tony Garnet had just climbed into bed for a much-needed sleep before he started a long overdue two-day rest period. Exhausted he lifted the receiver to his ear.

'That you Tony?' an emotional man's voice asked.

'Yeah,' he replied sleepily.

'It's Piet. I . . . I'm at Paybac Memorial . . . Julie's been hurt!'

'Hurt?' Tony repeated.

'Hurt . . . Hurt badly . . . A hit and run.'

He ruffled his hair and sat up. He was fully awake now; all thoughts of sleep gone.

She stared at the screen as the computer froze the image. She hadn't heard Dr Swartz's instructions, just the mumble of his words but, as the hologram of Tony Garnet faded into a fine mist, she heard the computer confirm. 'Section frozen.'

'You can get the Commander ready for her journey now Dr Turner,' Dr Swartz ordered, then turned his attention back to the programme.

While his deputy and the rest of team concentrated on preparing the commander, Dr Swartz instructed the computer to return to the hologram of Maria Becket immediately after the accident.

He watched as the car swung from lane to lane before Maria managed to regain control, rocketing on down the highway and out of the city.

Some thirty miles southeast of Paybac, and a little after 9.00pm, Maria turned into the parking lot of a deserted rundown motel, just off the main highway and switched off the engine.

Every bone in her body ached but not from tiredness. She felt strangely different somehow. Isolated but not alone. Angry but defensive emotions mounted inside her. Like the whistle of a kettle just coming to the boil, they suddenly broke free in an all out attempt to numb the incontestable pain that seared through her insides. It was as if an invisible force had severed her in two, leaving nothing in its wake but a degree of combustion equalled only by the very fires of hell.

In one deft move, Dr Swartz centred the eye of the hologram on Maria's white, luminous face. His heavily-lined brow creased anxiously as his eyes widened at the spectral vision that befell him in her glowing, distorted face.

Two deep red, pulsating cavities that were her eyes, sent his erratic pulse thundering in his ears and his eyes were drawn like a magnet to the sinister evilness they portrayed. Suddenly, Dr Maxwell's alarmed voice pierced his fear.

'Energy mass overload!'

But before she'd finished her sentence, Dr Swartz's nimble fingers had already begun to race across the speak keys, inserting what he prayed would be the right stabilizing code. As his eyes sought the soul readout section, waiting for the computer's acceptance, his inner fears mounted. If the computer accepted this particular code, then he would be right! He needed her stabilized but he prayed he was wrong.

He didn't have to wait long, for no sooner had he finished, than the computer's acknowledgement accepting his deviation was on the screen. The digital readout had neared maximum overload. His brow was covered in sweat as his eyes willed a descent. He was just two degrees from burnout. He was watching Maria's convulsing apparition when, just as suddenly as it rose, it dropped. Just one degree from dissipation, the energy mass was drained by his suggested quantum diversion and they started to fall, Maria's luminosity dimming as her apparition became solid once more and she slumped back in the driver's seat.

Dr Western's soul had built an enormously strong bond; not far short of an impregnability. An impregnability that must never be allowed to take hold.

As he waited for the energy to level and the hologram readouts to return to normal, Dr Turner, who was returning to his station, touched his shoulder, breaking in with a gravity of conviction that neared his exact thoughts. And he wondered just how much of the hologram he'd been privy to.

'The longer Dr Western's soul remains in her ancestor's body, the less chance we've got to bring her out unharmed.'

His face paled, not from Dr Turner's words, but from his own inspired fear. He knew his deputy was right but the energy mass that had appeared in Maria's eyes was something far more terrifying.

'And when and if we do succeed,' Dr Turner said as he retook his seat next to him, 'Her soul could well be split.'

'Split,' Dr Swartz repeated.

Dr Turner nodded, 'That is to say, taking on the traits of Maria Becket's soul. The more powerful traits. In this case making her somewhere close to a psychopath. A sociopathic killer!'

Dr Swartz swallowed hard, digesting his deputy's words. He wished that his colleague was right and that he was wrong. It would be a lot simpler.

'You see,' Dr Turner went on to explain. 'A psychopath, and I feel sure that Maria Becket is just that, feels no guilt. The guilt that we've seen. That is to say; the guilt that she has been feeling, is the guilt that is stored in Dr Western's soul. It is obvious what Gemma is trying to do. She's convincing Maria that the voice she hears is none other than the voice of her dead mother. And Maria, according to the history hologram I watched earlier, had this kind of mother worship. No, an obsession, would better describe it.'

He turned back to his control panel accepting the computer's deviation.

'For the present, it's the closest thing to love she is able to feel or understand!' Dr Swartz broke in.

Dr Turner turned his head again, regarding Dr Swartz. Just what did he mean by that? By the expression on his colleague's face he knew a lot more than he was prepared to say.

But now was not the time to ask and he finished, 'Nevertheless, Dr Western, I believe she has been homing in on it.'

'So, if your theory is right and Dr Western does eventually win control, she'll try to stop her ancestor killing?'

He'd purposely agreed with him, but knew he was way off track.

'It's not quite as easy as that,' Dr Turner explained.

'You see, Maria Becket is a sociopath. A killer . . . Dr Western on the other hand is not. The bonding between the two souls has resulted in tears from Maria, and as we know sociopaths don't have tears. They don't cry! They feel no guilt, so they've no need for tears. Tears are a sign of emotion. That emotion comes from Gemma Western's soul, and from that, we can see for certain that the bonding has progressed far beyond what we know to be safe. . . . Consequently Gemma's soul has undoubtedly been completely accepted by Maria's. What we've just seen is a result of that separation.'

He leant across from his consul and pointed to the smaller hologram. The dimming scarlet voids that were Maria's eyes were slowly receding, taking on their normal shape and colour and Dr Swartz knew he had seen it all.

Dr Turner rubbed the stubble on his chin, then ran his hand through his shoulder-length, fair hair. Then, still convinced he was correct, he referred to his theory.

'When we studied the possibilities of a theoretical conflict between souls, you'll recall I wrote a section about multiple occupations.'

Dr Swartz nodded. Then, satisfied his colleague had recalled the section to which he was about to refer, Dr Turner continued.

'Aligning that theory to Gemma and Maria's souls, I reiterate, as with multiple personalities, and saying that the soul is the personality, a person can have multiple soul-like personalities. In this case it's simpler: there are only two. The two being Gemma and Maria.

If you can understand a multiple personality; as to psychopathic tendencies within one of the personalities, you can understand what Dr Western is feeling.

'The difference in Gemma's case is that she's feeling it first hand! She's not just another person inside Maria, but a person who at the moment cannot stop the other killing. Consequently she is taking another route, guiding her, making sure that she gets away with it. That way she guarantees her own existence.

'In a case where there are multiple personalities, it's my belief that the not-so-strong personality becomes the protector. Making excuses for the psychopathic personality. Concealing its identity. Hiding the atrocities it commits, whilst the other sort-of sleeps. So that when the dominant personality awakes, he/she has no recollection of the events that have taken place. Hence the blackout. The sleep.

'Sadly, this is not the case for Dr Western. Therefore she has only one choice, if she wants to win the conflict, and that is to take on board Maria's actions as the norm. Her only hope would be to try to suppress some of them and if that's not possible she would just have to go with them, live with them, thereby, protecting her, even helping her to commit the perfect crime by using the "echo" facility she has so aptly mastered, to cover her traces.'

He paused a moment, turning to look up at the soul readout section, before concluding.

'What we've witnessed confirms that Dr Western's soul has bonded with Maria's in the way we've discussed. But what is even more alarming is that, if we leave it too long and the bonding becomes complete, when we attempt separation, there's a strong possibility that we could kill the body. In this case Maria Becket's body. The probability if that were to be the case, is that we would retain her soul within Dr Western.'

'I agree, leastways in part with you, Dr Turner.'

It was true, he did agree in part. But the part he agreed with was only the bonding.

Both scientists watched as the degree readout returned to normality. Then turning to Dr Maxwell, Dr Swartz asked, 'How's the freeze holding?'

'Not good,' she replied, entering her locking code instructions for the umpteenth time.

'Each time I lock in she manages to break free. She's fighting the restriction with every degree of energy she possesses.'

'Stay with it Dr Maxwell. Keep her frozen!' he finished with more emphasis than he'd planned.

He turned back to the main screen, catching Dr Turner's eyes.

They were a mirror of his own and confirmed their chances were becoming even slimmer.

Maria, meanwhile, had alighted from the car. As she closed the door a sharp gust of wind sent leaves and old paper bags skittishly across the surface of the parking lot to rest at her feet. As the rubbish touched her, she swung around. A crackling electrical charge shot out from her eyes. The deep glow of luminous crimson, that they'd seen earlier had returned, pulsating in defiance, distorting the almond shape of her eyes as they once again became two deep, swirling hollows.

Both Turner and Swartz watched in silence as she staggered back against the Pontiac's hood to steady herself. Her fiery orbs focusing on a newly-parked car about a hundred yards or so in front of her. Or was it them she could see? For she seemed to be staring straight at them. Almost as if she could sense something else. A time. An existence. Just outside the range of her perception. Something that hovered just beyond her limited vision.

Just then the driver of the parked car got out. To all intents and purposes he was in a hypnotic trance. Maria turned her head towards the office whilst the driver remained transfixed.

Meanwhile, the degrees on Dr Western's chart had begun to rise and once again Dr Swartz's nimble fingers dashed across the speak keys, augmenting yet another mathematical equation. A degree he hoped would finally dispel the steadily-mounting energy mass.

As he looked back to the hologram, Maria's attention had turned back to the driver. A twisted snarl of a grin spread across her face. She was scanning him, looking deep into his soul. Through tense muscles his back teeth ground against each other. Then suddenly, as the mathematical equation he'd inserted moments before started a secondary withdrawal of the mass, the fury in her scarlet voids ebbed, and his panic subsided. The degrees of Dr Western's soul readout dropped like the once spellbound driver, to the ground.

They watched in silence as Maria turned away from them. Then zipping up the front of her jacket, seemingly oblivious to what had just happened, she picked up the attaché case and walked in the direction of the motel office.

As she crossed the shadowy lot and mounted the wooden walkway to the office door, a disused soda machine close by, the humming and buzzing of the engine that drove it, long since dead, sprang to life. A stray, rusted can crackled with static electricity before clattering like a death rattle into the receiving tray.

Swartz and Turner glanced at each other, then back to the screen, Dr Swartz's anger at his own fear subsided as the driver found his feet and continued about his business as if nothing had happened. He followed his deputy's brief glance to the readout section, staying with it until it had reached normal.

When he returned his attention to the hologram, Maria had booked in, parked the Pontiac outside the cabin, unloaded the contents of the trunk and lay exhausted on the bed.

A single, laminated wardrobe, the same dirty white as the bedside table that held the coffee machine and its prepacked needs, stood opposite. Its doors were wide open as if the previous occupants had left in an almighty hurry. To the right of the bed was a threadbare armchair, beyond which was the bathroom.

Casting a weary arm across her brow, Maria fell into a fitful sleep. She dreamt of Bernie's face covered in blood, and his sarcastic laughter. She woke repeatedly, bathed in sweat, the dingy shadowy room spinning, until the noise of the driving rain as it steadily drummed on the motel's black slate roof, lulled her back to sleep.

As the early morning sun arose on the pink-streaked horizon, dirty water that had collected in the potholes of the parking lot surface steamed. Wet leaves of the trees and bushes glistened and dripped in the sunlight, as the strong south-easterly wind that had driven the downpour, ceased.

At seven thirty a weary Maria arose. After a quick shower and a change of clothes, she downed two cups of black unsweetened coffee, repacked her case and checked out.

Just after eight she was back on the road, invigorated by the fresh morning air and the inner voice's promises of the meadowland she'd come to understand meant Vegas.

'Yes,' she thought, 'In Las Vegas the future will take on its real meaning.' The voice had told her, although it had been silent of late, but then, that was its way.

Keeping her speed at a steady fifty-five, she lit up a cigarette then pressed the automatic select button on the radio.

Dolly Pardon's voice sang out loud and clear. 'We got chicken every Sunday and the preacher comes around.'

She tapped her fingers along to the beat, her empty stomach rumbling in a nagging accompaniment.

As the disc jockey faded out the last in a row of three records, pausing for a word from their sponsor, a large blue and white roadside sign loomed up on her.

She read the words aloud, "Chuck's Place. The Home of Mamma's Specials."

She watched for the exit then braked and turned off, following the signs on to a dirt track bordered with small bushes and rocks, just wide enough for two cars to pass.

At the end of the dirt track, and about five hundred yards further on, "Chuck's Place" came into view. The parking area was almost full.

Reversing into a space at the end of the row, she turned off the engine and slid out from behind the wheel, taking the attaché case with her. Locking the door, she walked across to the diner.

As Maria entered the crowded room, a lone highway patrolman's black eyes followed her. Slowly they moved up her long, slim legs, excited eyes, intently studying the way her tight blue jeans molded around the well delineated halves of her firm backside. With his coffee mug resting on his lower lip, his eyes just above the rim they moved with her. His lustful thoughts stripping her nude with each step she took. Then suddenly, she was nude. In his eyes.

He sat, both elbows resting on the table, both hands around his coffee cup; the other customers obliterated from the surroundings as his eyes digested her soft white velvet skin, the smooth line of her back, her tiny waist, the two full curved cheeks of her buttocks. As she hoisted herself up on the counter stool, he felt his loins tighten. . . .

A skinny young peroxide blonde took Maria's order, reeling off in a sluggish tone, the ingredients of Mamma's Special Breakfast.

'Ham un Eggs, sausages, burger, tomatoes, hash browns. How'd yer like yer Eggs?' she finished, without looking up from her ticket book.

'Easy over,' Maria replied, closing the menu card.

Impaling the ticket on a hook just inside the kitchen hatch, she poured Maria her coffee, at the same time shouting to a fat greasy-looking chef whose shoulder-length black hair was tied back off his face in a tail, 'Mamma's special. Eggs easy over,' then slid Maria her coffee, before taking the next customer's order.

Maria placed the attaché case between her legs at the bottom of the stool, sipped at her coffee then looked around the diner.

Two overweight truckers were just leaving, the larger of the two, trying to slip his fat fingers into a front pocket beneath his over-large stomach to get to his cash. She smiled and took another sip of her coffee, watching as a garrulous kid around eight years old was arguing with his father.

'I don't want the cheese . . . I want the pineapple,' he whined, before pouting. She watched as his mother fussed, trying to placate him, while his father, having had his fill of his son's griping, swung his hand outward swiping across the kid's face. She waiting for the impending howl, which followed a few moments later.

With the noise of the kid's howling taking precedence over the dull hum of conversation, the waitress pushed her breakfast under her nose.

An hour later with a full, satisfied stomach, she picked up the attaché case, threw three dollars on the counter, and walked across to the exit.

The patrolman's eyes followed, still seeing her naked, his excitement building as she turned sideways to pull open the restaurant door. He watched as her firm full, breasts, brushed against the glass door as a hefty middle aged woman tried to force her way in before she'd cleared the exit, and his loins stirred again.

As Maria slid in behind the driving wheel, the tall heavy set patrolman opened the patrol car's door.

The Pontiac moved slowly out of the parking area, back down the dirt track and on to the slip road that led to the freeway. The patrolman followed.

Ten minutes into her drive with the wide, grey road rolling under her wheels and the bright morning sun urging her onward, he was still there, just two cars back, cruising behind.

A few miles further disturbed by his presence, Maria pressed down on the accelerator, increasing her speed. The Pontic surged forward, weaving in and out of the traffic; overtaking some ten or more cars leaving him way behind, before she pulled off at a deserted picnic rest area, to let him pass by; the tall line of hedgerow hiding her from the roadside, but not blocking her line of vision.

Some minutes later as she watched the steady stream of traffic through the bushes, her anxious eyes seeking out the offending car, he pulled in, stopping a few yards behind her.

She glanced in the rear-view mirror, blinded momentarily by the sun's reflection on the chrome wing mirrors of the cruiser, before her large, green eyes narrowed suspiciously. She dropped down the flap of the glove compartment and her fingers curled around the butt of the gun. Her eyes followed his every movement as she slid it into her belt and pulled down her loose fitting blue sweatshirt to cover the bulge. She watched as he slid his heavy frame from behind the driving wheel and alighted from the car, looking around before he pushed his cudgel into his belt and walked across to her.

As he approached she thought she heard the faintest whisper of her mother's voice in warning.

Then, winding down the window, a quizzical expression on her face, she asked, 'Is there a problem officer? Did I do something wrong?'

The patrolman said nothing, just eyed her cautiously, his hand resting on the butt of his gun.

Maria's skin crawled as she studied his weatherbeaten face, recognising the same initial lustful expression she'd seen on the faces of Bernie's clients. Only his expression was different, dangerous somehow.

'Step out of the car Ma'am,' he said suddenly.

She opened the door and got out, standing with her back to the car facing him, suddenly aware of his great height.

'Where you heading?' he pressed taking a step closer, invading her immediate personal space.

'Vegas,' she replied warily, standing her ground, her eyes holding his in a brief challenge before his broke away and swept over her again. She was not as warm and responsive as he would have liked. She had no respect! he decided as his hungry eyes digested her smooth, white skin. . .

'You got a licence?' he quizzed. His tongue licked at his dry cracked lips. His dark eyes bore into her, his twitching hand still on the butt of his holstered gun.

'Yes Sir!' Maria replied, signalling towards the car. Her eyes sought his permission. 'You want to see it?'

Her voice sounded garbled and strange to him, almost as if she was under water. He nodded slowly, motioning with his left hand for her to get it.

As she leant across inside the car for her purse, his lusting eyes slowly lowered to her buttocks. His stimulated groin throbbed and pulsed with excitement. Removing his hand from the butt of his gun, he searched his back pocket for a handkerchief, to wipe his sweaty brow.

At the same time, the peripheral voice broke free from its restraint.

'Kill,' it urged repeating, 'kill him . . . before he kills you!'

Maria's head whiplashed around, her long fingers quickly curling around the handle of the gun in her belt. The patrolman was still mopping his brow, he hadn't anticipated her quick actions.

'What the. . . .' he started.

But before he could finish his sentence, Maria had slipped the gun from her belt and was pressing it tight against his large stomach, her narrowed eyes as black and menacing as his had been moments before.

'Kill him!' the voice insisted, repeating in a strained whisper, 'Kill him!'

At the same time, his large hand grabbed a handful of her hair pulling her head backwards, the strong craving for sexual gratification burning inside of him, his other hand reaching for her gun. Suddenly, the gun fired. . . .

The heavy-set patrolman swayed in disbelief, releasing his grip on her hair, his unbelieving eyes lowering to his bleeding stomach. As he touched the wound, she stepped aside.

A second later, like an angry, wounded bear he came at her again. She fired twice more, the dull echo of the muffled gun's discharge, sounding loud in morning air as each bullet, finding its mark, tore into his flesh, sending the patrolman's heavy frame backwards, his knees buckling beneath him. With one bloodied hand holding his stomach and the other stretched out clutching the air as he tried to reach her, she aimed again, this time at his head. The lethal projectile left the chamber and found its target, dead centre between the eyes and he fell, face down.

A familiar cordite smell, carried by the cool morning breeze, drifted into her nostrils and she grinned.

A few moments later, she'd returned the gun to the glove compartment and started the Pontiac, the patrolman's lifeless body, collecting the gravel and dirt that sprayed from the Pontiac's spinning wheels. . . .

4

BOSTON MAIN DOME LABORATORY: 18TH OCTOBER, 2384

From a parallel dimension, four hundred years in the future, Air Commander Irinka van Slijk's body lay torpid in the safety of a life support unit.

Trancelike, she lay sleeping the long sleep, surrounded by darkness. Her entity, drawn from her body, rising into a warm protective tunnel of a transporting black mist. Her detached soul, cocooned in the black mass, was turning high above the shell of the life support unit, slowly at first, then steadily building its speed as it span. A powerful magnetic force at the helm, steering through constantly changing seasons; through centuries. An alien entity pulsating in time, entering into the unknown, in the form of a single heartbeat, to join as one, in the void of another body, in another time.

As Dr Swartz and his team monitored the journey, the hologram settled on 6th November, 1984.

'Nurse Alison Caldry, a thirty-five-year-old spinster,' she reminded herself staring at her reflection in the mirror that hung over the wash hand basin of the staff room.

Securing her shoulder-length, fair hair at the base of her neck, she put on her white nurse's cap. It was almost time for her day to begin. One last look in the mirror told her she was as immaculate as ever. Opening the door, she walked the few yards to the nurse's station, on the second floor of Paybac's one and only Memorial

Hospital. At the same time the elevator came to a halt and the doors slid open.

'Good morning Dr van Slijk,' she said, smiling brightly.

'Morning,' he replied sombrely, preoccupied with his own thoughts.

Her almond-shaped, lavender eyes followed him from behind the counter of the nurse's station as his footsteps echoed on the grey, marbled floor of the long hallway opposite. Her heart was beating erratically, as was, and had been, the norm, whenever she saw him.

'Dr Piet van Slijk,' she whispered in adulation, before the beauty faded from her eyes and they formed two slits. The sudden pang of jealousy that tore through her mounting, as she shuffled paperwork into different sections.

'What was it? Almost three years, perhaps a little over?' She'd had several dates with him, nothing too serious, but she'd have gotten to that if only this Julie, this wife of his, hadn't spoilt it.

She remembered that fateful day well. They'd arranged to meet for dinner. It was a Friday. He'd cancelled at the last minute with the words, 'I'll take a rain check.'

Then later that evening whilst walking her ever-faithful spaniel Sophie, she'd seen them. Piet with his friend Tony Garnet. They were driving along the coast road in Piet's Jaguar. Two women were with them. He never did call after that. No explanation, no nothing!

The next thing she recalled was the hospital grapevine discussing his forthcoming wedding. She'd felt humiliated, belittled. . .

'It should have been me!' she exclaimed through clenched teeth, slamming the remainder of the paperwork down on the lower counter. This Julie had stolen him from her! But she was unconscious now, in a coma. Piet was grieving, but, if Julie never regained consciousness . . . if she died . . . she'd be there for him. Her, Alison Caldry.

The sudden bell of the telephone broke in on her lone conversation and her muddled thoughts were forced back into the deep rents of her subconscious.

'Nurse's station two,' she answered lifting the handset, 'Nurse

Caldry speaking.'

There was to be a new patient, with a private nurse, further along the corridor.

After attending to the necessary paperwork, she straightened her uniform and made her way along the hallway, retracing Piet's earlier steps.

For six long weeks Julie van Slijk had lain in a coma. Most of the time Piet had talked non-stop to her, trying to break in on her private world. She'd felt sick at the thought!

This morning he sat silently alongside her hospital bed deep in thought. His clear blue eyes, once sparkling, dimmed as they searched his wife's pale face; his mind willing her conscious.

Opposite him, on the other side of the bed, Dr Harry Nelson, a tall, thin auburn-haired man of some fifty-plus years, a friend and colleague of Piet's stood, notes in hand, pen poised, taking readings from the dials on the monitors in front of him. She stood to his side adjusting the tubes that fed Julie her nourishment, her mind willing the patient dead.

Outside, a storm raged. Lightning flashed, thunder rolled overhead as a sudden burst of rain ferociously beat down against the large window of the small room. Piet was far away, lost in his own solitary world.

In the background was mumbled conversation between Dr Nelson and herself, muted, excited mumbles mounting, becoming louder, as Dr Nelson's voice slowly penetrated Piet's calm. He turned his head in his colleague's direction.

Just then a bolt of lightning found its mark and the overhead lighting dimmed, the emergency generator automatically kicking in, before moments later full power was restored.

'Would you look at that!' Dr Nelson exclaimed.

He glanced briefly in Piet's direction, his grey eyes large with astonishment.

'It's unbelievable! I've never seen anything like it!' With a furrowed brow he studied the readings, whilst puzzling his incomprehensible innermost thoughts.

Piet rose quickly from his chair. A moment later he stood beside them, his eyes watching intently as the dials on the monitor continued to race. Pacing each other as they recorded two separate heartbeats slowly merging together becoming one, strong, vibrant pulse.

A heavy silence hung low in the air like the dark threatening clouds as Nurse Caldry and the two doctors stared at the machine, broken only by the omnipresent sound of Julie's now strong heartbeat, seemingly rebounding from every corner of the room; shattering the immediate stillness, and with it, Nurse Caldry's hopes.

Just then, Julie's hand stirred. The electroencephalograph needle zig-zagged wildly as her brain began to function. Her blood pressure reading rose rapidly from a normal 120/80 to 180/100, then dropped with equal speed, recording the normal 120/80 once again. She opened her eyes.

As the transporting black mist withdrew from the hologram, having deposited Irinka van Slijk's soul in her ancestor's comatose body, the first stage of Dr Swartz's rescue mission was successfully completed.

'Opening Receiving Sections,' Dr Turner informed. His eyes concentrated on the stability monitor, measuring the energy force within the commander's soul.

'Energy force holding . . . levelling at 2.59,' Dr Maxwell confirmed.

'Good,' Dr Swartz replied, tapping in his coded security clearance to release section two of the Probe.

'The Litchen Probe section you require is now clear Dr Swartz. Energy cell is at your command.' The computer advised.

As Dr Swartz drew the required energy for the second section, the Probe, in the form of a small green translucent arrow, appeared in the top right hand corner of the screen.

'Releasing Section Two,' Swartz informed Turner. 'Programme coordinates set.'

'Affirmative,' Turner replied.

'Lock in.'

Skilfully, Dr Turner's steady hands took control, whilst his keen eyes remained firmly fixed on the pulsating mass. Section two edged closer, following its preprogrammed course en route to Julie van Slijk.

In a short while they would have obliterated the Zone Time period and gleaned Julie's past sensations and knowledge. By feeding these into the Commander's awaiting soul, it would allow Irinka not only to have an open line to the laboratory, but to be able to read others' minds. She would be enabled to travel undetected through their thoughts, with the added ability of relaying them, in hologram form, through the thought process, to the receiving unit of the computer's brain.

In a few minutes, it would begin. In a few hours, she would have full control of Julie's body, all Julie's memories infused with her own thoughts and objectives, plus a constant, direct, open communication channel forward, into her own time.

Julie's soul would retain her memories and theoretically be still in "sleep" mode thereby not hampering the infiltration, allowing Irinka full use of her body. Due to the nature of Julie's injuries, the computer had advised that some parts of her memory might be inaccessible; that problem could not be helped.

Just then the Resident Elder's voice, on the hologram communication link, interrupted.

'How is the mission progressing, Dr Swartz?'

He looked into the communication hologram and accepted the call.

'All things considered, quite well ma'am,' he lied. His dark brown eyes held hers.

Mentioning nothing about the problems they'd encountered, he said, 'The infiltration of the Commander's soul has gone well.'

'A success then,' she confirmed.

'Thank you, ma'am,' he finished, and her hologram faded.

With a heavy sigh, he ran his hand through his greying hair then turned his attention to Dr Stevens, a short, dark-haired man of around thirty.

'Stay with Dr Turner on his monitor. Link up to his screen until we have the Commander mobile. In the meantime, I'll continue monitoring Maria Becket. It shouldn't be too long now, then we can work towards aligning the two time frames and freeze the paradox.' Dr Turner, nodded his agreement.

At the same time as Maria was passing another rest area, further up the Las Vegas Highway, an elderly woman screamed hysterically at the sight that befell her after depositing litter in the trash can of the isolated first rest area.

Officer Dave Parkinson and his partner Andrew Farcombe, both in their mid-thirties, heard the despatcher's alert on their radio. At Farcombe's acknowledgement, his partner turned the cruiser sharply around and, weaving through the heavy, slow moving late morning traffic, sirens blaring, lights flashing, he accelerated right to join the main highway. Swerving into the fast lane, they spend on. A short while later they drove up the incline towards the rest area.

A distraught old man and his wife waved frantically for them to stop. He brought the car to a halt at the top of the incline and the silver-haired pensioners hurried across. A few moments later two other patrol units converged. As Officer Parkinson slid out from behind the wheel, the old man pointed towards the line of hedging.

Lying face down on the dirt gravel road in a pool of his own blood was the crumpled body of Patrolman Edward John Gifford.

Officer Parkinson squatted down beside the body and checked for a pulse. A few moments later, the sound of gravel crunching under two pairs of shoes disturbed him. He looked up. Lieutenant Andrew Mason and Detective Sergeant Tony Garnet walked towards him, the latter about to become the chief investigator. He stood up, his great height towering above them as they approached.

'He's been shot,' he said, pointing to the dead officer. 'There's no sign of life. According to the 911 caller, his body's exactly as they found it. My partner's taking his statement now.'

Tony nodded and squatted next to the body. The Lieutenant followed suit. The patrolman's gun was still holstered. It had not been fired. Officer Parkinson squatted between the Detectives. 'His name's Edward John Gifford, he's from the same section as myself.'

Detective Sgt Garnet nodded again but said nothing, his eyes were trained on two tyre marks about three feet from the dead man's head. A closer inspection proved both to be devoid of tread negating the necessity of any cast making. The offending vehicle had sped rapidly away.

As his keen, trained eyes searched the immediate vicinity of the crime scene for clues, it looked as devoid as the tyre marks. They stood up and he ordered the area sealed, then signalled Detective Arnie Clinger, a balding fifty-two-year-old veteran to photograph the scene.

'I'll see the old couple now,' he told Officer Parkinson, as they walked back towards his car, 'Then you and your partner.'

It was going to be a long night.

Close to 6pm, Maria pulled up outside the Golden Palm Casino Hotel. It had been a long and hot drive. The air conditioning inside the Pontiac had been as temperamental as the previous day's weather. She opened the door and stepped out of the car. The cool, early evening breeze gently washed over her.

Dr Swartz's eyes took in every detail as Maria strode into the large hotel's foyer and over to the reception desk to book in. A teenage, fair-haired luggage valet unloaded her cases from the trunk, his ginger-haired counterpart driving off a few moments later to park the Pontiac. A few minutes later the luggage valet joined her at the reception desk, then escorted her to a large front-facing room, midway along the second floor corridor.

As he opened the door, Maria's eyes warmed to the pleasing pastel shadings of the peach decor. Laying her cases down on the lugging rack in front of the bed he started his well-rehearsed speech on the operations of the television, radio, coffee dispenser and fridge.

At Maria's nod of understanding he flashed a wide smile and finished, 'Will there be anything else ma'am?'

'No, thank you,' she replied and slipped him a ten-dollar bill. His deep-blue eyes glowed before he touched his cap, thanked her and left.

Hunger pangs nagged in her stomach. She hadn't eaten since breakfast. Dialling room service she ordered a steak sandwich and coffee, then unzipped her cases and unpacked. When she'd finished, she sank down on the luxurious king-sized bed, her hands clasped behind her head, her empty stomach sending urgent messages of remembrance of the succulent roasts that her mother used to make.

She closed her eyes.

She could smell the early morning rain as it fell on the green grass of the fields. Smell her mother's delicious apple pies cooking in the log-fired cooking range that stood in the corner of her grandma's spacious kitchen. She could see her grandpa as he rocked back and forth in his rocking chair on the wooden porch outside the kitchen window. Hear the chickens as they aimlessly pecked in the dirt. See the sun far away across the fields slowly sink in the sky and heard her mother's voice calling. 'Time to wash up now Maria.'

The smell of the yellow block soap that she used to wash her hands and face! Her grandpa, as he walked towards her with a towel, his wrinkled weatherbeaten face, gentle and kind as he smiled, just like her mother's. He dried her hands, then she skipped alongside him, back to the house for dinner.

'Room service.' A distant voice called, breaking in on her daydream.

She rubbed her eyes and slid off the bed to open the door. A dark-haired waiter of around twenty-five stood there, his eyes portraying his approval as his face lit up in a broad beam.

'Your steak sandwich and coffee, ma'am,' he said pointedly.

Maria signed the tab then slipped him a five-dollar bill. With a touch of his cap and a glint in his eye, he thanked her and was gone.

She sank down in the luxury of the hotel's plush armchair and ate her meal. When she'd finished she refilled her coffee cup, lit a cigarette, then sat back to enjoy contemplating a luxurious soak in the opulent bathroom.

Meanwhile, a few hours' drive away, Detective Sgt Tony Garnet and his partner Fred Hall had opened the dead patrolman's assigned locker. After removing a small black address book, he left Fred to see to the bagging, logging and itemisation, then drove the short journey across town to his office, where both patrolmen Parkinson and Farcombe were waiting to see him.

Neither officer could add much. Both knew him, but not well. Neither officer had shared any off-duty hours with him, or knew much about his private life.

Concluding the interview he turned his attention back to the address book, having assigned his partner to trace the dead officer's last movements.

At 8.40pm, he picked up the phone to further investigate the background of Patrolman Edward John Gifford. But several phone calls and an hour later, he was not much the wiser.

The officer had no known enemies that would want him dead save the normal crazies that all police were blessed with, and there were certainly a lot of those.

At 10.40pm Patrolman Arnie Bennet, a tall, slim bronzed, fair-haired man in his early thirties, who'd been Ed Gifford's partner for some three or more years, entered his office.

'I just can't believe it!' Arnie exclaimed, still shocked, as Tony motioned him to sit. 'Ed loved to live life in the fast lane but.'

He shook his head adding after a moment's thought, 'Now don't get me wrong. He was a good partner. Sure he'd fool around. That was just his way, but snuffed out.' He clicked his fingers. 'Just like that!'

After pouring the shocked patrolman and himself a coffee, Tony sat on the corner of his desk, facing him.

'Do you know of anyone who would want to.'

'Kill him?' Arnie broke in.

'Yes.' Tony confirmed, picking up the dead officer's address book. Arnie shook his head.

'What about his private life. Did he have a regular girl?' 'Yeah, Sandy. Sandy Ericson.'

He sipped his coffee, then suddenly exclaimed. 'You mean she hasn't been notified!'

'Well no,' Tony said. 'There was nothing on his file.'

'Christ! I'd better see to that.'

'Where can she be contacted?' Tony pressed.
'1538 Kellerman's Rise. Apt 2C. But she could be anywhere.'
'Anywhere?' Tony quizzed.
'Yeah. She's an air stewardess, flies for Pan Am. Ed kept her flight movement plan. She gave him one each month.'
'Where did he keep it?'
'Taped it inside his locker, and a copy at home on his information board.'
Tony picked up the phone and dialled.
'Have they finished itemising Officer Gifford's locker contents? Good, have them look for a Pan Am flight movement schedule, possibly taped inside his locker. When they've found it get them to bring it straight over.' He replaced the receiver.
'Is there anything else you can tell me about Officer Gifford? Anything that can shed some light on this?'
Arnie Bennet shook his head then finished his coffee.
'You want a refill?'
'Yeah, thanks.'
He refilled his cup, handed it to him then sat back on the corner of the desk.
'It's as I said before, Ed spent most of his off-duty time with Sandy or myself and my wife. He liked to live life in the fast lane now and then, but he loved Sandy. He never strayed far, and whenever he did it was usually one-nighters.'
He sipped his coffee his eyes wide. 'But none that would shoot him. Sandy'd castrate him if she ever found out!'
With an uneasy chuckle he shifted nervously in his seat.
'Do you know where these women can be reached?' Tony pressed.
'No. Yes, maybe. They were just one-nighters, as I said.'
Tony flicked through the pages of the address book.
'Could any of those women be in here?'
'I don't know. What's that?' Arnie questioned.
'It's Officer Gifford's address book.'
'Ed's little black book.' Arnie said slowly. 'He used to joke about that. You know the sort of thing, the way guys do.'
Tony walked across to the coffee machine to refill his cup leaving the dead officer's address book on his desk, watching

through the corner of his eye as the patrolman nervously sipped his coffee, an apprehensive expression in his eyes as they darted to the address book, shifting with the same swiftness to the floor, as Tony said suddenly: 'When they bring the flight movement details in, I'll leave it up to you to break the news to Sandy Ericson.'

He walked back and retook his seat behind his desk. Arnie was bathed in a nervous sweat.

'Perhaps you'd ask her to call in. Or, if she'd prefer, I could go see her.'

He nodded he would.

When the flight details arrived, Tony checked Sandy Ericson's location. It seemed she would arrive at London Heathrow within the hour. Asking the duty officer to photocopy the details, he told the patrolman he could use the station phone in the side office. Arnie drained his coffee and went next door.

As Officer Bennet closed the side office door, Fred Hall arrived.

'News?' Tony questioned.

'Sure have,' he replied. 'It seems that Gifford often used patrol cars when off duty. I've got George Martin taking a statement from the Duty Officer. His favourite place was Chuck's Diner, ten minutes from where we found his body. Used to use 'em just to cruise.'

'Cruise?' Tony questioned.

'Yeah, cruise,' Fred repeated, 'Seems he had a bit of a scam going down. He'd cruise, following lone women drivers, pull them over for some minor offence or document check, then offer to forget it for a piece of action.'

As the evening wore on Tony took a trip out to Chuck's Diner, while Fred took an unofficial look inside Officer Gifford's apartment.

The diner's morning waitresses had finished, but the manager remembered him sitting at a table on Jesse Talbot's station.

After taking the morning staff's details, he headed back to his car for the ten-minute drive to Wilsden Park and the waitress who'd served the dead officer his last meal.

Jesse was a talkative well-rounded forty-year-old divorcee, and although still shocked at the earlier news bulletin, she remembered clearly every detail. The patrolman after consuming three black coffees and two bites of an apple pie, had left the diner at five after nine that morning.

'He was acting kinda strange,' she said, 'I remember saying to Doris, that's my friend on the next station, he didn't seem his usual self. He was always joking with me. Said what I needed was a good man.' She giggled, adding, 'I told him, I'd had enough of those to last me a lifetime!' She rolled her eyes and smiled. 'I still can't believe it! He was always so polite an' all! Goodlooking guy. Always left a good tip. Used to come in all the time an' always sat in the same seat.'

'Did he ever meet anyone there?'

'Nope,' she said, shaking her head, 'Can't say as I ever saw him with anyone.'

It was close to ten-thirty when Tony drove back to his office. The other two waitresses had said much the same, confirming that Jesse had indeed gone to break at five after nine.

Arnie Bennet, the dead officer's partner, had in the meantime, managed to contact Sandy Ericson and would meet her flight at Los Angeles airport the following morning. It was close to two in the morning when both Tony and Fred signed out.

Maria awoke just after seven. She'd slept almost twelve hours. Slipping into her robe, she padded barefoot across the soft peach carpet to pull back the drapes.

The red morning sun shone brightly just above the horizon in a warm greeting. The wide street below was deserted.

'The best time of the day,' she thought and a smile of contentment spread across her face. Ruffling her thick, tawny hair she made her way into the bathroom.

By the time breakfast had arrived she'd transferred $5,000 from the stolen attaché case into her cream clutch bag, made up her face and slipped into her favourite figure-hugging emerald jersey dress and matching high-heel shoes, admiring her hour glass figure as she did so.

Today was the beginning of her new life. She'd not have to worry about money ever again.

Draining her coffee cup, she picked up the attaché case, tucked her clutch bag under her arm and made her way down to the reception area. It was 9.00am and the lobby was full.

Securing the case in a newly-acquired safety deposit box, she walked through to the casino. The first stage of her plan was about to begin.

The brightly-lit casino was crowded as she changed her five thousand into chips and cruised the tables. Then settling on one at the rear of the room, she stood behind a row of fully-occupied gilt chairs. An elderly woman with a blue hair rinse, sporting a large diamond bracelet on her thin wrist, pushed the remaining stack of chips in front of her on to the black 11 square. A loud laugh echoed inside Maria's mind.

'Dr Swartz!' Dr Maxwell called out suddenly. 'I think you'd better see this.'

He hurried across to her section and looked over her shoulder, his eyes following her pointed finger, to the soul readout section.

'The computer can't hold her. Dr Western's soul is moving in and out of freeze mode whenever she wants! She's draining the mode's cells, conserving the energy, adding it to her own!'

He watched as the digital readout crept up towards five degrees. 'Shall I disengage Freeze?'

Ignoring her question, his eyes studied the readings. Then, tapping in another command, he waited for the computer's acceptance which came almost immediately.

'That should hold her a little longer, but keep a watchful eye on her energy level. If it reaches five point two, sing out. If we disengage too soon, she'll bond too deeply to attempt a separation.' She nodded her head and he returned to his section.

'No more bets.' The croupier called out repeating himself as he turned the wheel. 'No more bets.'

Maria watched impatiently as the ball jostled and bounced

against the spinning wheel, before several seconds later it jumped into a pocket settling on a number.

As the wheel came to a halt, the croupier called out. 'Red 12,' then raked in the lost chips.

For a few, brief moments the elderly woman stared at the wheel, cursing her misfortune, then stood up, snatched up her handbag and abruptly pushed past Maria in a hastened exit.

She watched as the elderly woman hurried away, then taking her seat, she sat down facing the table. The gap behind her closed instantly.

When the croupier made his call for bets, she opened her handbag and took out her chips stacking them to her left.

'Red 20, $2,000 on Red 20,' the voice rasped.

Its difficulty in speaking passing unnoticed as Maria's eyes sparkled with anticipation. She placed the chips on the red twenty square and watched while the other gamblers placed their bets.

On her left sat a striking, rather than attractive woman of around fifty, with shoulder-length, golden blonde hair, greying at the temples. She glanced at Maria, twisting a $500 chip between her fingers, then smiled before placing it next to Maria's bet.

Just then the croupier called out. 'No more bets.'

'Just in time!' The woman muttered in a low whisper.

A moment later the croupier had started the wheel, the numbers fading into whirring oblivion before the ball was released and it jumped backwards and forwards over the numbers, bouncing teasingly with the sections before dropping into a selected pocket. When the wheel came to a stop, the croupier confirmed. 'Red 20.'

The golden-haired woman gasped, unconsciously gripping Maria's arm. 'I've won . . . I've won' She shouted excitedly.

Her strong southern drawl both pleased and warmed Maria, reminding her of her mother's voice. A low buzz of conversation erupted around the gaming table as the croupier pushed a large stack of chips towards the golden-haired woman, repeating his action in greater depth towards Maria.

'That's $15,000 plus my bet!' She exclaimed. Her warm, brown eyes wide as they met Maria's. Maria smiled but said nothing, just raked in her own chips, mentally totalling $62,000, including her stake.

'One more bet on Red 24,' the still-rasping voice managed, 'Put $2,000 on Red 24.' Maria's eyes sparkled as she obeyed.

The golden-haired woman watched as Maria placed her second bet, then quickly followed her lead with another $500 chip.

'No more bets,' the croupier called out, repeating as he started the wheel, 'No more bets.'

As the numbers faded into a spinning mass he released the ball. Once again, the gamblers watched as the ball jostled and fought against the wheel, the clicking sound vanishing as the ball selected a section and the wheel gently slowed, finally stopping.

A loud gasp came from the crowd as the croupier called out, 'Red 24.'

The golden-haired woman grabbed Maria's arm again as the excitement surged through her and the croupier pushed another stack in her direction. Cupping her hand over her mouth in disbelief, she glanced at Maria whilst the croupier pushed an even greater stack towards her.

Just then the voice returned. 'That's enough for now, we'll continue tonight.'

Maria obeyed, as was quickly becoming the norm, and raked in her chips. When the croupier called for more bets, she shook her head. The golden-haired woman did the same.

When she had finished, she stood up alongside Maria, and offered a handshake, her rich southern accent filtering into Maria's ears like music as she said, 'You always this here lucky?' Maria smiled as she shook her hand, 'I don't know. It's my first time.'

'Beginner's luck then,' the golden-haired woman quickly concluded, still holding her hand. Maria felt strongly drawn to her as she held her warm, brown smiling eyes, with her own.

'The name's Abigale Western. Abby to my friends.'

'Maria . . . Maria Becket.'

'Well, Maria, how's about I buy you a drink? You made me a good win. First time I come out on top for some time.'

'That'd be nice. I'd like that,' she replied smiling, unconsciously mimicking Abby's southern drawl; the same southern drawl that her mother's sister Geraldine had insisted she lose by advocating elocution lessons when she'd been forced to live with her, after the death of her beloved mother.

Maria, who'd never known any warmth or real kindness from her aunt, grew up hating her. In any clash of wills, Maria could never win. But clash of wills there was. For despite Maria being a total failure in her aunt's eyes, (and at that time in her own), she did excel in several fields of endeavour. But Maria's success at the shooting range couldn't win her a scholarship to college to study art; and art was not what her aunt had in mind.

So, ignoring the professional advice of Maria's teachers, she cut off these avenues and steered the artistic Maria into a secretarial study course, a course that Maria grew to hate almost as much as she hated her aunt.

The decision proved to be a fatal one, for, unable to take any more, Maria retreated inside herself, discovering after what was later diagnosed as a breakdown, a friend. A soft warm distant voice; a voice that placated her, that listened and advised her, that had grown with her; that was slowly becoming part of her. The same friend that had helped her to free herself, by the carefully planned murder of her hated aunt Geraldine.

The same deep, soothing, southern-accented voice that promised her an abundance of wealth. A voice that sounded like the voice of her dead mother. A voice that was becoming her mother.

The two women had made their way to the bar section, and occupied the stools adjacent to the counter.

'What's your poison?' Abby asked.

'Bourbon on the rocks.' Maria replied, not quite sure why she'd said that. She'd never really drunk hard liquor in her life before, preferring wine, but here she sat at a quarter to eleven in the morning ordering Bourbon.

'Make that two,' Abby confirmed to the tall, dark-haired, muscular man about to dispense their drinks.

'Here's to you an' beginner's luck,' Abby toasted, holding up her glass in a salute.

'Beginner's luck,' Maria agreed, clinking her glass against Abby's.

'Been here long?' Abby questioned, taking a pack of Marlboro from her shoulder bag.

'Got in last night.' She took the offered cigarette and fingered her watch as she waited for a light.

'Don't you find a watch puts you off?' Abby asked, flicking the lighter. 'Can't stand 'em myself. Only wear 'em when I have to. That is, when I'm flying.'

She knocked back her drink, then signalled the bartender to refill her glass, resuming, 'Run a flying school, a small air freight company at the edge of the desert.'

She turned to face Maria. 'Refill?' 'No, thanks. Not just yet.'

Abby took a sip from her refilled glass and resumed, 'It's my day off today. My husband Buck's outta town on a charter, so I thought to myself, why not treat yourself Abby?'

She took a handful of peanuts out of the bowl on the counter and dropped a measured amount into her mouth, then twisted around to face Maria.

'So. You on vacation?' Her soft brown eyes smiled, causing tiny wrinkles to appear at the sides.

'Sort of. Thought I'd sort of relocate myself.'

'Now, if you're looking for a house to maybe rent or buy, you should take a look up on Hunter's Ridge. They've built a number of real nice properties out that way. Backs on to the valley. Could show you myself, if you'd like.'

'Yeah, thanks, that'd be nice.'

'It'd be my pleasure,' Abby confirmed smiling, then nudging her arm added, 'No time like the present.'

Maria drained her glass whilst Abby settled up, then both women walked across to the cashier's office. Abby was first to hand in her chips, taking her winnings in cash.

'Thanks again.' She said, a broad beam on her face. She kissed the handful of dollars, then noticing Maria hadn't handed in hers, she asked.

'Ain't you gonna cash in?'

Maria smiled. 'No not just yet. I'm gonna try some more tonight.'

Abby grinned. 'Well now, I might join you myself.'

The two women made their way out to the front of the casino, to the car valet station.

'My Merc Rory please,' Abby said handing the tall young fair-haired valet her ticket, her eyes still sparkling from her lucky win.

'Yes ma'am,' he replied and ran off at top speed to fetch her car.

'Nice boy, parks my car carefully, an' in a prime position. He's in college you know, paying his own way. Wants to be a doc.' The broad beam returned to her face as she added, 'Got to keep in with him, never know when I'm gonna need one.'

Maria returned her smile, watching as the valet pulled up outside the casino with Abby's dark blue Mercedes. He stepped out and held the door. As Abby passed by him, she pressed a twenty dollar bill into his hand.

'Thank you ma'am, Mrs Western,' he said, his bright hazel eyes shining, before he closed the door to run around the other side to help Maria into the passenger seat.

'You both have a nice day,' he added, his face still beaming.

'We sure will Rory, and you too.'

'Yes ma'am!' he finished.

'Buckle up.' Abby told her, 'It'll take about ten minutes. We'll pass Hunter's Ridge on the way to the airfield.'

'The airfield,' Maria repeated. 'I thought we'd be driving.'

'Nah.' Abby said, wrinkling her nose, 'You can't see the layout so good.' She grinned, then turned to face Maria. 'Not scared of flying are you?'

'No,' Maria assured, 'On the contrary, thought I might take some lessons myself.'

'Now you're talking. I think everyone oughtta learn. Course I'm solely thinking of my business.' She chuckled loudly as they drove off.

Meanwhile, in Los Angeles, Detective Sgt Garnet stood looking through the window of his second-floor office, sipping his coffee, thinking about the autopsy report he'd just read. It was almost eleven thirty and the early morning smog was just lifting. He took another mouthful of coffee then walked back to his desk and leafed through the report.

Ed Gifford had been shot three times at close range. The last .32 bullet, passing dead centre through the brain, being the one that had killed him. Time of death was between 9.00 and 10.00am. As his eager eyes read on, an angry crease formed in his brow. At the time of his death, Officer Gifford had been high on cocaine.

He slammed the desk with the file, stood up and walked across to the window running his hand through his fair hair. Just then Fred Hall tapped on his door and walked inside. He swung around.

'Bud sent in some jelly doughnuts, says you didn't call by this morning for your normal fix of sugar.'

He chuckled, then placed the tray of doughnuts on the desk, his smile disappearing as he glanced across at Tony. 'What's up?'

'The autopsy,' Tony replied, pointing towards the file, his light-blue eyes dark and angry.

'Seems Officer Gifford was taking another trip yesterday, on Cocaine!'

Fred picked up the file, nervously licking his lips as he read the last page. Tony watched as Fred's face paled, noting the familiar signs of his partner's unease.

'Get Arnie Bennet back in. He knows more than he's saying. Bring in the girlfriend as well. He's meeting her at the airport in about twenty minutes.'

'Right away,' Fred replied and hastily made his exit.

The sun was warm and overhead as Abby and Maria drove towards Desert Road. Maria listened as Abby showed her the new shopping mall and various casinos they passed, giving her the lowdown on how much she'd lost or won in each.

'At the next light I'll make a right, that'll take us by way of Hunter's Ridge. It's the long route, but what the heck, we got all day. I guess I can show you it at ground level before we fly.'

As they approached the lights, Abby swept around to the right taking the inside lane. Desert Road stretched out before them, a wide four-laned road, that narrowed into two lanes further on.

Dr Swartz glanced across at Dr Turner's hologram, observing as Julie van Slijk's body, infiltrated by the soul of Irinka van Slijk, stirred.

'Don't let her awaken fully,' he ordered and his deputy adjusted the output.

Both doctors watched as the Probe throbbed and pulsed in

readiness before Dr Turner instructed Dr Stevens, 'Link-up.'

He depressed the link button and confirmed, 'Starting input . . . Programme running.'

The three doctors watched as the probe went into action transferring Julie's history, deeds, thoughts and feelings, into Irinka's soul. A short while later the operation was complete.

'Reset time,' Dr Turner ordered, 'On 9.30am.'

'Time reset,' Dr Stevens confirmed.

'Open communication channel.'

'Section opened.'

'Parallel reading?'

'49 of 100. holding steady,' Dr Stevens replied.

'Good,' Dr Turner said, and switched down the time link key.

'Hold the time space, we've got to bring Maria Becket to November 6th. What date is she in now Dr Swartz?'

'27th September, 1984. I have a semi-freeze on her there.'

'Okay, we can disengage freeze when you're ready.'

He turned to Dr Stevens. 'When the Probe has finished, freeze November 6th. We'll align the two time frames on the completion time.' Dr Stevens nodded his response.

'We're ready when you are Eric.'

Dr Swartz nodded, paused his hologram, then stood up and faced his team.

'How many weeks are we dealing with between the parallel programmes Dr Maxwell?'

'Five weeks, four days and four hours,' she replied.

'Okay. Set your parallel clocks with the main computer, at a frozen 9.30am November 6th 1984.'

'Time clocks set,' Dr Maxwell advised.

'Good. Now, set your time locks on an open access. I suggest a five times one parallel to start, but you can take it as it comes. This will slow down the hologram time enabling each one of you to have, if you so choose, a five minutes for five minutes in 1984. This I hope will be sufficient time for you all to do your jobs.

'When we're ready to fast forward, I'll give you the order on a countdown basis of ten. When you hear the order, start unlocking procedures at my count. Is that clear?'

He waited for their joint, "Affirmative" response before turning to Dr Turner.

'Freeze Commander van Slijk's soul as soon as the Probe's input has finished then disengage the Probe after it has eliminated Zone Time. Once we have parallels in the same time frame, the Commander can be awoken. In the meantime, feed every scrap of information, every detail known, into the commander's soul. But keep Julie in sleep mode. She must not be allowed to awaken under any circumstances.'

His deputy nodded and he turned to face his waiting team.

'We'll work in two groups, Group one: Dr Turner, Dr Maxwell and myself. Dr Turner will monitor Commander van Slijk. Dr Maxwell. You'll monitor Julie van Slijk's parallel for an alignment window. I'll be the third in group one, on the main computer with Dr Western and Maria Becket. When I need the necessary input, I'll ask.'

He paused momentarily, a meaningful expression on his face, his eyes searching out each team member's before he resumed, 'And when I ask, I'll want it immediately, so stay on top of it.

'Group Two: Dr Grey, Dr Stevens and Dr Blackmore. Dr Grey. You'll monitor the freeze on Julie's soul. Dr Stevens. You'll monitor the Probe's input. Dr Blackmore. You'll monitor and tend the Life Support Units. If there is any change in that area at all, however slight, I want to know about it immediately, so don't wait to be asked. Good luck team, now go to it.'

He retook his seat at the main computer.

Abby and Maria were on their way through Hunter's Ridge. The date and heading read, Las Vegas, Nevada. September 27th 1984. He watched as they continued their drive through Hunter's Ridge.

At the same time, a few hours' drive away in Los Angeles, Detective Tony Garnet eyed Arnie Bennet across his desk.

'I'll come straight to the point, Officer Bennet,' he said, 'I've had the results of the autopsy on your partner Patrolman Gifford. What do you know about his use of Cocaine?'

'Cocaine!' He exclaimed nervously.

Tony's statement and sudden question hit a nerve.

'I eh.' He stammered, attempting to clear his already clear throat whilst he thought, 'Not much.'

'How much is not much?' Tony questioned, looking him straight in the eye.

'It's difficult to say,' he faltered. He glanced at Fred Hall who was stood by the window.

'I'll make it easier for you,' Tony said shifting forward in his seat. 'You knew that your partner was snorting Cocaine.'

'Well, yeah,' he reluctantly replied.

'So you knew where he got it.'

'No. I was never with him when he purchased it.'

'I didn't ask you if you were with him when he purchased it, Officer Bennet. I said, you knew where he got it.'

He held his eyes with his own. The patrolman shifted nervously in his seat.

'Sort of,' he conceded uneasily. 'Ed used to stop off at Bud's place for doughnuts. Sometimes when he gave me the box, he'd say, the sweetness is not only in the sugar Arnie baby. So I sort of thought he got it there.'

'How long has he been using the stuff?' Tony pressed.

'I'm not sure. A while, I think.'

'Have you ever used Cocaine Officer Bennet?'

'Me! nah, never touched the stuff. Can drive you crazy. I was always saying, he oughtta quit it.'

Tony flicked through the autopsy report again, glancing every now and then at Officer Bennet, watching him as he looked towards Fred.

Fred turned around and stared out of the window.

'How long had Officer Gifford been using the cruisers?' He asked suddenly, breaking the short silence.

'About a year or so,' the officer answered without thinking.

'That long,' he said with a brief look at Fred, 'Always the same car duty officer?'

'Yeah. No. I guess so,' Arnie replied, sweating nervously.

'What was the name of the duty officer involved?'

'I can't be sure,' Officer Bennet replied.

'So, there were more than one.'

'I didn't say that. I don't know.'

'You spent a lot of time with your partner off duty?'
'Yeah, some.'
'Did you ever go with him, on these rest days?'
'No, never!'
'But you did see him on his rest days.'
'Yeah, sometimes he'd come over and we'd have a beer.'
Tony looked through the paperwork again, deliberately letting the silence that followed feel heavy before he resumed.
'Well Officer Bennet, thanks for your help. Detective Hall will escort you to Interview Room one, and we can get all this down on paper. I'll see you before you leave.'
He stood up. 'Have Detective Selby take his statement.'

When they'd both left the room, Tony buzzed the Duty Officer. 'I'll see Sandy Ericson now.'
A short while later, the attractive, slim brunette sat opposite him.
'Sorry to have kept you waiting, Miss Ericson,' he apologised, shaking her hand, 'Detective Sgt Garnet.'
Her small hand felt cold and clammy. 'Can I get you a coffee?'
She wriggled further back into the chair, brushing an imaginary piece of fluff from her uniform, 'Yes, thank you. Black, no sugar.'
Tony poured two coffees then sat on the edge of the desk.
'It's been quite a shock for you,' he said warmly, offering her the coffee cup. She took the cup and nodded.
'If you feel up to it, I'd like to ask you some questions, Miss Ericson, about your friend.'
'Fiancé,' she corrected.
'You were engaged?'
'Yes. Three weeks back on my birthday.'
She showed him the ring on her finger. He looked at the large emerald, at the side of which were two equally large diamonds and made a mental note to have Officer Gifford's bank details sent up immediately after the interview.
'It's a beautiful ring.'
'Yes,' she agreed sadly.
'Did you know him long?'
'Three years, maybe a little over. We were going to be married in December. The 24th.'

He leant forward and placed a comforting hand on her shoulder.

'We can go over these things tomorrow, if you'd prefer,' he offered, his thoughts racing ahead.

'Yes,' she replied. She took out her handkerchief to blow her nose. 'I feel too.'

'I understand,' he broke in. 'I'll get someone to drive you home.'

He walked with her into the large outer office, then opened the door to Interview Room one, letting the door stay open just wide enough for Officer Bennet to see her. Then, checking that the officer he sought was not there, he excused himself and ushered her to the duty officer's desk, to book her ride home.

Leaving her comfortably seated within the waiting area, he stopped at the duty sergeant's desk. He wasn't a hard man, but he'd had to bring her straight in if he was going to set a trap for Officer Gifford's partner.

'When the car drops her off, have her tailed. Tell the detail to report straight to me. Me only.'

'Yes sir,' the duty officer replied.

He walked back through the outer office and swung left, tapping on the door of Lt Mason's office to update him.

'I've got Officer Gifford's partner, Arnie Bennet, in Interview Room one. Detective Selby's taking a statement. He's not levelling with us. Knows much more than he's letting on. I'd like to have his phone bugged and suspend him, pending further enquiries. I think we've taken the lid off a hornets nest.'

'Problem is, if we suspend him, we've got to call in Internal Affairs.'

'Yeah, and I like to keep them out of it right now. See what he does.'

'He could take some time off, get over the shock. How long do you think?'

'Couple of days. A week would be good. I've let the girlfriend go for the present, see where she runs.'

'Nasty business.'

'Yeah,' Tony agreed. 'Sure is. I'll send Officer Bennet to you when we're through.

As he walked back toward his own office he could see Fred through the window in the hall doors. He was engrossed in a telephone call. He kept on walking, past his office and out into the main foyer. Fred's face flushed when he saw him approach. He took no notice and went over to the duty officer's desk.

'Any luck with those bank papers?'

'Be on your desk within the hour.'

'My eyes only, for now,' Tony finished and turned to walk back. Fred was just replacing the receiver.

'Problems?' Tony asked, feigning innocence, for his suspicions were more than aroused.

'Just June, wants her mother down for Thanksgiving.'

'Thanksgiving, that's two months away.'

'Yeah, she's on about it the whole time,' he lied.

Meanwhile, in Las Vegas, Abby's Mercedes climbed the long, winding hill amidst split-level brickbuilt houses most with wooden frontages set back off the road and centred in large well-tended gardens. Maria looked down at the tops of the tall maple trees. Below her, the valley and a trail of log cabins nestling between small clearings along the bends of the river. The September sun was high in the cloudless blue sky as they rounded the bend to start their descent. She could see for miles. Her eyes took in every detail.

The desert that faced them was vast, covered with giant and smaller cacti. Their tough, swollen stems reaching upwards towards the burning sun. Their arms each wide of their stems following suit. Abby glanced briefly across at her, smiling her approval as she followed her gaze.

'You should see it in March or April, when all the cacti are in bloom. Colours like you could never imagine.'

As they started down the other side Abby pointed, 'That's the airfield. My house is just the other side.' Her smile broadened before she accelerated and added, 'Wait til you see it from the air.'

Dr Swartz's brow creased with concern as Dr Western's energy levels dipped and rose. 'Any luck with an alignment window yet Dr Maxwell?' He called.

'Not as yet Dr Swartz. The computer is still searching.'
'Let me know as soon as you have it.'

He continued his monitor, watching as Abby braked to swing left across Desert Road and onto the approaching perimeter road, keeping her speed a steady twenty as the road twisted back on itself and out towards an elongated, whitewashed, wooden building.

Parking the car alongside one of the two hangars, she released her seatbelt.

'This is it,' she said and opened the door.

Maria followed her to the front of the office. A small, newly-painted blue and white sign, "Western and Eastly" hung outside, swinging back and forth in the gentle breeze. Opening the door she led Maria through the main office. The door closed behind her.

'Morning Ted, or is it afternoon?' she said smiling as she opened the wooden waist-high gate to his section.

'Morning Abby,' he said. Then stood up, his keen, bright blue eyes darted past her to Maria. Her smile broadened as she watched the flush of colour in his cheeks. She picked up the mail from his desk.

'Maria,' she resumed, her eyes still watching him, 'This here is Ted Ashly. Runs our booking section.'

The young clerk wiped his suntanned hand nervously on the side of his jeans before offering it out towards Maria.

'Maria Becket,' she said warmly, accepting his handshake. The young clerk's flush deepened.

Abby flipped through her mail, then returned it to the desk. 'Is the Cesna refuelled?'

'Eh, yeah,' Ted stuttered, his eyes still regarding Maria, 'You going up?'

'Yep, thought I'd show Maria here Hunter's Ridge, the only way it oughta be seen.'

Ted laughed, and his shoulder-length, sun-bleached fair hair fell over his eyes. He pushed it away and the waning flush in his face reappeared. Abby smiled, still amused at the effect her new friend had on the young clerk, then motioned Maria through to her own office at the rear.

'Just slip on my flightsuit, file a flight plan and check the weather, then we're off,' she confirmed, closing the door.

A short while later they were airborne.

The view from the air was magnificent. Hunter's Ridge was indeed every thing that Abby had said it would be. The houses looked so tiny, like an architect's model awaiting development.

As Abby banked to the portside, Maria looked down, her eyes picking out the river she'd seen from the car, smiling as the sun's reflection bounced across the blueness, making it glisten brightly.

She followed its route as it twisted and weaved its way through the rock-strewn valley, her eyes reluctant to leave the spectacular sight. Abby banked starboard, climbed then circled to fly in a criss-cross pattern over the top of the ridge. The red and white Cesna's engine hummed warmly in her ears as Abby branched out across the desert and finally over the many tall buildings that made up the city in the middle of the desert.

'You know what Las Vegas means?' Abby asked, not waiting for Maria's reply. 'It means Meadowland. Don't know why they called it that, because there's nothing but desert.'

'I know,' Maria agreed, but she was sold and the voice had been right. It all made perfect sense. She would stay.

When the flight was over Abby drove Maria back to her hotel. They would meet later for drinks and dinner.

Meanwhile Dr Swartz studied the various history parallels and although he could not obtain Maria's true parallel, from Abby Western's history there was no comparison. The history Dr Western's soul was creating had caused many a paradox. And something was gravely wrong. Just how the future would be affected if he couldn't rerun the true parallel, he didn't know. He just had to pray the freeze on this new-made history would hold, because without it they were lost!

Just then, Dr Maxwell interrupted him. 'I have that alignment window Dr Swartz.'

'How close?'

'24th October, 1984.'

Whatever he'd found would have to wait. If they lost this window, goodness knows how long they would have to wait for another.

'Okay. Prepare to take time-parallels off. Lock into 24th October, 1984. Set a five to one ratio on my count.'

Leaving the history parallel in pause, he proceeded with the count. 'Ten . . . nine . . . eight . . . seven . . . six . . . five . . . four . . . three . . . two . . . Lock in on one.'

The team watched as the hologram settled on 24th October, and the previous history was relayed.

Maria had built a strong, and what was to be a lasting, friendship with both Abby and Buck. She'd started flying lessons and was genuinely looking for the right house. Dr Western's use of the Echo at various casinos over the last two weeks had netted Maria $250,000. And that, added to her previous wins, made a total of $511,000.

Her system was to lose some before winning. This, she did to perfection, thereby keeping a low profile, before the big win.

When she'd win, she'd give the casino a wide berth for a night or two, and play elsewhere. The voice however by this time was the leader. Her guide, gaining more control, through Maria's natural greed. He watched as the hologram sped on. It was 9.00am 25th October.

The shrill beep of the alarm clock awoke her. Maria stretched her arms languorously into the air before slipping out from the bedcovers and made her way across to the window. The sun had long arisen and hung like a giant red ball painting the horizon with pink and purple streaks.

She glanced up the street. A loud group of teenagers were kicking a battered coke can around the grey concrete of the parking lot of a bar, much like she'd done at the same age. She smiled to herself, reluctantly leaving her memories to head for the shower. She had a busy day ahead of her.

By 10.30am she'd dressed and eaten, then made her way down to the bank to deposit her previous night's winnings.

Dr Swartz watched as she walked across the parking lot in the Bank's direction.

'511,000. Dr Western has most certainly mastered the use of the Echo,' he thought, recalling his own experience of the facility.

He heard his own voice instruct his team, during his morning lecture. 'The flash, that rebounds from the future, that mirrors in the first part of the soul, sending previous events in hologram form, allowing the transported soul a brief insight into the immediate future or past, as much as an hour in advance or behind.'

He recalled his conversation with Dr Western. The excitement that shone from her eyes. Her eagerness as he explained his experience. Her questions; an almost interrogation. He'd been like a transmitter and she his transponder, receiving his predetermined signals. . .

At the time, he'd taken her jubilant behaviour to be stimulated by wholehearted devotion and felt nothing but proudness that she'd shared his total dedication.

He glanced up at the soul readout section. Her energy level was still registering maximum. He had to get her out soon . . . He didn't know just how long his delay tactics would hold.

Just then the hologram Communication Link flashed and the voice of the Resident Elder spoke.

'How are things progressing Dr Swartz?'

He cleared a sentimental thickness from his throat.

'Very well ma'am. We will be aligning the two parallels shortly. We've frozen the Commander in her ancestor's body in 1984. November 6th, and have successfully transferred all the relevant information. There were a few areas of her ancestor's memory that were damaged, but we don't envisage any major problems.'

He could have bitten off his tongue as soon as he said it, for in the next moment the Elder questioned.

'Precisely what areas are we talking about, Dr Swartz?'

'We don't exactly know yet ma'am, but the computer has given us every indication that it isn't anything too drastic. Meanwhile,' he enthused, 'some good news. We are running Dr Western's miscalculated programme side by side with history. A majority of areas are actually parallel.'

'Good,' the Resident Elder said, 'I'll leave you with your continuance then.'

As the Communication Link faded, Dr Swartz breathed a silent sigh of relief.

He looked at the main hologram. It was light years away from the reality that was their history. This hologram was Dr Western's newly-constructed history; none of which so far, had happened.

And then it came to him. He could try using section four of the probe, to run interference, draw off some of Dr Western's energy. Hastily he tapped in the coded command.

A few moments later the main brain section raced with enthusiasm and a coded acknowledgement of its acceptance lined his private screen.

Satisfied, he waited, pondering Dr Western's reaction, watching as the soul readout section dropped two degrees, before turning his attention back to the screen.

Maria awaited Abby in the Hotel Mirage lounge bar, a bourbon and ice in her hand. She'd been waiting since 8.30pm it was now 9.10pm. Her stomach rumbled hungrily as she drained her glass and took another handful of salted peanuts from the bowl in front of her. Where the hell was Abby?

She signalled the bartender. 'Is there a public phone here?'

'Yes ma'am,' the balding bartender replied, and pointed to the lobby section of the hotel.

With a muttered 'Thanks,' she picked up her clutch bag, stepped down from the bar stool and made her way through the early evening crowd. Her seat was taken within moments.

Abby should have landed by seven thirty, seven forty-five at the outside. She'd shower and change at the airfield then jump in the car and be with her for eight thirty; eight forty-five at the latest. One thing about Abby, you could set your clock by her. If she said a time, she meant it.

Pushing a coin into the slot she dialled the airfield.

A few moments later the ringing tone rang out loud in her ear. She let it ring, tapping her long fingernails on the darkened glass hood of the booth. As she was about to replace the handset, the phone tone suddenly changed, the unobtainable sound abruptly following.

Her large green eyes darted from side to side in puzzlement. She dialled the airfield again. The monotonous, low, dull sound of the unobtainable tone droned out in her ear like an earnest and persistent cry for help.

Just then, the urgency of the voice rasped, 'She's hurt! She can't. . . .'

It faded brusquely, the sentence incomplete, but not before its alarmed warning had prompted her into action.

Leaving the receiver dangling where she'd dropped it, she tore out of the lobby and thrust her parking ticket at the valet. He sped off at double time, his prime objective, a nice fat tip. Minutes later he pulled up outside.

She was around to the driver's side in a flash, almost knocking him sideways in her getaway. The young college boy valet stood there, scratching the top of his head; puzzling her flight before shaking his head, muttering under his breath, 'Some lady!'

Then, with an ever ready smile, he turned to his next customer, reaping the sympathy as he took the middle-aged woman's ticket, his objective, a nice fat tip.

It was way past dusk and a distinct chill was in the air, the same chill that ran up and down her spine as she drove. If anything had happened to Abby . . . it was all she could think about. Her foot pressed down harder on the accelerator.

Close to nine thirty she brought the Pontiac to an abrupt halt outside Abby's office. Her eyes searched the shadows, her loud heartbeat, her only companion.

She dropped down the flap of the glove compartment and curled her fingers familiarly around the handle of her gun.

The voice was silent, but she felt its closeness as she slid out from behind the wheel and crept towards the open office door.

The building was cloaked in a silent darkness. Slowly she pushed back the door and looked inside. Papers were strewn across the floor and the wooden inner half gate torn from its hinges, the overhead strip lighting laying crushed midst the chaos. Through the half-open door of Abby's rear office, a lone dim lamp pierced the shadows in a strip, making the surround area seem twice as dark.

Silently she crept further inside towards the door and listened. A woman's muffled sobs filtered into her ears and, as she eased the open door wider, her eyes fell on Abby's outline behind her desk.

'What the?' She heard herself say, forgetting the immediate dangers that may lie ahead as she rushed across to her.

By the dimness of the light she could see her face. Her left eye and cheek looked grazed and puffy. She slipped her arm around Abby's shoulder.

'What happened?'

Abby took a deep breath stifling her sobs before she blurted out, 'Matt Figorelli's men.'

At the mention of his name, Maria felt a knot in her stomach tighten and her eyes narrowed.

'Later, we'll see to it later!' The voice assured.

A warm feeling swept over her as she contemplated the voice's promise, the narrowness of her eyes waning and with the same comforting warmth she turned her attention back to Abby.

'You want to tell me about it?'

She waited as Abby dabbed her mouth with her handkerchief.

'It was all so fast,' she began. 'I'd just landed an' taxied to the hangar. I knew Ted was off early today, but the office light was still on. I walked across and opened the office door . . . An' wham! Summut or someone just hit me!'

She paused a moment suppressing a sob.

'Next thing, I was pushed into the chair.'

She blew her nose. 'You gotta smoke?'

Maria slid the gun into her pocket and lit two cigarettes, passing one to Abby, then sat on the corner of the desk.

Abby drew deeply on the cigarette, and coughed. She was shaking like a leaf. Maria placed a comforting hand on her shoulder and after a few moments Abby resumed.

'There was three of 'em. The one guy, I've seen before, works for Matt Figorelli. The other two.' She shook her head shrugging her shoulders.

'Never seen 'em before. But they was hell bent on looking for summut!'

She drew again on her cigarette and a stray tear ran part way down her cheek. She wiped it quickly away and made a forced attempt at a chuckle.

'I bet I look a mess eh?'

Maria smiled reassuringly but said nothing, and after a few moments Abby continued.

'I asked 'em what they was doing? They was wrecking the place, throwing the files and things around. Then this big guy swipes me across the head an' says, "Shut your fucking mouth bitch an' sit still!" After they'd finished trashing the place, they still couldn't find what it was they was looking for. The big guy slaps me some again . . . I still don't know what they was looking for! Then, as fast as it begun, they was gone. . .'

She drew again on the last of her cigarette, then stubbed it out.

For a few moments Maria remained silent, digesting Abby's words. Then dropping the burnt-out filter of her cigarette in the ashtray she said, 'Can you stand up?'

'Yeah . . . ain't hurt too bad. Just a bit shaky, that's all.'

'Guess you are at that. I'll drive you home and get you checked over.'

'No!' Abby said firmly. She held up her hand in protest. 'Don't want no doctor pawing at me. Just drive me home, would you?'

Reluctantly, Maria nodded. 'What about your car?'

'Ted'll bring it over in the morning. I'll call him later, tell him what to expect in the office.'

It was 10.05pm when Maria turned into the dirt road that led to Abby's house. A few minutes later she'd pulled up outside the double front doors. The large split-level house was silent. Flicking on the lights Maria followed Abby into the lounge.

'Could sure use a bourbon,' Abby said, as she eased herself into the soft leather chesterfield.

'Coming up,' Maria replied and walked across to the maple-wood bar in the far corner of the room.

It was Tuesday 25th. Buck would be back tomorrow. She lit a cigarette, then took her drink from Maria's outstretched hand. She took a mouthful straight off and swallowed heavily. Maria lit up a cigarette and watched as Abby stared down at her drink, deep in thought.

A few moments later, she drained her glass, as if cementing a thoughtful decision, then held it out to Maria. 'Could you?'

Maria smiled, but said nothing just took the glass.

'Would you mind staying tonight?'

'Sure,' Maria said and walked across to the bar.

'Good,' Abby confirmed, more to herself than Maria, and her strained expression eased.

'Summut's going on,' she resumed as Maria returned.

Abby sipped her drink, slower now, her immediate thirst seemingly quenched.

'Buck wasn't his usual self when he took off for Portland Monday.'

At the sound of the word Portland, the same knot in Maria's stomach tightened. She drew again on her cigarette and sat down. Abby took another sip of her drink, the pain in her body receding with every mouthful.

'Buck flies a contract for Matt Figorelli. I don't know too much about it, that's Buck's side of the business. I just teach an' fly the odd charter. But Monday.' She paused shaking her head slowly. 'Monday, when Buck took off, he just wasn't his ole self. In fact he was looking mighty worried.'

She nodded her head in a silent agreement. 'I asked him if everything was okay. He said everything was fine, so I let it drop. But he sure looked worried. Real worried. And, as you know, my Buck's not one for worrying!'

She drew again on her cigarette then, feeling the warm glow, stubbed it out before it burnt her fingers.

'It was nothing I could put my finger on. Nothing he said or didn't say, just a sort of nagging in my gut. . .'

Maria took a mouthful of bourbon watching as Abby lapsed into another silence, then looked around the well-furnished room. To her right the bar. Some thirty foot further on, and covering most of the east wall, a panoramic window. No openings.

'Draw the drapes, would you?' Abby said suddenly, following Maria's eyes. 'And I guess I could use something on this lip. There's a first aid box behind the bar.'

Maria drew the drapes, then tended to Abby's lip.

'Don't look so worried,' Abby said as Maria replaced the iodine bottle back in the kit.

'Seems to me we've got good reason to be worried,' Maria replied tightly.

'Well, that's maybe, but that's my problem, not yours.'

'You and Buck are my friends,' Maria said deliberately, keeping her voice low and steady, 'So don't tell me you wouldn't be worried if the circumstances were about face.'

'Well, yeah,' Abby agreed with some reluctance.

'But there's no call.'

Maria cut her off mid-sentence and her voice rose an octave, 'And don't tell me there's no call.'

'Okay . . . okay,' Abby conceded, 'You made your point. But don't go making too much of this.'

Maria swung around to face her and their eyes met.

'Don't make too much! You've been beaten up, Abby, for chrissakes! Who you trying to shield or don't you care!'

Abby's bruised face flushed guiltily. She was indeed protecting someone, but that someone was Buck.

'Look, just sit down and listen! Can you do that?'

Maria sighed heavily and sank down opposite her. A few moments later Abby began.

'I don't knows that I should be telling you all this, but hell, I gotta tell someone.

'It all started about six months back. The business hadn't been doing too good. The bank was sending letters almost every week. We was so far behind with the mortgage that we was in danger of losing the whole goddam thing! Then in comes Chuck Atkins one bright and sunny morning. Buck and me hadn't seen him in a whole mess of Sundays.'

She paused a short moment, thinking to herself, and sipped her drink.

'Who's Chuck Atkins?'

'You might well ask,' Abby said, smirking to herself.

'I don't think even Chuck Atkins knows who Chuck Atkins is! Anyhow, Buck and good ole Chuck used to fly together, way back in the sixties. They go way back before college. He, that is Chuck, took off in the early seventies some place, and we didn't hear from him, save for the odd postcard.'

She paused again to think.

'Yeah, must be way over ten years. Anyways, says he's looking for a good pilot to help him with a charter to Portland and Mexico.'

She sat back in the chesterfield, a loose smile on her lips.

'At that time, it was like the answer to our prayers. Cash up front every trip. Course Chuck paid Buck himself, keeping the actual business close to his chest. And we never paid no mind to it. Just glad of the business. Then one Monday morning Chuck didn't show. Buck waited around for a while, then rang the number Chuck had given him. It seemed that good ole Chuck had disappeared again. But we never knew for sure. That is, at the time.'

She sipped at her bourbon, wincing as the whisky touched the gash on her lip.

'Next thing was, we had a visit from Matt Figorelli himself. Don't know if you know him, but that's one guy you don't mess with, I can tell you!'

She drained her glass and put it on the coffee table, her eyes wide as she recalled her husband's account of Matt Figorelli. She could hear her husband's voice in warning after she'd moaned about him being at his beck and call. 'Don't get in his way, just stay out of it Abby!' Buck's face had been red with anger. 'Don't you understand?'

'No Buck!' she'd replied, 'I guess I don't, so why don't you tell me!'

'Sit down,' he'd said. She'd sat down in his chair. He'd sat on the desk just in front of her, silent for a few moments, his hazel eyes wide and serious and she'd suddenly felt scared.

'He's an underboss Abby. Runs the West Coast operations. You know what I'm saying?'

'Mafia?' The word had drained the colour from her face. 'Oh Buck, why?' she started.

'Money,' he said. 'Plain and simple. I guess when Chuck walked in that day, I would have done anything.'

'This is Chuck's doing!'

'Yeah. No. I don't know. You can lead a horse to water and all that.'

'Can't the police do anything?' Abby had pleaded, frightened for her husband. Buck had laughed, stood up and running his hand over his thick unruly hair, walked back and forth in front of his desk. His face had taken on a serious expression again before he spoke.

'Let me explain something to you Abby. Matt Figorelli has been brought to court three times in the last few years, and not by the piddlin' police but by the FBI.'

He'd thrown his arms in the air in a gestured hopelessness. 'Three times! And three times he's been freed. No case to answer!' He'd chuckled to himself, his eyes still wide as he resumed. 'An operation that included four combined law enforcement agencies. They targeted his HQ! Undercover men carried out audacious exercises to obtain evidence. And he was freed on a few technicalities! No, if they get him this time.'

Buck's ghostly voice faded from her mind as Maria's penetrated. 'Abby, you okay?'

Abby looked across at her and nodded, then dropped what was left of her cigarette into the ashtray, picking up where she'd left off as she lit another.

'Well you just don't mess with Matt Figorelli! Anyways, Buck took him into the little office to talk. Next thing, Matt was leaving. Buck tells me he's got Chuck's charter, permanent like. He picks me up hugs me an' puts an envelope containing $50,000 in my hands to take to the bank. The bank was more than satisfied I can tell you. Then, regular each week, Buck makes the Portland trip. Every month, the same guy I recognised earlier, comes to deliver the envelope; same day, same time.

'A while back I asks Buck about Chuck. He'd not heard a word from him, but then that wasn't unusual for Chuck. As I said, we'd not seen him for some time before he'd shown up that Monday morning. So, Buck for the last six months, bin flying the accountant to Portland with the occasional trip to Mexico.'

'Who's the accountant?'

'Yeah,' Abby replied with a smirk. 'Gave him that name myself, on account that he always had on those funny little glasses. You know the type, wired behind the ears so's they don't fall off. He asks me one morning, real nice like, can he use my office. Buck was doing some last-minute checks, and I says, sure, make yourself at home. A little while later I take in some coffee. He was counting out what had to be half a million.'

'What did he do when you walked in?' Maria interrupted.

'Nothing much, just looked me straight in the eye and said, "You never seen that. Got it!" '

'I says, quick as you like, "Seen what!" I left his coffee on the desk and got the hell outta there.'

She drew on her cigarette. 'And as to me being beaten up, if I hadn't been so difficult, I dare say I wouldn't have been touched. I'm sure when Buck gets back he'll sort it.'

'So, that makes it alright, does it?' Maria said angrily, 'They pulled the office apart looking for summat they thought you had, then when you tried to stop them, they beat you up.'

'Now hold on there,' Abby started.

'No,' Maria interrupted, 'You hold on there . . . You heard from Buck?'

'No, but that's not unusual. Ted's probably heard from him. I bin out most of the day, and when I got back, Ted was gone.'

'So, phone Ted.'

'What now!' Abby exclaimed.

'Yes now!' Maria insisted.

Abby picked up the receiver and dialled.

'It's ringing,' she told Maria, tapping her fingers nervously.

'There's no reply, is there?' Maria said pointedly.

'No,' Abby conceded reluctantly. 'What do you think?'

'Plenty,' Maria replied, standing up. 'Where does Ted live?'

'Just off the strip, not far from Dino's Bar. You don't think something's happened?' She stopped mid-sentence.

'Could be,' Maria said.

'Oh my God!' Abby said, 'We should get over there.'

'No!' Maria said tightly, 'That's just what we shouldn't do. We'll call him again later. See if he's in then.'

She rubbed her brow. She had to think.

'Have you locked up all round?'

'I . . . I, don't know,' Abby stammered, 'Why . . . do you think they'll come here?'

'It's a possibility. If they couldn't find what they were looking for in the office, it seems logical to me that they'd search the house. And we can see that they've not yet been here, so it's probable. I'll get my things from the car, then we'll lock up.'

Outside the wide turning space was deserted save for her Pontiac. She looked through the still night air to the storm shelter doors and felt a strange sense of foreboding. The voice was silent.

Opening the car door, she reached inside for her handbag, then dropped down the glove compartment and took out her gun. Another probe inside and her fingers closed around the silencer. She pulled it close to her chest, stroking the coldness of the barrel before reaching for the clips, then placed the gun, clips and silencer inside her handbag.

Closing the glove compartment she locked her car and, with a last look around, she went back inside.

After she'd secured the front door she made her way down the hallway to the kitchen. The rear door was already bolted and the window that overlooked the desert securely fastened. Drawing the blind, she left the kitchen light on and returned to the lounge. It was 11.24pm. They'd been talking for almost two hours. If Matt Figorelli's men were coming, they wouldn't have long to wait.

'Is there any other way in on the ground floor?' she asked Abby.

'No. Yeah,' Abby said, confusingly.

'Well which is it?' Maria quizzed, impatiently.

'Yeah. The cellar. The door from the storm cellar outside leads to the hallway.'

'Okay, show me.' She motioned Abby up with her hand.

'It's that one,' Abby confirmed, pointing to a five foot high cupboard-like door, beneath the stair housing.

'Where's the key?' Maria asked.

'On the hook inside.'

'Is there a light?' Maria questioned, opening the door.

'Yeah, next to the hook. On the left there.'

Maria flicked the switch but nothing happened.

'It must be the bulb,' Abby suggested.

'You got a flashlight, and a spare bulb?'

'Yeah, hold on I'll get them.'

Abby hurried off to the kitchen, returning a few moments later.

She switched on the flashlight and handed it to Maria.

With the broad beam of the flashlight leading the way, they descended the rough wooden stairway into the darkness of the musky cellar.

Suddenly a loud creak broke the stillness, and they froze in mid-step. Abby gasped aloud almost dropping the bulb before the creak registered.

'It's just the stair,' she said, 'Buck's been meaning to fix it.' Maria shone the beam on the light fitting.

'Hold the flashlight,' she said, passing it to Abby, 'I'll unscrew the bulb.'

A few moments later the new bulb was in and the musky dark cellar was bathed in a warm glow.

'The storm doors. Do they lock?'

'Not exactly. There was some sort of catch, but no, they don't exactly lock.'

Maria took the flashlight from Abby and shone the beam up the three approaching stairs. The wooden catch housing had rotted away. Two nails had been hammered in the wood each side and a cobweb-infested piece of string tied to each nail was a vague restraint to stop the doors rattling. She couldn't do much with those, but forewarned was forearmed.

She moved a rusted watering can from the cellar floor to the first step and threaded the piece of string through the handle. When they pulled the storm doors open, the watering can would go with them hopefully clattering to the floor as it slipped the string.

She climbed back down the steps and up the stairs towards Abby. Then, taking the key from the hook, she switched off the light and locked the door. Not that it would have mattered, because one hard shove and the door would be open.

'No more entrances downstairs?'

'No, that's it,' Abby confirmed.

'Okay, then we better go up.'

Maria switched on the upstairs lights and led the way. Abby followed close behind.

'We'll start at the rear and work forward.'

Abby nodded an agreement.

When they had checked the entire upstairs, and locked all the spare bedrooms, they returned to the lounge.

'You don't really think they'll come here do you?' Abby questioned nervously.

'Don't know. But if they do we'll be waiting. Meanwhile.' She opened her handbag and took out her gun.

'What's that for?' Abby questioned.

Maria's eyes met hers, 'Protection.'

'But surely,' Abby started.

'Oh come on Abby. Get real. Don't you have any guns in the house?'

'Buck. Buck's got a rifle,' she faltered and pointed to a maplewood gun cupboard, adjacent her. 'But I never was much good with guns, just don't like them.'

'No one can fault you for that Abby, but this is necessary. Is the rifle loaded?'

She looked Abby direct in the eyes. A cold chill ran down Abby's spine. It was almost as if a stranger was looking back. 'No. Buck don't keep no gun loaded.'

'Good!' Maria said, then returned her attention to the gun.

Abby lit up a cigarette, trying to mask her unexplained fear, then watched as Maria loaded the clip and fixed the silencer into place. It was not only Maria's actions that distressed her, for her gut ached with nothing short of impending doom.

She drew on her cigarette, arguing silently. Maria was just . . . just being careful . . . looking out for her.

She picked up her empty glass and walked across to the bar for a refill. When she'd returned Maria was finished.

'What do we do now?' she asked.

'Not much we can do except wait.'

She lit a cigarette and picked up her drink.

'Is there a number you can reach Buck on?'

'No, not really. He'll call me around six in the morning before he takes off from Portland.'

She glanced down at her wristwatch. It was almost 1.00am. 'Shall I try Ted again?'

Maria nodded and Abby picked up the phone. 'They'll be here. They'll be coming.' The voice suddenly warned; its sadistic laughter echoed around her mind.

For the next two hours Abby called every half hour. As the chimes of the grandfather clock announced 3.00am, they still hadn't reached him.

Stubbing out her umpteenth cigarette as she stood up, Maria picked up her things and looked across at Abby.

'I guess we'd better go up. I'll take the bedroom opposite you, that way I can hear from across the hall.'

Abby nodded in agreement, then stood up facing her across the coffee table. She leant forward and with a weak smile, hugged Maria.

'I know you mean well, but I hope you're wrong.'

'Yeah. I hope I'm wrong too!' she lied, for she knew they'd come. The voice was never wrong. 'Now come on, let's go up. You look like you've about had it!'

By 3.15am Abby had fallen into an exhausted, deep sleep. The large old house was silent, nothing moved save for the settling creaks of the thick old rafters.

From inside the bedroom opposite Abby, Maria listened carefully to the voice's instructions.

Dr Swartz watched as she smeared on the scarlet lipstick, pulled on her black leather gloves, then slipped her gun into her cardigan pocket.

'They're almost here . . . go check Abby.' The voice informed.

Maria hurried into the wide dimly-lit hallway. The bright stream of light that filtered through Abby's partially open door, told her Abby's bedside lamp was still on. She crept into the room and switched it off; the light of the almost-full moon shining through the bedroom window, casting her milky-blue shadow across the foot of Abby's bed.

She moved across to the window and looked down at the dirt track. An eerie strangeness washed over her. A oneness with the night.

As a cool breeze from the open top window rustled her hair, the sound of footsteps crunched on the gravel below. Her searching eyes peered out into the moonlit night scanning the dry bushes.

Suddenly, two long shadows fell against the porch. She stepped back and drew the drape part way. Through the open top window the sound of their whispers filled her ears. Closer, they were coming closer. Just then there was the creak of the storm doors and the clattering of the can. Her heart raced wildly.

'Downstairs. Quickly!' the voice ordered.

For a few brief moments she paused at the top of the stairs listening to the silence then, with her back hugging the wall, she began her descent. It was almost 3.25am.

When she reached the bottom of the stairs she heard the first creak . . . seconds later another creak. The stair. They were nearly behind the door.

Like a hungry black panther cornering its prey, she waited in the shadows, the balustrade and grandfather clock her cloakment.

As the sounds of the twisting door knob shattered the stillness, the clock announced the half hour and the small five-foot door was forced open. Less than a moment later the first man appeared; a second later his accomplice followed.

Dr Swartz watched intently. Two deep burning hollows began to smoulder in Maria's eyes, the accentuated paleness of her face shimmering like a halo around the illuminated firelike glow. As Dr Western's energy readout started to rise, Maria's tawny hair stood out like tentacles grasping the immediate darkness and she emerged from her cover to stand like a glowing statue by the side of the stairs.

The two men froze mid-step startled by the eerie illumination as their eyes met hers. The heftier intruder's gun was the first to clatter to the floor before the pulsating mass that was her eyes slightly dimmed.

She was playing with them, like a cat with a mouse. Releasing them from an invisible holding force. She allowed them to regain the use of their limbs.

As they turned to flee back down the wooden stairway into the cellar, she followed, her mere presence driving them onwards. The electricity in her body crackled as her loud, sadistic laughter echoed behind them.

Gripped by a terrifying fear they scrambled on and out of the cellar doors. A lone wolflike howl of a dog pierced the stillness. Maria or the thing that now was Maria regarded its prey with disdain, the floating spectre hovering above the stairs.

The two men had reached their car. But as they opened the doors and climbed inside she'd caught up with them.

Powerless, Dr Swartz could only watch as once again Maria's fiery orbs held them in an invisible force field. His previously adjusted calculations, powerless to stop her.

She opened the rear door of the car and climbed inside and the car moved off in the direction of the desert.

5

The sleek, black Dodge came to a halt at a turning space midway along a narrow, rock strewn desert track, just off the main Las Vegas desert highway. It was 3.44am, the moon had started its descent in the glittering star-clad sky. Slowly the rear door opened and Maria's glowing apparition floated outside.

Spellbound, Dr Swartz watched as the ghostlike spectre slowly lifted its arm and pointed a forefinger towards the two shadowy figures in the front seats.

Simultaneously, the car doors creaked open and, in a Zombie-like trance, the two men stepped out. As the two figures faced her, their frames bathed by the light of Maria's glow, the governing heat degrees on the thought section of the Probe reached maximum.

'Open relay!' Dr Swartz's low but urgent voice instructed the computer. His dark eyes were wide with disbelief as he witnessed Dr Western's mastership of the Echo facility. With an amazing skilfullness she drew the precise amount of energy to infiltrate the transfixed men's minds; gleaning their past and immediate memories.

Suddenly, a woman's loud shrieks filled his ears as a hologram of their stolen memories filled the thought section of his private screen.

A single desk lamp lit the room as the eye of the hologram projected the scene. Abby was cowering in a chair behind her desk, the hefty intruder's bulk casting a giant shadow in the dim light as he towered over her slim figure. Fiercely, his fingers entwined in her hair, he tugged her head backwards and lowered his face close to hers.

'What kinda chicken shit you talking?' he menaced.

'Your ole man's been pissing in somebody's pool, and that somebody ain't too pleased!'

He twisted her hair tighter and she shrieked again. His raucous laugh filled the room as he straightened his back.

Then turning to face his accomplice, he mockingly offered, 'You wanna be first Deke?'

His grasping hand tore at her flightsuit. Her bruised face was wet with tears as she fought against his strong hold, biting into the back of his hand. Suddenly, he swung out striking her cheek with a crashing blow and she fell into a silent slump.

With a deliberate calmness, for at that moment his emotions were running high, Dr Swartz checked. 'What reading do you have on Dr Western's soul Dr Maxwell?'

'Four point nine-eight . . . And rising!'

'And the freeze?' he pressed.

'Non-existent.' She glanced across at him, her anxious eyes wide as they briefly held his, before he turned back to his screen.

The thing that was Maria was raising its arm, her glowing finger pointing to the shorter of the two men. The other had dropped to the ground in a crumpled heap in what Dr Swartz believed to be a state of unconsciousness. Trancelike, the shorter man obeyed the silent command and ventured towards her.

Suddenly, Maria's two scarlet orbs dimmed; the eerie light that engulfed her being, fading before the burning voids that were her eyes slowly disappeared and they began to take on the light green beauty of their normal shape and colour, he had unknowingly begun to love. He turned to Dr Turner.

'We'll have to release the freeze. Dr Western's almost drained section two and her soul readout is nearly five.'

Quickly, Dr Turner paused his parallel and released the freeze. Anxiously they watched as her energy chart waned.

'What reading do you have now Dr Maxwell?' Swartz asked.

'Four point five.'

He glanced at Dr Turner. 'We'll try it again later.'

Dr Turner nodded. He was unaware of Dr Swartz's personal

dilemma and Dr Swartz saw no reason at this moment to enlighten him.

Both doctors returned their attention to their individual screens, Dr Swartz watching as the shorter man staggered and swayed in a vain attempt to regain his senses as he turned to stare at his accomplice's crumpled body. The invisible force that had held him, broken for the moment as Maria's eyes continued to regain their innocence.

Pale-faced Dr Swartz studied her, recalling his own suffering. The extreme pain that had wracked his body as it surged through him, the stored electricity that Dr Turner had fought to earth, long after the team had been dismissed, his violent, uncontrollable thoughts and urges, that could only be explained as pure madness, and his blank, blacked-out weekend, were just a few.

In truth, the terrifying side effects he'd had to combat when his soul had returned were vast. From what he was witnessing, it seemed that Dr Western's transported soul was experiencing them all at first hand. He was powerless to help! These same side effects both he and Dr Turner had decided to bury for the present, in the name of science.

Dr Turner had theorised that Maria Becket was a psychopath, he was not so sure; they only had his theory to support that assumption. For himself, there were so many unanswered questions. . .

Would Maria have killed her aunt if Dr Western's soul hadn't infiltrated her body? They only had the computer's suggested parallel on that score and the facts and figures for the parallel were given by Dr Turner. Because of the malfunction they were unable to run a true parallel.

Would Maria Becket be killing today, if Dr Western's souls were not trapped inside her?

Just who was the psychopathic killer . . . Maria or Gemma? Or could the stored energy, that Dr Western had needed to combat the conflict between the souls, be responsible. Was that the actual cause of Maria killing?

If only he could run the complete history of Maria Becket. See if she truly had been a murderess. Both Dr Turner and the computer were working on the malfunction, but how long he'd have to wait he didn't know and there seemed no point in sidetracking Dr Turner with what he'd seen just now.

He'd kept so much of his true pain hidden; even from Dr Turner . . . all in the name of science; or so he'd told himself when he'd recovered and had time alone to think.

After all, he reminded himself, they'd both agreed they'd be able to work through them, overcome them, to work something out! He wiped his brow and glanced briefly at his colleague. If they hadn't kept quiet and with what he'd just witnessed, it could well mean the end of their experiments. . . . The end of his dreams.

Why the hell couldn't she leave it alone? he thought. There was so much he had to do before it would be possible for any soul to be able to travel in complete safety. He just hoped Commander van Slijk's soul wouldn't pose any similar problems.

Suppressing his feelings of annoyance and anger he returned his attention to the hologram. Maria's now innocent expression said it all.

Her ghostlike appearance had to be the result of a build up of static electricity between two occupying souls he reasoned. The same static electricity in him that Dr Turner had managed to earth. A kind of burn out similar to the problems previous scientists in the twentieth century had had to combat, when they'd constructed primitive heat shields, so that their deep spaceships could return safely through the atmosphere.

'Yes,' he told himself, satisfied with his reasoning. 'That's what this is.'

'Deke,' Maria began again with the same childlike southern drawl. Her eyes questioned expressively, as only a child's can, 'How d'yer know if'n someone's dead?'

She looked at the crumpled heap of the hefty man's body, waiting impatiently for Deke's reply.

He stood there, his wan face lit by the moon, his throat tight and dry unable to form any words, his muddled mind racing frantically as it tried to grasp at the distant shadows that were his thoughts.

'Deke!' she shrieked suddenly, her facial expression now thunderous, with rage, before it changed quickly to the previous innocence.

'I. . . I guess,' Deke faltered nervously, the sudden awareness of her gun and that his partner might be dead, paramount. 'I guess they don't breathe any more.'

'Yeah,' Maria agreed. With a crooked smile she nodded her head then questioned, 'Better make sure though, eh?'

Undauntedly she walked past him to his partner's body. Deke remained fixed to the spot. It was as if his arms and legs were ton weights. He stood like a frozen statue with only his eyes able to follow her. It was the only part of his body he sensed he could move.

'Where am I?' he asked himself, 'How the hell did we get here? What's happened to Tony? Is he dead? The last thing I remember was . . . was.' He tried to recall, but his memories continued to elude him.

He watched as Maria crouched down next to his partner's body; watched silently as she put her ear to his mouth to listen. Then standing up she shook her head with indecision.

'Never could tell when anyone was dead. Hey Deke,' she called, glancing back over her shoulder, 'Would it be fair to shoot him again, if'n yer not sure?'

Deke didn't answer. She was quite mad, he thought, quite mad!

'Aw shit!' she said then leant over and placed the gun to the hefty man's temple. A second later, a muffled shot rang out.

'Wow!' she called out to Deke, excited, as the familiar cordite smell drifted into her nostrils.

'It's a good thing I was stood this side.'

She stepped back from the body, her eyes wide in amazement, pausing to view her work, before she reached inside the dead man's breast jacket pocket and took out his wallet, her gloved fingers fumbling as she removed the identification card before resuming convincingly, 'I think he'd dead now Deke.'

Her deep-red lips twisted in a half chuckle as she read the name aloud, 'Antonio Mancetti,' then turning to glance at Deke she assured, 'Yep Deke, I reckon he's dead now!'

Deke swallowed hard, as she slipped Tony's I.D. Card into her back jeans pocket and threw the wallet on the ground alongside the body.

She walked back towards him and his immediate thoughts confirmed the woman's madness as her childlike voice resumed, 'Deke. I've got a problem. It's Abby. You remember Abby, the woman you and your partner here had so much fun with. . .'

She paused, whilst her large green eyes held his, as she emphasized the word fun, before resuming, her eyes still fixed on his.

'Abby's like my own Mamma . . . and Buck . . . well he's just like I wanted my Pa to be. My Pa died you see . . . when I was just a little 'un. I can't altogether remember, but my Mamma told me about my Pa.'

She paused again, still looking at him. 'And if Buck was dead then . . . then . . . then I don't know what I would do!'

She looked down at the gun in her hand, stroking the silencer as she caressed and embraced the tube, before returning her eyes to Deke's pale face. Nervously he averted his eyes.

'Well yeah,' he started. He cleared his throat. If it was at all possible he was gonna stay alive! 'We don't know that Buck is dead.'

'Yeah?' Maria questioned before agreeing eagerly. 'You know Deke that's just what I've been hoping you'd say.'

As her wide eyes held his expectantly, the voice's solemn words bit into her. Menacingly, her eyes narrowed. She looked down at her gun, the last words of the voice echoing over and over. 'Buck's dead . . . he's dead . . . dead . . . dead . . . dead.'

A twisted snarl etched its way across her scarlet lips and Deke felt a tingling sensation in his legs. Summoning all his strength, he stepped back quickly, his anxious eyes still on her. Suddenly a burning knife like blade of pain stabbed his ribs, halting him midstep, preventing his further retreat. He grabbed his chest.

'What's the reading on Gemma's soul?' Dr Swartz called with urgency to Dr Maxwell.

'Four seventy-five,' she replied, 'but her sudden power surge is draining her soul's collective energy.'

'Good!' he replied, looking back at the hologram, hoping he'd made the right decision. She may well bond further with Maria's soul but she'd not have the chance to draw any more energy from the Probe.

He watched as Maria walked towards Deke; the scarlet glow in her eyes had disappeared.

'A little voice inside here,' she resumed, ignoring Deke's pained expression as she pointed to her temple; her lips a tight thin line, 'told me he was!'

Deke swallowed again, the burning blade in his ribs easing slightly as he managed, 'Now I'm not saying that Buck is dead, but you gotta face the fact that he may well be.'

Maria thought for a moment, momentarily doubting the voice's wisdom. Just then, the loud echoing sounds of the voice's last word rushed forcefully through her. 'Dead . . . dead . . . dead!'

As the words bit into her, she spat out menacingly, 'Quit shitting me Deke!'

Nervously he licked his lips. His throat felt like sandpaper, it was like a nightmare! He lifted his heavy, aching arm to wipe away the sweat from his brow and tiredly conceded, pointing to his partner's body. 'Tony shot him! But I ain't saying he's dead . . . he was left in some alley.'

'I figured as much!' But her eyes were sad now, as she tried to swallow a large lump in her throat. He watched as a stray tear rolled down her cheek.

Just then the voice returned, 'He killed Ted,' it said, echoing the name in the same manner around her head, 'Ted . . . Ted . . . Ted. . .'

Helplessly, Deke stood there. He knew his time was limited. She turned to face him. He could see from her expression, that his last thought had been confirmed.

'What did you have to kill Ted for. Why did he have to die?'

He was about to answer, when her eyes glazed over and she stared straight ahead. It was almost as if he wasn't there. He tried to run, but he couldn't move. He was frozen to the spot; the invisible force that had previously held him was back.

The voice was silent as it flashed the pictures in Maria's mind; pictures of Ted; the agony he'd endured; his last breath of life; his death and now his face, lying in a pool of his own blood.

As the glazed expression cleared from her eyes, Deke pleaded, 'It was an accident . . . an accident!'

She faced him, her vengeful eyes holding his.

'Where was Ted shot?' she questioned kicking the sand absent-mindedly with her foot, impatient now, like an unruly child as she waited for his reply.

'Through the head,' he said, almost without thinking and watched powerlessly as she cocked the trigger of the gun.

Her full red lips were all his frightened dark eyes could see as she whispered, 'He was so young an' all. Never did no harm to no one.'

As she raised the gun pointing it at his head, he pleaded loudly, 'It was an accident! an accident!'

'An' how did this here accident happen?' she mocked, reprieving him momentarily; cocking her head to one side not wanting nor waiting for his answer; the evilness in her eyes quickly returning in a glowing flash of scarlet, as her voice rose and she raged, 'He kinda fell into your gun with his head! right?'

Deke wrestled in vain, but the invisible force held him fast and the projectile had left the gun striking him dead centre in the forehead. As the force broke, he fell backwards to the ground.

Maria stepped closer, standing over him, staring down at the hole in his head then, lifting up his jacket, she took out his wallet and slid out his I.D. Card. Slipping the card in her back pocket she tossed his wallet to one side and aimed the gun again slowly depressing the trigger. Less than a moment later a second bullet tore into his chest and his already lifeless body jerked with the impact.

The voice was but a whisper now as she followed its instructions and took his handkerchief from his top pocket. Wiping her gun clean of prints, she took out the remaining bullets and carefully wiped each one.

'Yes Mamma,' she assured softly, as she pressed the newly-wiped bullets between Deke's fingertips.

A moment later her gloved hand had reloaded the chamber. Then placing the revolver in his hand, she pressed his forefinger to the trigger, ensuring his fingerprint, as she fired the gun. When she was satisfied his prints would be detected she smudged some of the barrel prints then replaced his handkerchief and slipped the gun back into her belt.

As the moon dropped lower in the early morning sky her deep red lips parted in a piercing shriek of laughter and she slid in behind the wheel of the Dodge, muttering almost incoherently, 'Never could tell when anyone was dead.'

6

Close to four thirty, Maria turned into the almost-full rear staff parking lot of the Starlight Casino and reversed the Dodge into a space close to the wall near the exit. Switching off the lights she got out of the car and closed the door.

'Hurry!' the voice whispered with urgency.

Just then, the staff exit of the casino swung open and a couple's laughter drifted through the early morning air. Her heart skipped a beat as, afraid of discovery, she ducked down behind the trunk of the Dodge, listening until their footsteps had faded from her ears.

She peered over the trunk then, at the sound of their car door opening, she weaved her way through the cover of the parked cars to the corner pedestrian exit and into the main street. It would be a long tiring jog back to Abby's. She'd have preferred to take a cab but the voice had been insistent and she'd learnt a long time back not to argue these points. . .

Just before five, she'd reached the end of the dirt track that led to Abby's. Hugging the dried hedgerow, she looked up at the bedroom window. The drapes were the same as she'd left them. The big house still silent.

By the light of the waxing moon she could see the storm cellar entrance, the doors were open wide. Sprinting across the turning space in front of the house, she stepped inside the dimly-lit cellar and down the three small steps. She stood on the concrete floor, her eyes searching the shadows, her ears listening to the sounds of the creaking rafters above her, her senses acknowledging the familiar smell of death. . .

Suddenly, from the corner of her eye she caught the quick movement of a small dark shadow. Her head whiplashed around, drawn to the far corner of the room. The voice remained strangely silent...

As she started to walk towards it, a low scuffling noise beneath the stairs startled her. She stopped in mid-step and took the gun from her belt, straining her eyes against the milky-blue darkness beyond. Her heartbeat was quick and loud, as the small dark shape darted across the floor just a yard from her feet. She followed it with her eyes.

As it reached the second step to the cellar exit, it arched its back and turned to face her. Two luminous green eyes glared back at her, before it hissed wildly.

Just then a gust of wind lifted the open doors. Her eyes followed the doors' movement as they shuddered before the gust subsided, and they fell back heavily against the ground. When she looked back at the second step, the creature was gone.

As she turned her attention back to the corner, the voice broke its silence, rasping, 'The guns!' Slowly, she started her ascent to the hallway then bent down to pick up the intruders' guns, listening to the voice's utterings as she placed Deke Richardson's silver-handled revolver in her belt before returning to descend halfway down the cellar stairs.

As the dim cellar light swayed back and forth in the early morning breeze, she threw Antonio Mancetti's snub nosed revolver through the open back of the steps and into the dark hollow beyond. A dull thud echoed back and she repeated her actions with her own gun before making her way back up the steps.

As she reached the top, the strange foreboding feeling had returned. She would have investigated further but the strained whisper of the voice ordered, 'Hurry!'

Leaving the hallway cellar door open, she hastened up the wide mahogany staircase to her bedroom opposite Abby. The grandfather clock in the hall struck five as she closed the door.

It was noon when Tony called Abby. He was at the private airstrip. 'I'll grab a cab and be with you soon,' he promised.

Replacing the receiver, she walked across to Maria's bedroom and opened the door. She was still fast asleep. Closing the door quietly she walked back to her room and ran a bath. She stared at her reflection in the mirror, the horrors of the last seventeen hours came flooding back.

Lowering herself onto the bathroom stool she rested her arm on the wash hand basin and wept. The black and blue swelling around her right eye had almost reduced it to a slit. Her cheek had turned a yellowy purple and the graze had started to form a crust. Her sleep had been restless, waking periodically throughout. As the hands on her bedside clock neared 5.15am, she'd been fully awake waiting for her husband's call.

Just after six thirty, when he hadn't rung, she'd called her godson Detective Sergeant Tony Garnet, at his Los Angeles office. The duty sergeant informed her he'd signed out at 11.00pm the previous evening. Hastily, she'd dialled his apartment, explaining, through her intermittent sobbing, the turmoil of the previous ten hours.

She shook her head in disbelief and eased herself up, wiping away the well of tears from her tired, puffy eyes. Then, stifling a sob, she tested the bath water with her fingertips before slipping off her nightdress to step into its soothing warmth.

Thirty minutes later, as Abby made her way downstairs, Tony's cab pulled up outside. She opened the door and her aching body fell into his strong circling arms. He held her for several moments kissing the top of her head whilst she sobbed, then gently releasing her he tilted her chin up to face him and comforted, 'You're alright now, I'm here.'

Fresh tears ran down Abby's bruised cheeks. She swallowed hard before closing her eyes, as she nodded her head. She hugged him again, feeling safe and secure before, drying her eyes, she led him inside. Dropping his case in the hallway, he closed the front door and followed her down the hallway.

'What the. . ?' she started, halting just before the cellar door, 'The door . . . We locked it last night.' He ducked his head under the five-foot door frame and peered down the dimly lit cellar stairs.

'The storm doors are open.'

'We locked them . . . we locked them all!' Abby exclaimed.

He descended the first three steps. She followed, standing on the top step, twisting her hands nervously in front of her.

'Can you see anything?' her voice just above a whisper.

He glanced back at her and shook his head then descended further.

'Stay there,' he said. His eyes searched the shadows as he slowly made his way across to the storm doors. They'd been forced. One of the nails that had held the rope was missing, the other bent. He descended the three small steps and made his way back across the cellar and up the stairway.

'Did you call the police as I asked you, Aunt Abby?' he questioned as he came up the flight.

'No. . . I thought I'd wait for you,' she faltered.

'I guess. . . Oh, I don't know what I thought.'

'It's alright,' he calmed, 'I'll do it now.'

'I'll make some coffee?' she said shakily, meeting his eyes, her suggestion more of a question. He was about to answer when Maria, descending the stairs, caught his eye.

'Maria!' Abby exclaimed. 'I'd forgotten you were here.'

She smiled and walked towards them.

'This is Maria Becket . . . my friend . . she stayed with me last night.'

He nodded as she approached.

'I was just about to make coffee.' Abby resumed, looking at Maria, her voice thick as she faltered, 'Some . . . someone's broken into the cellar.'

Maria placed her arm around Abby's shoulder.

'Come on, I'll help you with the coffee,' she comforted and led her through to the kitchen.

Tony went into the lounge and dialled the Las Vegas Police Department. Just as he'd finished his call and replaced the receiver, the phone rang.

'That you Tony,' the sombre voice questioned.

'Yeah,' he replied.

'Bad news,' Lieutenant Mason advised, 'They've found Buck Western.'

Tony swallowed hard, 'Where?'

'Rear of an alley. . . Single bullet, back of the head.'

A long silence followed, before the Lieutenant called, 'Tony . . . you still there?'

'Yeah,' he managed, his voice thick with emotion, 'I'm here.'

'I've written you out for a week's leave,' the Lieutenant resumed, 'But take as much time as you need.'

Buck had been like a father to him. When he'd lost his parents it was to Buck and Abby he'd turned, they'd both been. . . He swallowed again wiping his eyes, then replaced the receiver and sank down in the chesterfield, his throat tightening as he held back the sudden grief that swept over him.   When Buck had first come to him, with the disappearance of his friend Chuck and his part in Matt Figorelli's illegal operation, he'd insisted Buck stay out of it. But Buck, being Buck, had been equally insistent he be the man on the inside.

'After all!' he'd explained, 'I'm already employed by them, have been for six months. They'd have no reason to suspect me. I'm just the pilot!'

'Just the pilot,' he whispered, before his shoulders shook in a silent uncontrollable sob.

Just then, Maria's clear crisp voice called from the hallway, 'Coffee's ready.'

'Yeah,' he acknowledged, composing himself as he stood up. How in hell would he tell Abby? He ran his hand through his sunstreaked hair and made his way down the hallway to the kitchen.

'Any news?' Abby questioned as he approached. Her tear-welled eyes were wide with hope, holding his as he sat down next to her. 'I heard the phone ring. . .'

Her heart thumped heavily as his arm slid around her shoulders. She'd hoped he'd tell her it was all a horrible mistake . . . but she knew; she knew from the expression on his face.

'Oh God!' she whispered.

He took her slim hand in his. She'd known him from a child, his eyes said it all.

'No . . . no . . . not my Buck!' she sobbed.

He swallowed back the lump that had formed in his throat, then nodded, closed his eyes, and confirmed, 'They found him a short while ago.'

He felt her fingertips press against his lips to silence him and opened his eyes. For a few, brief moments her eyes held his, then she nestled her head in his chest. He hugged her close, each comforting the other.

Maria sat silently opposite, before a moment or so later, she whispered, 'I think I'd better call the doctor, he'll give her something to make her sleep.'

'No!' Abby exclaimed through her sobs, 'I don't want to sleep.'

Maria looked across at him, her eyes questioning, waiting for his agreement.

He nodded and, with his voice just above a whisper, confirmed, 'Go call the Doc.'

It was 1.15pm when both the Police and Dr Derrier arrived. After examining Abby, he gave her an injection to help her sleep.

'She should sleep for a good six, seven hours, maybe a little longer,' the old doctor told Maria as they descended the wide stairway, 'You'll stay with her?' he questioned.

'Of course,' Maria confirmed nodding.

He was a kindly old man, portly with silver hair, not far off retirement; more like a country doctor, not like the flash ones you normally find in Las Vegas.

When Maria returned to the kitchen, Tony was deep in conversation with a Las Vegas detective.

'The cat was dead, shot through the head!'

She heard the detective finish as she retook her seat on the stool and looked out over the desert, her thoughts centred on the cellar and the strange foreboding feeling she'd had earlier.

Just then, another of the detectives called them and both Tony and the detective walked quickly into the hallway. A short while later Tony returned to the kitchen. His suntanned face was flushed with anger.

'They've found Ted Ashley. Single bullet through the head . . . same way they found Buck.'

Suddenly the room spun and the coffee pot crashed against the counter as Maria stumbled.

He stepped forward, catching her, apologising, 'Sorry. I didn't think. . . Blurting it out like that.'

'It's okay,' Maria assured, not quite sure why his statement had shocked her, for she knew, although she hadn't known where his body was.

'Come sit down,' he resumed, 'I'll pour you that coffee.'

Gently, he guided her to the breakfast stool. As he poured her coffee he glanced back. It may have been the sun's rays, or a trick of his tired eyes, but he thought for one moment he saw a flickering red glow, burning in the centre of her eyes.

He placed her coffee in front of her. 'You okay?'

'Yeah. Thanks, I'm fine,' she assured. He slid on the stool, opposite her.

'You didn't hear anything last night?'

'No . . . nothing,' she lied, 'Abby and I locked up and went to bed around three. I couldn't sleep straight off. I checked in on Abby around four, then went back to bed.'

She looked across at him, the light green of her eyes convincingly earnest as she shook her head. 'Didn't hear a thing.'

'What time did you and Abby get in last night?'

'Don't know exactly but I think around ten. Abby was supposed to meet me for dinner around eight. I waited for a while and when she didn't arrive I called the airfield. . .'

'You found her?' he interrupted.

'Yeah, she was in her office. I wanted to call the doctor right off, but she wouldn't let me. Said she'd be okay, so I drove her back here. Later on we tried to call Ted. Poor Ted,' she faltered, blowing her nose. 'We tried to call Ted . . . Abby. Abby was worried you see, but we couldn't reach him . . . so about three, we locked up and went to bed.'

'That's a strange course of action, why didn't you just call the police?'

'I wanted to. I wanted to call them when I first found her, but Abby wouldn't let me. She insisted she was fine and that it was all a mistake. It was later when we got back here that she explained why she didn't want the police involved.'

'What exactly did she tell you?'

'Not very much,' she replied thoughtfully, 'Just that Buck was working a contract for Matt Figorelli . . . said that Buck needed the money . . . that he was flying some accountant back and forth to Mexico. That they'd had some problems with the bank and that it would all be alright when Buck got back.'

He studied her for a moment, sipping his coffee . . . God! she was beautiful! He'd never seen such a shade of light green eyes. Amongst all his grief he felt his heart skip a beat as he imagined her alabaster skin close to him.

Just then the detective he'd been talking with earlier stood in the doorway and beckoned to him. He slid off the stool and walked to him.

'The photographer's finished and we're about to remove the body,' the detective informed, his voice hushed.

As both men disappeared into the hallway, she slipped off the stool to freshen her coffee, watching through the corner of her eye as they spoke in whispers. A few moments later he returned to the kitchen.

'Would you mind if I call at my place and pick up a few things?' she asked, 'Abby wants me to stay a while, so I need to.'

'Sure,' he interrupted, not waiting for her to finish, gladdened by her intentions, 'Would you like me to get someone to drive you?'

'No, I'll be fine.'

'It's no trouble,' he insisted.

'No, thanks all the same, I've got my car outside.'

Her eyes challenged his briefly before he saw the innocence return and she turned to leave. He sipped his coffee and stared out over the desert.

An hour had passed before Tony placed his empty cup in the sink. He was glad his Lieutenant had extended his leave and pleased that Maria would be staying with them. There was so much to organise and he still hadn't let Buck's brother, Andy, know.

He went into the lounge and flicked through the Roladex then, sitting on the arm of the chesterfield, he picked up the receiver and dialled.

'Western Air and Sea Freights,' the cheerful voice of the telephonist answered.

'Put me through to Andy Western,' he said sombrely.

'Mr Western is out of town at the moment. Would you care to leave a message?'

'No,' he replied, pausing a moment. 'It's Detective Sgt Garnet, Los Angeles Police Department. Where can I reach Mr Western?'

'One moment please.' Handel's water music filtered weakly through the line before a few moments later a Bostonian woman's clipped accent informed.

'Good morning, Mr Western's personal assistant Miss Palmer speaking. Can I help?'

'Dt. Sgt Garnet. I'm trying to contact Mr Andy Western rather urgently.'

'Mr Western is in England Dt. Sgt. Can I help you?'

'No, it's of a personal nature. It's imperative I contact him as soon as possible.'

'He'll be at his hotel within the hour. Would you like me to leave a message for him to call you?' she enquired.

'Yes, thank you. Ask him to call Tony Garnet as soon as possible. I'm at his sister-in-law's, Las Vegas home number.'

'He has the number?' she checked.

'He most certainly has,' he finished, replacing the receiver.

He hated the so-called personal assistants. He knew she was only doing her job, but they could be so irritating at times. And what kind of message could he leave.

He pictured it in his mind's eye as Andy was given his messages upon his return.

Mr so and so called . . . please return call.

Mr whatever called . . . please return his call.

And a message from Dt. Sgt Garnet. . . Your brother's dead!

He didn't know how long it would take before his request reached Andy, but at least he'd set the wheels in motion. He walked back out into the hallway and picked up his suitcase, then made his way up to his room. It had been far too long since his last visit and now this.

When he was a kid he'd spent almost every summer here. Abby'd been his mother's best friend, her lifelong friend, and when his mother has passed away some twenty-five years back, it was to Abby and Buck he'd turned. His father, unable to come to terms with his grief, had died six months later.

The painful memories crowded his mind. He was crushed at the time, but both Abby and Buck had been there for him. Abby had not been able to carry children, she'd lost two in a miscarriage, so, as far back as he could remember, she'd been like his second mother and Buck, his father. . . No! he corrected himself, Buck had been more than a father. And now he was gone. His throat tightened again as he forced a swallow, trying to get rid of the persistent lump that had been there since he'd first received the news.

As he approached his bedroom door he paused and smiled sadly. He'd been allowed to make his own personal choice of his room. He was just six years old. Abby had brought him back after the funeral. He'd cried that first night, so she'd stayed with him. He wiped a stray tear from his cheek and smiled as he stared at the nameplate on the door. "TONY'S ROOM", the memories flooded back. He ran his fingers over the brass plate. He'd chosen it at a "swapmeet" with Abby.

Buck was taking him fishing later that day, when he returned from Los Angeles, so while they waited for him, Abby took him to a swapmeet. He'd bought himself a real snazzy fishing hat, bright red with numerous flies pinned to the peak, and then he'd seen the nameplate. Abby had pointed it out to him and given him fifty cents to buy it. He'd stuck it in his blue jeans back pocket until they'd got home. She'd let him fix it to the door himself. He'd centred it just right. . .

He opened the door and placed his case on the bed, tracing his fingers over the double mattress. The bed had seemed so big to him when he was a kid. Abby had suggested getting a smaller one, but Buck had told him it was a man's bed, and waiting for him to grow to fill it. He'd laughed with Buck that day, as he did most days. Buck's powerful arms had lifted him up and tossed him high in the air. He could still hear his boyish laughter and Buck's deep chuckle, still feel the love and security of his hug. He sat down on the bed, his shoulders slumped, as he gave way to his grief and sobbed.

It was 3.00pm when Maria loaded up the Pontiac. She'd hand in her keys to the realty office en route to Abby's. The phone company would disconnect later that day. After calling at the bank, she'd stop at the store and pick up some steaks for dinner, then drive out to Abby's. Taking a last look around her rented apartment, she closed the door. When Abby was able to manage without her, she'd look for that house she'd promised herself up on Hunter's Ridge.

The bank was crowded. After a tedious half hour of form filling, she'd rented herself a safety deposit box. A tall dark-haired, uniformed guard of around twenty-five accompanied her to a cubicle and asked her to wait. Flicking the light on, he closed the door. A short while later he returned carrying an oblong grey steel box. Placing it down on the table in front of her, he flipped back the lid, leaving her with two silver-coloured keys, explaining she should lock the box when she'd deposited her belongings inside.

She opened her attaché case and took out the bundled notes, placing them inside the box then, leaving $10,000 in the case, she closed the lid and slipped the first key into the lock. A light click followed and the box was secure. Opening the door, she signalled the guard as she'd been instructed then followed him as he carried her box downstairs to the vault room.

After placing her box in the designated slot he pulled down the outer cover and inserted his key in the top lock, inviting her to follow his lead in the lock immediately below. Maria repeated his action and secured the second lock.

'All secure,' he confirmed smiling before leading her back up the steps to the ground floor.

Whilst Maria handed in her keys at the realty office and picked up the steaks for dinner, Tony unpacked his case, then after a quick shower he changed into blue jeans and sweatshirt.

It was close to 4.00pm when Buck's brother returned his call. A death notification was a difficult task to undertake when you weren't emotionally involved, but to have to tell Andy that Buck was dead, and when he was some six thousand miles away . . . . .

He sat thinking over their conversation, sipping the much needed bourbon he'd just poured. Andy had taken it badly. He was returning on the next available flight.

Just then, Maria's bright, smiling face appeared in the doorway, 'Hi,' she called, loaded up with bags, 'I've just picked up some steaks. I hope you like steak?'

She dropped her bags in the hallway, not waiting for his answer, as she resumed before disappearing down the hallway, 'Could use one of those myself.'

She was feeling quite cheerful despite the voice's rasped objection to her suggested night of gambling. She'd argued with it on the way back to Abby's and, after repeating its objections, it had remained sullenly silent. The voice soothed and helped her but if she argued too much it depressed her. She hated the depression. . .

7

The next eight days came and went. Andy Western had taken the first available flight from England and the room next to Maria.

He was eighteen months older than his brother but with the same hazel eyes and receding hairline and stood about the same height, a little over six feet, but with a more serious stance about his person. Not that she'd had too much time to get to know him because the voice had set her a routine.

Each morning after sun-up she'd watch Matt Figorelli's house then trail him throughout his day.

At 8.00am he'd rise and breakfast. At 10.00am his car would come to the front of the property and take him to his penthouse office in the Starbrite Casino. At 1.00pm sharp, he'd lunch at Luigi's Pasta House, just off the strip, until 3.00pm when his car would return him to his office.

By the end of the first week she was at ease with his movements, but it puzzled her why she'd had to watch him. The voice had given her no explanation. And why hadn't it just informed her of his routine?

Each time she followed the next step of the voice's instructions, she had this strange feeling, a feeling like she almost knew the reason. It was on the tip of her tongue, then suddenly it was gone . . . slipped away. When she'd asked the voice had become angry, so she'd not probed further but she still felt the excitement course through her and knew it was going to be something she liked. She smiled to herself as she went over the voice's instructions.

'Leave the envelope at the Pasta House.'

Dr Swartz watched as the hologram sped on, the date and time flashing in luminous green in the righthand corner of the screen, THURSDAY 3RD NOVEMBER, 1984. 1200 hours. . .

Tony, Abby and Andy were sitting in the lounge, the television tuned into the news. Since Abby had made her statement, the news channels and press had reported every new turn of events, covering widely the death of Ted Ashly. Police were still searching for Antonio Mancetti and Deke Richardson, wanted for questioning in the murder enquiry of the young clerk.

Head-and-shoulder photographs were splashed across national and local front pages, along with speculations of their whereabouts and a traducible statement of their past and links to the mafia.

'Turn it off!' Abby pleaded, as if by doing so the whole, still unbelievable hurt, would go away.

Tony switched off the set and she lit another cigarette, fidgeting as she settled again in her chair.

'Have you seen Maria this morning?' Andy questioned.

'Yes, she went out about an hour ago.'

'Did she say where?'

'No, she didn't.'

He hadn't meant his answer to be so curt but Andy's question had irritated him. He'd called after her, but she'd not heard him. He too wanted to know where she was going, but by the time he'd come downstairs and opened the front door, she'd driven off.

At 12.24 pm, Maria strode into Luigi's Pasta House just off the strip. She wore a pale blue, long-sleeved, calf-length dress with matching stretch turban that concealed her tawny hair. A large pair of dark glasses completed her look. Smiling complacently, she sat at a rear table and browsed through the menu.

A few minutes later a short tubby waiter of Italian descent took her order of Spaghetti Bolognese and a half carafe of dry red wine.

By 1.00pm Maria was well into her meal. At the sound of the restaurant door opening, she glanced up, Matt Figorelli and his entourage flooded in, taking their usual table in the far corner, opposite.

From behind her dark glasses she watched as he tucked a white table napkin in his shirt collar and broke a breadstick in half, smoothing the crumbs away absent-mindedly with his hand as he talked with the taller man of the group, a mean-looking Scandinavian type of around forty, with a deep scar running from just underneath his right eye down his cheek to the top of his lip. The three others in the group were of Italian descent, a head shorter and more rounded.

'Phillipo,' Matt called out affectionately, as the tubby waiter hurried towards his table.

'Mr Figorelli,' the waiter reciprocated, with a broad beam.

She sipped her wine. Suddenly, Matt Figorelli was staring right at her. Her flesh crawled as she recalled that same look. It was definitely the same man that Bernie had entertained in Portland.

She lowered her eyes to her food and picked up her fork. When she looked back at him he was talking to the fatter Italian, describing with his hands, as was his trait.

Signalling the waiter, she asked for the tab, then counted out her money to settle it. Whilst the waiter was busy taking another order from a newly seated customer, she opened her purse and took out the previously-prepared, long white envelope. Then slipping it underneath a ten-dollar bill, she finished her wine and left.

From outside the restaurant, she watched unobserved as the waiter returned to her table and picked up the money and the envelope. With a puzzled expression he read the name on the front then walked across to Matt Figorelli's table and handed him the envelope.

She couldn't hear what was said, but a few moments later Matt Figorelli was slitting it open. She studied him as he looked inside, then took out Antonio and Deke's identity cards. Placing them down on the table he took out her note. She smiled to herself as she watched him read it.

When he'd finished, his face flushed with rage. She felt the excitement mounting inside her and wished she could hear what was being said as he handed it to the Scandinavian opposite. After a few more hurried words, he signalled the waiter, who'd returned to the bar section.

As the waiter approached he replaced the two identity cards in the envelope and picked up his glass of wine. The Scandinavian leant across the table and said something more. Matt's lips tightened. She watched, enjoying every moment of his displeasure.

It was evident from the waiter's actions that Matt had asked him to describe her. She smiled again. Her description would do him no good. After a few more minutes Matt dismissed the waiter. The tall Scandinavian leant across and whispered once more. At Matt Figorelli's reply he nodded then stood up to leave. As planned, she stepped back around the corner and entered the adjoining boutique, watching through the glass door as the Scandinavian left Luigi's and made for the parking lot. After a few moments he drove off.

'Can I help you ma'am?' the young, brunette shop assistant's cheerful voice said from behind.

'Yes, thank you,' Maria replied, 'I do believe you can.' She smiled as she turned around to face her. 'I'd like the outfit in the window.'

'The scalloped black and white,' the assistant checked.

'Yes,' Maria confirmed nodding, 'Size 8.'

The assistant disappeared to the rear of the shop, returning a few moments later with the dress over her arm.

'If you'd like to follow me ma'am,' she requested with a bright smile. Maria followed her to the fitting room and slipped on the dress. It moulded to her figure like a glove.

'I'll take it, would you box these?'

'Certainly ma'am,' the keen assistant smiled and picked up Maria's things.

A few minutes later her sale was complete and she left the shop in her new outfit, her hair swinging freely around her face as, pleased with herself, she walked across to her car.

The note she'd left Matt Figorelli thanked him for his half a million and promised he'd end up like the enclosed I.D. Cards lying in a one lane track five miles north in the desert if he insisted on pursuing the matter further.

It was almost three when Maria pulled up outside Abby's. As Tony opened the front door she swept past him and up the stairs, the faint smell of her delicate perfume lingering in his nostrils. A short while later she'd changed into blue jeans and sweatshirt and joined them in the lounge.

Meanwhile, a disgruntled Matt Figorelli had returned to his office in the Penthouse suite of the Starlight Casino. The nerve of the broad!

'She's got balls,' he whispered to himself.

'What's that boss?' his bodyguard questioned.

'Get me Portland,' he ordered.

The thick-set swarthy-skinned guard obeyed and passed him the phone, confirming, 'It's Gino.'

'Hey Gino,' Matt said, 'How's yer father doin'?'

'Much better Mr Figorelli,' Gino started respectfully.

'Good,' Matt said. The pleasantries over, he got straight to the point. 'That problem you sorted. Cost me a pilot.'

'Not me, Mr Figorelli,' Gino defended. 'Met Antonio as you suggested. Said he didn't need my help, he could manage. Said the pilot was leaking and the best place for a leak was at the end of an alley!' He chuckled loudly at his joke, then added, 'So he plugged the leak!'

Matt's brow creased with anger as he pictured the youngest son of his counterpart Enzo Rossini, sitting at his father's desk, a cocky smirk on his face.

'That right?' Matt questioned, adding after a short pause, 'Any sign of the money?'

He listened as Gino fumbled an explanation.

'Not as yet, but we're closing in. Got a detective on the inside . . . bin working for me for a couple of months now. Leave it with me. I'll get it.'

Matt dropped down the receiver amused at his counterpart's son's nerve and concluded under his breath, 'Yeah Gino, you and me both.'

It was close to five before Scarface returned to the Penthouse.

'What did yer find?' Matt questioned looking up from his paperwork.

'Antonio and Deke,' he replied flatly.

Matt threw down his pen and leant back in his chair.

'Where are they?'

'We buried 'em, Boss!'

Sighing heavily, Matt shook his head. 'This whole business is beginning to give me a bad taste in my mouth.'

He pushed back his leather chair and walked across to the darkened glass wall of windows, staring pensively down on to the strip. The traffic was heavy, the car parks were full. Knots of people stood waiting as various car valets ferried cars to the front of the hotel opposite. Running his hand over the top of his thinning hair, he turned around to face the Scandinavian.

'Get back to Luigi's. See if he can shed any more light on the girl. See if anyone's seen her before!'

Scarface nodded then left the room and he walked back to his desk and sat down in his chair.

Who the fuck was she? Had she been sent by a rival to get rid of him? And if so, why?

He stood up and retraced his earlier steps. He'd find out soon enough. He'd find out Monday when he saw his counterpart in Portland.

After their evening meal Tony helped Maria clear up. Abby excused herself with a headache and Andy followed moments later.

It was just after nine when Tony and Maria settled themselves with a bourbon and ice in the lounge.

'I'm worried about Abby,' he confided, 'She's made of strong stuff, but Buck was her life.'

Maria nodded her agreement, 'How long can you stay?'

He shrugged his shoulders and lit a cigarette,

'You'll stay a while though?'

'Of course!'

'Good,' he nodded, then sipped his drink, 'She's got a lot to sort through.' He stared at the coffee table and the room fell silent. She watched as he drained his glass.

'Refill?' he asked. She finished her drink and gave him the empty glass.

'Andy's a good sort,' he said, picking up the earlier conversation as he walked across to the bar, 'But Buck's death has really shaken him. He's not long buried his own wife.'

He unscrewed the cap on the bourbon. 'He married, I guess you'd say late in life. Miriam, his wife was twenty years his junior. They've a son. He'd be around four years old now.'

She walked across to the bar and sat down on the bar stool opposite him.

'She, that is Miriam, was crushed by a runaway truck. Not a hundred yards from their house.' He replaced the cap on the bottle. 'Turning in, she was, to the start of their driveway. The truck came over the hill so fast she didn't know what hit her.'

He took a handful of cubes from the ice bucket and dropped them into their drinks then pushed Maria's towards her.

'How long ago did it happen?' she questioned.

'About six months back,' he replied, adding after a moment's thought, 'So you see Buck's death on top of that. . .' His voice trailed off and he stared straight ahead lost in his thoughts.

It was close to ten when their on-off conversation ended. For the last fifteen minutes they'd been sitting in silence.

She stood up and stretched and, yawning, said, 'I think I'll take a shower and turn in. It's been a long day.' She slid off her stool. Tony didn't reply and she doubted he'd heard her.

He was tired, but he knew he wouldn't sleep, there was too much on his mind. He scooped another handful of ice and poured another drink then walked across to the chesterfield, vaguely remembering her exit. Pulling the phone towards him he lifted the receiver and dialled.

The results of his phone calls confirmed it. It would be a few more days before Buck's body could be released. He would have liked to have got it over with as quickly as possible for Abby's sake, but it couldn't be helped. His last telephone call was to his partner Fred Hall, in Los Angeles.

'Tony! I was just about to call you. . . How yer doin'?'

'I'm doing okay Fred.'

'Have you come up with anythin' new?' Fred questioned overeagerly.

'New maybe not, but I'd like you to run a further check on

Antonio Mancetti and Deke Richardson. Call in a few favours. See what the feeling on the street is?'

'Sure Tony. . . Sure.'

A sudden cold shiver in Fred's spine accompanied his recollective thoughts as he recalled his last meeting with the menacing duo. At the same time Tony's brow creased as he puzzled Fred's tone. He'd known him a long time and the nervous tremor in his voice, that he'd tried unsuccessfully to mask, didn't fit the light tone with which he'd couched his question.

'How goes it with that last lot of paperwork Buck sent in?' Tony pressed.

'Still ploughing through it. Course what we really need is hard evidence; drugs trafficking even tax evasion will do.'

'Yeah.' Tony agreed, his voice housing a sarcastic edge as it turned from a question to an order.

'Maybe when you've finished ploughing you can unearth what we're looking for in Buck's paperwork, detective!'

'Yeah,' Fred managed, weakly noting the sarcastic quip before Tony broke the connection.

What was it with Fred these days? he asked himself. He'd had that paperwork for over a week. He'd seen stumbling rookies get more results in half the time. Knocking back his drink, he turned off the downstairs lights and made his way up the stairs.

After checking in on Abby, he crossed the hall to Maria's door and tapped lightly. 'Maria, you asleep?'

When she opened the door, her robe was draped loosely around her shoulders. She wiped the salty wetness from her eyes. She'd never been an emotional person, however her new-found emotions were running high. She'd not shed a single tear at her beloved mother's funeral but lately she'd awaken on a damp pillow. Sometimes she felt convinced the voice was none other than her mother and others she knew it wasn't. She missed her so much and the sound of the voice made it worse. She longed to feel her mother's loving arms around her.

Seeing her distress, Tony's arm circled her shoulders and he ushered her back inside. Closing the door, he sat her down on the bed and cuddled her close to his chest. He needed her, wanted her; had to have her. No words were spoken as he felt her hot breath against his cheek. Lifting her chin to face him, he gently kissed each side of her cheek. It seemed the most natural thing in the world as her warm moist lips found his.

Her arm closed around his neck pulling him closer and together they sank back on the bed. He could feel her strong heartbeat, in tune with his own as her robe fell away from her shoulders and he cupped her small, firm breast in his hand.

She pressed her body against him, moulding into him, her light green eyes searching his as they warmly invited him. Her soft slightly parted lips touched his neck, sending shivers of exalted rapture right through him.

Slipping out of his clothes, he laid next to her smooth, lithe body and kissed her breasts. Suddenly, the gentleness that had drawn him to her vanished. She was like a voracious tigress; an unremitting sexual time bomb, devouring him of his will as she mounted him.

Unable to understand his willing response, his manhood stood tall and proud; then suddenly, she clasped his hands tightly above his head, her almost superhuman strength outweighing his as she held them with great pressure back against the bed.

To her . . . he was the necessary seed.

She moved rhythmically above him, satisfying the inner voice's incitement. . . .'Take him! Take him!'

The sudden warning signals that tore through his subconscious were swept away on the full tide of ecstasy as his sexual need was fulfilled; he was in a state of oblivion now, feeling only triumphant in his immediate climax.

When it was over, she rolled off him and closed her eyes. He lay there staring at the ceiling. He felt as if he'd been raped . . . and yet . . . he'd been willing. He'd gone to her room wanting her . . . needing her . . .

He turned his head towards her, studying the beauty in her face and his excitement returned. As his manhood stirred again he knew she'd be like a drug, a fix he'd have to have regularly. For a long time he'd had an enormous vacuity inside that no one had been able to fill . . . except now, this beautiful woman . . . This Maria, his Maria.

It was dawn when Maria awoke. Tony was asleep at her side. Startled, she turned to look into his face. At the same time the voice returned, its previous raspishness replaced by a cruel determined tone as it spat out, 'You are impregnated . . . his child . . . my future!'

Like a bolt of lightning out of the blue, a piercing shriek of laughter shot through her mind and she felt a hot tear burn a path down the furrow of her nose, for she remembered nothing of the previous night. Confused and shaking she slipped out of the covers and hurried into the bathroom. She turned on the shower and stood underneath, her silent tears mingling with the relaxing warmth of the water as it cascaded over her shoulders.

In the shower she would find comfort; had done since she was a child when her mother had bathed her. As far back as she could remember, she'd done most of her thinking in the shower. Not that she could do much of that lately, for the voice would always intervene.

She'd just sponged her body with shower-gel attempting to rid herself of his smell, when suddenly with a mocking laugh the voice informed, 'A daughter . . . you'll have a daughter.'

Exhausted, she slid down the tiles and sat on the floor, the force of the angry water like giant needles beating against the pain in her head. There was no fight left in her. The voice was dominating her every thought.

As the hologram relayed Maria's thoughts, both doctors turned to face each other. The brief silent statement in their eyes acknowledged Dr Western's victory before Dr Swartz asked, 'How is the history parallel holding?'

'Steady for the moment, although we've still a lot of static.'

'Have we obtained any access to Dr Western's thoughts?'

'Negative. The computer is still trying.'

His face was dark with frustration and anger as he walked across to the life support unit. He stared down at Gemma's comatose body. She looked so pale, yet so peaceful and his expression softened. The mere sight of her had always had that effect on him. Slowly he regained his composure.

'Any problems Dr Blackmore?' His question had been a cover

for his unwarranted check for he knew if there had been he'd have been the first to know.

'No sir,' he replied confidently.

He nodded, then glanced back at Dr Western, before he returned to his seat.

Meanwhile, the computer had fast forwarded the hologram settling on Friday 4th November, the day of Buck's funeral.

Maria, wearing a black dress and matching shoes, sat at her dressing table powdering her nose, her hair twisted into a chignon. He watched as she made her way downstairs to the kitchen.

It was 8.43am. Tony and Andy had been up for hours and as Maria entered Tony motioned her to sit, then slipped his hand into an oven glove and withdrew a breakfast of ham and eggs from the hotplate. He placed the breakfast in front of her and kissed her cheek softly.

Her slim hand touched his cheek lightly and Dr Swartz felt a sudden unexplained pang of jealousy surge through him.

Just after 9.15am Abby joined them. Her face looked pale and drawn over her high-necked tight-fitting black suit. Her golden, normally free-flowing shoulder-length locks were unflatteringly pulled straight back off her face and fastened with a black ribbon. She poured herself a coffee then sat down next to Andy.

'Did you sleep any?' he asked, concerned.

'Some,' she nodded, looking down into her coffee cup. Tony placed her breakfast in front of her.

'I don't know's I can eat anything?' she protested and stared out across the desert, in her own private world.

After a few moments, Andy picked up her fork and put it in her hand. 'You have to eat something,' he insisted.

She looked at her breakfast, then half-heartedly forked the scrambled eggs around the plate. 'What time will the car be here?'

'10.15am. You've plenty of time.'

'I really can't eat this,' she said, then laid down her fork and lit a cigarette, her eyes returning to the peacefulness of the desert. The sun shone brightly against the light blue of the sky but in Abby's saddened eyes there was only grief.

At 10.15am prompt the black limousine pulled up outside. The driver opened the door and they settled themselves inside.

The small chapel in the centre of the cemetery was full.

Through misty, red eyes Abby stared at the brass-handled walnut coffin, at its isolated loneliness centre stage, at the flowers that lay on the lid, Buck's favourite, roses, tiny buds of white and red. She wiped away the well of tears that had built up in her eyes. It all seemed so unreal.

She had an overpowering urge to stand up and scream, 'It's a mistake . . . All a terrible mistake!'

She looked up at the multicoloured stained glass window high in the chapel wall, at the sunrays that fell across the coffin lid in strips . . .

Just then, the Chaplain placed his hand on her shoulder and whispered words into her ear. His sudden presence had startled her. She nodded, more from politeness for she'd not heard a word, her silent inner sobs of grief masking out the sound. She felt Andy take her hand in comfort, then raised her head as the Chaplain took his place behind the lectern.

She could see his mouth moving as he spoke, his actions, their actions, all in slow motion, but could hear no sound, just Buck's voice as he'd kissed her goodbye that fateful bright Monday morning.

'See you, pussycat,' he'd said kissing her cheek.

'See you. . . .'

Her hand rose to her cheek touching the spot. And now there was nothing, just this fierce, lonely coldness inside, a walnut casket taking centre stage alone and the Chaplain that didn't truly know him, starting a eulogy about her husband.

Suddenly the Chaplain's words broke into her thoughts. 'His widow,' he'd said. She'd heard him! and the well of tears flowed . . .

Andy's arm slipped around her shoulders. 'Oh dear Lord,' she thought, 'What now?'

When the Chaplain had finished speaking, he asked if there was anyone who'd like to say a few words.

A tall thin man of around sixty stood up and came forward. As he passed her, she recognised him. He'd been a long time friend of Buck's, his name was Frank Masters. It seemed like yesterday he'd spoken at their wedding; was it really almost thirty years ago?

Her mind wandered again, and his kind words were lost, as her memories flooded back. When she looked at the lectern again, the Chaplain was laying down his book . . . the service was over.

The coffin was carried shoulder-high to the graveside.

Andy took her arm and together they led the cortège. It was all like a dream; a nightmare she was living with no one to wake her . . . and then the coffin was lowered.

She threw a single red rose and watched as it floated down into the grave. Andy circled her shoulders with his arm, then she accepted the outstretched hands of mourners offering their condolences, as they broke away from the graveside and filed past them. With glazed eyes she stared at the coffin.

Gently, Tony tried to lead her away. She turned to look up at him, and through swollen tear filled eyes assured, 'I . . . just need a minute or two.'

He kissed her cheek, then joined Andy and Maria as they walked down the incline to the waiting car some thirty yards away. Settling himself inside, he turned back to look at Abby. A lone, tall figure of a man walked toward her. He watched through the darkened windows of the black limousine whilst they spoke.

Suddenly, Abby stepped back from the man, angrily brushing his hand from her sleeve. He reached for the handle of the door and was out in a second, running full speed towards her.

The tall man startled by Tony's intent, hastened the few yards to his waiting limousine and as Abby fell into his arms, the limousine sped off and it was over.

'Who was that?' he questioned, biting back his anger, following the limousine with his eyes.

'One of Matt Figorelli's men. Just paying his last respects!' Abby confirmed.

His eyes narrowed meaningfully, as he led Abby away from the grave.

It was 4.00pm exactly when Tony closed the door on the last mourner. Maria had escorted Abby to her room and Tony and Andy were in the lounge. Andy drew back the drapes and the large room flooded with the late afternoon sun.

'I remember when Buck had this window fitted. There was just a tiny window this side. We were out on the back porch, looking out at the desert. It was spring and the cacti were all in bloom. We'd never seen such a magnificent sight . . . That's when he decided . . . He did the same in the kitchen. Within a week he'd got on to the builders and both windows were in.'

For a few, brief moments he stood looking out over the desert, nodding his head at his statement, then turned to walk over to the bar where Tony had poured them both a drink, then settled himself on a bar stool.

'I'm glad we're alone,' Andy started, 'I was wondering how the murder investigation was progressing. And how the leads panned out, with the list Buck handed in?'

'It's going just fine,' Tony placated, anticipating Andy's thoughts and not wanting to lose him the same way he'd lost Buck. 'Ballistics have confirmed that the gun found next to Ted Ashly's body not only killed him but also killed Buck and both Mancetti and Richardson's prints were all over it.' He paused and regarded Andy, then resumed, hopeful he'd stifled a further question.

'What was an added bonus and solved a murder enquiry for the Portland police was the discovery of a second gun found just a few feet away. That gun killed a Portland Private Eye, name of Bernie Walters and although most of the prints were smudged, there was a clear thumb print belonging to Deke Richardson. Needless to say, neither gun was registered, but with Mancetti and Richardson's prints . . . '

'No leads on their whereabouts?' Andy interrupted.

Tony shook his head. 'Not as yet, but as they both work for Matt Figorelli, they'll surface sooner or later.'

'Yeah. Matt Figorelli, head of the West coast; the guy that gives the orders,' Andy ranted angrily, 'The Mr Clean. The whiter-than-snow-white Mr Clean! Why is it that the higher up the chain you look, the cleaner they get?'

It was a question Tony had asked himself over the years, more than once and the only answer he'd come up with was power! Andy took a mouthful of bourbon and lit a cigarette. The vengeful expression in his eyes said it all.

'Well, maybe Matt Figorelli is not as clean as he'd like to be. You know I spoke to Buck just before he was killed and a week prior to that he mailed me a copy of his notes, in case anything happened to him. Said he had a new route. From his notes I'd say he'd found out exactly what was going down.'

'You still got the notes?'

'Got some of 'em right here. The rest, and they include two files, are back at the office, in my safe.'

He put his hand into his inside pocket and pulled out a brown manilla envelope which he gave to Tony then, draining his drink, he refilled his glass while Tony read through them.

'Buck made no mention of this when he spoke to Detective Hall!' Tony exclaimed.

'Told me he gave Fred Hall exactly what he'd mailed to me, but in case you got any doubts, I'll tell you what Buck told me. And I've got the files to prove it! The firm, as he put it, was about to move part of their operations from Portland to Shreveport.'

'Shreveport! Why Shreveport?'

'Good question,' Andy nodded, 'And one I asked Buck. It seems he'd overheard a conversation between Matt Figorelli and his counterpart Enzo Rossini, they mentioned something about that private eye, Walters being murdered. Anyhow, Buck didn't say where or how, just that he'd heard they were definitely moving part of their operations to Shreveport. After all, we all know there's no mob activity there.

'Anyway the conversation went on about tax fraud. It would operate like every other company they owned. They'd file a nice and clean, proper tax return each year, reporting a fraction of the income, etc. It's no secret they set up legitimate companies with dirty money. Figorelli seemed to think the Shreveport base could handle about two million a year! Dope, gambling and protection.'

'Did he know how? Where? What bank? Country?'

'Said Matt Figorelli had a big meeting in Portland and he was gonna fly him. Course he was murdered before he could. But those two files he took from the accountant sure make good reading.'

'Why didn't you tell me this before, Andy?'

'I thought you had what I had. Buck told me he'd given the originals to Fred Hall. He called you, but you were out, so he asked Fred to meet him and he came straight away.'

'That's right, but all Buck gave him was an envelope with a couple of lists in, mostly companies where he thought deliveries would take place. There weren't any bills of lading. Had I documentation like these, or what you tell me you have . . . '

'Well you got it now!' Andy broke in, 'First thing tomorrow I'll fly down and get the files. Maybe it was the files they were looking for and not the half a million.'

'Maybe both! One thing's for certain, if we can solidly tie them in with Matt Figorelli's operation.' His voice trailed off.

Andy wasn't listening just staring down into his bourbon.

'When you get back Andy, how long can you stay?'

'Haven't really given it much thought. I guess as long as Abby needs me. But I'll be in a better position to answer that tomorrow. Why?'

'It's just . . . I'd like to get back to L.A. as soon as possible and knowing you were here with Abby and Maria would make it a whole lot easier.'

Andy nodded his understanding. 'Guess I'll go up now. I've got to be up early and it's been a long day.'

Tony was on his fifth large bourbon by the time Maria had joined him.

'Any left?' she quizzed, facing him across the bar. He held up the almost-empty bottle and forced a smile, then turned around to get her a glass.

When he turned back, she was next to him. Her arm circled his waist and she kissed his cheek. A moment later she was in his arms, her determined eyes luringly inviting. Slowly, but deliberately she loosened his necktie, opening the top button on his shirt with her teeth, before nuzzling his neck. His head spun. He could feel his whole body ache for her. He couldn't help himself; his innermost thoughts told him no, but he couldn't refuse her.

Roughly, he pulled her close to him, his eyes wide. He wanted her, needed her. His hand slipped to her thigh and her toe traced the outline of his powerful thigh. He held her eyes with his as he slid her dress up, and felt the bareness of her firm buttocks. She smiled, her lips moist, as she unzipped his trousers and let them fall to the floor, her fingers caressing and searching.

She moaned with delight as he lifted her onto him, moving with him, feeling his masculinity inside her. As her soft wet lips found his, they clung to each other on a tide of ecstasy, their hearts pounding in synchronisation as he thrust forward and they both reached their ultimate goal.

As the excitement exploded inside them his hands bore deep in her buttocks. She clung to him, nuzzling into his neck then, brushing her lips across his, she slid down him and left.

It was all over within minutes. It wasn't as he had wanted it to be. A strange feeling swept over him; he'd wanted her; she gave herself, and yet he felt so . . . so . . . He stood there, his hands resting on the bar, his head bent between his shoulders, exhausted. The scent of her body still lingered in his nostrils; his sweat, soaking through his shirt. He took a handful of ice and ran it over his face. He couldn't think straight. . . . He had to get some sleep. He pulled up his trousers and zipped his fly then, picking up his glass he drained his drink, turned out the lights and made his way upstairs.

At 5.00am Buck set off for the airport. He'd be gone most of the day. By 6.00am Tony was awake. For two hours, when he'd finally turned in he'd tried to reach Lt Mason, but he'd had no luck and what little sleep he had managed had been restless, to say the least. The nagging ache in his guts hadn't helped.

Was Fred involved? And if so what had happened to the rest of the paperwork? As for the rest of the lists, Fred should have made some sort of progress! But then, if he was totally honest with himself, there were a lot of things Fred had done of late that didn't seem to make a whole lot of sense.

It was about six or seven weeks back, he recalled. He'd handed in a revolver. The last time he'd seen it was when he'd bagged it. He'd written up the required paperwork and left it in the evidence bag on his desk, awaiting collection. He went through every movement he'd made in his mind. It just didn't make sense!

At the time, Fred had been reading a file opposite him. He'd signed out about eleven. Fred had signed out at midnight, an hour after him. When he'd left, there were a few other detectives mulling around the outer office. It was like a thorn in his side, a nagging ache that wouldn't go away. He'd taken the gun himself, from the dead man's hand. The corpse wasn't wearing any gloves. There had to be fingerprints, if only from the dead man! Yet when the ballistic report had come back, the gun bore no prints . . . none!

The thing that bothered him even more was the disappearance of the two bullets. When he'd called ballistics they'd insisted there were no bullets. It was either ballistics or Fred. He'd have preferred it to be ballistics, but the more he investigated, the more he came up with Fred's name.

He'd talked to Lt Mason, told him about his suspicions. He'd hated to do it. The outcome of their conversation had been an unofficial enquiry; just Lt Mason and himself. Without Fred's knowledge, they'd check it out.

He swallowed heavily, the nagging ache throbbing as he continued with his thoughts. Fred in the meantime remained his usual self; that being, the usual self he was accustomising himself to, which was slightly more nervous than he deemed Fred's norm.

Then there was June, Fred's wife. She'd always been able to spend more than Fred earned. It had been a constant bone of contention between them, but these days Fred didn't seem too bothered. June was still spending and Fred was still smiling.

What happened to the bullets? he asked himself again.

The corpse was a local hood and well known as one of Figorelli's odd job men. The gun in question had no registered owner. The corpse had been shot through the head with all the signs of a contract-type "hit" that left not a trace, except that the gun was in the corpse's hand and, from the position of the body, there was no doubt that it had been put there for them to find. But, why go to so much trouble, then buy someone on the inside to mess with the evidence. Whichever way he thought about it, it all came back to Fred. He hated the guilt he felt at suspecting his partner, but it certainly explained where Fred was getting the extra monies that June liked to spend.

He'd been partners with Fred for three years, they were friends . . . . . He threw back the covers and headed for the shower.

The more he thought, the more he became convinced. Fred had to be working with them. Lt Mason had been convinced that someone on the case was and Fred had done a lot of things that had no explanation; just like three weeks back, a Saturday morning. If he'd not gone down to the evidence section and signed for the belongings of an old timer that had been knifed, he'd never have seen it. But there, as plain as the nose on your face, was Fred's signature, just two lines up from his. He'd signed out the evidence on one Ricardo "Totto" Sandini, a well-known runner about town. The case in question had nothing to do with Fred, wasn't even his section. What had he been looking for? He'd checked the list against the evidence . . . nothing missing.

He held the picture in his mind as he lathered his body.

Fred was pouring himself a coffee. When he'd mentioned it, he'd told him with a quick glance. 'Just doing a pal a favour.'

But there was something . . . something, in that glance, almost as if Fred was checking that he'd accepted his reply. He'd taken to doing that a lot over the last six or more months.

As the computer sped on the hologram changed. It was Saturday 5th November.

Fred Hall sat behind the wheel of his new, two-tone beige convertible in the empty parking lot of a disused warehouse. The hour on his illuminated watch showed 11.00pm exactly. He looked in his rear view mirror. A set of headlights moved slowly towards him. As the black Dodge positioned itself alongside him, the window lowered half way.

At the driver's signal, Fred got out of his car and slid in beside the driver.

'Got it?' Fred questioned, closing the door.

'Yeah,' the driver confirmed. 'You done good Fred.'

He put his hand inside his overcoat pocket and pulled out an envelope then, with a wide grin he tossed it to Fred. Returning his grin, Fred put the envelope into his breast pocket.

'Thanks Gino.'

'Ain't you gonna count it?' Gino joked.

'No need. I trust you.'

'Yeah,' Gino agreed, 'That's what it's all about, ain't it?'

'Sure is,' Fred finished, reaching for the handle of the door.

'I'll be in touch,' Gino called, as Fred stepped out of the car.

'Look forward to that Gino,' Fred replied, then closed the door.

He patted his breast pocket, watching as the Dodge moved off. He hated Gino. He was such a crazy sonofabitch but then he was Enzio's son and therefore commanded a certain amount of respect and what did he care who paid him for the files.

'Yeah Gino,' Fred thought, as he climbed into the driver's seat, 'You keep in touch!' But for now he was tired. It had been a long and arduous day.

The hologram clock sped on. As it approached 7.47am Dr Maxwell's urgent shout broke his concentration.

'Section two energy cells draining fast!' she exclaimed.

Hastily his eyes sought out the readout section, whilst his fingers sped to the speak keys with a correction code. It didn't seem to take Dr Western long, for each code he'd used she'd broken. Her power was becoming extremely frightening. He felt the tension build inside as he waited for the computer's acceptance but Dr Maxwell's voice was first.

'Section two holding . . . climbing . . . two degrees . . . three . . . four . . . approaching full power.'

'Full power restored Dr Swartz. Parallel synchronisation 24.2 hours,' the computer confirmed over Dr Maxwell's voice.

He turned to Dr Turner. 'Try to maintain full power. We're almost ready. We'll freeze Dr Western's soul then merge the two parallels. This is one alignment corridor we can't afford to miss!' His deputy nodded his understanding.

Fast forwarding the programme as much as he dared, for he knew to interfere too much would alter the alignment sequence, he watched as Tony and Abby kept their appointment with Lt Smithers in his office.

'May I offer my condolences Mrs Western,' the lieutenant said as they seated themselves opposite him. She nodded her head and accepted his handshake.

'I'm afraid we have no fresh news on the whereabouts of Antonio Mancetti and Deke Richardson. They seem to have disappeared without trace.'

He glanced at Tony, his blue-grey eyes holding his before he looked back to Abby. He was still not completely sure Abby should be involved, but if the files Tony had taken to Lt Mason were anything to go by, and after his previous meeting with them both, the plan to install two detectives at the airfield was the only course they had.

'I've asked you to come here today because we need your help.'

She lit a cigarette and he pushed an ashtray towards her.

'We propose to set a trap for Matt Figorelli. Our sources lead us to believe that they are moving part of their operation, so it may be our last chance. Your husband flew a Walter Pinne to various destinations.'

'The accountant,' Abby interrupted, 'He makes a regular run every Monday. Dangerous, beady-eyed little man.'

She flicked the residue of spent ash into the glass ashtray, then looked across the desk at him. 'So what do you want me to do?'

He stole another glance at Tony then returned his attention to Abby.

'First of all, you have to know how dangerous it is. If you start asking too many questions you could end up the same way as your booking clerk.'

He ran his hand through his thick greying hair, walked across to the window and looked down at the street.

Then, turning to face her, he said, 'I don't know how much you know about their operation, but it looks certain that the break-in was connected to a missing half a million and it's our belief that your husband was murdered because of it! You see, the money was clean, already laundered.'

'But Buck never had any half a million!'

'We know, Abby,' Tony broke in, 'He called us immediately he'd delivered it.'

Lt Smithers walked back to his desk and opened his file.

'Now we have several options open to us. But we're hoping Matt Figorelli will still use the company. So in case he does, we'd like to put two men out at the airfield. Detective Voite, who has a pilot's licence and Detective Waverley. Voite would take over contracts and Waverley the bookings.'

She thought for a moment, her finger unconsciously picking at the skin around her nail then, stubbing out her cigarette, said, 'If Matt Figorelli's contract is still on, I'm gonna do it myself!'

'Abby!' Tony cut in quickly, 'Listen to the lieutenant! Let the Detectives handle it. Please! It's far safer.'

She turned to face him and saw the concern in his eyes. With Buck gone, she was all he had and it showed. Reluctantly she turned to face the lieutenant and nodded a silent agreement.

He stood up and walked around his desk sitting on the edge facing Tony.

'Their operation has been interrupted now and they don't know who to trust, so maybe they'll start making mistakes.'

8

BOSTON MAIN DOME LABORATORY: 18TH OCTOBER, 2384

With great diligence, the team members at their stations applied their skills. The two parallel time frames edged closer together.

'Approaching alignment,' Dr Swartz informed,

'Alignment on four . . . three . . . two . . . We have parallel . . . lock in,' he finished excitedly.

Simultaneously each team member secured their stations and the two time frames became one in unification.

Each member's eyes were eagerly expectant, awaiting the clearance of the hologram's blue, smoky mist. The computer unfroze the section and the Commander's soul, in her ancestor Julie van Slijk's comatose body, stirred.

At the same time on a smaller hologram screen, Maria Becket slept.

Both Dr Turner and Swartz monitored as the freeze on Dr Western's soul, that had constantly dogged them, slipping in and out throughout the entire operation, was officially discarded.

'You have a full parallel alignment, Dr Swartz,' the main computer advised.

It was nine thirty precisely, Sunday morning 6th November, 1984. The second phase of their rescue mission was complete.

A loud cheer rang in his ears as his team clapped and voiced their congratulations.

Dr Turner stood up and shook his hand. 'Congratulations Eric!' he enthused.

'Still a long way to go Harry,' he replied, as he shook his hand, amidst the applause, 'A long way.'

On a wave of euphoria, the team retook their seats for the next step of the rescue mission.

'How's the energy level holding on Dr Western's soul Harry?' Dr Swartz quizzed, simultaneous to his colleague's check.

'A steady 4.8 degrees,' he replied.

'Good. Have we enough stored energy to ease the Probe into Maria's dream state?'

Dr Turner looked his colleague straight in the eye. He knew exactly what he had in mind.

'The stored energy is not a problem but it'll be risky if Gemma's soul is fully awake, she could drain it again.'

Dr Swartz thought for a moment, then whispered a suggestion.

'If we use the thought pads, we'll minimise the risks. If Gemma does try to draw the energy, the failsafe should break the connection.'

'But we have no authorisation!'

'I know, Harry, but if I'd waited for authorisation on the Probe.'

'You mean.'

'I obtained it after. There shouldn't be a problem. The failsafe WILL disconnect. Do it, Harry . . . Do it now!' Reluctantly, Dr Turner programmed the necessary information into the computer. When it had accepted his intention, he released the appropriate section of the Probe and eased it into the sleeping Maria.

Both doctors waited, the palms of their right hands firmly pressed to the Receiving Pads as the Probe penetrated Maria's dream state.

The Receiving Pads were still classified information and, on the Counsel of Elders' strict instructions, would remain that way.

When Dr Swartz had discovered Dr Litchen's sketchy outline, he had streamlined the system. The plates now measured just a two-inch square and were situated on both Dr Turner's and his station, thus enabling them to privately view various projects by a simple touch.

Maria's dream-state thoughts, therefore, could be transmitted directly into their own minds. It had been a major breakthrough and one to which, with the exception of the Counsel, he and Dr Turner only, were privy.

Suddenly Maria stirred . . .

A great whoosh of energy swept through them and their hands became semi-transparent. Blue, crackling energy cells danced over their fingers, gluing their palms to the pads like a powerful magnet, as Dr Western's soul, discovering their intrusion, tried to draw the stored energy.

For the first time, in the following fleeting moments, they experienced the great depth of bonding between Gemma and Maria's souls.

In the next instant it had gone. The preprogrammed failsafe, had severed the connection and the receiving pads were cold.

Disappointedly, both doctors turned to face each other.

'When this mission has been completed, that area merits our urgent attention,' Dr Swartz said.

Dr Turner agreed. 'It would certainly eliminate the necessity of having to send another soul back to retrieve.'

Dr Swartz's angry dark eyes flared, his voice now a whispered growl, 'This catastrophe will not happen again! Of that you can be sure!'

He held his eyes, defying him to argue the point, before he turned away, watching as the computer fast forwarded to 6th November, 1984 . . . on a settled 4pm.

The sound of a telephone ringing filtered through the hologram's blue haze. As the mist cleared a hand reached towards the receiver.

Both doctors watched as a sombre Tony Garnet answered the call. Less than a moment later, a wide beam replaced his dismal expression as he listened to his friend's news.

'Piet . . . that's wonderful . . . wonderful news!'

'Julie came out of the coma at nine thirty this morning . . . I still can't believe it.' he confirmed emotionally, 'Recognised me immediately! At this precise moment, she's sat up in bed eating soup! Can you believe it! Soup!' He paused a few moments to take a breath and Tony broke in.

'You're one hell of a lucky guy, Piet.'

'I sure as hell am!' he echoed.

'I'll be back in Los Angeles Tuesday afternoon. I'll fly up Wednesday evening.'

'Great!' Piet enthused, 'We'll both look forward to seeing you . . .'

'It's been a long time since you've been able to say that,' Tony joked.

'It most certainly has,' Piet agreed, smiling broadly as he replaced the receiver.

'Good news?' Andy enquired.

'Unbelievable news!' He was hardly able to contain himself. He looked across at Abby, his jubilance radiating through his light blue eyes as he reminded.

'You remember I told you about Piet's wife, Julie, being run over by a hit-and-run driver.'

She nodded, her eyes expectant as she shared her godson's joy, 'Some time back.'

'She came out of the coma nine thirty this morning! Recognised Piet straight off!'

'Well that certainly is good news!' Abby beamed.

Just then, Dr Turner nudged Dr Swartz, and pointed to the soul readout charts. Both doctors watched in silence as the energy level of Maria Becket's soul divided into two parts. Suddenly, the smaller reading, measuring two degrees, disappeared altogether. Less than a moment later the degrees of Dr Western's soul shot up rapidly, rising by the missing two points; signifying to their horror that she'd taken yet another part of Maria's soul.

Whilst they were still watching, Maria's reading dropped again by another half point and Dr Western's rose by the same amount. It was an all-out battle to stop her as the computer automatically fought their balance, releasing an emergency energy realignment.

Both doctors' pulses thundered loudly as their eyes remained with the readings. A moment later Dr Swartz's hopes were dashed. He stared long and hard at the computer's written response. 'Energy Realignment Code unacceptable.'

Anxiously his fingers darted to the speak keys. But the same written message glared back at him.

'It won't accept any deviation!' he gasped, still staring at the screen.

Just then Dr Western's soul levelled at 5.4 degrees.

Both doctors watched helplessly as Maria Becket conversed with the voice; the one-sided conversation obliterating any doubts they may have had of the power Dr Western now held.

They listened as Maria's whispered pleas lost the argument. They couldn't hear Dr Western's voice, but there was no doubt in their minds that Maria now believed the powerful influence belonged to her mother.

The computer following its pre-programmed course sped on and the blue mist faded the scene.

The time, 11.00pm. The date, 6th November, 1984. When the haze had subsided, Tony and Andy were talking outside Tony's bedroom door.

'Yes, I am looking forward to seeing Piet again. I haven't been able to get up to Paybac lately. With this case taking precedence, I've not been much of a help to him. He's been through hell and back!'

Andy patted his arm. 'Still, it's great news Tony. Give Piet and Julie my best. And say hello to Stan for me. It's been a long time since I saw him, must get up there one of these days.'

The two men parted company and Tony went into his bedroom.

Maria's face was pale and tired as she eased her bedroom door closed. She hadn't meant to but had overheard their conversation.

'Why does the name Paybac seem so familiar?' she asked the voice.

They watched as Dr Western's energy level fluctuated and knew she was conversing. It was evident from Maria's answers, she had no recollection of passing through the city. Equally she didn't know she'd been the hit-and-run driver and, at this stage of the one-sided conversation, it was more than apparent that Dr Western was not going to enlighten her. He wished he could hear what Dr Western had said.

'Soon,' he told himself, 'Soon, when the Commander comes in contact with Maria.'

Maria got into bed. The one-sided conversation continued.

'Who is Julie van Slijk?'

They couldn't hear Dr Western's reply, but from the sharp rise in degrees on her energy readout chart it was obvious she was using the Echo facility.

'You'll meet her soon,' the voice assured, the words fading into her subconscious, as Maria drifted off to sleep.

Suddenly, Dr Maxwell's voice broke the calm.
'Maria Becket's soul readout decreasing rapidly!'
Swartz and Turner looked up at the energy level.
It was registering 1.78.
'Computer refusing to accept deviation,' she resumed.

As Dr Western's reading rose, they were helpless. 'She's taken another section of Maria's soul Eric,' Dr Turner whispered, 'We'll have to try separation.'

'Not yet Harry . . . not yet!'

'We can't afford to wait . . . She could. '

'We can wait as long as I deem necessary Dr Turner!' Dr Swartz cut in.

His dark, defiant eyes held an expression Dr Turner thought close to madness.

Why the hell was Eric delaying? Now that both parallels were aligned, why hadn't he frozen them then run the alignment forward to a suitable interception and just taken both souls? Dr Swartz was head of the unit and fully aware of the dangers.

Swallowing hard, he suppressed his objection. When Eric was like this it was useless to argue. But his angry, silent reasoning had convinced him this wasn't just a rescue mission. It was another, unauthorised, in depth experiment. An experiment that could cost Gemma Western her life! And at this stage, there was nothing he could do . . . . . or was there?

He turned back to the hologram promising himself that he'd try separation of the souls at the first available moment . . . with or without the good Dr Swartz's permission.

Releasing a subdivision of the third section of the Probe, he instructed the computer to activate separation procedure at the first available moment, then sat back to wait . . . Dr Swartz was obviously not himself.

'A thought for you, Harry,' Dr Swartz resumed. His voice was calm now; the previous outburst of moments earlier clearly forgotten.

'We have no real research into the Echo, apart from my own limited insight. Dr Western, on the other hand, has both! She monitored the experiment when we sent my soul through time, she now has experience in both fields. What if she were able to use the Echo to flash into Julie's future?'

'Not possible!' he replied, still angry at his colleague's previous rage.

'Not possible!' Dr Swartz contradicted, 'Think about it man! If Julie's life affects Maria's then Dr Western will have access to that period!'

'But only that particular period,' Dr Turner reluctantly conceded.

He thought quickly, maybe Eric wasn't so crazy.

'Even if that does happen, she won't be able to see into Irinka's thoughts. In that time frame, Irinka has no history! We are controlling Commander van Slijk, so theoretically as Julie is in a coma, all Dr Western will see is a blank.'

'True . . . ' Dr Swartz agreed nodding, 'Or she'll see what we want her to see. Nonetheless, worrying.'

He rubbed his chin as he thought, then called across to Dr Maxwell.

'Keep a close watch on both Maria Becket's and Dr Western's

soul degrees. I want to know immediately of any change.'

He turned back to Dr Turner.

'Gemma doesn't know the Commander's soul is in Julie's body. It'll be interesting to see how she interprets the situation.'

He wished again that they had developed the Litchen Probe to its fullest potential. He'd just have to be patient and wait!

At least he'd learnt something from this mission. The Probe could not penetrate an alien soul when it was inside a body already occupied by its conscious, rightful soul. According to the main computer's computations, the living soul was blocking out the Probe's channel of communication. But, by the same token, and a plus as far as he could determine, an alien soul wouldn't be able to use the Echo facility to read the thoughts of another suchlike soul.

'A question,' Dr Turner said, interrupting his colleague's thoughts.

'When Dr Western comes into contact with Commander van Slijk, and we open the channel of communication with the Commander, will Gemma be able to hear us?'

'I've already pondered that very thought, Dr Turner. I don't believe it's possible, but if it is, I'm more than ready. I've programmed the computer to operate the scrambler. All Dr Western will pick up is heavy static.'

'Time corridor choice available,' the computer advised.

Dr Turner depressed a switch, and the availability was on the screen.

'Shall I take the first option?' he asked.

'No, it's too soon!' Dr Swartz exclaimed.

'Well, what option should I take?'

He was impatient now and it showed.

'You will take an option, when I tell you to take an option and not before, Dr Turner!'

He turned back to the hologram, disregarding his deputy's objections and watched as the blue mist faded the vision, and the computer, following its preprogrammed course, raced forward to the next applicable date.

They listened to the narration before it settled on 30th December, 1984.

Buck Western's brother Andy and his small son Tommy, a sandy-haired five-year-old, had moved to Las Vegas permanently.

Overseeing his brother's section of the company, he'd infused a great deal of capital. Delivery of new and larger aircraft, plus new and re-negotiated contracts ensured business was booming.

The seven-weeks pregnant Maria, had bought a house on the millionaire's side of Hunter's Ridge and had just taken occupancy.

Tony Garnet had returned to Los Angeles. They were close to cracking the case. He and Maria had kept in touch, but until Abby inadvertently advised him of Maria's condition, had been none the wiser.

Under Dr Western's guidance, Maria still enjoyed the fortunes of the casino and had duly amassed a fortune. Through careful investment and a new business venture in computer design, her fortune grew healthily.

Using the stored voice of Maria's mother Lillian, and having taken possession of three sections of Maria's soul, Dr Gemma Western had obtained almost total control.

The sun shone brightly through the windows of Maria's study. The two doctors watched as she sat behind her desk in her new home, her thoughts prominent.

Dr Western's soul had had great influence. True to Dr Turner's previous theory, she'd successfully blanked out most of Maria's past life. All that was left was a hazy fog. Consequently, Maria had only one direct aim and the emphasis now was on building on the abundance of created wealth; the same wealth and power that would come to future generations through the child she carried. With her mother's guidance Maria needed no one except, it seemed, Abby.

The voice had been all-insistent on that score. 'You be good and kind to Abby.' It could affect her whole future. And the future was all that mattered.

If anything happened to Abby, her brother-in-law Andy would return to his home; the consequence of which would be that her unborn daughter would never meet her intended husband, Abby's nephew Tommy. The vision she'd experienced had been explicit! She'd seen her daughter's future in a dream. She was head of her multi-million dollar computer corporation.

'You are not dreaming. It's a glimpse into the future. ' the voice had placated, 'A future of your making that you, and you alone, have the absolute power to control . . . and when mere mortals die, you'll live on in me as I live in you!'

And she knew her mother was right!

She turned and looked over the valley. The large split-level house stood in eight acres of magnificent gardens, giving both privacy and seclusion.

The lower level sported an enormous square kitchen, to the side of which, and overlooking the valley, was an equally large dining room. A large open-plan lounge, with a centred fireplace off which was a squared hall, completed the ground floor.

Upstairs on the first split-level section was a further lounge and study, plus en-suite master bedroom. This was her private domain!

At the top of another stairway, facing east, ran a long corridor of ten bedrooms, eight of which were en-suite. At the rear of the property, a wall of darkened windows ran floor to ceiling.

Outside, to the right of the property, stood a six-car integral garage, which at the present time housed her new white Porsche. Above this was a three-bedroom apartment, the home of her gardener/handyman Jeff Fowler, a very fit fifty-five-year-old and his forty-year-old wife Jeanette who, together with two live-out daily cleaners, tended the house. Mrs Carrera, a short plump Mexican of around forty-five, completed her staff.

'Iz vor you Miz Maria. A Mizter Garnet,' Mrs Carrera advised in her heavy Spanish accent, whilst trying to master the new phone system Maria had had installed. Satisfied it hadn't beaten her, she transferred the call and continued with her preparations for lunch.

'Good morning. Iz dat Miz Maria?' Tony mimicked jovially.

'Well, good morning yourself,' she laughed.

'I'm coming up to Vegas tonight. Thought I'd come straight across and see that magnificent house I've been hearing about.'

She chuckled again. 'Abby been boasting?'

'Now how did you guess?'
'Call me psychic?'
They both laughed together.
'Should be there about eight . . . . . too early?'
'You're never too early,' she teased.
'See you around eight then.'
'I'll look forward to it.'

It would be good to see him again. She had so many questions. Since their last visit to Lt Smithers' office she'd been kept in the dark. Matt Figorelli had spent a lot of time out of town and when she'd asked Abby about him, she'd quickly changed the subject. For the moment she'd let it lie, her mother insisting he was not an immediate threat. When she'd voiced her objection she'd experienced the most awful of headaches. Still, when the pain had subsided and with her mother's blessing, she'd treated herself to a night she would never forget! Prior to her treat, her mother had introduced her to a sort of sixth sense. This new ability, enabled her to "see" into the future. An insight, she never knew her mother had possessed! It was eight thirty. Matt Figorelli's Starlight Casino was full. With her usual two thousand dollar stake in her purse, she'd cruised the tables.

Then suddenly it happened. She saw it! The number 20. It stood out in her thoughts so vividly. The scarlet, pulsating figure twenty.

When a chair became vacant she'd taken it quickly. The unexplainable urge to place the whole two thousand on Red 20 was most prominent.

A moment later, when the tall, blonde female croupier called for bets, she'd done just that, watching as the wheel became a spinning blur.

Then suddenly the ball was released. As it clattered and clicked against the gravitational pull, her fingernails dug into her palms. Through the entire process the voice had remained silent. A few seconds later the wheel had slowed. The ball had chosen its slot. As the croupier confirmed, 'Red 20,' she could hardly contain herself. As the croupier pushed a large stack towards her, she saw the Red 20 flash again and heard herself say, 'Let it ride! Let it ride!'

She was still standing, the crowd a jumbling buzz, as the dark-haired Pit Boss walked across and stood to the croupier's side.

Like music soothing her aching breast, the ball's familiar clicking filtered into her ears . . . round and round, faster and faster . . .

Her excited eyes remained firmly on the wheel, her hands clasped together. Then the wheel stopped. The crowd gasped and the quaking voice of the blonde croupier confirmed, 'Red 20!'

The look on the croupier's face was quite perfect! She'd stood riveted to the spot whilst the Pit Boss had walked around to congratulate her. With two bets she'd won $1,922,000, including her stake.

She'd felt herself blush as he took her hand. She'd glanced over his shoulder and witnessed the most imperceptible motion of the blonde's head as, still in a state of shock, she tried to listen to his whispered words. Then, closing the table, he'd escorted her to the manager's office, where, after placing a glass of champagne in her hand, she'd been presented with a banker's draft for almost two million dollars. It had been a terrific night, and she'd done it all herself!

Refusing the casino's hospitality, she'd returned to Abby's. She could still feel the euphoria. The voice had been right. It was certainly a night to remember. She'd never dreamed it would feel so good!

Although only 11.00pm, Abby's house had been silent and still. Everyone had retired to their rooms. Part of her wanted to race up and wake everyone, tell of her success, but the voice had restrained her and she'd waited until morning.

All through the night she'd drifted in and out of an excited sleep; waking just to look at the banker's draft, her stomach turning somersaults as the voice told her, 'As much as you want. You can do it as much as you want!'

Just after six in the morning, she heard Abby pass her bedroom door. Pushing the banker's draft into her dressing gown pocket, she'd followed her down to the kitchen.

Abby had plugged in the coffee machine, switched on the television, and was about to light a cigarette. After expressing her surprise to see Maria up so early, she'd turned back to look at the news.

Maria felt the excitement course through her again as she relived the memory.

She'd just filled a glass with orange juice, when she heard the newscaster's excited voice declare, 'And now for some good news. An unemployed secretary from the West Coast has won almost two million dollars at the Las Vegas, Starlight Casino!'

'Did you hear that!' Abby exclaimed turning to glance at her.

A moment later her head whiplashed back on a double take as she saw Maria's expression.

'You? It was you!'

Her mouth fell open as Maria smiled broadly and nodded her head.

'My God! . . . my God!' Abby exclaimed. She slipped down from the stool and hugged her tightly. At a loss for words, Maria pushed the banker's draft into her hand. 'Here it is!'

Abby stared at the cheque her eyes wide in disbelief.

'Can you believe it?'

Holding the cheque out in front of her, she walked back across to the stool. She shook her head. She had the cheque in her hands. It was incredible!

'Do you want a drink?'

'Do I want a drink?' Abby repeated laughing, 'Girl! I need a drink!'

Yes, Maria reflected it was truly a magical time. 'And there's more magical times to come,' the voice suddenly whispered.

Maria's eyes beamed.

Noting the fluctuation in Dr Western's energy level, Dr Swartz turned his attention back to the screen.

What he would have given to be able to hear Dr Western's voice . . . . .

At 8.00pm exactly, Tony Garnet pressed Maria's bell. Inside the hall it chimed loudly.

'Some house!' Tony thought, as Mrs Carrera showed him into

the upstairs lounge where Maria was waiting.

She stood up and welcomed him with a hug. 'Would you like a drink?'

She walked across to the bar. He followed, waiting as she poured him a bourbon and herself an orange juice, then sat on the bar stool opposite her.

'Not joining me?'

'Bad for you.'

'Coffee too?' he quipped.

'Coffee too!' she agreed, eyeing him suspiciously.

He stood up and took his drink across to the window, his back towards her.

'Why didn't you tell me?' he said.

'Tell you what?'

'That you're pregnant!'

He turned around to face her.

She felt her anger rise. It could only have been Abby!

'Easy now . . . easy,' the voice chastised.

She walked across to join him, then hesitantly slipped her arm around his waist and, as she looked up into the blueness of his eyes, a strange but wonderful feeling swept over her. It was almost as if she could see into his very soul. He was her destiny; her fate; her future. With him she would be safe and secure.

'You . . . you seemed so distant lately. I . . . I . . . '

'Maria,' he said softly, slipping his arm around her shoulders.

For some unexplained reason she felt herself stiffen. His face flushed with embarrassment and he pulled his arm away. He wasn't handling this the way he'd planned. Pushing his hand deep into his trouser pocket, he shifted his weight from one foot to the other, then drained his drink. He placed the empty glass on the table to the side of him and stared out over the valley. After a few moments he spoke.

'I've never felt like this about any woman. I guess I've loved you from the first moment I saw you. What I'm trying to say is, if you'll have me . . . I'd like you to be my wife?'

He turned to face her, his blush fading as he took her hand in his.

This time she didn't pull away for she heard her mother say,

'He'll protect you. You need him; your daughter needs him.'

He watched as a single tear tore a path down her cheek, before she lifted her eyes to his and nodded her head.

Elated, he swept her up in his arms, then with a tenderness she'd never thought possible he kissed her and set her down.

A moment later he slipped a large, diamond solitaire ring on her finger.

'You were sure?' she teased, laughing through her tears.

'I was sure,' he lied, then hugged her and whispered, 'Forever!'

'Forever!' the voice echoed.

'But which one is he really marrying?' Dr Swartz thought, 'Which soul, Gemma, Maria or IT?'

Early next morning, while Maria was asleep, Tony crept out of bed and made his way down the hill to Abby's. Just ten minutes later he'd spread the news. There was to be a surprise New Year's Party to announce their engagement.

As the computer fast forwarded to 8pm that evening, Dr Swartz watched intently. Soon he would witness the confrontation between Commander van Slijk, Dr Western and the hidden IT!

Just then Dr Blackmore's voice broke in on his thoughts.

'Dr Swartz, Commander van Slijk has a rapid temperature rise.'

He rushed across to the life support unit.

At the same time the life support computer advised, 'Body temperature 39C. Corrective programme intercepting . . . ' A moment later Irinka's temperature dropped to 36.4.

The computer had registered a massive feedback of energy.

'Run a parallel on the Commander,' Dr Swartz called to Dr Turner, then returned to his station.

Moments later he watched as the parallel hologram showed Piet and Julie van Slijk.

'How do you feel?' Piet asked.

'Fine, just fine,' Julie insisted.

'You don't look so fine to me,' he said, 'I'll call Tony and cancel this evening.'

'No,' Julie protested, 'Please don't do that.'

'Darling, I must.' He cuddled her and placated, 'We'll see them when you're feeling better. For now, I want you to rest.'

They watched as Piet dialled Abby's and made their excuse.

Dr Swartz cursed, as he took the explanation from the smaller hologram's readout section. The explanation was a simple one; the Commander had eaten a piece of chicken and the result had caused her temperature to rise as her soul drew the necessary energy to combat it.

The computer assured him that the Commander's soul had released the necessary antibodies in Julie's bloodstream. In the meantime, Piet had cancelled the meeting.

At 8.15pm, Tony and Maria drew up outside Abby's house. There were no visible lights.

'We should have called,' Maria said disappointedly, as Tony helped her out of the car.

'I did, but I expect she's been delayed. No worry, we'll wait for her.'

Opening the front door, he switched on the hall lights and led her through to the darkened lounge. As he switched on the light she heard a chorus of voices.

'Surprise . . . surprise!'

Everyone spoke at once. Hands appeared from everywhere, congratulating her on her engagement and a long red and white banner across the large rear window read: "Congratulations Tony and Maria". He took her hand and led her into the party.

'I'd like you to meet my partner, Fred Hall, and his wife June.'

She shook his hand. As she moved on to shake the hand of his wife, Fred's eyes followed her.

Almost without thinking he touched her shoulder, 'Haven't we met before?'

His wife blushed and, turning abruptly, she glared at him, recognising, or so she thought, her husband's attempt at a pass.

Tony laughed, 'That's very original, Fred.'

' 'No . . . No seriously!' Fred protested, wincing from his wife's sudden pinch.

Maria smiled, amused, whilst her innocent eyes held his earnestly. 'No, I can assure you we haven't'

She paused and a mischievous glint crept into her eyes as she teased, 'I'm sure I would have remembered.'

Tony smiled, winking at his partner before leading Maria on to another colleague. As the party moved into full swing, she glanced across at Fred. She'd felt his eyes constantly and knew he was studying her. Each time she'd stolen a glance she'd caught his puzzled expression.

'Bernie Walters,' the voice reminded, 'He came to meet Bernie.'

A picture flashed in her mind as she recalled their meeting. It was a hot day, some eighty degrees. After parking her car, she'd exchanged a few pleasantries with Ned, the night porter, then climbed the stairs to her office. The door was half open. As she entered she heard their voices. She'd closed the door and the conversation had stopped, that's when she'd seen them.

Bernie and Fred Hall. Only at the time, she hadn't known the visitor to be him. They were sitting opposite one another at Bernie's desk, a small mirror between them, upon which were two lines of white powder. Bernie had just handed his guest a straw. It was the first time she'd seen Bernie with drugs.

Placing her shoulder bag on her desk, her back to them, she'd walked into the small kitchen. When Bernie had called to her, she acted surprised and, popping her head around the door, said, 'Oh, I didn't see you there. Good morning. Can I get you both a coffee?'

The mirror had disappeared and Bernie'd replied, 'Yeah. Cream and sugar for my guest.'

When Fred had left the office a short while later, Bernie had given him an attaché case. She'd watched as he grinned and patted the case before the two men walked out into the hallway talking, their voices low.

As the computer followed its programme, the mist reappeared and the hologram faded. A moment later it had settled and the date and time in luminous green flashed in the corner of the screen; 3RD JANUARY, 1985 . . . 0755.

'See you in four days, darling,' Tony said, hugging Maria before he climbed into the light airplane. He turned around as he opened the door and winked. 'I'm missing you already.'

'Then don't go!' she pleaded.

'Got to. It's my job,' he replied.

He blew her a kiss and closed the door. She waited as he revved the engine before taxiing to the runway. A few minutes later the red Cherokee took off. She watched as it climbed, shading her eyes from the bright morning sun, until he was just a speck in the light blue sky.

As she turned to slip in behind the wheel of her Porsche, her eye caught the rear of Matt Figorelli's limousine, parked at the side of Abby's office building.

A bodyguard, one of the Italians she'd seen at the restaurant with Matt, stood by its hood smoking a cigarette, his back towards her. Stealthily, using the cover of two parked aircraft she crept across to the other side of Abby's building. Her heart beat fast as she crept closer to the open rear window. She could hear Matt's menacing voice as she approached but his words escaped her. Crouching down she peered through a corner of the small window.

'I'll be here at 7.00am prompt!' he growled, 'And you'll be ready!' Reluctantly Abby nodded her head.

He stood up to leave and, with an almost imperceptible nod to the tall Scandinavian behind him, said, 'Remind her what to expect if she messes in things that don't concern her.'

Scarface grabbed Abby's wrist then slapped her full across the mouth. She watched as Matt grinned then moved away from the window, her face a contortion of anger. Just then she heard the limo start up and she made her way to the far side of the building out of sight. As the limo moved off she hurried to her car.

A short while later in the privacy of her locked bedroom, she went into her dressing room and slid back a rail of clothes.

The vision she'd just experienced confirmed Matt's fate. If she didn't kill him then he would most certainly kill Abby. She took out the rifle and stroked the barrel, her eyes an expectant glow. Then, opening the bottom drawer in a chest, she took out a box of ammunition and slinging the rifle strap over her shoulder she made her way undetected down to her car. Her destination the desert, the sun, like a giant magnet, pulling her forward in an urgent quest.

A short while later on a one-lane desert track, she switched off the engine

Large red boulders and giant cacti were her only witnesses, as she slid the rifle strap over her shoulder and walked across to the edge of the track. After loading the rifle she checked the sights.

'The tip of that tall cacti,' the voice incited.

Releasing the safety, she aimed and fired. A loud crack followed, the impact of the projectile piercing the tip of the cacti.

'Lucky shot!' the voice teased.

'That ain't luck Mamma,' Maria's southern drawl contradicted as she repeated her actions twice more, 'That's excellence . . . pure excellence!'

For a further ten minutes she practised her skill. Not one bullet missed its intended target.

'That's some shooting!' Dr Swartz whispered excitedly to Dr Turner.

He watched as she aimed again. A small stone on top of a far distant boulder disintegrated into tiny pieces before his eyes. He'd never seen such accurate marksmanship.

Pleased with herself she picked up the empty shell cases and walked back to her Porsche, depositing the rifle in the trunk.

The large dip in Dr Western's energy level went unnoticed as they watched Maria drive back to her home.

'When Mamma, when?' they heard Maria ask.

'Tonight,' the voice promised, 'Tonight from the Ridge.'

'Run a trace on Matt Figorelli's death Dr Turner,' Dr Swartz instructed. A few moments later the trace revealed. 2141hrs. 3rd January, 1985.

'You'll have only one shot,' the voice warned.

'Mamma.' she replied with a heavy sigh, 'One shot is all it takes!'

Two and a half hours later, back in his Los Angeles office, Tony sat behind his desk studying a report from ballistics, while his umpteenth cigarette of the day burnt away in the ashtray as he tried to control his steadily rising anger. The truth was plain, however unpalatable he found it to be. He pulled the phone towards him and dialled Bill Marshall in ballistics.

'That you Bill?'

'Yeah. Who's that?'

'Tony Garnet.'

'Tony! Bin meaning to call. Heard yer got yerself engaged.'

'I sure did Bill,' he replied with a broad beam, his anger for the moment forgotten.

'Who's the unlucky gal?' Bill kidded. Tony smiled acknowledging his old pal's humour.

'Her name's Maria. '

'My congrats to yer both,' Bill finished. The pleasantries over with, 'Now, what can I do fer yer?'

'How's your memory Bill?'

'Ain't never let me down before. Why?'

'Cast your mind back to September, last year. I sent in a revolver for dusting.'

'Yeah,' Bill acknowledged, 'But I don't need a good memory for that one. I take it we're talking about the revolver that's the centre of Lt Mason's current investigation.'

'One and the same Bill,' Tony confirmed, 'I've been checking your paperwork and I've a question for you. Who'd you send across to pick it up?'

'Hold on, I'll just check the log.'

The line went quiet and Tony could hear Bill flipping through the daily log.

'Says here. ' There was a rustle of papers as he double checked. 'Yep. It was dropped in by Detective Fred Hall. 12.15am 27th September, 1984.'

'You're sure about that?' Tony questioned.

'Yep, no doubt about it.'

'Who was the night officer?'

'Old Tom Edwards. Retired now. Went to his retirement party just afore Christmas.'

'Is he still in the area?'

'Sure is, lives out yer way . . . apartment 2B, 4928 Glenoaks.'

'That's just off Sunset?'

'Yeah.'

'Say Bill, keep this to yourself, eh?'

'Sure thing. Say, I'm over your way later in the week. We'll have that drink.'

As Tony replaced the receiver the door opened and Fred came in. 'That was some party,' he grinned as he walked towards the filing cabinet. 'Familiar face your Maria.'

'Yeah, Fred. So you kept saying.'

Closing the ballistics report, he tucked it under his arm and took his jacket from the back of his chair.

At 3.13pm he drew up outside Tom Edwards' apartment complex.

Slipping on his jacket, he walked along the flagstoned pathway to the entrance of the main building. Then he ran his finger down the row of name plates, stopping at the retired officer's name. He pressed the appropriate buzzer, and a few seconds later Tom's voice answered.

'That you Tom?' he checked.

'Yeah. Who's that?'

'Tony Garnet, L.A.P.D.'

'Yeah . . . Bill just called . . . said you'd be dropping by. I'm on the second floor, first on yer right.'

He pressed the door release and a buzzing sound released the outer security door. Tony pulled the door towards him and went inside.

Mounting the stairs two at a time, he turned right. Tom was waiting, a half consumed can of beer in his hand.

'Tony. ' he acknowledged as Tony came towards him, 'Thought I knew yer voice. Last time I saw yer, yer dropped off that old army pistol, back . . . let me see, when was that?'

He chuckled to himself as he led him inside then concluded, 'Yeah, 'bout two year back.'

'That's right Tom, I did. You got one hell of a good memory there.'

'Yer bet yer. Ain't senile yet eh?'

'No Sir!' Tony agreed, smiling.

'Sit yerself down. I'll get yer a cold beer.'

'Thanks Tom. That'd go down real good.'
'Now, what can I do fer yer?'
'Don't know as you can Tom. It's just a hunch.'

He lifted the can to his lips and took a swallow, then opened a packet of cigarettes and offered one to Tom.

'Do you remember back to the night of 27th September, 1984. Fred Hall handed in a .22 revolver. It would have been around midnight.'

The old man thought for a moment then wiped his mouth with the back of his hand, gesturing with the beer can.

'Yeah . . . I remember, tall guy, thinning red hair.' He ran his bony hand over the top of his bald head and eased himself back in his seat.

'Yeah . . . real nervous he was. Kept looking at his watch. It was after midnight. I told him he could leave it on the desk, I'd do the paperwork later. I was halfways through my sandwiches yer see.'

He paused a moment and sipped his beer. 'Told him it wouldn't get seen til mornin'.'

He gestured again with the beer can. 'Said it was never mind an' asks me for an evidence bag. I takes one from under the counter opens the seal an' he drops it in.'

'Evidence bag?' Tony quizzed.

'Yeah, it's like I just said. He unwraps his handkerchief and drops it in . . . What's a matter, yer deaf?'

Tony smiled apologetically.

'Ain't no big deal. Load of cops ask fer evidence bags. Kept a stack of 'em under the counter.'

Tony nodded and sipped his beer. His suspicions had been confirmed. Fred had switched guns. The gun that had been planted in the corpse's hand had not been the one they wanted the police to find. So Fred had switched them. It was all coming together.

The hologram sped on. It was 9.29pm.

Maria took a handful of shells from her chest of drawers and pushed them into the back pocket of her black ski pants. Dr Swartz watched as she took out the scarlet lipstick and coated both lips. Then, covering her hair with a black bobbled hat, she zipped up the front of her black jacket, slid open the french window and stole silently out into the night, closing the window behind her. With panther-like movements, she made her way down the veranda steps and around to the front of the house. As the threequarter moon emerged from behind a dark cluster of clouds she opened the trunk of her Porsche and removed the rifle.

It was 9.34pm. The night was quiet and still as she disappeared into the trees that bordered the side lawn. At the end of the drive she sped across the deserted two-lane road and into the growth of bushes bordering the ascent of the ridge. A short while later she'd reached the top.

Matt Figorelli's large house was a blaze of lights, the well-lit high, black, double wrought iron gates firmly closed. Two guards stood either side.

By the light of the moon, she knelt down and loaded the rifle. When she was finished she laid on her stomach and released the safety, resting her elbows on the bankside to line up her sights. He was close, she could sense it.

A few moments later, the gates slowly opened and Matt's black limousine swept through.

With her sights trained on the glistening limousine and her finger curled tightly around the trigger, she followed its approach to the house.

'Only one shot,' she heard the voice remind, and watched as Matt's limousine came to a halt.

The tall Scandinavian slid out of the front passenger seat then, ever watchful, he opened the rear door and Matt Figorelli was in her sights.

At the heavy dull "clunk" of the closing gates, she pulled back on the trigger. He dropped like a stone to the ground. His body motionless. She had taken him out with one clear shot straight through the temple. His bodyguards rushed forward. His two large, specially-imported Rottweiler dogs went wild as they smelt the blood.

She kept her sights on Matt's body, the echo of her shot still buzzing in her head.

As the Scandinavian pointed towards the ridge, she lowered her rifle and picked up her spent shell. Then, using the bushes for cover, she hurried down the ridge.

Minutes later, while the guards were scrambling up the front of the steep slope, she sped unobserved between the trees that bordered her lawn.

A short while later, when Mrs Carrera tapped on her door with her nightly hot milk, she'd showered and changed and lay watching the news.

Just before 7.30am the following morning, Mrs Carrera drew back Maria's drapes and placed her orange juice on the side table. Rubbing her eyes, Maria sat up and smiled a good morning.

'Iz a beautiful day,' the housekeeper confirmed brightly, returning her smile.

'Breakfast in ze 'alf 'our?' she checked before leaving.

'Half an hour is just fine. Thank you Rosetta.'

Maria sipped her orange juice and turned on the television. The female newscaster's face was stern.

'Early last evening Matt Figorelli, a leading member of the Las Vegas community was gunned down on the steps of his Hunter's Ridge home. Mr Figorelli was the owner of the Starlight and Startorch Casinos.'

She watched with great enthusiasm as the outside broadcast unit filmed the Figorelli's house. Matt's tall Scandinavian bodyguard stood on the marble front steps, two Rotweilers close to his heels. Suddenly a hand went over the lens of the camera and the screen went blank. A few moments later the newscaster's face was back on the screen.

'We apologise for the break in transmission, we hope to have a more in depth report in a short while. Meanwhile on a lighter note. '

Maria switched off the set and took a shower.

It was just after eight when Abby burst into the kitchen.

'Good morning Miz Abby,' Rosetta started, 'Miz Maria is . . .'

'Here,' Maria cut in, 'Good morning Abby. What a pleasant surprise! Want some breakfast?'

She turned to her housekeeper without waiting for Abby's reply.

'Set another place for Mrs Western, Rosetta, she'll join me.'

'Si, Miz Maria,' Rosetta replied, studying Abby's sombre face.

They walked out on to the veranda where Rosetta had laid Maria a table.

'Have yer seen the mornin's news?' Abby questioned.

'No. ' Maria lied, 'What's happened?'

'Matt Figorelli . . . . . he's dead!' She gripped the veranda rail tightly and looked out across the deep valley of Maple trees.

Maria was puzzled at Abby's behaviour. She'd thought she'd be pleased that Matt was dead!

Just then, Mrs Carrera returned with Abby's place-setting and poured her a juice.

When she'd finished Maria joined Abby at the rail. 'How did it happen?'

'Newscaster said a Hit! Contract they think.'

'Well,' Maria said, 'He *was* in the business of contracts.'

She placed her arm around her friend's shoulders.

'You sound sad that Matt Figorelli's dead.'

'No. ' Abby faltered, 'Not sad . . . jus' . . . robbed!'

'Robbed?'

'Yeah . . . don't suppose it matters now but I was helping the police to put 'im away . . . an' now . . . 'im dead . . . is just . . . too good fer 'im . . . ' Her thick southern drawl trailed off and she stared down at the valley.

'Well, look on the bright side,' Maria comforted, 'At least he's dead!'

As the hologram sped on, choosing the next item of importance, Maria had returned to her bedroom.

It was 2.00pm and time for her rest. Drawing the drapes she lay down on the bed. They witnessed as, worried about Abby, she used her newly-acquired sixth sense to look into her future.

Abby looked so happy, the radiance beaming from her eyes as she talked with two dark-haired men in morning suits.

Immediately Maria's mood lightened, and she questioned excitedly, 'Do you see her Mamma? . . . Do you see her?'

'Yes child. I see her.'
'Oh Mamma. I miss you so much.'

As Maria lay thinking, wishing she could feel the comfort of her mother's arms, she felt a strange burning sensation sweep through her.

At the exact same time Dr Western's energy chart rose rapidly.

'I see it Dr Maxwell. Let it rise. Don't interfere.' He ordered. Dr Turner flashed Dr Swartz a glare, but he was oblivious to all around him, watching as a fraught Maria sat up and stared straight ahead, listening to her mother's voice . . .

'Fear not child . . . because fear is the greatest gift God could ever have given to mankind; for his gift is your protection. For the present I am your fear, as I am your life's protector, but soon I'll be no more, so you must taste fear, be akin to it, use it. Hold out your arms child. Feel the life force as it flows through us. We are as one.'

As Dr Western's energy field reached maximum the invisible emanation, that was her aura, flowed through Maria's outstretched arms and out through her glowing fingertips, the energy manifesting itself in the mirror image of her mother Lillian.

From a seated position next to Maria the shimmering apparition held her hands, and she opened her eyes.

'Oh Mamma. It is you!' she exclaimed, her fraughtness long since gone.

Suddenly the computer, following Dr Turner's previous orders, released the preprogrammed recovery subsection.

The alarm on the life support unit roared into life. Dr Western's comatose body reading was registering nil.

They were powerless to do anything. The unit was dead. Then, just as suddenly as it had blared into life, it was cut off and the laboratory fell silent. It was as if they were trapped in a third parallel; a parallel in which there was no time.

They could only watch as the luminous green arrow edged closer; watch as Lillian's manifestation spun around to face it, her chilling laughter welcoming the intrusion, enticing the pulsating light as it sank into her. She was feeding from it; replenishing her store; draining its energy.

As Dr Swartz fought for strength to depress the speak keys, in a vain attempt to destroy the subsection, the arrow was gone, consumed in its entirety . . . . . the apparition had won . . .

A loud scream filled their ears and Maria's head slumped forward.

With the speed of light, the now-contorted head of the apparition snapped back to look at Maria. Less than a moment later it had dissolved into a grey mass of mist, retreating, back through the fingers of her slumped body; Dr Western's aura had rejoined her soul . . .

At the same time, the life support unit sprang back to life and the readings were normal. Dr Swartz looked at the laboratory clock. It was 11.00am.

They'd lost over an hour! Just then, the Weather Computer announced.

'Warning . . . Electrical storm approaching outer boundaries . . . ETA. One hour.'

The preprogrammed computer sped onwards, settling on January, 11th 1985.

The funeral of Matt Figorelli was a massing of great names; like a reading of *Who's Who* of the underworld families.

The January sun was high in the near-perfect blue sky.

Maria watched from the upstairs lounge window as the flower-smothered hearse moved slowly past her house carrying Matt's coffin. A long line of black limousines followed. The cemetery was packed to overflowing.

An unsettled, nervous buzz fell over the entire West Coast, its tentacles reaching as far as the east. Mass coverage by the press and TV Stations milked it daily.

A contract was put out on the "hit" which quickly became wide public knowledge as it was purposely leaked out, through various contacts, to the press and police.

Gang wars erupted in a "roll-on" effect in New York, Chicago and Los Angeles. New York suffering the worst. Las Vegas, in stark contrast was, to say the least, extremely quiet.

A few days later, Abby had a visit from the tall Scandinavian, who informed her during his flight to Los Angeles, that her services would no longer be needed, adding if the company required her in the future, they'd be in touch. He handed her an envelope which was to be her last.

A short while later, after they'd landed in Los Angeles, he alighted from the aircraft and was gone.

For a few minutes she sat there, still unable to believe what had happened, then stepped out herself. She took a deep breath; her first real breath of fresh air since before her beloved Buck had died.

9

Both courage and determination had taken Julie and Piet traumatically through the last two months.

It was 11th January, 1985 and according to Piet, Julie had made remarkable progress; defying all odds.

She had filled in her memory gaps, learning again with great dedication the skills of her work. He'd watched in silence, sipping his "wind-down" nightly brandy as his wife sat crosslegged on the lounge carpet, books strewn around the floor.

He saw the swiftness of her reading, the inexhaustible depth of retention she now possessed. Her conversation told of her unbelievable memory of pages, books, case histories, she'd previously defended. She'd met her patchy amnesia with military precision. The objectives she'd set herself, warranting very little sleep. To her it was no laborious task.

With an iron-clad will, she drove herself on. Sometimes, when he'd awoken, he'd found her in more or less the same position, except the books she'd devoured were stacked in neat piles ready to be returned to the library shelves.

He'd spoken to his friend and colleague Harry Nelson a while back. He too had become increasingly concerned. But, like himself, could still offer no medical explanation or solution.

He could recall every word of their conversation; he could still hear the solicitude in his colleague's voice as it echoed around his troubled mind . . .

'In my opinion, with the injuries Julie has sustained, any normal patient would still be in hospital . . . In or out of a coma, who knows . . . but one thing I am sure about!'

At this point, he'd unlocked the drawers to the right of him, and slid open the top file. Delving inside, he'd removed two large buff envelopes.

As he laid them on the desk in front of him, his eyes bore into Piet's and he stressed, with a rigidly raised forefinger:

'Your wife is no textbook case! I have never, in all my years as a doctor witnessed anything, quite like this! I've seen patients come out of a coma time and time again . . . you too! But never like this.'

His expression was one of graveness as he sorted through the group of x-rays, then took out the two to which he referred. He stood up and walked across to the white x-ray board, motioning Piet to follow.

With Piet at his side, he positioned the two x-rays side by side, then switched on the light and pointed out the initial extent of damage to the cranium.

A few moments later he moved across to the second x-ray.

'This is the most recent, taken just last week . . . Explain that to me?'

He pointed to the "healed" section. There was certainly no sign of any injuries now; he'd go so far as to say that the cranium they now studied, had never been damaged . . .

Then there was her electrocardiograph reading; the reading that was taken the morning she'd regained consciousness. It clearly showed two individual heartbeats; two definite signals . . .

The firm, stronger trace, beat a definite parallel path. They'd watched as it merged with the weaker . . . fusing together to become one vibrant pulsating heartbeat; a heartbeat that had awoken her and given Julie her life.

His colleague's words continued to bounce around his subconscious, and had done since she had first regained consciousness. That, he reminded himself again, had been two months ago. Harry Nelson was still seeing her, but was no closer to solving the mystery and the questions still remained unanswered. With a heavy sigh, he stood up and stepped between Julie's open books, to refill his glass.

'Drink Darling?' he asked, as he manoeuvred his feet.

She smiled her refusal and shook her head, briefly glancing up at him. After pouring himself a generous glassful he returned to his seat.

'You work too hard,' he told her, then ruffled her hair affectionately.

She smiled, glancing up again, then, closing her book, she stretched her arms into the air and yawned, 'Mmm . . . maybe you're right.'

She stood up and rubbed the back of her neck, then walked across to the drinks cabinet. Opening the small bar fridge, she took out a bottle of beaujolais and poured herself a glassful.

Once again Piet's brow creased with puzzlement, but he said nothing. For the four years he'd known her she'd never liked red wine; an occasional sweet white with dinner, but never dry red! Her favourite tipple of an evening, whilst he indulged in his brandy relaxant, had always been gin and tonic; not that Julie had ever been a drinker, as such. But then, her sudden liking for red wine was only one of the things that had puzzled him since her accident. Take the chicken she'd eaten a few days back. She'd never been able to eat chicken; was allergic to it, as she was fish . . . Now she ate both, in abundance. It had not only confused him, but the housekeeper Mrs Beale as well. He'd even go so far as to say chicken was her favourite! And sometimes when he'd found himself studying her, just as he'd convinced himself that she was a total stranger, she'd do or say something completely typical of Julie and his fears would subside. But then she'd always been able to melt his heart. He sometimes wondered if he loved her too much; not that he could do anything about it nor, for that matter, did he want to. There were days when he doubted his own sanity, and was thankful for his colleague, Dr Nelson, with whom he could discuss her.

The Commander's soul, fully in control of Julie's body sipped at her wine, her eyes on her ancestor's husband, her mind probing his as he wandered through his torment. She was fully aware there were areas of Julie's memory, the Probe hadn't been able to reach; important areas, that had been damaged in the unfortunate accident.

Dr Swartz had laser-healed Julie's injuries, thereby allowing her full control of a healthy body, but these inaccessible areas would remain a complete blank. And on his suggestion she'd had to improvise. It had, and was not, going to be easy . . . . . There was still so much she didn't know about her ancestor.

She walked back across the room and curled up on the sofa by the side of his chair.

'You may be right,' she teased, turning to face him. Her soft, alluring blue eyes portrayed an unmistakable twinkle.

'Maybe an early night would be in order.'

He smiled and stretched his hand out towards her, his puzzlement for the moment forgotten, as she clasped his hand with hers and leant forward to kiss his fingertips, the way she'd always done.

Meanwhile, Dr Turner's eyes followed her every move, but his thoughts were still with the electrical storm. Surely Dr Swartz would fast forward to the suitable, designated corridor. Surely now.

The storms, when they came, were quite fierce. It was standard procedure, mandatory, to reduce all power in the laboratory. His brow creased again. If Dr Swartz continued in this vein, the rescue would not be possible; they'd run out of time! And if they took a direct hit, they could lose not only Dr Western's and the Commander's soul, but the Probe to boot! At the very least, it would be hours before they regained their power.

Still questioning Dr Swartz's intentions, he wondered if the energy detoxification he'd been forced to perform on Dr Swartz's soul after their last experiment, hadn't somehow returned; his reasoning was certainly meriting his closer attention. There was no time to set up the tracer unit now; if this was indeed the cause, then he'd have to take over . . .

As the Weather Computer's voice broke in on his thoughts, he turned to Dr Swartz.

'Do we reduce power?'

'We can't . . . we have to stay with it!' he replied curtly.

Just then the Resident Elder appeared on the direct-link.

'Dr Swartz,' she called.

'Yes, ma'am,' he replied, accepting her interruption.

'You are aware of the approaching storm?'

'Yes ma'am.'

'Are you able to continue operations on reduced power?'

'No, ma'am,' he replied, 'We are using all three sections of the Probe, we need full power.'

'Are you not able to hold the parallel in freeze mode until the storm has passed?' she pressed.

'With respect, ma'am, the power we would need to hold the parallel, would still be too great. It would make very little difference.'

'The weather computer has advised that the storm is through the outer boundaries, and is moving in a south circular pattern. ETA approximately forty-five minutes. How long do you envisage before you have both souls safely returned?'

'Forty-five minutes should be more than ample, ma'am,' he pacified.

'I see,' the Elder said, pausing a moment, her suspicions of his non committal reply uppermost in her mind.

'You may continue as you are for the present Dr Swartz. I will monitor the storm's progress and report your present position to the Head Elder. But if the storm continues in its favoured path, you must follow mandatory procedures and reduce power until it has passed.'

'It's not that simple, ma'am,' he protested.

'Is it not Dr Swartz!' she exclaimed, her dark eyes challenging. She was not used to having her orders questioned in this manner.

'No, ma'am!' He hesitated, softening his voice, 'With respect, if we abandon the programme now, and let it run its course, even on a minute-by-minute existence, because we couldn't freeze it without running the same risk as we are now, it could be hours before we were able to return. During this time, if the Commander needed our guidance and we were not able to give it, she could inadvertently change history by making her own decisions.

'The results could well be catastrophic; so much so, that we would not be having this very conversation.'

'I see,' she said, the suspicion, although on the wane, still in her eyes.

'I'm sorry, ma'am,' he resumed, impatient now, 'It really is crucial we continue.'

'Well, Dr Swartz. It seems, for the moment at least, that we have no choice!'

The hologram faded and Dr Turner, concerned with his colleague's quick mood change, turned to regard him.

'Are you alright Eric?'

Dr Swartz nodded his head, simultaneously depressing the communication button to sever the connection. He ran his hand through his thick greying hair.

'Fast forward to the next relevant event.'

Dr Turner shook his head.

'No, Eric!' he exclaimed. He looked quickly around at the rest of the team, not sure whether they'd heard his objection. When he was satisfied they hadn't he resumed with his whispered opposition.

'You can't run this rescue mission as another experiment! I understand your feelings, but you have to find a corridor immediately! You must retrieve the souls!'

Dr Swartz turned to face him, his eyes glaring with rage, their faces just inches from each other.

'You understand my feelings! How magnanimous of you. How in hell could you understand what I'm feeling?'

His face was blood-red with anger as he drew in a breath and spat out his questions, questions that demanded him not to answer . . .

'Have you ever had your life-force detached from its housing; felt the excruciating, torturous pain that seers through your very being? Understand! You don't know the meaning of the word!'

His voice was tortuous now, his nostrils flaring. Sharply, he drew in another breath.

'No, Dr Turner! Not yet! We have twenty minutes before the storm poses a real danger and I intend to use every last one of them!'

Dr Turner sank back away from him. His suspicions were right. Dr Swartz was urgently in need of another detoxification; there could be no other explanation. He'd always known Eric was pigheaded and adamant about his beliefs, but this was sheer madness! But the long and the short of it was, there was no time . . . no time for detoxification . . . no time for arguments!

The best he could hope for was that he could keep Eric calm, because if he were angered the poison would take over and all sense of reasoning would be history! If Eric could remain calm and control himself until they rescued the souls, they might all stand a chance.

'I hope you're right, for all our sakes!' he concluded. His whispered tone was more desperate now as he fast forwarded to February 12th, 1985.

Theoretically, however, they did have a safe twenty minutes. But if the storm moved faster, if it picked up speed, if they ran out of time and were forced to reduce power, then the problems Dr Swartz had detailed, could and most probably would arise.

He understood why Dr Swartz didn't want to reduce power; equally he could see why he wanted to continue. Nevertheless, the last storm had been with them some eighteen hours, and the one before had lasted three days. During the three day storm, they'd been lucky. The funnel they'd used to channel the energy, running on reduced power, had taken two hits, but if they were forced to run on full power, it would act like a magnet, drawing the electrical storm to them; they'd be a homing beacon.

To his mind, Dr Swartz had only one decision to make: fast forward, withdraw the souls! But to Eric's crazed thinking, the decision wasn't in the frame.

He watched as the hologram sped on but his mind still lingered over his grave misgivings.

Tony's red Corvette sped through the evanescent mist.

'What a wonderful view!' he heard Maria exclaim.

Tony glanced across at her and covered her hand with his own in a quick, brief, affectionate squeeze then, changing down through the gears, he turned into Piet's long, gravelled driveway.

As the gleaming Corvette swept around the large old grey stone fountain and halted in front of the magnificent old house, the two heavy wooden front doors opened. An elderly white-haired butler appeared at the top of five wide, bevelled-with-age stone steps. Tony's face beamed.

'That's Rogers. He's almost as old as the house, although he only admits to fifty.'

She watched as the old man descended the steps and opened her door.

'Welcome Miss Becket. I trust your journey went well?'

'Thank you Rogers.' She returned his smile. 'The journey was most enjoyable.'

Closing the car door behind her, he nodded politely then turned his attention to Tony and with a warmth, most would have thought alien to his reserved British nature, said, 'Welcome Mr Tony. It's always a pleasure, to see you sir.'

'Rogers,' Tony acknowledged, with equal warmth, 'The feeling is quite mutual.'

He winked at the old man and the butler coughed, embarrassed, but there was no doubt in her mind, that both held each other in the highest esteem.

'Shall I take the cases sir?' Rogers resumed.

It was more of an order than a question as he bent over the open trunk.

'No, thanks. I've got 'em,' Tony smiled, saving the old man's strength, as he took out the two cases, 'But you could close the trunk.'

'Yes sir . . . the trunk,' he repeated bewildered by Tony's quick actions.

Just then Piet came bounding down the front steps.

The two men shook each other's hand, then hugged each other.

'Good to see you,' Piet said, taking one of the cases then, turning to Maria, he offered his hand.

'And this beautiful lady must be Maria?'

Blushing at his remark, she shook his hand.

'Did you come up the coast road?' he said quickly, trying to put her at ease.

'Yes,' she nodded, 'Such a breathtaking sight.'

'It surely is,' he agreed, holding his eyes with hers. His hand still held hers. 'You can let her go now,' Tony joked, and Piet looked down at his hand. His face flushed as he laughed and transferred it to her back, leading her up the steps.

'Julie will be a few moments,' he explained, 'We've just arrived ourselves.'

Leaving the suitcases in the vast, square hallway, Piet led them through to the sitting room, where a large, open log fire burned brightly.

'Get's a bit chilly this time of year,' he joked, 'At least, that's Roger's way of thinking.'

He rubbed his hands and held them close to the fire, then motioned them to sit. As Rogers took their coats and Piet walked across to the drinks cabinet, Julie came in.

'Well, you're a sight for sore eyes!' Tony said hurrying across to hug her. She squealed with delight as he lifted her up and spun her round, then, putting her down, he kissed her cheek exaggeratingly and took her hand, leading her towards Maria.

'Julie, this is Maria.'

'Congratulations to you both on your engagement,' she said warmly, and shook her hand.

'Tony has told us so very much about you. I just know we're going to be good friends.'

'Likewise,' Maria enthused, 'I've heard such a lot about you, too.'

'All good, I hope,' she quipped as she turned to Tony with a knowing look in her eyes.

'Well. ' Tony teased, as his hands portrayed the up and down movement of the scales.

'Drinks?' Piet asked, amused at his actions,

'Maria?'

'Bourbon,' Tony cut in quickly, 'Straight.'

'And I never saw her lips move!'

Julie threw him a knowing glance. 'I'll have a glass of beaujolais please darling.'

The two women had sat down on the two-seater chesterfield close to the fire, Julie admiring Maria's ring.

'Doesn't take them long, does it?' Piet said, indicating with a nod of his head, as Tony came up behind him.

'Yeah,' he agreed, adding 'What's with the wine?'

'You may well ask,' Piet replied, placing their drinks on a tray.

Dr Swartz watched as the two women talked, then anticipating the interruption when both men returned, opened the communication channel.

'Commander. ' he called.

The slight turn of her head went unnoticed and he pressed eagerly, 'Ask Maria something about her life . . . something that will incite Dr Western to intervene. Gently though, I don't want either to be suspicious. Dr Western will have already used the echo facility and as yet we have no idea what she knows.'

He paused a brief moment, then concluded, 'She won't be able to glean your thoughts, or anyone else's, unless they affect Maria but, if Maria's immediate future or past is part of your future, she'll certainly be privy to those. '

'Understood,' the Commander confirmed in her thoughts.

'You can begin whenever you're comfortable, the communication channel is operational.'

'So, how was the engagement party?' Julie resumed, joining the conversation during a brief pause between Piet and Tony.

'Yes,' Piet said, 'That was certainly a surprise, eh Maria?'

'It certainly was!'

She looked at Tony, her thoughts skipping through the party and to the voice's warning about Fred Hall.

'Did the whole of the department turn up?' The Commander directed her question toward Tony, but her mind still probed Maria's.

Maria smiled politely, but her thoughts were elsewhere; listening as Dr Western, using the stored voice of Maria's mother warned, 'You'll be hearing again from Fred Hall.'

'Perfect, Commander . . . just perfect. Dr Western's voice is as clear as a bell. The reading is almost off the scale.'

Whilst Dr Turner's hopes sank, Dr Swartz's eyes shone greedily.

Dr Western had built an immense bond; not far short of total domination. And, as far as he could deduce, Maria had been a more-than-willing participant, accepting the voice as that of her deceased mother Lillian.'

'So, when are you returning to work?' Tony asked.

'That's a sore subject at the moment,' Piet cut in, throwing a meaningful glance at his wife.

'Not for me,' she contradicted, adding in a sarcastic whisper, 'Perhaps for you.'

She looked across at Piet, then smiled at Tony, 'As soon as possible.'

He smiled weakly, detecting the annoyance in Piet's attitude, then changed the subject. 'Anyone for a refill?'

Julie and Maria drained their glasses. Maria warming to Julie as she fought her husband's obvious dislike of her returning to work. Tony stood up and took their glasses, then followed Piet across to the drinks cabinet.

'Not a good subject of conversation, then,' he said as he approached.

'A sore subject to my mind. It's only been seven, eight weeks since she came out of the coma. She's been studying, reading and digesting law books at a rate you wouldn't believe. And now she has visions of accepting a post in the District Attorney's office as a prosecutor! Her whole outlook has changed!'

'Prosecuting!' Tony exclaimed, 'What happened to her belief in strong defence?'

'You may well ask!' he said with an impatient sigh. 'I seem to be using that cliché a lot lately . . . Truth is, I don't know how to explain it. I guess you have to be living here . . . seeing it. She's just not the same Julie we all know and love. And yet . . . it's the weirdest thing . . . she *is*! Sometime when you have a spare year or two, I'll try to explain.

'Now is not a good time. For all our sakes try and change the subject . . . if she stays with that one, we'll never escape!'

He laughed, trying to lighten the mood, but the concern in his eyes said it all.

Through the whole weekend, Tony'd found himself observing Julie. By the time Sunday evening came around, he shared not only Piet's concerns, but several of his own. Julie had cross-examined Maria with such rapidity, his head spun. And, far from avoiding the questions, Maria had reacted warmly. Almost baring her soul. To say the women had become firm friends would, in his estimation, be an understatement, to say the least! Both Maria and Julie had exchanged such deep secrets, that even he'd not been privy to . . .

He zipped up his case and placed it next to Maria's at the foot of the bed, then closed the top drawer of the tallboy. A silver-framed photograph on the top of the chest, toppled over. He picked it up, and stared at the grinning trio; Piet, Julie and himself. How happy they all were.

It had been taken on their last fishing trip of the previous summer, outside Jackson's bait and tackle shop. Old man Jackson, who had taken the snap, had since died. He traced his finger over Julie's face. She'd always been an intellectual, but now she was much more intricate; more complex. And, if it were at all possible, more determined.

'Almost ready?' Maria interrupted, slipping her arm around his waist. He hadn't heard her come in.

'Sure am,' he replied, shelving his thoughts as he replaced the frame.

'Good!' Maria warned, mischievously, 'Because Rogers is on his way to collect the cases.'

'Is he now . . . ?' he smiled.

As the hologram sped on to March 4th, so did the storm. It was now just thirty-five minutes away.

'Lock in at 7.13am on a five to one with our time,' Dr Swartz instructed.

'Locked and running,' Dr Turner confirmed and watched as June, Fred Hall's wife, pulled on her dressing gown.

'Fred, I have to have a new outfit! You can't expect me to go to Tony's wedding in the rags I have!'

She stressed the word "rags" meaningfully, pouting as she tried to catch his eyes in the mirror. Rinsing the toothpaste from his mouth, he picked up his shaver and switched it on.

'Fred! Are you listening to me?' she prompted over the dull buzz. He sighed heavily and switched off the razor.

'You've got a wardrobe full! . . . No,' he paused, correcting himself, 'Several wardrobes full . . . overflowing with clothes! Why the hell do you need something new? For chrissakes! why buy something new?'

He stood there, tired by her constant whine.

'It's different for you! I can't go to the wedding looking like a . . . like a . . . '

She searched frustratedly for the words before resuming, 'A bundle of rags!'

He laughed sarcastically, ignoring her frustration, something to which he'd become a master, of late, then continued in a condescending voice, 'You could never look like a bundle of rags Junie.'

He winked and turned back to face himself in the mirror, checking his chin, 'Anyway, I don't know why you should worry about Tony and Maria's wedding. She's just a glorified secretary!'

He stopped in mid sentence; the words had tumbled out of his mouth before he'd realised what he had just said.

'A secretary!' June exclaimed, 'Oh, Fred, do keep your mind on what we're discussing. I don't know where your mind is these days, but it most certainly isn't on me and my needs!'

'Yeah . . . yeah,' Fred answered, still puzzled at his own reply, unable to catch his own thoughts through June's constant whining.

'Go buy yerself a new outfit,' he conceded, giving in; anything for her to leave him alone.

'Thanks Fred,' she said, her face a broad beam.

She blew him an exaggerated kiss and disappeared from the bathroom. He stared at himself in the mirror.

That's where he'd seen her. He knew he'd seen her before. Yeah, it was all coming back. She was Bernie Walters' girl . . . Bernie's secretary; the girl who'd interrupted their early morning meeting.

'Of course!' he exclaimed. His voice was a hushed whisper. He grinned at himself in the mirror . . .

The whole 'family' had come to the conclusion that Buck Western had never delivered the money; hadn't Gino told him so?

'And all the time,' he said aloud, 'It was the secretary, Maria Becket . . . yeah.'

She'd taken the case! What was it that Tony had said? She had had a big win on the wheel. She had to have a stake.

Everyone has to have stake monies.

'Wait!' he told himself, seeing a slight flaw in his way of thinking. Bernie had sacked her weeks before his death. He had that blonde. What was her name? Sally something . . . "Sally Big Tits" he recalled smiling. He felt a stirring in his loins as he pictured her vital statistics, before resuming with his train of thought.

If Maria had stolen the attaché case then she had to know something about the shooting. Maybe . . . maybe she'd even shot Bernie herself!

He continued with his shave, weighing up whether or not she could shoot a guy.

If she did kill Bernie and take the case, then it would be his duty to apprehend her. He smiled to himself as he continued with his thoughts.

Better still, he reasoned, she might be grateful to share her new-found wealth with him; that is, if he kept his mouth shut. And he'd certainly had a lot of practice at that.

Yes, that bit of the action had been quite satisfactory, and would have been a lot more satisfactory, had someone not killed off the golden goose. So, if it turned out that she did kill Bernie, it was only right, she pay for that!

He'd had a good thing going there with ole' Bernie. Yeah. She'd cut off that avenue and now he was stuck with Gino!

When Buck Western had passed the stolen documents to his department, hadn't he informed them, and taken his time processing what they'd given him in return. Course the family had moved the stuff now, so whatever leads they might have had were gone.

He'd even switched the gun that Tony had taken from that fool Toto when he'd been careless and got himself shot by the opposition. It had been the opposition that had planted the gun. A gun that had been used to kill the mayor.

Matt Figorelli had been well pleased with him! Although it had turned out to be a hairy task.

He'd intended just opening the evidence bag and switching the gun. But that stupid rookie Day, had chosen that very moment to interrupt him and he'd torn the darn thing. Like greased lightning, he'd stuffed it in his pocket. He'd not had a chance to switch it and replace the evidence bag so, a short while later, he'd signed out and gone down to his car in the staff parking lot to the side of the station. He'd searched the pockets for another evidence bag, cursing because he'd run out, then remembering that the old guy in ballistics kept a stash under the counter, he'd taken himself across for a replacement. He could still see him standing there, halfway through his sandwich.

'Yeah,' he said aloud, 'A visit to Miss Becket, just might be in order.'

He pulled on his lemon shirt and buttoned the front then with a satisfied smirk, mused, 'Should be worth at least $50,000.'

That at least would do for a start, enough to satisfy even June's extravagant spending for quite a while.

'Fred . . . Fred! Breakfast is on the table . . . going cold!' June's shrieking voice interrupted.

'Where did I go wrong?' he questioned, staring at his reflection in the mirror. Then reaching for his tie, he sighed as June's voice shrieked again, from the hallway.

'Fred . . . . . Fred. What are you doing up there?'

Frowning, he knotted his tie. 'What happened to the sweet thing I married?'

With no answer forthcoming, he snatched his jacket from the hanger and made his way downstairs.

Just before 9.00am Fred scrawled his name in the duty book, then headed for the washroom phone. Satisfied the cubicles were empty he thumbed through his black book. Tony had given him Maria's unlisted number a few weeks earlier, in case he was needed.

Lifting the receiver, he dropped in a coin and dialled.

'Miz Becket's residence.'
'Yeah. Let me talk to Maria Becket.'
'Who is eet?' Rosetta questioned.
'Tell her, Fred.'
'Fred who?' Rosetta insisted.
'Just tell her it's Fred. She'll know,' he said impatiently.
There was a few moments of silence before a reluctant Rosetta

resumed, 'One moment, I see eef Miz Becket in.'

A short while later Maria's voice filtered into his ears.

'Yeah,' Fred acknowledged, 'This is Fred Hall.'

'Yes. Of course! Tony's partner. Hello Fred, what can I do for you?'

'Yeah, one and the same, and it's more what I can do for you.'

He cleared his throat and glanced down at his nails.

'I believe we've got . . . or had . . . a mutual friend.'

He paused, waiting for a response.

'And what friend is that?'

'Bernie. Bernie Walters, your ex-boss.'

He waited, his ear pressed tight to the phone, his thoughts spinning around in his brain as she admitted lightly.

'Yes. How is Bernie?'

'Dead!' Fred replied flatly, 'Very dead!'

'Oh, I'm sorry to hear that Fred. What was it, his heart?'

Fred laughed loudly, then replied sarcastically. 'I guess you could say that.'

He chuckled again then added, 'It kinda stopped . . . stopped you might say, when the bullets interrupted it.'

The line went silent for a few moments before Fred resumed, 'It's Bernie I wanted to talk to you about.'

The line was silent save for his breathing. He listened for a few moments then asked, 'You still there?'

'Yes Fred, but how can I help you?'

'Well, we'll just have to see about that but I'm confident you can.' He waited for her response but the line was still silent.

'I'll get back in touch with you in a few days, when I've worked something out. In the meantime, I wouldn't mention our little conversation to anyone else. I'm sure we can work this thing through.'

'I don't understand what you mean Fred. Does Tony?'

He cut her off mid-sentence.

'Then I'll tell you. Tony doesn't know a thing about our little talk . . . and I think when we meet and I've explained, you won't want him to. D'yer get my drift?'

'Not exactly,' she lied.

'Look!' Fred exclaimed impatiently, 'I'll be blunt . . . a black leather attaché case! How's that for starters?'

'A black leather attaché case?'

'Yeah,' Fred confirmed, 'The property of one Matt Figorelli.'

'What's that got to do with me?'

'You think about it. I'll be in touch in a few days.'

He replaced the receiver and rubbed his hands together, then opened the washroom door and walked down the corridor to his office.

Maria replaced the receiver, deep in thought.

'A removable problem,' the voice assured.

'Yes Mamma,' she agreed, for her newly-acquired sixth sense had already eliminated him.

Dr Swartz and Turner watched as Maria's twisted sardonic grin faded from the screen and the computer fast forwarded to March 8th and the next of Fred Hall's calls.

Maria had just finished lunch.

'Iz that Fred person vor you Miz Maria,' Rosetta said, with obvious annoyance. Maria walked through to her study, closed the door and picked up the phone.

'What exactly do you want Fred?' she asked impatiently.

'Exactly $50,000,' he replied.

'$50,000!' she repeated.

'Yeah.'

'Now why would I want to give you $50,000?'

'To stop me going to the late Matt Figorelli's family . . . not to mention Tony.'

'Matt Figorelli!' Maria repeated.

'Yeah,' Fred said, pausing to light a cigarette, 'Matt Figorelli . . . the missing attaché case; the one with half a million bucks; the one you stole from Bernie's office; the one and the same case Buck Western paid for with his life!'

'I'm getting tired of this, Fred. You go to Tony, or Matt Figorelli, or anyone else you want. I don't know what you're talking about!'

'Easy now, easy,' the voice chastised.

'Is that so!' Fred said sarcastically, pausing a moment to think.

'Kill him . . . kill him. ' the voice incited.

'Fred,' Maria said suddenly, drowning out the voice's words as she rubbed her forehead, 'Fred, you still there?'

'Yeah,' he grinned, startled by her voice, 'I'm still here. You're not getting rid of me that easy. I've got enough proof to put you away for a long time. What I'm saying is, no money, no wedding! You think about it and give me a call tomorrow.'

He dropped the receiver, and the line went dead.

Maria's sudden surge of anger sent her reading almost off the scale and prompted Dr Western into action.

'Easy child . . . easy,' her mother's voice soothed.

'Yeah Mamma,' she promised, 'But he'll get his!'

Her hologram faded and time numerals span. It was 10.00am, March 11th, 1985.

Maria was sitting behind her desk, crushing yet another of Fred's messages between her fingers. He was becoming a deep-rooted nag in the pit of her stomach; a nag she knew she could put off no longer.

With his interference she couldn't concentrate on her business. He wanted his money and if he didn't get it he'd stir up a whole mess of trouble. With her wedding less than a week away she couldn't afford the risk . . .

Picking up the phone, she dialled Fred's number.

'It's Maria,' she said calmly.

'Well, hallo there little lady, I've bin wondering when you'd call,' he drawled smugly.

'Fred,' Maria said, ignoring his sarcasm, 'I've been thinking. Perhaps we should meet, discuss things.'

'My sentiments exactly.' He grinned spending the fifty thousand starter in his mind as he spoke.

'You and June are coming up to my wedding next week.'

Just then Tony walked into the office and Fred interrupted her, 'I'll call you back on another line, this one's not too clear.' Replacing the receiver, he dashed off down the hall to the washroom. Tony's head followed Fred's flight.

'Was it something I said?' he joked, calling after him.

'Bad case of the trots,' Fred shouted, rubbing his stomach.

Tony shook his head and walked across to his desk. At the same time, Fred pushed open the washroom cubicles, and checked he was alone. A moment later he was dialling Maria's number.

'Now, where were we?' he resumed complacently, 'Oh yeah . . . no money . . . no wedding!'

'When exactly are you coming up to Vegas?' she questioned, ignoring his remarks.

'Sometime Friday,' he chuckled, 'Can't say exactly but. '

'Alright Fred, let's cut the crap. I don't know what you think you've got, but you are entirely wrong in what you're assuming. Nevertheless, I think we ought to talk about this, maybe I can help you with what I know about Bernie's operation.'

'As you just said, let's cut the crap! You know exactly what I mean, so you'd better start counting out my money. It still stands, no money . . . no wedding!'

He grinned greedily as he chewed on his gum, waiting for her response.

'You'd better come see me.'

'Sounds good to me, small bills though, nothing larger than a hundred.'

Ignoring his remarks, Maria finished, 'Call me Friday before 8.30pm to arrange a time.'

'Wait, can't we meet before?'

'Sure . . . what day do you want to come up?'

He thought for a moment, his brain racing. There was no way he could get up to Vegas and he knew it was too risky for her to come down.

'Nah, guess it'll have to be later.'

'Good. ' Maria finished, 'Call me Friday before 8.30pm.'

Dr Swartz and Turner watched as the computer sped on. It was 17th March, 1930 hours, the eve of Maria's intended wedding.

At eight thirty, Abby and Julie would arrive. June, Fred's wife, had called Rosetta earlier, explaining her predicament. She'd contracted a mild case of measles and thought it better to stay put.

When Maria received June's cancellation her face had beamed. It was just what the doctor ordered! It couldn't have been better! With June safely in Los Angeles there would be no one who would initially miss him. And if and when they did, they'd presume he'd been delayed somewhere and she would be home free.

After the small celebration tonight, just her, Abby and Julie, she'd retire to bed by 11.00pm for an early night. Julie was staying with Abby, leaving just herself and Rosetta in the house. The rest of the staff would be long gone.

Tony, Andy, Piet, Fred and four other colleagues would be staying at the Starlight Casino Hotel. They'd each booked a separate room, and apart from Piet and Tony, would arrive separately meeting up later in the evening for their intended celebrations.

She'd arrange a time to meet Fred before he had a chance to meet Tony, that way no one would know he'd arrived and later, when they found his body, as she knew they would, they would presume it a contract hit!

She in turn, would have a well corroborated alibi, not that she needed one; in fact she knew she didn't. Who would suspect her?

At 8.20pm exactly Fred Hall called.

'You got the money?' he questioned immediately she picked up the phone.

'Where are you?'

'Still in Los Angeles. Got delayed.'

'Perfect!' she thought.

'What time will you arrive in Las Vegas?'

'I'm about to leave for the airport now. The next flight's nine thirty.' He slipped a cigarette from his pack, stuck it between his lips and lit the end.

'Good!' Maria said quickly.

'Can't wait eh?' he chuckled complacently then adding with the same smugness, 'There's no need to panic. As long as you've got the money, you got no problems.'

'No problems! I'd sooner get this over with. '

'Yeah,' he agreed, smelling the money.

'Will you have collected the car by 11.15pm?'

'Should be right in the process.'

'Okay, after you've got your car, drive out on to the old Cemetery Road.'

'The what?' he interrupted.

'I don't have time to argue Fred. Just listen. Drive out onto the old Cemetery Road. There's a pull-in where you can wait. You can't miss it, it's just up from the rear gates. I can see it from my house. I'll meet you there.

'Why don't I come straight out to the house?'

'Why don't you do just that!' she said flatly, 'I'll leave the money with Rosetta!'

'Okay . . . okay,' he soothed.

'Look Fred,' she started. She was calm now as she dangled the bait money. She knew that even if his gut-feeling warned him off, the mere thought of $50,000 would change his mind.

'You can't come out to the house in case Rosetta sees you, equally I can't come into town in case I'm seen. So if you want your money, you'll have to meet me. '

'I can pick you up on Desert Road,' he offered.

'If you're going to do that, Fred, you might as well take your chance, and come to the house.'

A long awkward pause followed then, dangling the bait again, she said, 'Second thoughts Fred. Go straight to the hotel. I'll come down to see you and we'll tell Tony what I'm doing. It'll be better all round. A wife shouldn't have any secrets from her husband, and I'm sure he'd be pleased to know you came to him first with your suspicions.'

'Now hold on there. No need to go off half-cocked! The rear of the cemetery'll do fine . . . just thought. '

'Well, don't think Fred!' she cut in, 'Do you want the fifty thou or not . . . either way's fine with me!'

'I'll be there. I'll be there!'

He dropped down the receiver. He had the distinct feeling she was backing him into a corner but for fifty thou it was a risk he was willing to take and he'd make sure he'd be more than prepared.

By 11.15pm Julie and Abby had long gone.

As Rosetta's light went out for the night Maria slipped out

through the French window and on to the veranda, her scarlet-painted lips glistening in the light of the full moon.

Like a sleek, black panther hungry for food, her silent sneakered feet stepped down the veranda stairs and onto the soft, green lawn.

A few minutes later, she'd crossed the open span and sought shelter in the tall bordering trees of the drive.

Through the silence of the night her lone figure sped to the bottom of the drive. As the moon slipped behind a cluster of clouds she made her way across the deserted road and into the ruggedness of the waste ground opposite.

The bright headlights of a car moved slowly along the rear of the cemetery. She watched as it pulled off the road and the headlights went out.

It was 11.31pm and Fred was in position. He looked down at his watch, his gut feeling working overtime, and touched the bulge underneath his jacket.

Using the bushes for cover, she hurried over the rocky wasteland and crossed Cemetery Road. He lit up a cigarette and she stopped dead in her tracks.

Just then, the moon moved out from the clouds. Hugging the bordering bushes, she crept closer, her hungry eyes feasting on her prey . . .

She took the gun from her belt and released the safety, then silently crept on, coming level with the rear passenger door.

As quick as lightning, she pounced. And the driver's door was open. Startled, he turned to face her. But it was too late, she'd fired.

The bullet passed through the middle of his head, the force pushing him across the passenger seat. With her scarlet-painted lips grinning widely, she emptied the chamber into his chest, then dropped the previously-wiped gun on the floor of the car.

Slipping off her black leather glove, she felt for a pulse, the familiar cordite and blood odour filling her nostrils, sending thrills of excitement coursing through her before, satisfied he was dead, she hurried back across the waste ground towards home.

A short while later she crept up the side veranda steps and into her room. The hour on her digital watched showed 11.55pm.

Tomorrow was her Wedding Day!

10

On March 21st, 1985, Julie took up her position as Prosecuting Attorney in the District Attorney's Office, beneath the Los Angeles County Courthouse.

In the three months that followed, and much to the dislike of her husband Piet, her strong reputation for winning grew daily. Like the Mounties, she always got her man. This prompted unaccountable perjury warnings from numerous judges to her many victims.

To her colleagues, she seemed to possess a rare insight; an insight, which became more prominent with each of the ever-prolific cases she prosecuted.

She would recall and turn the most difficult of defence witnesses, who'd previously offered strong, stable, seemingly unbreakable alibis in evidence, into gibbering idiots within minutes.

The most clever of liars couldn't escape, she'd lull them into a false sense of security, then rapidly fire an onslaught of questions, with quick, sharp repetition, rendering them precariously inept.

This incredible insight, made possible by a section of the Litchen Probe that Dr Swartz had laid open to her, enabled her to see into the very soul of a person and, guilty or innocent, a well-rehearsed liar or just plain truthful and honest, she'd know immediately and build her case accordingly. From then on it was a foregone conclusion.

Defence lawyers feared her indignation, but respected her nonetheless.

As each day passed, Piet became more and more concerned.

She'd thrown herself totally into her work, staying at their beachside house in Los Angeles from Monday through to Friday. Apart from Dobie her dog, from whom she refused to be separated, her newly-appointed Mexican housekeeper Riccardo and her husband Manual, brother of Rosetta, Maria's housekeeper, plus the regular visits from Maria, she stayed alone, flying up to Paybac on an occasional weekend.

This was one of those favoured weekends. A weekend that had resulted in Julie's head being buried within a multitude of paperwork, statements and the like, that she'd been given the Thursday prior to the coming weekend.

Her colleague, Jim Farrel had suffered a massive stroke and she'd been asked to step into his shoes. Whilst the State had a mound of cases, this had taken precedence, a priority, a serial rape case that demanded an urgent result!

She'd accepted the challenge with open arms, eagerly diving into the paperwork.

This, like so many other things still puzzled Piet. There would have been a time, before the accident, when she'd have spent all her time defending the suspect. Now, she worked obsessively to prove the suspect's guilt. Once she would have offered the very best defence and a rehabilitation programme. Now, it was jail.

As each day wore on, he became more and more convinced. This Julie, the Julie that had awoken from the coma, was vastly different, almost a stranger. She looked the same, even spoke the same, but her character, her whole being, had changed. He mourned her, his grief silently eating away inside.

He'd found himself watching as she slept, studying her facial outline. It was only then that she looked like the beautiful woman he'd married.

When she'd awoken, she was different or, if not different, then changed. The way she threw her hair back over her shoulder, her style; the flamboyance of her personality, both in and out of the courtroom.

He cast his mind back. Dobie would have been the first to agree.

After her accident, when Julie had been reunited with the dog, Dobie had backed away from her, had in fact growled. It hadn't lasted but a few seconds. But during that time he watched as their eyes met and slowly the dog had belly crawled toward her. Dobie never left her now.

Then there was Julie's odd mannerisms; her delightful idiosyncrasies he'd learnt to love and live with during the past three years. They were gone, changed, vanished!

The way she had interrogated Maria that Saturday in her new-found courtroom approach, he could still see them, quite vividly.

He'd found Maria to be charming, beautiful, if not a little shy, but full of energy and vitality nonetheless.

When he'd told Tony during that weekend how lucky he was to have found such a woman, he'd meant it. Maria was, in his opinion the girl for him.

He sighed and shifted himself into a more comfortable position in his chair; his drink, his pipe and the warmth that the log fire exuded relaxing him as he recalled.

It was February, almost a full month before Tony and Maria's wedding. Outside there was a distinct chill in the evening air, a chill that profligately found its way into the lounge, in the form of a cold shoulder from Julie.

Rogers, he recalled, had just set a fire. It was Saturday afternoon around four, they were having coffee and some of the wonderful English scones, Rogers had shown Mrs Beale how to make, with some of Mrs Beale's famous homemade jam and cream.

Julie'd kept up her onslaught of questions on Maria for a good ten minutes. He, like Tony had felt awkward.

She'd pried into areas that were obviously private and somewhat painful for Maria. He'd watched closely, seeing a side of his wife that deeply worried him, that isolated him from her affection, her love. He'd begun to doubt his own feelings.

He'd been a silent observer, just watching, whilst Maria's light-green eyes slowly narrowed. And, fearful of what would happen next, he'd been forced to intervene, to conciliate between them.

Julie had sat there as if suddenly struck dumb, a blank expression on her face, and he wondered if she had heard him at all. It was like she was having a private, inner conversation with herself and he was intruding. He'd felt that same total isolation many times since.

Then, out of the blue, she'd spoken, her sullen mood suddenly changing to one of sweetness and light and with the next breath she'd invited Maria to accompany her in her walk with Dobie along the shoreline.

Silently, he'd caught both Maria's and Tony's expression. For a few brief moments they both seemed thrown too. Then, with a weak smile and an obvious reluctance, Maria had nodded her acceptance.

In his mind's eye, he could see them now setting off towards the beach, along the ill-fated pathway. He drew again on his pipe, watching as the flames devoured the log he'd just put on the fire.

Julie sat opposite, Dobie at her feet, leafing through her files, his mind, unbeknown to him, an open route that she'd walked through many times. She stared at the paperwork, wandering unnoticed through his thoughts, recalling the part that Piet would never know.

'Commander,' Dr Swartz had called, his voice travelling down through time, through history, to its destination inside her head. She'd stopped her questioning immediately; the familiar glazed expression that Piet had referred to during his thoughts, present as his voice continued.

'We've had the main computer run the parallel programme through to a possible time corridor; we think we may have one.'

She'd waited, listening as he spoke with his colleague, before he'd resumed moments later.

'When Maria gives birth to her child, her heart will stop beating for 2.4 seconds. We can take Dr Western's soul then. In the meantime, we need your help to gauge the full depth of her bonding.' He paused a brief moment before resuming.

'Commander, we are getting an incredible amount of static. This may be due to the fact that other people are too close to you both; at least we think that this may be partly to blame.'

Dr Turner raised his eyebrows, to his mind the static was nothing to do with the problem; the real fault of the static build-up was the impending storm. Although travelling in a circular movement, it had moved a lot closer.

'The beach is quiet this time of year,' Dr Swartz said 'and the fresh air just what you both need. Talk to her about her childhood.

The objective is to try to get Dr Western to communicate with Maria. But please tread carefully. Try not to generate any hostility.

'When we have the correct reading, the computer will be able to adjust its computations of Dr Western's force and we will be able to begin separation and retrieve her soul.'

'Affirmative,' she'd thought.

Dr Swartz cursed silently as he thought of the Litchen Probe's malfunction. When he'd originally frozen Dr Western's soul in her ancestor's body, it had successfully transported her voice. He'd heard it.

Then, moments later, the computer had detected a malfunction. One of the sections that made up the third part had blown. It was a vicious circle. With the Probe in use, he couldn't get to it. And if he withdrew the Probe to repair the section he'd be back where he started. Still with quick thinking he'd overcome the problem and sent the Commander's soul back, thereby seizing the opportunity to complete another experiment. The Elders meanwhile hadn't picked up the fact that he'd already listed it in his last brief. Even Dr Turner hadn't questioned him too deeply.

However, and unbeknown to Dr Swartz, Dr Turner had his own thoughts!

He knew full well that the so-called rescue mission had turned into nothing short of a full-scale experiment. Using the Commander's and Dr Western's souls alike, Dr Swartz was attempting to solve the problems they'd been unable to answer in the previous experiments. No doubt Dr Swartz believed that the means whatever they may be, would justify the end.

From his point of view, it could mean an unnecessary sacrifice, but he also knew that the information they'd obtained so far would be deemed, in the Elders' reasoning, for the betterment of society. He wondered if the Elders truly knew? For if that were so, then what did they hope to achieve in allowing him to continue?

He'd worked as Dr Swartz's Deputy for almost five years. And he knew him to be a dedicated scientist. But a dedicated scientist in need of an urgent detoxification! And the Elders could have no way of knowing that.

He glanced up at the laboratory clock, then caught a glimpse of

Eric, before returning his attention to the hologram. At least for the moment he seemed to be rational. And they did still have fifteen minutes left.

Julie had stood up announcing she was taking Dobie to the beach. 'Do join me Maria. The fresh air will do us both good.'

Her change of mood had been sudden, quick to say the least! Piet watched as she stroked the dog's head, smiling benignly. His confused thoughts, feelings towards her, beat an angry path to his brain. He'd glanced across at Tony. The expression on his face told him he was feeling much the same.

Outside, the sun shone brilliantly, but heavy dark clouds threatened in the distant sky. Both women pulled their coats tightly around themselves.

When they reached the cove, the tide was on the turn, the waves, making a thunderous roar each time they crashed into the large boulders further on down the beach. The excited dog ran on ahead, her strong paws digging into the hard-packed sand as determinedly she chased the gulls and various sea birds which had settled in search of food.

Side by side, they walked slowly on across the beach, Julie's tall frame dwarfing Maria by a good foot. When they reached the line of boulders, Julie climbed up on to a flat top rock, then stretched her hand down toward Maria and helped her up.

Settling themselves comfortably, they watched as two fishermen further on down the rocks, packed up their fishing boxes and reeled in their lines.

'I'm sorry about my cross-examination earlier,' she said apologetically, 'I guess it comes of being a lawyer.'

She turned to face Maria.

'Since my accident I don't seem to have too much patience. But I truly didn't mean to offend you, or for that matter pry into what doesn't concern me, and certainly not to the extent I unfortunately did. I won't make any excuses for my behaviour. I just don't know what came over me! I only hope you will forgive me?'

The warmth that Julie exuded had initially confused Maria. She hadn't expected such sincerity. But the candidness in her words had touched her, and she felt strangely drawn to her.

'Of course,' she said, meeting Julie's troubled gaze. 'Don't think any more about it.'

Julie, satisfied for the moment that Maria had believed her, resumed excitedly, in another complete mood change.

'It's all so exciting. Wedding and a baby to look forward to. When is the baby due?'

'First week of August,' Maria replied, returning her smile as she thought of her impending child.

'And what do you want . . . boy or girl?'

'I don't really mind.'

She'd lied, for she knew. The voice had already told her. She looked out over the sea and smiled complacently.

'Be careful!' the voice boomed suddenly.

At the same time, as Commander van Slijk relayed the power-force of the voice to Dr Swartz and his team, an unexplainable rush of fear swept through her.

'This is too dangerous Eric,' Dr Turner whispered, 'If Dr Western. '

'Harry,' Dr Swartz cut in, 'We've worked together for a lot of years. Your contribution to the programme is not in question, neither for that matter is your concern, but none of us is indispensable!' His brown eyes darkened emphasizing his words.

'Through her own meddling Dr Western has placed us in this precarious predicament. But as a scientist, it is an opportunity I can't let slip by. At this stage I can do without your fraught connotations!

'Harry, I need you, but I'm not going to argue the point. I neither have the time nor the energy. The storm is getting closer with each precious minute and I intend to retrieve both souls!

'You understand full well the situation. And equally, you know what the outcome would be if we are forced to reduce power. Now let's get on and do the job!'

He turned and looked back at the hologram but the flush of his anger was still present. He was tetchy, or maybe tetchy was too tame a description for his true feelings. He knew Dr Turner was right. His only real objection was that he'd voiced it at the wrong time. He glanced across at him, then back to the screen. He'd apologise later.

'Just look at her,' Julie pointed.

Dobie ran at full speed, her thoughts centred on a gathering of gulls further on down the beach. They watched as the gulls took off, screaming and shrieking into the wind, a mass exodus of flapping wings as the dog sped full speed through them.

Just then, a loud rumble of thunder echoed around the dark, gathering clouds.

'I guess we'd better start back,' Julie said, with some reluctance.

It was the first time she'd walked on the breach, and she had begun to enjoy the peacefulness. She whistled to Dobie. The dog stopped dead in its tracks and bounded towards them.

The two women walked back across the sand, the dog running on ahead of them.

'You know, I feel Tony's suggestion of my being an attendant at your wedding, has caused you a lot of bother.'

'No, on the contrary,' Maria cut in, 'I have no objection. I admit we haven't discussed it, but having at last met you and Piet and, with the circumstances as was, I think it's a delightful idea.'

She smiled and they walked on, another loud rumble of thunder forcing them to quicken their pace as the first spots of rain fell.

Piet drew again on his pipe, oblivious of his wife's infiltration into his thoughts. His mind now on the conversation he'd had with Tony, after the women had left for the beach.

'When did you first notice the change in Julie?' he'd asked. 'When indeed,' he heard himself reply.

If the truth were known, he thought, almost immediately. And, there was still the unexplained readout of Julie's heart monitor. They, both he and Dr Nelson had never seen anything like it.

Goodness knows what Nurse Caldry had thought. He only hoped she'd not discussed it with anyone else. Still, what could she say?

He'd thought Harry Nelson's explanation at the time a might thin, but as far as he knew Nurse Caldry had accepted it. He smiled at his colleague's immediate interpretation, albeit for the nurse's benefit.

'It's a shadow. ' he'd explained calmly, 'Just a shadow.'

Then, a few moments later when Julie had stirred, Nurse Caldry had immediately tended her. She'd not seen what they had. And, until they could make some real sense of it, they'd agreed they would keep it a closed book. Consequently, Dr Turner had kept the incriminating evidence in his desk drawer, under lock and key.

His thoughts turned back to Julie's behaviour. She'd insisted that Nurse Caldry be removed from her room. He'd tried to calm her, but she'd insisted, got herself in quite a state. So, he'd given in, as he'd done with most things during their three year marriage. And the nurse had been transferred to maternity. He knew then, that Julie had changed; she was not the woman he'd married.

She'd known he'd been seeing Nurse Caldry but from the first moment he'd met Julie, the nurse was history. It was all in the past and she never referred to it. But now she didn't want the nurse near her. He'd never known her to be jealous, but what other possible reason could there be?

His thoughts moved on.

It was after five. Julie and Maria had returned from the beach. Dobie was completely worn out and strode quickly across to the fire. The storm was almost overhead and she just hated them.

He smiled as he looked down at the sleeping dog then ruffled her fur. She lifted her head and glanced up at him, then lay back down and turned over on her back, legs askew, as was her way, when she wanted her stomach scratched. He chuckled and obliged then, patting her head, he leant back in his chair and puffed on his pipe.

The next few weeks had passed quickly. Julie and Maria had become more than firm friends. They were almost inseparable.

Julie stayed with him in his thoughts, sharing his puzzlement, hurt and joy, her heart joining with his as she felt him express his dearest wish for a child. An overwhelming feeling swept over her to ease the pain that he felt. She was drawn to him; wanting to have his child; wanting to have him. What was happening to her? Then suddenly Dr Swartz interrupted.

'We have a date and time for you Commander. Maria Becket's baby will arrive at precisely three seconds past 10.00am, July 2nd. And at the very same time Maria's heart will stop for 2.4 seconds.

We will take both yours and Dr Western's souls then.'

'But, the baby's not due until August!' she corrected.

'Maria will give birth as I've said,' Dr Swartz argued, 'In the meantime Commander, your ancestor's soul has regained consciousness. It's nothing to be unduly alarmed about as we have her in freeze mode. But if you feel any changes within her body, let us know immediately.'

'That gives me about five weeks,' she thought, dismissing his warning.

'Yes, Commander,' Dr Swartz replied, 'Invite them both for Independence Day celebrations early, on the Friday before.'

Piet turned to face her. Julie had that faraway LOOK in her eye, the LOOK that alienated him.

'How's the rape case progressing?' he asked, staring right at her. She turned her head towards him but her eyes were far away.

'Sorry Darling?' she questioned.

'The case,' he repeated, 'How's the case progressing?'

'Yes . . . sorry, I was thinking.'

'About the case?'

'Yes,' she lied. 'I was thinking about this witness's statement. I've a meeting with one of the victims on Monday morning.'

She closed her file and the same faraway, glazed expression came into her eyes. She stared straight ahead.

'God!' he thought, 'How I wish she wouldn't do that.'

It was getting to be a habit. They'd be in the middle of a conversation or discussion and she'd get that LOOK in her eyes. He hated it. The LOOK that just dismissed him. No! banished him, in actual fact, not only from her mind, but from the room! He felt it didn't matter if he was there or not. She'd absorb herself with her notes and files. She was beginning to exclude him from her life!

'You go on up,' she suddenly said, 'I've got work to do.'

Her ice-blue eyes were cold as they bore into the new file she'd opened.

She'd done it again. Dismissed him! 'I'll take Dobie out in the garden first,' he challenged. He felt almost disobedient.

'As you wish,' she finished, busily scribbling in her notepad.

He opened the door and walked into the hall for his coat, beckoning Dobie. But the dog stayed put then looked at Julie, wagging the stump that was her tail.

With her eyes still on her paperwork, she gave the dog her approval, 'Go on girl.'

Dobie barked, as if answering, then bounded after him. He shook his head. Even the dog wouldn't obey him. Not that Julie ever would or did. Not that he'd ever thought of it in that way. But consideration would have been something!

He looked back at her before closing the door, but Julie was absorbed in her notes.

She paused, pen in hand. Her head ached, the words she wanted so desperately to write, lost in her thoughts. The rain pattered against the window. Piet must be mad to go out on a night like this! Then, with great haste she started to write, picking up speed as she hurried onwards not stopping to insert commas or colons, barely remembering full stops.

'Dr Swartz!' the Resident Elder called as the hologram link buzzed into life. 'Yes, ma'am,' he replied, accepting the interruption.

'The Head Elder and Counsel agree. You may proceed until the storm is deemed dangerous, then safety procedures must be adhered. You will reduce power and return to the mission whenever it is safe to do so.'

'But ma'am. '

'No buts, Dr Swartz!' she said sternly, as she severed the connection.

Infuriated, he thumped the console with his fist.

Commander van Slijk finished the preparation of Julie's opening speech and worked on her summing up. If Dr Swartz was right, she'd have little enough time left before she would vacate her ancestor's body. She had to leave her a conviction. A winning maximum penalty conviction and a summing up speech, that would put the likes of Richard Scott Wilkinsen away for a hundred or more years. With no chance of parole!

'Fascinating,' Dr Swartz commented.

'What's that?' Dr Turner said. Swartz pointed to the hologram.
'How the Commander has engrossed herself in her ancestor's roll.'

His deputy nodded.

It was all too late now. Whether the Commander wanted it or not, she was a prosecuting attorney. How long she'd remain so was anyone's guess. How long the trial would take was another! She didn't know if she'd still be here at the end! And yet, she'd had the strangest feeling this morning; a complete contradiction to Dr Swartz tellings.

'I'd say it's a case of love' Dr Turner said. 'The Commander has fallen in love with her ancestor's husband.'

'Rubbish!' Dr Swartz contradicted, 'Dr Stevens, read-out on the Commander's soul?'

'2.59,' he replied, 'I tried to tell you earlier.'

'Is it still rising?' he interrupted.

'No sir. It's levelled at 2.59.'

He turned to face Dr Turner.

'She's pregnant!'

'That would be one explanation,' Dr Turner agreed.

'Run the history parallel. Let's find out when exactly?'

Dr Turner gave the computer the necessary details and the history programme settled on the appropriate time.

'It's parallel. Julie's three months pregnant,' he confirmed.

'That's all we need!' Dr Swartz exclaimed. He leant back in his seat and ran his fingers through his hair. He'd been so involved in pursuing the evil side of both Dr Western's and her ancestor's soul, he hadn't given Julie van Slijk's history parallel much thought.

'We've got to get her out fast!' he said.

The new life in Julie van Slijk's body had a soul. Why hadn't such a possibility occurred to him sooner? He should have paid more time to her history. It was only nature, natural that the Commander would bond with it. If he didn't act fast they'd have a far greater problem. Instructing the computer to fast forward to the designated corridor he waited impatiently for its confirmation.

Then he became alarmed as it continued with the present hologram, ignoring his instructions.

That evening at the beach house as they toasted the start of the trial, Julie told Piet her news.

The love she saw in his clear blue eyes made her sad. She held his eyes with her own and watched his joyous tears explode.

She loved him so deeply. She, Commander Irinka van Slijk. She from the future yet to be made. She that had to leave him soon; for she had no control over this part of his life . . . or hers for that matter. If these feelings she felt were true love, then this was her destiny.

If she never loved again during her lifetime, then she would have had a lifetime of love in this life. For the present she would spend as much time as was possible with him, because at this time he belonged to her.

They talked long into the evening, watching the golden sun meet the sea, feeling the evening's light breeze as it gently washed over their bodies as they lay naked in the sand making love. She felt the tenderness in his strong hand as it cupped her small breast and her nerve endings tingled with the excitement he generated inside her.

When the waves of their passion exploded, he held her closely, declaring his love in whispers, until she felt her heart would burst wide open.

And later, as they drifted off to sleep in each other's arms, she knew she could never replace him. When it was time to vacate Julie's body she would be for all intents and purposes a widow! A widow that had lost her husband in time, but a widow that would leave him her child, their future . . . her future . . .

The section of the Probe that dealt with the soul readout, one of many Dr Stevens had monitored throughout Julie van Slijk's controlled unconsciousness, consisted of five parallel white lines on a hologram screen.

The first four, each representing a different area of the soul were normal and steady; the fifth line was the one that gave him concern; moving across the hologram erratically, with heavy huge irregular strokes. Its movement indicated an incredible amount of excess activity in that specific part of the soul. He was convinced that Julie's subconscious, the dream section, was fighting against the controlled coma.

'Dr Swartz,' he called anxiously. 'We have a serious problem. Julie van Slijk's soul is becoming stronger by the second. The probe has automatically increased her sleep state by fifteen degrees in the last two minutes. It'll break up if it is allowed to continue. There's only another five degrees before overload!'

Dr Stevens quickly checked his calculations.

Julie's soul was definitely functioning independently. He had no other choice than to withdraw the Commander for, if they froze the programme, Julie would regain consciousness immediately and their conflict would begin.

'We'll have to try to accelerate the programme,' Dr Swartz told him, 'Release the minute-by-minute time lock. If we're to succeed, we'll need full power.'

Dr Stevens faced his screen and carried out his orders and Dr Swartz walked back to the main computer and retook his seat.

'Accelerate the programme Harry and lift the failsafe,' he said, trying to hide the deep desperation he felt inside.

'It's the only way. The computer won't accept any deviation if you don't! And I have no other way to drain Dr Western's stored energy.'

While he inserted the necessary instructions into the computer's memory, in the hopeful attempt to drain as much as he could of Gemma's static energy, Dr Turner lifted the failsafe. Then Dr Swartz informed his team of the further development.

'The malfunction is in the first stage of overload. Unfortunately it's not the kind of repair that Dr Turner and I can make while it is still in operation, so, as you can see, we have very little time. Dr Turner is at present trying to accelerate the programme enabling us to retrieve both souls immediately we reach the corridor.'

'July 1st 1985 imminent. Confirmation corridor 10.00am.' Dr Turner interrupted, 'Storm ETA fourteen minutes.'

'Set parallel clocks for three minutes on a time of 1700 hours July 1st, 1985. We'll take both souls in the 10.00am corridor.'

11

As the blue-grey mist of the hologram cleared, the sky was a deep blue, free from clouds. A light plane droned in the distance leaving a white cloud trail in its wake.

Swartz and Turner watched as Julie threw a ball for her dog Dobie to retrieve. The excited Doberman bitch jumped high into the air enthusiastically snapping at the ball then, with a sudden higher leap, caught it firmly in her powerful jaws before turning to run full pelt towards Julie to drop it at her feet.

The eye of the hologram moved on, capturing Tony at the window. As he turned away a hologram of the guest bedroom filled the screen. Maria was resting on a four-poster bed. Tony had just sat down by her side.

'Peewee giving you a hard time Darling?' he asked. His eyes softened and his brow wrinkled with concern. She nodded her head and closed her eyes.

'Rest darling,' he soothed, stroking her forehead, then leant over and kissed her cheek. 'I'll look in on you later.'

At 6.30pm he gently woke her. She felt much better after her nap and the nagging ache in her right side was gone. She slid her legs over the side of the bed and eased her way on to her puffy ankles, then made her way into the bathroom.

She looked at her swollen middle in the mirror. She felt like she was ready to burst and knew the forthcoming event was near. It was way too early. She'd tried to draw on her sixth sense but nothing happened and the voice was silent. For the first time since as far back as she could remember, she felt totally alone and scared.

The hologram moved on to 7.00pm. Dr Swartz rubbed his eyes then straightened his aching back. He watched as the two couples ate their evening meal, his thick, dark brows drawn together as he puzzled over his troubled thoughts.

Could the Probe have truly discovered an area of the soul that could function independently, even when frozen. A kind of brain within? Because Julie was in sleep mode and there could be no other explanation. And equally, could he, they, inadvertently have discovered a nucleus to the five parts? The spherical or ovoid compartment of the soul, protected . . . bound by the other parts. The subconscious soul, the being?

He rubbed his eyes again.

What if they couldn't get the Commander and Dr Western out? He'd not really allowed himself the doubt before. But what would happen if his theory was well founded . . . if the evil sides of both souls had merged? For he had no way at present of confirming his suspicions. Or, for that matter, separating them.

He prayed the parallel time zone would hold and that the computer would be able to drain, if not all, then most of Dr Western's energy. He had grave doubts, for the Probe had already malfunctioned and overheated.

If they couldn't get both souls out . . . was this the way it was supposed to be? Was this their true past; future?

Why on earth had he started this?

Why had he not just gone straight for the rescue? What the hell had possessed him. What could he have been thinking of?

The hologram sped on to 10.00pm.

Julie helped Maria upstairs. She felt nauseous, the nagging pain in her right side had returned. Tony and Piet had retreated an hour or so earlier to the study and when she and Julie had looked in on them to say goodnight, were engrossed in a game of chess.

'How do you feel now?' Julie asked, as she helped Maria into bed.

'Not so good. I've got this dull ache.'

'Where exactly?' Julie questioned, trying to relay to Dr Swartz an as-near-perfect account as was possible.

'All over, I guess.' Maria replied.

Julie sat on the side of the bed. Maria was tired but managed a faint smile. 'It's probably your passion fruit cocktail.'

Returning Maria's humour, Julie smiled then affectionately covered her hand with her own. 'Lie back and relax. Close your eyes and try to rest.'

'Don't disturb Tony,' Maria said, as Julie turned to leave, 'It's the first bit of relaxation he's had in quite a while.'

Julie smiled she'd understood.

'I'll stay with you awhile if you want. Then if the ache doesn't settle, we'll ask Piet to take a look.'

She nodded and closed her eyes. Julie settled herself in the bedside armchair, conveying her fears, in thought form with Dr Swartz.

'Everything's going well, Commander. There is no cause for you to be concerned,' he assured, 'Maria's child will be born soon.'

She rested her head back in the chair and closed her eyes.

At 2.00am, Tony made his way upstairs and awoke Julie.

'Did you both fall asleep talking?' he joked, his voice a whisper.

She smiled, then sat up and yawned. He glanced at his wife.

'How is she?'

'About the same,' Julie replied, with the same hushed whisper. 'She complained earlier of an ache in her side but she seems to be sleeping now. Still, if she awakens and doesn't feel so good, come get Piet.'

She stood up and moved the chair back to its normal position then walked towards the door.

'You've got a "nappy" event yourself soon then?'

'Piet told you?' she questioned with a broad beam.

'Sure did.' He winked. 'Didn't think the old guy had it in him. Congratulations to you both.'

At 5.00am, the nagging pain's reoccurrence awoke Maria. She looked at Tony asleep at her side then eased herself up and switched on the reading light.

Disturbed by her movement, Tony turned over to face her.

'Are you alright dear?'

'I . . . it's a kind of heavy ache.' She stroked her stomach.

'Oh God!' she exclaimed suddenly. And felt the whoosh of her waters break.

He sat up and put his arm around her shoulders.

'Go get Piet. Now!'

Reacting to her panic, he threw back the covers and made for the door, hurrying along the corridor.

'Piet. Piet. ' he whispered, rousing him from his sleep. He opened his eyes and sat up.

'Tony! What is it?'

'It's Maria. I think the baby's on its way!'

He slipped quickly out of bed and into his robe.

Just then, Julie stirred.

'What time is it?' she said sleepily.

'A little after five. Too early for you darling. Go back to sleep.'

He slid his feet into his slippers and followed Tony back to his room.

Julie rubbed the sleep from her eyes and looked at the clock. It was 5.03am. She sat up and switched on the bedside lamp.

'Maria has started in labour,' Dr Swartz informed her. 'Five hours to countdown.'

She slipped on her dressing gown and hurried after them.

Maria held on to the mahogany chest of drawers. She pointed to the bed. The sheets were soaking.

'I'm sorry,' she apologised. 'Something just whooshed!'

Piet smiled knowingly.

'There's nothing you could have done about that,' he said gently, 'Your waters have broken.' He helped her over to the bedside chair and turned to Tony.

'Go get my car from the garage, the keys are on the hookboard in the kitchen. Bring it round to the front of the house.'

He turned back to Maria and said in a reassuring manner, 'We'll just get this little lady into the maternity section.'

'The baby is coming? It's too early!' she said anxiously.
'Now don't you go worrying yourself about that. You'll be fine,' he placated.

Meanwhile, Tony had quickly dressed himself and gone for the car.
'The baby?' Julie questioned, kneeling down beside the chair.
'Yes,' Piet nodded, 'Would you stay with her, I'll get dressed.'
He patted Maria's arm, 'I'll let the Memorial know we're on our way.'

At 5.30am, Piet's silver Jaguar drew up outside the Maternity Section of Paybac's Memorial Hospital. Standing just off Main Street in the centre of Paybac, the large modern brick-built edifice was a blaze of welcoming lights.

By 6.25am Julie had arrived.
'Hi,' Tony said with a wink as Julie peered around the door, 'You made it then?'
'Wouldn't miss it!' she assured, her smile masking the guilt of her ulterior motive.
'I've brought a few things I thought Maria might need.'
She placed a cream leather overnight case at the side of the bed. Maria held out her hand and Julie clasped it tightly.

Swartz and Turner watched as Commander van Slijk talked with Maria, taking what he hoped would be the last soul readouts of both subjects before their return, forward, to their own time.
Just then, and simultaneous to the Weather Computer's updated verbal warning, the Resident Elder called from the hologram link:
'Dr Swartz. The storm is just nine minutes away.'
'Yes ma'am,' he acknowledged, taking her call.
'You will of course follow mandatory procedure?' she questioned.
'Yes ma'am,' he repeated again, hoping he would have both the Commander's and Dr Western's soul by that time.
The communication link faded, leaving him with his thoughts,

and he turned back to the main hologram, watching as the door opened and a petite, attractive brunette entered, followed immediately by two female student doctors.

'Dr Peters,' Tony acknowledged with a nod.

'Good morning again,' she said, 'I'd like to take another look at your wife, see how she's progressing. So if you both wouldn't mind waiting outside, I'll call you when we've finished.'

'Yes, of course,' he replied then, drawing his wife's hand to his lips, he kissed her fingertips and said, 'See you in a little while darling.'

The comfortable second floor waiting area, overlooked the hospital's vast gardens. Tony lit a Marlboro and drew on it nervously, then walked across to the window.

The early morning sun had long arisen. He stood, one hand in his pocket, the other holding his cigarette. Concerned thoughts came and went and, in between, he watched as the sun's rays, blocked by the low white cloud, forced yellow beams through the thinner puffs.

'I'll get you a coffee,' Julie said, but he hadn't heard. She walked off down the corridor, in the direction of the staff room.

A short while later when she returned, he was in the same position. She sat down and placed his steaming coffee on the table. He hadn't noticed, his mind was on other things. The baby was five weeks early.

'Tony . . . Tony,' she called.

'Uh . . . what? Sorry. Did you say something?' He turned around to face her.

'Your coffee,' she pointed.

'Yeah. Thanks.' He picked up the cup, his lips eagerly drawing the steaming black liquid.

'She'll be fine,' Julie comforted, as he replaced the coffee cup and lit another cigarette from the butt end of the other.

He nodded his head, sighing inwardly, but said nothing, just glanced at his watch. It was 7.29am.

At 7.55am, Nurse Alison Cauldry secured her cap to her hair, then made her way to the Maternity Section.

After the normal takeover procedure had been completed, she walked along the adjoining corridor to the staff room, to set the coffee machine for her later mid-morning break.

Just as she was about to open the staff room door, the loud ringing of a telephone on the desk at the unoccupied nurses substation, opposite the waiting area where both Tony and Julie were sitting, took her attention and she continued down the corridor to answer it.

Tony stared at the recalcitrant thing, before the nurse's solitary footsteps took his attention. His tired red eyes watched as she picked up the receiver and held it to her ear. There was a firm almost grating resolution in her voice. The stark white of her uniform glared back at him. He rubbed his eyes and turned to Julie.

'What are they doing in there?'

He hadn't really wanted an answer. It was more like an inner question. He stood up and walked back to the window and Julie followed.

'She'll be just fine,' she comforted, then slipped an arm around his shoulders and led him back to his seat, smiling mischievously as she whispered, 'I'll steal some more coffee.'

Collecting the two empty mugs, she walked off to the staff room. Tony lit another cigarette and stared at the coffee table.

The fair-haired nurse had finished her conversation and was busily making notes on a clipboard. When she had finished, she hung it up and came over to him.

'Would you like a coffee?' she asked, the smooth tone of her Los Angeles accent gentle now, her light lavender eyes smiling. He looked up at her. Just then Julie came out of the staff room.

'Oh!' the nurse said pointedly, 'I see you have one.'

Her gentle manner disappeared as Julie approached and the previous harshness he'd witnessed earlier, returned.

'Good morning Mrs van Slijk,' she said sharply.

He watched as their eyes locked together like a magnet, before Julie repeated curtly, 'Good morning Nurse.'

The fair-haired nurse blushed and unlocked her eyes, then with a weak smile walked off down the corridor.

He watched as Julie followed her with her eyes, her curt expression fading as she turned to face him.

'A problem?' he questioned as she handed him his coffee.

'No . . . not really.' She shrugged her shoulders, adding in a whispered afterthought, 'Hers. Not mine.'

He sipped his coffee, it was obviously an area to avoid.

She sat opposite him, her thoughts still on Nurse Cauldry and the day her soul had been awoken.

It was this nurse who'd tended her every need; this nurse who'd listened as she'd spoken aloud to Dr Swartz, before she'd realised she need only think her reply. This nurse who'd eyed her suspiciously and told Piet about her waking conversation. The same nurse who'd been Piet's lover before Julie, who'd tried unsuccessfully to become Mrs van Slijk, and who now so obviously resented Julie. Her ancestor had had a lot to put up with. But she, Irinka van Slijk wasn't going to put up with any more.

She smiled inwardly . . . she'd complained, prompting the nurse's transfer to the maternity section . . . . . nevertheless she could still pose a threat.

Nurse Cauldry had watched the Probe's magnetic pull as it had passed through Julie's memories. She hadn't been able to understand what she'd seen, but still, she had seen it!

She was without a doubt, one troubled human being, with an immense amount of burning hatred for Julie. But, and thankfully so, she still was unable to decide just what it was, she'd witnessed. And as the days passed, and together with Dr Nelson's explanation, the nurse's thoughts had reasoned it was some sort of malfunction.

She'd smiled to herself at the doctor's clarification, even though she knew for a fact that he, and for that matter Piet, didn't believe it.

Meanwhile, unbeknown to both Piet and Dr Nelson, Nurse Cauldry had listened to their conversation. She'd had hours of pleasure eavesdropping, and had learnt plenty.

'Dr Western's soul computations are a green Commander,' Dr Swartz informed, breaking in on her thoughts. 'We'll start rescue procedure at 9.57am precisely.'

'Affirmative,' she thought and glanced down at her watch, it was almost 8.13am.

'They're a long time,' Tony said suddenly, 'It's been almost three quarters of an hour.' He paused to draw on his umpteenth Marlboro. 'What time do you have?'

'Almost quarter past,' she replied.

'What's taking them so long?' he said impatiently, stubbing out his half-finished cigarette.

She watched as the still-burning Marlboro's smoke rose from the ashtray. Why, with all the medical evidence, even in this primitive time, were people so stupid as to smoke? She shook her head. At least the body she had infiltrated had not smoked; that would have been another thing that would have puzzled Piet, because she was sure she could not have condoned that one!

She reached across and stubbed out the offending smouldering weed. Tony stood up, glanced at his watch again, then retraced his earlier steps to the window.

The sun had receded behind the thickening clouds.

Just then, Dr Peters came out of Maria's room.

'You can go in now,' she said as she approached. He turned around at the sound of her voice.

'How is she?' he asked nervously.

'The doctor's deep brown eyes softened. 'She's doing fine,' she placated, adding in the same manner, 'I've asked for a colleague of mine. '

'A colleague?' he questioned anxiously before she'd time to finish her sentence, 'Is there a problem?'

'No,' she said, pausing a moment to choose her words, 'A second opinion, you might say. I'm waiting on him now.'

She smiled confidently, but Tony swallowed hard, not convinced. He glanced at Julie then back at the doctor.

'I want to do a caesarean section,' she told him.

'Caesarean. But why? Why?' he stammered.

She motioned him to sit and sat down herself before she spoke.

'The baby is premature, as you know. It's lying in the wrong position. We've tried several times to turn it, unsuccessfully so, I might add. But then, that is often the case, so don't be too alarmed. Mother and baby are otherwise healthy. I just think a caesarean would give them both a better chance.' She patted his hand gently then stood up finishing, 'You can see her for a short while, if you'd like.'

The seconds on the parallel clock ticked by. Dr Swartz mopped his brow. It had been a long morning, and one that had stretched his nerves to breaking point.

He was acutely aware, although his team were ready, waiting to retrieve both souls, of the mounting pressure that surrounded him.

It was their first real chance; edging closer and closer as was the storm, with every carefully controlled micro-second that passed.

He would have liked to have had more time. But the imminence of the electrical storm had changed all that. The opportunity with which Dr Western had inadvertently presented them; although mostly conducted as a rescue mission, had given him the ideal circumstances to complete the rest of his experiments. Sadly it was not to be.

He turned to glance at the parallel clock. It was 9.44am.

He watched as Tony and Julie walked either side of the trolley, each holding Maria's hand, the blue-coated orderly pushing it down the long white-walled corridor towards the operating theatre, making light conversation as he greeted various other orderlies en route.

As they reached the double doors of the Operating Theatre, Julie leant over the trolley and kissed Maria's cheek.

'See you in a little while,' she promised, then slipped her hand free. Maria nodded, returning a weak smile . . . the relaxant she'd been given earlier was beginning to take effect.

At 9.56am, Julie settled herself in a red leather armchair in the small waiting area, to the left of the operating theatre. The time had almost come. . . . . .

She could hear the hypnotic voice of Dr Swartz giving instructions and, with her head resting against the high back of the chair, she closed her eyes, her soul relaxed now, as the calmness Dr Swartz's voice exuded, spread through her being like a sedative, preparing her to vacate the safe housing that Julie's body had provided.

Her mission, to escort Dr Western's soul to the future.

Then suddenly she sensed Julie's soul stirring . . . awakening. She was fraught with panic . . . she had no armour . . . no protection! Then it was back. Dr Swartz's deep, gentle placating voice.

She could feel the Probe's mounting vibration, the pulsating heat as Dr Swartz's velvet-edged voice, defusing her panic, confirmed, 'It's almost time.'

As the surrounding haze that impaired her vision slowly cleared, she looked down. She was inside the Operating Theatre. Floating high above them . . . waiting . . . hovering above Maria's anaesthetized body . . .

The surgeons had begun the operation.

A black, rubber-like mask covered most of her face. A doctor sat alongside, pressing a black oval rubber ball, the size of a football, between his fingers.

She watched as he turned his attention to a small ring-like handle on a long, black cylinder, opening the jet wider.

Tony was sitting to Maria's right, still holding her limp hand. He was wearing a long green gown; the same colour surgical cap covered his hair and his mouth was masked.

The only visible part was his forehead and eyes. She looked at his sweat-covered, glistening brow, then down at his anxious light-blue eyes, as he gazed tenderly at his anaesthetized wife.

Glancing across to the anaesthetist, she followed Dr Swartz's instructions implicitly, watching intently; awaiting her cue, as he adjusted the heart monitor's brightness.

At that exact moment, and just behind the ghostly bounce of the main heartbeat, she saw it; a shadow; a further weaker heartbeat; the same vision Piet and Dr Nelson had witnessed when she had infiltrated Julie's body . . . the heartbeat that Dr Swartz had so carefully described to her.

The Operating Theatre clock showed 9.59am and forty seconds.

She listened as Dr Swartz's hypnotic voice returned.

'We're almost parallel.'

She watched as the black mist tightened around her. Then she felt the warmth as it touched her being; binding her soul, before opening an exit. She felt herself floating, being drawn to the clearing, bathing on the edge.

Soon it would engulf Dr Western. She felt the excitement course through her, then the sadness as she realised she was leaving . . .

'Piet!' She heard herself cry out in desperation. 'Piet!' 'It's time,' Dr Swartz announced, and once again she felt the pulsation of the Probe as it surged through the mist, supplying her with the energy she needed.

Suddenly, and simultaneous to the Theatre's flickering bright lights, she felt herself descending, her invisible being, searching, drawing and enticing, inside Maria's still body, for Dr Western's renegade soul.

Just then, she touched it. She could feel its powerful force as it came to investigate the intrusion . . . the entity, drawn to her homing beacon, contiguous to her own.

She embraced it, calmed and soothed it; guiding, leading the spirit upwards into the home vessel, into the safety of the centre of the transporting mist then into the depth of the blackness . . .

When they were safely cocooned, the invisible mist rose, turning slowly at first then building its speed, spinning faster and faster, soaring in height, like the spiral of a tornado, surging, forward through time; through history yet to be made by the mortals they'd left behind . . . homeward, to their time . . . their world, their waiting bodies.

As the warm, black mist divided into the separate receiving chambers, the Commander's soul, in her designated funnel, moved side by side with the other.

Steadily it edged its way across the laboratory in the direction of the life support units, to deposit its precious cargoes into the waiting recipients . . .

It was then that she felt it. A strong, forceful, overpowering oppressive evilness.

'Dr Swartz!' Dr Turner called anxiously, as he monitored the readings. 'The ablator on Dr Western's soul. It's weakening!'

He paused, checking the time corridor readout.

'T.C. readout is 2.59. It should read 2.79. It looks. '

Dr Swartz's exclamation cut him off before he had a chance to finish his sentence.

'My God! No! No!' It had happened. He shook his head, his mind refusing to accept the readings. The colour drained from his face as he waited, seeking the computer's confirmation, his voice a denying whisper.

'It's not possible!'

She'd sent the evilness.

He ran his hand through his thick, greying hair, his face still white and shocked. He couldn't bear to admit it.

Both doctors stared at the hologram parallel. The surgeons had just lifted out Maria's baby and they witnessed the breath of the new-born life.

'Reverse the Probe,' Dr Swartz called out suddenly.

'Not possible,' Dr Stevens confirmed, 'Time corridor closed.'

He watched as the life support units throbbed and pulsed, the black mist depositing its cargoes . . .

The two souls had returned to their separate receivers, each heartbeat registering on the separate monitors.

As the black mist subsided, the first unit cover slid aside and Irinka's eyes opened. Dr Blackmore extended his hand, helping her up. 'How do you feel?' he enquired, as she stepped out of the unit.

'A little tired,' she replied, 'But otherwise alright.'

Smiling tentatively, he led her across to the Scan Table adjacent the unit, as was the normal procedure.

Tilting the table to the upright position, she stepped into the footholes, grasping the two hand levers either side of her.

When she was secure, he depressed a button and the table tilted back to its normal position. A moment later, she heard a great whoosh of energy as a large globe of translucent light was released to scan her body.

Slowly, the bright globe moved up her body, from her feet to her head, the data collecting on the monitors above her. Then, automatically reversing on its preordained course, it slowly proceeded back to its resting position and the scan was complete. The Commander's readout was normal.

Dr Blackmore smiled confidently as he tilted the table forward and helped her off. She felt as if every sense in her body had been razor-sharpened.

'Everything is a okay' he confirmed as he poured her a beaker of orange liquid. 'Drink this slowly and rest a few minutes.'

She nodded and did as he said, watching as the lid on the second unit opened . . . . . Dr Western's body remained perfectly still.

Returning to his station, Dr Blackmore assisted by Dr Turner, lifted the slim limp body of Dr Western from the unit and placed her flat on the scanner table.

Whilst Swartz and Turner, secured her hands to the two levers, Dr Blackmore depressed the scanner's control button.

A moment later, she heard the same whoosh of energy as the large globe moved into position hovering over Dr Western's feet.

She watched, as the globe moved slowly over every inch of her still body, in much the same way as it had moved over hers.

Although Gemma's body was functioning, the difference that registered on the monitor above, left the three concerned doctors in no doubt.

The split soul they'd retrieved, was alien . . .

With the unwitting help of Dr Turner's interference; by his thoughtless actions of releasing the Probe, thereby infiltrating the apparition of Lillian Becket, he'd inadvertently solved Dr Western's dilemma.

In the split second that followed, she'd seized her chance. Drawing the Litchen Probe's mass energy, feeding and draining, storing every last drop. And from that fatal, careless process, a massive burst of energy had been put at her disposal, affording her the ability to detach the evilness and retain the fourth part of Maria's soul; the vital part she'd so fiercely fought for. The essential element needed for her soul to remain permanently.

Dr Swartz stared at Gemma's still body, her fine chiselled features, her pale ivory skin and her soft tawny curls.

Suddenly, her eyes sprang open. He gasped as they stared accusingly, straight at him.

Dr Turner hadn't heard his gasp for he was already studying Gemma's readout, mentally reconstructing the events that led up to his previous blunder. He cursed his own incompetence!

As the vacant, hypnotic emptiness of her eyes held him, an eerie scarlet glow flickered to life.

He watched, unable to move as the two deep red masses grew, swirling madly to forge two deep cavities of burning fire . . . hypnotically whirling, faster and faster . . . down and down, into two never-ending, bottomless pits.

His eyes were wide with terror, his lungs fighting for breath . . . his whole being transfixed to the spot.

Suddenly, the fire was in full flame . . . two vivid orange jets leapt out towards him, yet strangely there was no heat and he felt a ghostly cold . . .

It was then that he heard it. His heart beat wildly with shock. An icy blast hit him full in the face. He retched with the stench of her breath as the unearthly deep growl penetrated his whole being.

For the first time he felt an immense fear.

Alien blue lips drew back into two thin lines across spiked yellow teeth in an evil, contorted grin. A malevolent chuckle, low and coarse that dominated every other sound, filled his ears . . .

'Sedate it . . . sedate it!' he managed urgently, clasping his hands over his ears. Turner and Blackmore spun around, but saw only the pale, still body of Dr Western.

In the next instant, Dr Swartz had grabbed the sedation gun and shot the body with a full dose of sedative.

Slowly, he felt himself freed, and his laboured breathing subsided. The scarlet glow was receding and her eyes were returning to normal. He felt Dr Turner's hand on his sleeve.

'Are you alright, Eric?' he questioned, with concern, but Dr Swartz couldn't hear him. He just stood there, staring down at Gemma's face.

Suddenly the room spun at an incredible pace and a vice-like pain gripped his whole body. His voice rose to an almost scream . . .

'Help me!' he managed, as his legs gave way and he fell heavily to the floor.

Unable to prevent his colleague's fall, Dr Turner knelt down at his side.

'Eric. Eric. ' he called, opening the top of his colleague's tunic. But Dr Swartz's eyes were half closed, only the whites were showing and his face was rigid. He could hear Dr Turner's distant voice, but the monstrous oppression was still with him.

Rushing across to the medical section of the laboratory, Dr Turner filled the inoculation gun with a 20cc dose of detoxification serum and sped back to Dr Swartz. Placing the gun to his neck, he fired the pellet.

Dr Swartz moaned loudly, but Dr Turner's distant voice was becoming louder, penetrating his unconscious, his colleague's words somehow filling him, saving him from the deep, black void that awaited him; from the two burning orbs that drew him downwards. Invisible cold hands were all over him, pulling, tugging with a seemingly infrangible force.

Fraught with anxiety, Dr Turner, felt his colleague's pulse . . . it was jumping like crazy and his hand was freezing.

He watched helplessly, as Dr Swartz fought against the invisible force that gripped him, his body a mass of contorted twists as it jerked violently.

Then, just as suddenly as it had begun, it was over, and Dr Swartz's face regained its normality . . .

Convinced it was a convulsion due to the much-needed detoxification, Dr Turner instructed, 'Lie still Eric, you've had a seizure. I've given you shot.'

The manifestation had seemingly been in Dr Swartz's mind, for no one had seen it but himself . . . the horror of its warped features; the evil it had exuded; were in his own fear.

As the detoxification shot began its stabilisation, Dr Turner helped him to sit up. He took a deep breath. The overpowering pressure that had held him in a vice-like grip was gone, but in its place an uneasy stillness.

'I'm alright,' he insisted sluggishly, as he regained his senses. 'Help me up.'

'What happened?' Dr Blackmore questioned.

The question went unanswered as Dr Turner helped his colleague stand, and motioned the team back to their stations.

A moment later Dr Swartz stood at the side of the scan table, his knuckle-white hands gripping the safety rail as he stared at Dr Western's comatose body. It was still and silent.

Dr Turner followed his colleague's stare.

As Dr Blackmore lifted Dr Western's body and placed it back in the life support unit, a single tear ran down the furrow of her nose and her light green eyes stared blankly into space . . .

Suddenly, a chilling, desperate voice called out.

'J U L I E E E E . . . '

The single name had echoed emptily around the spacious laboratory, the helpless plea, so fearfully shouted, was heard only in the minds of the Commander and Dr Swartz . . . . . for Dr Western's lips had not moved.

Irinka hurried across to the unit. She stood there for several moments, her unbelieving eyes searching Dr Western's small, white face that housed her empty, vacant stare . . . . .

Suddenly, her heart hammered out a beat at double time, as the lid sprang to life, and the pale, white, still, body was sealed inside.

Coldly, his skin still tingling with fear, Dr Swartz returned to the main computer. Dr Turner followed.

'What happened Eric?' he questioned, his voice a whisper, as Dr Swartz slumped down in his seat.

Slowly he turned to face him. 'You didn't see it?'

'See what?' Dr Turner replied in the same whisper.

A long silence followed, as Dr Swartz stared vacantly ahead. Then, just as Dr Turner was about to speak, a cold steel-like expression in Dr Swartz's narrowing, dark eyes stifled his question.

Eric was in desperate need of a full detoxification. Whether or not Dr Swartz was aware of the pressure building up in him, he was not absolutely sure, but he himself, was acutely aware. Eric's convulsion and now hallucinations, gravely concerned him. But for now he was powerless, the present situation required all his concentration. He could only wait and hope; hope that the detox-serum he'd administered earlier would hold.

'Has the Probe finished input Dr Stevens?' he heard Dr Swartz question.

Confirming that it had, he turned full around in his seat to face Dr Swartz, then, with a quick brief glance to Dr Turner, resumed, 'Every memory that the Commander created has been infused within her own.'

Dr Turner watched as Dr Stevens turned back to face his monitor and shouted alarmingly.

'Wait . . . something's happening to Julie. Her soul is dying!'

'Freeze the parallel. Display readout!' Dr Swartz commanded with the same urgency.

'Parallel frozen. Readings displayed,' the soft voice of the main computer confirmed.

As both doctors studied the readout, the weather computer interrupted. 'Electrical storm ETA 6.5 minutes.'

'We've got to return Commander van Slijk's soul,' Dr Swartz said reluctantly.

'No!' Dr Turner protested, 'It's madness Eric. There's not enough time!'

'We have to Harry. There's no other way!' He turned to face him and saw the insistence in his dark eyes. He knew he was right. Dr Swartz stood up and laid his hand on his colleague's shoulder.

'There really isn't any other way, Harry.'

He nodded reluctantly, and Dr Swartz walked across to the Commander.

'We have to return your soul Commander,' he told her wearily. 'Julie's soul can't function on its own. We'll try to find out what the problem is but in the meantime you'll have to remain in her body or she will die. And I'm sure you understand the gravity of that!'

She nodded her head, 'For how long?'

'We'll try to get both you and Gemma back before the storm's arrival.'

He turned to look at Dr Turner and Irinka felt her heart skip a beat as she thought of Piet.

'If we have to follow mandatory procedure and the storm . . . '

His sudden further explanation panicked her and, afraid he might retract his decision, she cut in with assurance, before he'd finished his sentence.

'I understand Dr Swartz.'

He turned back to face her and she held his eyes with her own.

'We'll get back to you immediately it's safe,' he promised. But his eyes told her different. And she knew there would be no guarantees. She nodded again. She didn't care . . . she was going back to Piet.

'Prepare the Life Support Unit for the return of the Commander's soul.' 'Yes sir,' Dr Blackmore replied.

He went over to Stevens and Grey.

'Return Julie van Slijk's soul to freeze mode. Dr Grey, monitor the operation. As soon as we've successfully replaced the Commander's soul, pull section three out. Dr Turner and I will check the break-up then.'

He turned around and spoke to Dr Maxwell. 'I need a parallel time corridor, co-ordinates and full power. We are returning the Commander's soul.'

After nodding her understanding, she set about his instructions.

Swartz's legs were still unsteady as he walked back towards the Life Support Units. Dr Turner caught his eye in a silent concern before Dr Swartz's almost imperceptible nod answered his unspoken question.

He stood by the side of the unit, resting his hand on the rail . . . Irinka had just settled herself inside.

'At best, it'll be five, six minutes. At worst . . . '

His voice trailed off as he felt his fear return and the trepidation surged through him.

She placed her hand over his, her eyes holding his in an unspoken reiteration. She sensed his great fear, but her love for Piet was greater.

As the Life Support Unit lid closed over her head, he mouthed a silent goodbye and walked back to his station.

'All section checks completed. Time corridor opening,' Dr Turner confirmed.

His tired eyes watched as the main computer drew maximum energy, the laboratory immediately bathed in the red hue of emergency lighting.

Slowly the transporting black mist crept forward, the screen registering every beat of energy as it cocooned its precious cargo before speeding backwards through time into history. Centuries quickly disappearing as the Commander's soul raced to her ancestor's dying body.

If the storm arrived before he had a chance to get them both out and they took a direct hit, it would obliterate both parallels and both the Commander's and Dr Western's souls could end up in infinity!

Time would race on, the parallel clocks would surge forward. Theoretically, the time frame both souls had infiltrated would no longer exist. Consequently as the ancestors' bodies reached the end of their lifespan and died, the two souls would make their departure. And the computer, having been knocked out by the storm, would not be able to receive them.

The thought was just too horrific! He shook his head in an effort to get rid of his doubts and returned his attention to the hologram.

'Julie. Julie,' Tony whispered, trying to rouse her from the sleep he believed her in. He leant closer and whispered in her ear, his face beaming,

'It's a girl. 5lbs 4oz.'

She opened her eyes.

'Wonderful . . . just wonderful. Congratulations!' she replied sleepily, collecting her bearings. Her grogginess, she knew he'd attributed to her nap. She stood up, her instant elation second only to his, and flung her arms around his neck in a hug.

'And Maria?' she questioned with the same elation.

'She's fine . . . came through it just fine,' he assured.

Swartz and Turner watched, their immediate attention initially diverted, as the first roar of thunder echoed in the distance.

'Storm approaching, ETA to mandatory procedure 4.5 minutes . . . ' the Weather Computer advised.

At the same time, the Resident Elder appeared on the direct link.

'Dr Swartz. Just four minutes to mandatory procedure.'

'Yes ma'am,' he replied, assuring her his intentions would be honourably so, but knowing he would do quite the reverse should the situation merit. For his prime objective was to rescue both souls, no matter what threat the storm posed.

As the seconds ticked by, Dr Stevens replaced Dr Turner and worked non-stop with Dr Swartz to repair the Probe's burnt-out section.

Dr Turner meanwhile, studied the readout on the alien soul. He had to admit, it really was quite an extraordinary achievement, and one that were the circumstances different, would have commanded all his devoted dedication.

Inadvertently they'd completed a part of their experiment that should have come much later. Disappointedly he shook his head. If only they had the experience to control it fully, but not, he hastened to admit, with the grave consequences they now faced.

An incomplete soul was not what they'd intended, but it was nevertheless what they had. And a sedated soul to boot!

Is it right to keep it sedated? he asked himself staring at Dr Western's body. Just then Dr Swartz approached.

'We've found it Harry,' he told him excitedly, 'Another moment or two we'll be on full power again.'

'Is it right to keep her sedated?' Harry said aloud, staring down at the still body of Dr Western, 'I know we have to send it back . . . but whilst we have it . . . '

His voice trailed off, and Dr Swartz's face flushed with anger.

He was normally a calm, logical man, but his colleague's insensitive suggestion made him not only fearfully alarmed, but tetchy and impatient too. He felt the shell of his newly-regained imperturbability breaking down, revealing the same fraughtness in his defensive demeanour.

'No!' he said, his tone reflecting the fiercest hostility.

'She stays sedated! We'll return it immediately we have full power!'

He stared at Dr Swartz, following him with his eyes as he walked back to the main computer.

'Full power has been restored Dr Swartz,' the main computer informed.

Slowly, Dr Turner turned back to face the sedated body, his scientific mind racing ahead.

A few days ago, Eric would have jumped at the opportunity . . . only a few hours ago, he'd been using the rescue mission as an experiment, now his only intention was the safe return of both souls. It just didn't make any sense . . . did Dr Swartz know something that he didn't?

Just how much time did they have, did they need?

'Dr Turner!' Dr Swartz summoned impatiently.

He turned round, but so had the rest of the team. His face flushed. Dr Swartz's summons had made him feel like a disobedient junior, not the senior assistant he was, still, now was not the time to argue and he knew his colleague better than he knew himself.

Something else . . . . . something far greater than the detoxification was worrying him. As the embarrassed team turned back to their tasks, he walked back to his station and retook his seat.

The hologram screen had chosen a time corridor. January 4th, 1995. They could return the alien soul within seconds.

Acknowledging the computer's co-ordinates, the history was set before them.

Maria would almost drown in a boating accident, whilst water skiing on a late holiday. Historically, Tony would dive into the water and save her, but for a vital three seconds . . . her heart would most definitely stop beating.

Just then, and simultaneously to the Weather Computer's announcement, the voice of the Resident Elder on the direct link, spoke.

'Dr Swartz.'

'Yes ma'am,' he acknowledged.

'The electrical storm is stationary. It looks as if you may get a short reprieve, although just how long that will be. '

'Yes ma'am. Thank you, we've just heard,' he cut in.

'Good luck Dr Swartz,' she said and severed the connection.

He thought for one fleeting moment he'd caught just the hint of smugness in her expression, then dismissing the thought, he turned his attention back to the computer.

Meanwhile the Resident Elder, having taken a reading from the main computer of the present situation, during her planned interruption, reported her findings to the Head Elder.

'Do you realise what this means Zoniac?'

'Yes sir, I do.' The determination of her nod enforced her words and his eyes sparkled. He was more than pleased with her findings.

'It means we now have the ability to successfully transport a soul. No several souls back. We can take the present soul . . . even destroy it . . . send it into oblivion!

'We can rewrite history . . . history before the great war . . . assassinate past, troublesome dictators at the touch of a button. We can build . . . lead history our way . . . whatever way we wish!'

His watery-blue eyes bulged with excitement as he spoke his private thoughts aloud. 'We can send our own souls back! And with our superior intelligence, we can create a perfect world! I can be immortal through the ages. Why! when one body is worn out, I can go onto the next! Hold the occupying soul in freeze mode . . . in oblivion! Generations . . . hundreds of years . . . lifetimes, in each century.'

He paused a moment, enjoying his thoughts, the expression on his face portraying his greed and hunger.

She'd listened as he'd raved. He was mad . . . totally mad!

This was not what it was all about. She had to do something!

'Zoniac,' he said suddenly, jarring her free from her thoughts.

'Yes sir!' she replied, startled by his sudden interruption, but trying to hide the terror he'd created inside her.

'You've done well. Keep a constant monitor on Swartz.'

'Yes sir!' she replied. But she knew her enthusiastic reply was a falsehood to keep him satisfied.

'Zoniac,' he called, as she opened the chamber door to take her leave.

Her heart thundered loudly as she turned to face him. 'Sir.'

'Does Swartz know we've intercepted the main computer?'

'No sir,' she assured.

'Good,' he replied, 'Will the storm pose any further problems?'

'No, sir,' she lied convincingly, then left the chamber.

Dr Swartz's attention stayed with the hologram. The distant sound of thunder rumbled in his ears. It was a fight for survival . . . their survival and the survival of future generations that would go the way history intended . . . as history had happened.

Calling his team's attention, he briefed them as fully as he was able.

'From parallel interception, we'll have just three seconds. The time corridor will close immediately. We'll send the alien soul first, then at the closest time to death, and during the infusion, we'll take Dr Western's.'

His eyes mirrored the great determination he felt inside, as he paused before adding, 'There's no room for error . . . full concentration, team.'

As he bid them all good luck and retook his seat, the Resident Elder entered the laboratory. He turned around to face her.

'Ma'am,' he acknowledged.

'No, don't get up Dr Swartz,' she said, raising her hand, 'Just carry on. I know how precious time is.'

She sat down next to him and watched as the parallels accelerated. It was 1.59pm, January 4th, 1995.

The hot, red sun was like a great burning disc in the azure sky. Tony turned the bright red-and-white twin-engine speed boat into Waianae Bay. They watched as Dr Western's soul, almost totally alone in Maria's body, laughed excitedly as she skied behind the boat, her bright-orange life jacket reflecting in the smooth, blue water of the Pacific Ocean, just off Kaena Point.

Suddenly, her joyous laughter turned into a piercing scream as a dark-skinned youth came from nowhere.

In the split second that followed, his bouncing Jet Ski Scooter had severed her ski line, knocking her sideways with terrific force.

Tony watched helplessly as his wife skimmed across the water, then disappeared from his view. The Jet Ski rider sped on, out into the open sea.

Frantically his eyes scanned the surface . . . his voice mirroring his desperation as he shouted hysterically, 'Maria. Maria!'

It was then that he saw her.

Less than a heartbeat later he'd dived over the side, his powerful arms beating a path through the water, at an incredible speed.

Whilst his heartbeat accelerated at an amazing rate, sending a shockwave of pulsation thundering in his ears, he turned her over and saw the gash . . . her lips were blue.

'Oh Dear God No. No!'

With shock, fear and anger, he summoned his remaining strength, swimming as fast as he could, pulling her unconscious body back towards the boat.

'Almost parallel,' Dr Swartz informed, loudly.
'Sending alien soul on my count of three . . . two . . . one. '
'En route,' Dr Blackmore confirmed.

As Dr Western's soul in Maria's body lay in limbo, the Life Support Unit sprang to life in readiness and the main laboratory lighting took on the familiar red hue.

The Resident Elder watched in silence as the transporting black mist, supporting its alien cargo, started its journey. Back through the dark corridors of time; through the pages of history; back into Maria's own time; into her own body, into the year 1995.

Devastated, Tony tried with all desperation to overcome his grief. Praying inside, with every snatched breath he took, he tried to blow life into his wife's limp bloodied body.

From almost four hundred years in their future, the anxious team watched as Dr Western's screaming, irascible soul began its journey towards the hovering black mist, visible only to their eyes; in their time; for her transportation home to their future; the present, 2384.

They watched as the alien soul reached its destination, infiltrating her pale, still body, caressing the other en route. A moment later, the transporting black mist appeared in the receiving chamber of the laboratory.

Dr Swartz watched a moment longer as Tony, satisfied his wife was breathing, made her warm and comfortable, then pushed the small boat to maximum speed in the direction of Waianae Bay and the hospital.

He turned to Dr Turner.

'You take over, monitor their every move. I'll check the receiving unit.'

He strode quickly across to the receiving unit. The Resident Elder followed him with her eyes. The black mist was already clearing.

Impatiently, he waited standing alongside Dr Blackmore, watching as the monitor gave them her readout.

'It's 2.89!' Dr Blackmore exclaimed, pointing to the screen.

Dr Swartz's face drained of colour.

'Are you sure?' he questioned.

'Positive!' Dr Blackmore said.

Dr Swartz strode determinedly back to the main computer, and bent over Dr Turner's shoulder to whisper in his ear.

'It's no good, Harry. She's brought the fourth part with her. She won't let go!'

'Maybe she can't let go!' he said gravely, then turned to face him, 'Eric you know what you have to do.'

'Yes,' he agreed, 'But it doesn't make it any easier.'

He turned to face the Resident Elder.

'You're going to send her back,' she said, her eyes wide.

'Yes, ma'am,' he confirmed, 'She'll have to live out Maria's life. It's the only way we can ensure the future. When Maria dies, we'll take Dr Western's soul.'

'But the storm!' she protested.

'Ma'am,' Dr Turner enforced, quickly interrupting, 'there's no other way. '

She turned abruptly to face him. She couldn't tell whether it was fear or curiosity in his eyes, perhaps both, but she knew he was right. Her small face was ashen as his words spun around in her mind and she nodded her head.

'Reverse Probe Dr Stevens. Return Dr Western's soul,' Dr Swartz commanded then turning to Dr Turner, said, 'Run the parallel forward Harry, we need the final time corridor.'

'Their deaths?' the Resident Elder said, her question more of a statement. He nodded his head.

They watched as the parallel sped on, the hologram settling in the year 2001.

As they studied the detailed plane crash and both Maria and Julie's impending death, a loud clap of thunder boomed a violent threat.

'Storm approaching. ETA three minutes,' the Weather Computer advised.

The Resident Elder stood up and protested, 'There's not enough time. Mandatory procedure.'

'With all due respect ma'am,' Dr Swartz cut in, 'We have no choice.'

'I don't think you understand, Dr Swartz!' she challenged, disdainfully.

'The main computer has been programmed to override your instructions! It will operate mandatory procedure, immediately the storm . . .'

Her voice trailed off, as did the surge of contempt she had felt towards him. She held his deep-brown pleading eyes with her own. What she saw there, said it all.

His sudden, earnest appeal had tested all she believed in; her confused loyalties spun around in her head, his words begging her.

'Ma'am please! Please help us. That mustn't happen! We will lose them both!'

The Head Elder's mad ranting earlier statement had distressed her considerably. It raced through her thoughts. His intentions were plain. Even a fool could see it. It wasn't the way it should be. And if she didn't do something quickly, then she'd be responsible for both the Commander's and Dr Western's certain death! The notion distressed her further, and she wondered if the Head Elder's principles that she was employed to enforce, had become too rigid.

Breaking away from his eyes, she sat down and faced the main computer. She had an overwhelming feeling of doom. Her slim, manicured nails hovered indecisively over the speak keys. But maybe this way, they'd have a chance . . .

With a brief glance up at Dr Swartz, her decision was made and in the next instant her slim fingers sped quickly over the letters. Less than a moment later the soft calm voice of the computer spoke.

'Verbal password?'

'Zoniac 2RE.'

The computer confirmed, just moments later, in bold script.

'Automatic Shutdown Aborted. Manual Control in operation.'

She looked up at Dr Swartz.

'Thank you,' he mouthed silently. The expression of intense relief she saw in his eyes, spoke volumes.

Whilst Dr Turner programmed the intended retrieval of both souls, they watched in silence as Maria lay in the Honolulu hospital bed, her husband Tony at her side.

Slowly, as the Probe began the transportation of Dr Western's soul and the subsequent inoculation, Maria's body stirred.

Dr Swartz, sighed heavily. He looked drained. The detoxification he so badly needed, was costing him. He knew he would have to fight to keep his thinking rational.

The Resident Elder hadn't helped. Her interference, and previous restraint, had made him both angry and alarmed. He had to stay calm, anything less would accelerate the poison.

Just then the computer advised, 'Time corridor available. One minute thirty-five seconds. Co-ordinates on screen.'

Silent moments passed as he studied the figures.

'Do you wish automatic logging?' the computer asked.

'Affirmative,' he replied.

'Co-ordinates logged. Interception at one minute thirty-one seconds . . . countdown begins.'

As the hologram clock ticked off the seconds, Dr Turner glanced across at him, 'It'll be over with soon Eric.'

Dr Swartz turned to face him, 'But will it?' he questioned.

His anxious eyes darted quickly to the Resident Elder's. Her expression equalled his own.

As the computer searched for the exact time of interception, the storm rumbled louder. It was almost overhead. Zoniac looked up through the laboratory's clear dome ceiling, the sky was black. The heavy, portentous space above like a huge cauldron overflowing with threatening sounds.

A second later, the first bolt of forked lightning was discharged. She watched as it bounced off the intercepting conductor directly above them. Like a gigantic torch it lit up the blackness, turning it pink, then grey.

She lowered her eyes. She knew they were at a grave disadvantage.

Dr Swartz's eyes met hers. A weak smile touched the corners of his mouth for an instant and then it was gone.

He looked around at his team.

They were anxious, nervous. Each member rueful as they looked up through the dome ceiling. They'd stayed with him, loyally carrying out his commands, witnessing his own impetuousness, that exuded from him now as noticeable as the sweat that glistened on his brow.

It was make-or-break time, he concluded, more to himself than anyone else. Zoniac had resigned herself to just that fact a while back, when she'd lifted the automatic shutdown.

As the computer went through the normal procedure, committing the co-ordinates to its memory cells, the main hologram suddenly froze.

Dr Swartz's heart missed a beat as his mouth opened in a gasp.

'What the?' Zoniac started, but her question was cut off midsentence as another deep, resonant rumble of thunder boomed around the unrelenting heavens. Moments later a fierce crackling streak of lightning speared earthwards, leaving them bathed in the red glow of the emergency lighting.

As the main computer fought against the sudden surge of power, earthing the unwelcomed burst, the hologram suddenly sprang back to life.

They watched, their eyes wide in disbelief, as a broad hollow pathway of heavy static energy tore like two giant sparklers, in a blaze of cracking light, straight through it.

Just then, the computer's calm unfaltering voice informed.

'Co-ordinates set Dr Swartz. Do you wish to proceed?'

Astonished by the normality it brought to him, he managed. 'Affirmative. On a thirty second countdown.'

He looked around at the four other members of his team. They were each taking delivery of their retrospective information.

He turned back to the speak keys, his fingers urgent in their request.

'Confirm previous history reprogramme and inserted corrections . . . Maria Becket . . . Julie van Slijk.'

A few seconds later the computer had confirmed.

The parallel history programme would be automatically reset, upon the successful return of both souls.

The laboratory silence was deafening as the storm continued in its path of destruction, the ferocious forked lightning seeming to prod them with each earthbound strike, driving them onwards in their desperate attempt as the parallel hologram, oblivious to the storm's obstruent behaviour, relayed the fight between the newly reunited souls. They witnessed the jealousy, the resentment and finally the immense hatred that Maria's soul exuded . . .

They watched as Dr Western's soul suppressed and defied it, until it retreated, licking its wounds, becoming nothing more than a pathetic whisper in the back of her mind.

The parallel sped onwards, slowing only as it approached the thirty second countdown of their final hours, setting on 30th October, 2001 . . .

They watched as the hologram clock settled on 1.00pm, twenty-nine hours before their deaths.

The breeze had developed rapidly into a strong wind, driving the swollen dark clouds of heavy rain straight at them. Maria opened the collar of her beige overcoat. Despite the chill and damp air, she was perspiring profusely.

Julie's hand tightened on the stem of Piet's large black umbrella, as she struggled against the elements to keep it upright.

Together, with heads bowed, they made their way across the large parking lot towards the welcoming lights of the brightly-lit restaurant.

The restaurant was crowded to overflowing. The bar area, where customers awaited their tables, packed tightly with mostly women. Probably came in for an early lunch, to dry off, she reasoned. She'd never seen it so packed.

Placing the wet umbrella in the stand, she removed her coat and hung it up. Just then the portly, bald-headed English major-domo approached.

'Good afternoon, Mrs Garnet, Mrs van Slijk. How nice to see you both again,' he said warmly. He took Maria's coat and hung it up.

'Your table is waiting,' he resumed, with a broad smile.

As they followed close behind him, waiters weaved and darted their way through the rows of tables, balancing trays laden with drinks and empty plates, precariously on the fingertips of their upstretched hands, over their heads.

Having seated them both, and with the pleasantries over with, he gave them a menu.

The sound of crashing china shattering a few tables over, brought the hushed mumbles of several conversations to an abrupt halt.

A fat ginger-haired woman of around fifty stood up and yelled obscenities at a young, dark latin-type waiter, who was trying somewhat unsuccessfully to mop up several platefuls of spilled soup she'd knocked from his hand.

The major-domo, seeing the young waiter's plight, excused himself, then hurried over to placate the irate woman. Her henpecked, red-faced husband cowered weakly as she redirected her anger towards him.

They watched as the hologram sped on.

At almost forty, Maria was still a beautiful woman. The years had been good to her. And, to Dr Swartz, was a beautiful anachronism.

It was 3.30pm when they left the restaurant.

Outside, the downpour continued, the heavy skies showing no sign of respite, black clouds making the day seem darker than usual.

Maria looked up at the sky, the strange feeling she'd tried to push from her mind had returned. It was like a distant voice crying for help . . . refusing to be dismissed.

As they made their way to the car, the feeling stayed with her but she couldn't quite reach it. It bothered her, like the words on the tip of your tongue, you can't quite recall.

Dr Swartz had eased the Probe forward, drawing her energy, and in doing so had had temporarily blocked Dr Western's ability to use the echo facility. His actions would hopefully enable him, upon the body's death, to separate her from Maria's tormented soul.

With the Commander keeping Julie's body alive, and both deaths imminent, he couldn't afford to let Dr Western gain the knowledge to change this part of the newly-written history. And there was no doubt in his mind, she would most certainly do just that!

'When is it ever going to stop?' Maria questioned, as she opened the car door.

Julie laughed and closed the umbrella then, sliding in the driver's seat, she tossed the sodden umbrella into the rear.

'Let's hope it stops tomorrow. We're all flying up to Las Vegas.'

'Now how could I forget that,' Maria replied, with a chuckle, her mood lightening. She was looking forward to her week at the tables. Paybac had since become her residence, but Las Vegas would always be her home.

He watched as Julie drove out of the car park.

'Commander, we have a corridor to take both your souls,' he informed.

'Yes, sir,' she acknowledged, the conversation between them, now a skilled thought projection.

'October 31st. 1800 hours.'

His statement made her shudder. It was so close.

Dismissing her apprehensiveness, he turned to his team.
'We'll take Dr Western's soul first then the Commander's.'

The hologram screen sped on through the limited time they had left.

The Resident Elder watched intently, the storm thundering above in an undisputed, constant reminder of their peril.

Tony's red-and-white Comanche light aircraft taxied into position. The fateful flight was moments away.

Just then, the main computer's voice confirmed the pre-set thirty-second countdown.

'Parallel. 5.59 and thirty seconds . . . twenty-nine . . . twenty-eight. '

The team watched as the light aircraft gained height before the eye of the hologram caught a large brown hawk circling in the far right of the screen, as if the labouring drone of the light aircraft's engines had inadvertently given it life.

Determinedly, its powerful wings skimmed the tops of the giant fir trees that grew up the side of the shadowy mountains. Then, banking steeply, it spiralled upwards, gaining the same height as the plane, completing a full 360-degree right turn before following the path of the red-and-white aircraft, its solitary presence, trailing behind in the doomed plane's wake, seemingly pushing it to its death.

As the vital seconds dropped away from the parallel clock, the powerful bird soared high into the clouds; its speed much in excess of the Comanche.

Suddenly, Piet grabbed Tony's sleeve and pointed.

He looked up from his map and followed his friend's eyes out through the front cockpit window.

The menacing hawk was in front of them . . . just moments away . . . its cold, black eyes seizing its prey . . . staring straight at them.

In one deft movement, Tony flicked off the auto pilot and grabbed the controls. As the Comanche climbed higher, in a desperate bid to shake off the bird he banked, sharp port, then starboard. Up, down, it sped through the air, shuddering with the quick directional pull, but no matter what he did, the undeterred hawk remained, an unwanted defiant extension, held by a powerful forcefield . . . an invisible bond, invading their immediate space . . .

Maria gripped the back of her husband's seat, staring over his shoulder, her eyes locked on to the bird, the knuckles of her small slim hands white with panic.

Tony dived again. But it was too late . . . for at the very same instant, with the speed of a bullet, the devilish monstrosity, its black vengeful eyes trained on the cockpit, came straight at them in a frenzied attack.

With an immense force, it shot through the front cockpit window, its glass-riddled, broken body whistling past Tony's right ear. He struggled, fighting the controls and the fierce wind that followed. By some miracle he still had his sight. Like a heavy lead weight thrown into a sea, the Comanche plummeted down and down, the ground rushing towards them at an incredible rate, the steep dive and the great force of wind tearing through the cockpit, pinning them back in their seats . . .

Suddenly the hologram image froze. The noise and the rushing wind had ceased. An eerie silence replaced the violent bedlam. Through Maria's eyes, they saw the mangled heap that was the hawk. Slowly it moved its head, its red, pulsating eyes found hers. She could sense its demonic soul, but she was unafraid.

She turned to look at Julie. The side of her head was a mass of congealed blood. She was still, almost statue-like, her lifeless eyes staring straight ahead.

It was as if time stood still. She turned away from Julie and looked at her husband. He too was statue-like, his face a frozen, contorted twist as was his hands, locked in a fierce grip at the controls. And Piet, with the same lifelessness, had a gaping head wound. But like Julie, the blood was not flowing.

It was then that she heard the low, menacing chuckle. It was coming from the bird; echoing around the glass-strewn compartment, out through the hole in the cockpit window.

Suddenly, a chorus of demonic howls and she felt the rush of cold air. Others had come to join it. They were anxious to claim her.

The broken bird screeched in triumph and she looked down at its glowing eyes.

It was waiting . . . waiting for her to go with it. She would go. They wanted her to go, for they were her protectors, her guardians.

She felt no fear, no hatred, just a deep belonging . . . a release and the flush of knowledge that her death or new life, was imminent.

As the hawk's dark, shadowy presence rose up and took her, the frozen hologram sprang to life and the red-and-white Comanche met the ground, the fuselage breaking apart on impact.

They watched as a wheel from the severed landing gear rolled down the side of the mountain. Then heard the creak of the metal as the port-side door was forced open.

Miraculously, Tony crawled out from the wreckage.

Less than a second later Piet followed, dazedly staggering to the starboard side of the crippled aircraft before clawing at the passenger door.

'Tony!' they heard him call. 'Help me. Help me!'

In a state of stunned confusion, Tony stumbled around to join him. Together they wrenched the door free.

Blood trickled down his face from the wound to his forehead, as Piet pulled Julie's still body toward him. Still stunned, Tony fell back against the mangled wreck and clung on to the aircraft's hanging door. Piet lifted Julie into his arms and staggered towards a clearing . . . shouting back to him. 'Get Maria!'

Piet's urgent command jarred him to life and he wiped the blood from his eye with his sleeve. With the remainder of his failing strength he reached into the aircraft and pulled her towards him. He lifted her out and staggered after Piet, collapsing in an exhausted heap. Moments later the Comanche suddenly exploded.

A great ball of orange flame shot high into the swollen, dark sky. A soaring, monstrous flare, scorching everything in its path, was followed seconds later by a cloud of dense black smoke.

Piet knelt down alongside his dying wife, cradling her head in his arms. A dark, cold shadow flew across them and he looked up.

The great hawk was back.

He stared unbelievingly as it circled, screeching clamorously overhead, then swooping with great speed before soaring straight up into the dark sky, disappearing into the low clouds.

As Dr Turner released the retrieval section, Piet's anxious eyes searched the dark heavens.

Suddenly, a beam of brilliant light broke through the blackness. His hand rose to his eyes, to shield them from the glare. When he looked again, the great hawk had emerged. His mouth fell open in amazement as a pulsating halo of blue surrounded the giant bird. He watched as it descended, its wings full spread, its once dark feathers, glistening, radiating a pure, snow white . . .

Just then, it broke free, swooping by him . . . circling again, climbing high on the wind, its lone piercing cries echoing ubiquitously.

As the sudden wind grew greater in strength, gusting angrily, the swollen black clouds moved steadily closer. Moments later Julie took her last breath and with it the ambiguous hawk was gone.

He hugged her lifeless body close to his chest, rocking backwards and forwards, stroking her long, blonde, silky hair, then leant forward and kissed her paling lips.

She was dead . . . gone. He could taste the salt of his tears as he laid her gently back on the grass and held her hand.

Thunder rumbled loudly, followed moments later by a crackling fork of lightning that struck a nearby tree, splitting the trunk in two.

Seconds later the same halo of blue light engulfed Julie's entire body. He could sense, but not feel the heat and he watched through watery eyes as her hand slowly slipped away from his, her whole body fading, disintegrating into fine, grey dust, leaving only her platinum wedding band between his fingers.

His hand formed a fist in the air and his teeth clenched with a fierce anger, as the gusting wind carried the grey, powdered remains high into the sky.

Still unable to perceive what had happened, he looked back at the grass, stretching out his hand, touching the burnt patch where she'd lain.

'Reprogramming activated,' the computer's voice confirmed.

As the blue-grey mist transported both souls, Piet held his head between his hands. His whole body, dazed and confused, his mind unable to reason his thoughts.

The main computer sped on, activating the reprogramming Dr Swartz had set, obliterating Piet's memories, thoughts, events as it took him backwards in time, to the point he'd selected for their history to begin. Back before Julie's accident, back the way it should have been; the way it was.

They watched as Piet tried to focus his eyes, looking for Tony. A fine mist covered the area . . . the wreckage was gone . . . for it had never existed. There was nothing . . . no mountains, no trees, just the fine, grey mist of his history, thickening as it surrounded its subject, preparing his journey.

He sank back on the grass. A long frenzied scream escaped him . . . the long, wild ululation of desperation, before his hand reached out once again to touch the spot where his wife had lain. Then his head hung low between his hunched, heaving shoulders in a desperate sob.

Lethargically he tried to stand, but his legs refused to obey him. He was burning, swelteringly hot, then cold, a shivering icy coldness, his anxious breath forming gossamer like clouds, which floated before him as he exhaled, inhaled, with a panicked rapidity.

His hand found his forehead in search of his wound. It was gone. The moisture he felt was not blood . . . he was sweating profusely. He looked up at the sky, but there was none, just a silent, still, huge, black nothingness, moving toward him, enveloping him in its entirety.

Then suddenly, it was gone! The air felt light, clear and blue. The breeze . . . he could feel the warm breeze . . . fresh . . . redolent of country flowers.

A giant presence was lifting him, higher and higher, spinning faster and faster . . . around and around in a great vacuum. He could hear soft music drifting towards him . . . could see a dim glow flickering in the far, far distance . . . then, suddenly, the light became brighter . . . moving towards him. He squinted his eyes and saw a misted silhouette.

'Piet,' he heard Julie call out as she approached. 'Your candle's blown out.'

'He looked up through the steam of his bath as his wife put her burning candle to his to light the wick, her beautiful features outlined in the glow.

'Have you fallen asleep again?' she asked, kneeling to the side of the bath. 'Rogers has almost fixed the generator, we should have light in a jiffy.'

She wrinkled her nose in the way he adored as she mimicked Rogers' English accent, then joked, flicking the bathwater into his face, 'How long are you going to sleep in there?'

She stood up, not waiting for an answer. He followed her with his eyes as she placed her candle on the bathroom shelf and moved various small pots of cream, looking for something.

'Have you seen my ring, Darling?' she questioned, 'I could have sworn I'd left it here.'

He looked down at his clenched fist; it was like a bolt of lightning had shot straight through him. He opened his fingers.

Just then the bathroom was a blaze of light.

'Marvellous!' Julie exclaimed, smiling, 'Rogers is a genius!'

She turned to face him, her eyes meeting his as he offered out his hand, the ring nestling in the palm.

'Now what in the world are you doing with that?' she questioned, with a puzzled expression, adding as she took the ring, 'And what's this?"'

She held up a long, single blade of wet, green grass.

'Now how in blazes did that get there?'

She wiped the ring in her hand towel and slipped it on her finger.

'Come on Darling, do hurry. We're all waiting for you.'

She replaced her towel, then glanced back at him. 'And they say women take their time!'

She smiled as she went into the bedroom.

'By the way,' she called, 'We've another guest for dinner. I've left her with Tony. She got caught in the storm. Car trouble. She's waiting for the auto club, and you know how long they take!' She emphasized the word *they*, before dabbing a spot of perfume on her wrists then, replacing the stopper.

She patted her upswept hair into place absentmindedly finishing, 'A young girl. Maria something. Maria Becket.'

12

BOSTON MAIN DOME LABORATORY: 18TH OCTOBER 2384

As the deep-velvet, black mist appeared in the receiving chamber at the far end of the laboratory, the electrical storm thundered and raged overhead.

Dr Swartz and his team watched as the dense mist, holding both the Commander's and Dr Western's soul divided, infiltrating the two waiting recipients.

'History programme re-aligned,' the voice of the main computer confirmed, 'Soul transportations are now complete. Do you wish mandatory procedure to commence?'

At the exact same moment as Dr Swartz gave the shutdown order, a loud clap of thunder boomed overhead. Less than a moment later, his anxious eyes were drawn to the clear dome ceiling above him.

A monstrous spinning ball of burning, crackling fire, propelled earthwards by a giant fork of blue lightning, hit the top of the laboratory dome . . . its great mass of electrical energy ricochetting onto the lightning conductor, attracted by the main computer's magnetic field. In the next instant, and intensified by the rod's electromagnetic coil, it rebounded, travelling with enormous velocity backwards, towards the dispersal link of the main computer.

Helplessly, he watched in horror, an overwhelming panic mounting inside him as the computer fought in vain against the enormous power surge, an unwinnable battle to redirect the megacharge, Dr Swartz's last given order, flashing on the screen, in a brilliant green script, before the letters disintegrated as the main computer's normally firm, steady voice, shrieked in a mutated high-pitched frenzy . . . computation after computation, the screen filling with mathematical equations in a desperate last bid for survival.

Moments later the battle was lost and the screen was black; a haunting, dense blackness that told them the computer had died and they were bathed by the back-up computer's dim orange glow.

Dr Swartz turned towards the Resident Elder; he felt dizzy, sick; it was as if he was in a long soundproof tunnel with no way out. She touched his arm. Her gentle, brown eyes held his. He concentrated on them, holding the gentleness they exuded and felt his panic recede.

'It's burn out!' he managed, faltering, 'It . . . it'll take years to repair!'

They'd pushed it to maximum and the lightning bolt had done the rest. The dedicated years of work that Dr Litchen had prized, that he had held sacred, had been totally obliterated.

She squeezed his arm reassuringly, and he thought just for one second, he saw a glint of relief in her eyes.

'But we've got them back,' she whispered, repeating, 'We've got them back!'

He nodded, trying to swallow the large lump in his dry throat.

He watched as she stood up to walk across to the life support units and felt the panic come upon him again. It should never have happened. Never . . . . .

'Dr Swartz,' she called. He turned to face her, and she beckoned him over.

The soul readouts were completely destroyed.

'Did you get a readout before the bolt struck?' he asked Dr Blackmore.

Dr Blackmore shook his head. 'No . . . nothing.'

'We can't check the degrees on Dr Western's soul?' Dr Swartz questioned.

It was more a statement than a question, for he didn't really need his answer. He knew before he'd asked the question.

A moment later they heard the great swoosh as the seals on the life support units were broken and the clear lids slid open, both Dr Western and the Commander sat up.

EPILOGUE

24TH APRIL, 2386:

It was eighteen long months before Dr Swartz was to see Dr Gemma Western alone again.

Whilst he and his team worked steadily to rebuild the Probe and its governing computer, the Counsel of Elders had, in their infinite wisdom, imposed an eighteen months custodial sentence upon Dr Western, a condition of which was that she attend a specified course of treatment with a top psychoanalyst. Thereafter a report would be submitted to the Counsel for their deliberation.

Shortly before completing her sentence, and with the specified period completed, Dr Mary Peterson, a middle-aged no-nonsense type psychoanalyst, began her evaluation.

On the 20th March, 2386 Dr Swartz was summoned to give evidence, evidence as it turned out that supported the psychoanalyst's recommendations, and evidence that angered Dr Gemma Western.

He could tell nothing from her cool light-green eyes as they silently swept over him whilst the security police led her away.

After a long, six-hour deliberation, the Elders' decision had been unanimous.

Dr Gemma Western, his star pupil, his protégée would not be returned to his programme and a subsequent suitable relocation was made.

Dr Western would be sent to the larger, dome farming section, where she would assist a team of young scientists developing a new technique in food growth.

Over the following five weeks, Dr Swartz had visited the farming laboratories every week and written with the same frequency. She in turn had answered every letter.

His deep feelings for her had never faltered and tonight, 24th April, 2386 she would come to him.

At 6.30pm, he waited impatiently, silently staring out through the large window of his bachelor second-floor quarters in the accommodation section of the main dome, adjacent the laboratories.

The white carpet of snow that covered the fields and trees was peaceful, soothing to his eyes. It was April and the harsh, long, winter temperatures had receded. The huge outer protection dome had been opened.

As the minutes ticked by, his mind raced ahead . . . there was so much he wanted to say . . . to do . . . to help. He'd tried to explain in his letters, begging her forgiveness . . . he'd told her it wasn't her fault!

A few seconds later, he heard her lone hollow footsteps echoing in the underground transportation system tunnel that led to the steps of his private entrance.

He raced down to the already-open exit, his waiting arms outstretched in a welcoming embrace.

'Gemma . . . dear Gemma,' he whispered. Then led her inside.

Her scarlet, full lips made her slim face pale. Her light-green normally sparkling eyes, were dull and moist as his strong arms encircled her in another long-awaited embrace.

His heart pounded loud in his chest . . . he'd waited so long for this moment. He kissed the top of her head, hugging her tighter. As she buried her head in his chest, her deep red painted lips parted in a familiar sardonic grin.

He lifted her chin to kiss her.

Suddenly, he found himself staring deep into her eyes, into two, bright, alien orbs, which emitted a force of pure hatred he could almost taste.

But wait! There was something else too! An intense fear.

Could the fear that her eyes held be *her* fear . . . or was it merely a reflection of the fear in his own eyes.

He backed away from her, his eyes still holding hers and was suddenly aware of the fierce coldness that enveloped the entire room.

He felt the chill as it moved up his legs, touching his spine, his head, his entire body. He was freezing now, held in a vice-like grip.

It was the last thought that passed through his brain before she fired three times . . . point blank . . . the peripheral voice returning in a loud, ubiquitous, malevolent shriek of inner laughter.